THE FALCON OF NAVARRE

✳ ✳ ✳

C.B. NEVINS

ISBN: 0615872565
ISBN 13: 9780615872568

1

Ray Solner watched as a red Ford Prism crept through the gullies and uneven slopes of what was once his driveway. The car bounced along until it came to a barely legible No Trespassing sign,-paused, and then continued its slow approach. Ray decided to look busy. He grabbed his Jack Daniels from the seat of a tractor and took a long swig, waving a wrench at the trespasser emerging from the idling vehicle.

"Well, what can I do for *you*?" Ray yelled.

The man faced Ray. He was dark-haired, tall and thin, dressed in a light gray suit and a charcoal tie. Like a preying mantis, he cocked his head, his inky green sunglasses riveted on the rancher.

"Are you Fletcher Lawson?" the stranger queried.

Ray grabbed a fencepost and stood quietly, examining the creature. 'Heavy accent. Mexican? He couldn't be sure.

"Nope," Ray finally replied.

"Do you know where he is?"

"Nope."

"Do you know him?" the insect persisted.

Ray didn't care for Fletcher Lawson, but alcohol only intensified his belligerence. He wasn't about to divulge any coveted information, especially to a foreigner.

"What do you want?" Ray hissed. "You get outta here!"

The sunglasses remained fixed on Ray. Despite the heat, a sudden chill ran down the neck of the small man. He glanced around him, trying to locate his wolfish dog. Not seeing him, Ray returned the stranger's stare, motioning a dismissal. Then, he turned away and teetered toward his tractor, feeling the predatory gaze on his back. He flinched as the car door slammed. Slinking down the rutty driveway, the red Ford Prism disappeared.

2

"Heh Fletch! *Fletcher!* Quit it, Oliver! Quit it! No! Get down! I said *get down!*"

Fletcher's pitchfork clattered against a rail as he dashed from the paddock and lunged for his dog. Seizing the collar, he yanked the slobbering onslaught from the appointed intruder.

"Good Lord! I'm so sorry, Corey!" Fletcher panted, "I didn't hear you. . . ."

"I tried phoning," she chuckled through clenched teeth, dusting off her new turquoise jacket. "But you didn't answer, so I thought I'd stop by. I have a family from out of town that would *really* like to come this afternoon, O.K?"

He shooed the dog away. His jaw tightened.

"Don't worry if it's not immaculate," she gushed. "You know, these people are country people. They understand. No one expects a man to clean all day." Her face reddened. Fletcher was *always* immaculate. His home of two decades hadn't seen a dirty dusk nor had she ever seen him disheveled or unshaven, despite his downing scotch on an as-needed basis, which – during those terrible years - was about one an hour. It was hard to believe he could survive such a tragedy – his wife killed that way – but somehow he had managed, and did it tidily. Even today, with his lean, 6'1" frame awash in gray shadow, it was clear that his shirt was bleached and medium starched, his pewter hair pulled neatly into a pony tail. She flecked microscopic lint from her skirt. She could feel the weight of his rare indigo eyes as he formulated his "Not Today" speech.

"Corey, I just don't think. . . ."

"Fletcher, if you don't want to sell, believe me, I understand. I mean, now that it's spring . . . you know, it's beautiful in Colorado and you've probably got the most beautiful ranch this side of the Rockies. . . ."

"It's not that," he said softly. "It's just not a good day. I really do need twenty-four hour notice. We *did* talk about it. Oh come on now. Don't look that way. If they're serious, they'll wait. Look, since you're here, how about coffee?"

She sighed, about-faced and marched toward his back door. "Will tomorrow morning work then, say around ten-thirty?"

"Absolutely."

She hesitated at the stoop. "I thought Englishmen didn't drink coffee."

"I wouldn't know." He hastened to open the door for her. "This one'll drink anything."

3

Fletcher's habit had been to have a glass of port and a cigarette when the day's work was done. The day, however, had turned to night, and his habit was going to have to wait. He had secrets, and secrets required tending. As with the previous house showings, Corey's clumsy rifling had to be anticipated. He left certain drawers stuffed with innocuous statements and mail offers, enough to keep her frustrated but occupied. He smiled at the thought, surveying the kitchen. The appliances were polished; the tile floor washed. He stepped over Oliver into the dining room. Nine Rococo Chippendale chairs flanked three walls of the dining room, with the tenth at the head of a massive mahogany table, every inch covered with reference material. Corey wouldn't be interested. Still, he would lock anything suggestive in the closet. He swept through the foyer, checking for dust by wiping his hand over a 17th century French credenza. An Aubusson's faded flora trembled under the fractured cast of a crystal chandelier. He switched on the humidifier, straightened the rug and strode to the study.

It was soothingly dark save the occasional flicker from a gas fireplace. He headed for a small painting attributed to Sir Thomas

Lawrence, then stood arrested for a moment by the portrait. Hanging above the desk, it was a masterpiece of simplicity. Although the attire of the young subject suggested aristocracy, there was no attempt to conceal his modest demeanor. Trapped in time, the youth reached across the centuries with a warning; his large eyes incisive and sad. It was a lifetime ago, when - not much older than the adolescent so exquisitely rendered - a busboy seized the message and the painting, stealing it from a posh London gallery, never to return, either to his employer or to his bleak heritage.

He removed it from the wall and placed it behind another deposed oil, then collapsed on his desk chair, stretched his legs over his dog, poured a drink and watched a Fortuna's virgin smoke swirl through his fingers. Spain: he could smell it; Marbella: the Mediterranean holding its humid breath against the ambrosial scent of orange blossoms. He could hear it: her laughter in a steamy bar in Madrid, raucous with life in the hollow hours of morning, her footsteps skipping across the silent, medieval streets of Seville. He closed his eyes, wondering if she thought of him at all. His head lolled to one side as he studied the painting he had yet to store. Her contours loomed through the haze, her rich auburn hair framing her pale visage. The portrait was painted from a sketch done in Burgos. She was looking squarely and solemnly at him, inescapably in love and deeply aware of the pain he could inflict. The woman on the canvas was pleading with him not to leave her. But, in the end, he did, too wretched to allow his happiness – or hers – to endure. "Sonsoles." he murmured.

He extinguished his cigarette, delivered the paintings to a concealed closet, then crossed the room and opened the desk's center drawer. Yawning, he deposited the key. His eyes stung from exhaustion. Still, he couldn't resist reaching beyond the stationary tray to the rear compartment, feeling for the object so priceless that he shuddered when his fingers skirted across its edge. Fletcher took the hand forged medallion from its felted coffer and held it to the desk light; its fiery orb igniting his shadowed confines into an aurora borealis. Centered on the piece, an elaborate filigree cross was flanked by two finned creatures with baroque pearl heads, each encircling an enormous, embedded blue sapphire. The cross itself was studded with twelve blood red rubies. Traces of centuries old enamel were still visible. Along the bottom was a Latin inscription. Solid gold and as large as his palm, he allowed its countless karats to guide his hand back to the safety of its hidden sanctum. It was a spectacular piece, no doubt of immense importance, and he was the only living soul to know of it.

As he had done for the last twelve years, he bypassed the master suite to sleep in a smaller bedroom on the east end of the house. It was a British expatriate's sanctuary, complete with a barrister bookcase, a gramophone and assorted collectables from Victorian India and Arabia. Adorning the walls, vintage photographs and postcards were tossed together in shadowboxes, the faces of turn-of the-century adventurers comforting the solitary man as he untied his hair, donned his sweat pants and climbed into bed. It was 1:30 a.m. according to the only modern accoutrement in the room. From far away, somewhere in Spain twenty-three years ago, Fletcher heard Oliver's deep, menacing growl trying to alert him as he drifted away.

4

A shaft of pale light crept across the eastern valley to Fletcher's windswept bluff. Stealing through his window, it stirred him with a promise of a new day. He had not slept well. Visions of his wife had invaded his dreams, her blond hair tucked under her riding hat, her accusing whispers piercing the armor of his subconscious. He greeted his muzzy consciousness with relief as Oliver's distant barking prodded him from the sheets. The dog must have slipped through his portal to pee, and for some reason, couldn't get back in. Bare-chested, Fletcher shuffled to the kitchen, opened the door to the cold air and called him. No show. He crossed to the southern dining room window and inspected the landscape. He identified Oliver at the top of the drive, yapping at some mystery. He moved through the foyer and out the front entry, shouting to the dog to come. It was then that he saw the dew drenched Prism. It was parked down the hill at the foot of his driveway. He stared at the car, and then scanned the terrain around it. He saw no one. Perhaps someone broke down, but here? He lived at the end of a dirt road. Someone must be lost. Oliver's continued fuss was getting on his nerves.

"Quiet, damn it!"

"Mr. Lawson."

Fletcher flinched and spun to the sound of the voice. The dog was silenced by the stranger's detection. The tall man stood at the west corner of the house, as if he had come from the barn. Fletcher waited for an explanation. There was none. Instead, the man adjusted his sunglasses and ruffled Oliver's long hair. "A rare dog, no?"

"A Briard," Fletcher snapped.

"Briard," the man repeated softly, his thick accent hovering just above the morning wind.

"Who are you?" Fletcher demanded, acutely aware of a chill.

"Mr. Lawson," he said slowly, "I have come to find you to give you a letter." His head was slightly tilted, regarding the older, half-naked man.

"That's all? Why didn't you mail it?"

"Because, Mr. Lawson," the foreigner took a step toward Fletcher, "I wanted to see you . . . for myself."

Fletcher took an involuntary step backward. He ransacked his memory for the familiar lingual cadence and found it in Madrid.

"You've come a long way, then. You're from Spain?" he asked, beginning to shiver.

"Yes," The Castilian reached in his pocket and pulled out a letter. "For you," he said, offering a tan linen envelope. "Perhaps you should go to your house," he added.

Fletcher took it. It was addressed Ryan Egan. The writing was distinctly feminine, the embellished capitals unmistakable. He felt a flash of sweat across his face.

"How did you find me?" Fletcher stammered, riveted on the envelope. *"How do you know her?"*

There was silence. Fletcher looked up at the lean, motionless figure, the material of his gray suit whipping in the wind like a sail across a fragile mast. The handsome visage was returning his gaze through dark sunglasses, his expression betraying nothing. A gust caught his shoulder length hair, pulling it forward, framing his face in a familiar way. It had a copper sheen.

"Oh, my God," Fletcher cried softly, "Of course. Of course! *How could I be so. . . . Her son! You're her son?*"

The man nodded. Fletcher searched for something to say - something appropriate - but in his shock, all he could muster was an invitation for coffee.

✳ ✳ ✳

The visitor was seated at the kitchen table when his host reappeared wearing a pair of jeans and a much needed sweater. The coffee maker was gurgling as he pulled eggs from the refrigerator.

"Breakfast?" Fletcher asked, waving the carton. "Huevos?"

"Si," the guest said absently, "thank you."

"What's your name?" Fletcher queried, hovering over a skillet of crackling olive oil.

"Pardon?"

The chef poured the egg batter into the frying pan; it flared with a loud sizzle. "*Your name.* What do they call you? Como se llama?" he shouted.

"Tristan." The young man leveled his sunglasses against the searing light of the window.

"Oh. Yes. She would choose that name . . . an archaic name, a beautiful name."

There was no reply. The Spaniard appeared hypnotized by the pacing of a huge horse.

"That's Little John," Fletcher informed him as he placed a cup and saucer on Tristan's placemat. "I know. He's enormous. Do you take cream or sugar?"

"Nothing, thank you."

Tristan embraced the brew with both hands and drank it in nearly one swallow. Noting the signs of jet lag, Fletcher refilled his guest's cup and handed him a glass of orange juice. Then, he quietly resumed breakfast preparation, returning to the table with two sizeable tomato omelets, toast and grapefruit. They ate in silence, Fletcher studying his new acquaintance between bites. Washed and warmed by the rays of the morning sun, the wayfarer looked pious and resurrected. He was an El Greco painting, Fletcher thought. Everything about him was long, formal and soulful. When Tristan finally met his host's curious stare, Fletcher placed his fork on his plate and cleared his throat.

"So, Tristan," he began, "why was it so important that you *see* me, as you said?"

The visitor was quiet. Fletcher persisted. "I assume your mother spoke of me. How is she? Well? Happy? I presume married. What did she tell you?"

The Spaniard placed his utensils diagonally across his meal. He dabbed his mouth with a napkin.

"I will take a cigarette outside. Excuse me." He rose from the table and reached in his right jacket pocket.

"There's no need for that," Fletcher countered. "Please, sit down." He slid his saucer toward his guest. "Please. It doesn't bother me."

The guest remained standing.

"I'll open the window for good measure," Fletcher added, cranking out the casement. "Right, then. Please." He gestured to the chair. "Sit down."

Tristan reseated himself and leaned back out of the sun, lighting his cigarette. He loosened his tie.

"What's in the letter?" Fletcher asked.

The visitor shrugged. His index finger tapped an ember onto the dish. "She writes this to you. It is not for me to. . . ."

"How is she?" Fletcher searched the pale, chiseled face.

Tristan exhaled and turned toward the window. "She passed, many years before."

"Passed?" Fletcher sputtered, *"Passed? You mean. . . ?"*

"Yes."

A spasm of nausea rocketed Fletcher to his feet. *"What happened?"*

The young man answered in a monotone, gazing into the white light. "She was in the water, in the sea." He took a drag from his cigarette. The sea take her. That is all I know."

Fletcher felt short of breath. "*When*? How long ago?"

"I had ten years, so . . . twelve years back."

"*What?*" Fletcher was thunderstruck. "*What about the letter?* It's from *her*, from Sonsoles, your mother, isn't it? When did she write it?"

Tristan extinguished his cigarette in the saucer. "This letter, I believe, has - perhaps – fifteen years. I must go." He stood and sidestepped his chair like a panther. Fletcher tracked after him as he strode down the hallway.

"What does the letter *say*, Tristan? Why are you here? *Why did you want to see me*?"

The departing messenger paused at the front door, turning to confront the Englishman. "Why do you not read the letter, Mr. Lawson?"

Fletcher sighed. "I'm not sure I can. I'm not sure you can understand. It's difficult. I *will* read it, but I need the right time. I . . . I. . . . *Oh my God, did she forgive me?*" he whispered, shaking his head. His eyes welled with tears. He fixed on the floor.

Eternity passed before the old, young man spoke. "Mr. Lawson, I am very sorry for your loss." He hesitated and rubbed the bridge of his nose. "I do believe she forgive you . . . always. Thank you, Sir, for your kindness."

Fletcher smiled weakly, forcibly sealing his emotional floodgate, preparing an apology and a stiff-upper-lip send off. But when he finally faced the Spaniard, he could barely find his breath, much less utter a word. With his sunglasses in his right hand, the man before him was not an El Greco painting; the large, pensive eyes studying him did not belong to a Spaniard. They were the eyes of a Sir Thomas Lawrence portrait closeted in his study. They were the eyes of an Englishman. They were - unmistakably - the indigo eyes of Fletcher Lawson, and, suddenly, the contents of the letter were manifest, etched in the features of an Iberian harbinger.

5

Ray Solner squinted at the lilac filled bucket on his kitchen counter. It was something his mother used to do, which made him wonder if he was still alive. The room was filled with a heavenly scent and a heavenly light, a side-effect - as Ray slowly realized - of the windows being washed. He was in desperate need of aspirin, and there it was – a big bottle of it - right on the kitchen table, anchoring a note written by his angelic baby-sitter of forty years: Corey Martin. Ray sauntered over to the refrigerator. Instead of finding a hair of the dog that bit him, he found something twice as vicious: orange juice. He groaned, grabbed the carton and sat down with his back to the flowers. Four pain relievers later, he read Corey's Ten Commandments:

1) I found you under the tractor. You were blabbing about some terrorist in the driveway. You're killing yourself, and I'm sick of it. There's no booze. I threw it all out and took the garbage with me.

2) I paid your phone bill with my credit card, so it will be back on tomorrow. You owe me.

3) I'm going to ask Reverend Peters to come by. Be nice. I mean it.

4) I still need three bluebird houses.

5) I bought you some water. Don't drink out of the tap. I dumped some Clorox down the well.

6) Eat something. You look like crap. Instant dinners in the freezer.

7) I have buyers for your south quarter section. You don't have much choice, so sign the papers on the counter. . . .

Ray finished the list of do's and don'ts with a swig of Florida Natural. He found the contract on the counter, crumpled it in a ball and dropped it on the floor. He'd never sell his daddy's ranch, not one acre of it. Still, he was in trouble. His truck wasn't working, and without his truck, he couldn't get to town. If he couldn't get to town, he wouldn't have any beer. He'd have to look at the truck right away. With the aspirin taking effect, Ray pattered down the hallway. At the sight of his sterile bath room, it occurred to him that he might be dreaming. Then, rotating the faucet, he smelled the bleach, assuring him that he was quite awake. He waited for the shower to warm up, stepped out of his jeans, and slipped under the hot water. The sweet scent of shampoo and soap nurtured him; his freshly cleaned, fragile physique inspiring him to make changes. But, as he sunk to the side of the tub, he realized that he was too weak for a metamorphosis. He emerged from his steamy bathroom with his knees shaking. Staggering to bed, he knew Corey's bluebird houses would have to wait.

6

"*Fletcher!* You can't be *serious!*" Corey had a stranglehold on the phone. "These people have to get back to Grand Junction! How many people do you think can afford your place, anyway? *They don't come along every day, you know!*"

She fumed through his excuse. "I can't postpone *again*! The market's awful; you know that! *What* exactly has come up?"

She heard the conciliatory tone but the words were meaningless, something he was unusually good at when he didn't want to fess up. It was futile to argue. She clicked off and slammed the handset into its base. Composing herself, she reached for it again, gripping it between her shoulder and jaw as she turned to dump her coffee.

"Hello? Hello?" A male voice was speaking.

"*Hello?* This is Corey Martin. Who's this?"

"Corey, that's odd. This is Pete. I just called you but there was no ring."

"Oh hi! Huh! I just picked up the phone to cancel a showing. *Fletcher!*"

"Ah. Sorry. Well, I got your message. Is there anything else I need to know about Ray, other than he's worse?"

"Well, as I said, he looks bad. 'Doesn't remember much. I don't know; he looks yellow."

"Hmm. 'Nice color for spring. I'll go over this afternoon."

"Thanks. Let me know."

"Will do."

Pete, aka Reverend Peters was not exactly what the church elders had had in mind for a pastor, but they had learned. Their former minister was so mesmerizing that he managed to abscond with a sizeable portion of the church funds without one question about his bookkeeping. It was only when his serpent-like charm coaxed the jeans off the veterinarian's young wife that his conduct became alarming, but by then it was too late. The money and the wife vanished with a man looking very much like the good preacher last seen playing the slots in Nevada. Humiliated and without a pastor, the church elders hired Reverend Peters before he could hand them a resume. They enthusiastically complied with his suggestion that they call him "Pete" and gave him immediate rein to lift their depressed Christian spirits. With two PhD's, Pete was exceptionally bright, energetic, and persuasive; in less than a year, he had doubled the congregation. But more to the point - as a devoted father of four - Pete cherished family, commitment and community as much as he did barbeques and bake-offs. Weighing in at nearly four hundred pounds, Pete was not perceived to be a threat to the matrimonial bliss of the otherwise tempted, much to the relief of the hiring committee.

7

No one had slept in the Master bedroom since the night of the accident, so the room's noonday occupation sent Fletcher's precious English reserve into an uncomfortable exile. Like a bird, his heart kept fluttering between fear and exhilaration. As his young arrival slept, Fletcher collapsed on his chair, trying to fathom what had triggered his son's daring journey. It hadn't been hard to convince him to stay. Tristan had been in the States for well over forty hours and awake for all of it. He had left Denver International Airport with a rented car and a hundred dollars in a foreign version of traveler's checks - worthless in a rural area – and drove straight to Fletcher's township. Unfortunately, people were few and far between, and even fewer were helpful. Google was of no use as the property was incorporated. As Fletcher had always maintained a post office box, the mail clerk felt no reason to concede Lawson's existence, much less his whereabouts. Consequently, Tristan's first day in the United States was spent finding out how big a Colorado county could be. With evening approaching and his only credit card maxed out, Tristan was forced to drive all the way back to Denver to trade a traveler's check for a meal and some cash. Rehabilitated by several cups of coffee, he returned that night armed with a flashlight and a carton of cigarettes. By some strange process of elimination, he had determined where Fletcher did not live, while searching for a name or something telling on ranch signs and mailboxes, covering probably a hundred square miles of new territory. Half past midnight, the beleaguered young Spaniard walked into Billy Bronco's Bar and asked for a coke, stunning its Wolf packing patrons into a predatory vigil. Sensing the stranger's peril, an affable Navajo named Elan sidled up and asked if he was lost. Tristan simply wrote *Fletcher Lawson* on a cocktail napkin. Elan laughed and announced the name. The crowd howled; everyone knew him. At one thirty a.m., the Navajo's truck disappeared into a starlit night, but not before a red Ford Prism was guided safely to the foot of Fletcher's driveway. Four hours later, emboldened by a vivacious dog and the dawn's reassuring glow, a nervous foreigner inched up a hill to meet the man who had fathered him twenty-two years ago.

Fletcher smiled at the irony. Tristan would not be walking this earth had it not been for his own quest: to confront a fugitive father, only he never found the man. Instead, in fields of saffron and olive trees, he discovered a love so complete that he felt unworthy of it, and ultimately fled. He never knew what became of his Irish sire, or whether he ever detonated another bomb or maimed another British officer in the name of independence. All he knew was that he went to Spain in search of him, hating him, but her love extinguished the hate and ultimately, even his curiosity about the man. It was the love that saved him, and the love - he feared - that took a life far more worthy than the one he had thought to destroy. He covered his face with his hands.

8

Venturing out of his bedroom like a furtive rodent, a naked Ray Solner peered into the hallway toward the kitchen, swearing he could smell bacon. A dark, massive figure filled the kitchen doorway, waving what appeared to be a spatula.

"Good! You're up!"

"Jesus!" Ray screamed, covering his crotch with his hands.

"*Nooooo*, but the next best thing," a deep voice boomed. "Come have some breakfast, Ray!" The silhouette disappeared.

Semi-crouched, Ray took another step into the hall, his mouth agape. The shadow reappeared.

"Put your pants on, Ray," the voice commanded. "I know. We're all naked before God, but you'll just have to believe me, I'm *not* your maker. If I could make it any bigger, I would."

Ray rushed into his bedroom and slammed the door. He wiggled into his jeans and threw on a shirt. The best he could scavenge for weaponry was a science trophy. He cracked open the door, but was losing his nerve.

"Who are you?" he hollered.

"The ghost of breakfast yet to come!" a jovial voice replied. "Come on, Ray. It's Pete. Reverend Peters, Pete Peters. In lieu of whiskey, your road to salvation! Come on, Bud – oh, no pun intended - it's getting cold."

"Reverend Peters?" Ray whispered, rubbing his eyes, the fog lifting. "Oh, yeah," he mumbled. He opened the door and shuffled unsteadily down the hallway.

"For some reason," Ray shouted as he approached the kitchen, "people don't seem to mind just barging into my house without knocking."

"So true, Ray. So true. We don't mind at all."

His red eyes wide open, Ray surveyed the table's gleaming dishes with a gasp. The meal waiting for him was nothing less than a culinary masterpiece. Reverend Peters had shaped a cantaloupe into flowers; parsley becoming the stems and leaves. The four eggs were sunny side up and fashioned into daisies, growing out of the earthen bacon. Obviously bored, the artiste had actually whipped up some cornstarch concoction to create a side dish of white, puffy clouds above a wavy field of hash browns. Even the crowning pancake had a syrupy smiley face and a peeled banana hat.

"Whoa," Ray murmured.

"I have to agree, Ray. *Whoa.*" Pete puffed up like a military statue in front of the stove, twirling his spatula like a baton. "As close to perfection as a mere mortal comes! Sit down, Raymond."

"I can't eat all of this."

"Just eat what you can. *Try!*"

"Um, O.K." Ray took his seat at the table and fiddled with a fork.

"I don't suppose you made any coffee?"

"Well, yes, as a matter of fact, I did!"

Only a moment passed before the chef de jour plopped an enormous, oozing, whipped cream latte in front of the astonished rancher. With an exaggerated flounce, Pete capped the frothy volcano with a cherry and cried "Voila!"

Ray vaulted out of his chair and rushed to the bathroom.

Pete was as good a guide to nutrition as he was a path to redemption, which left Ray snoring on a full, antioxidized, vitamin-enriched, albeit force-fed - stomach. Having rinsed the last of the pots and pans, the epicure reached for a towel and glanced at his watch. He still had a couple of hours before a much needed unwind with Fletcher, otherwise known as "Two Hawks Night." Chess was Pete's passion and Fletcher was certainly an able player. But over the last year Pete had developed as much a dependency on his opponent's dry wit as his wet cordials, Cuban cigars, and – oh yes – the game. Since late was not an option for the pastor's weekly fix, he figured he had just enough time to visit a couple of elderly people needing a little remedial work, and a quick hello to a couple of foster kids needing a complete overhaul, with the overhaul waiting for the weekend. He checked on Ray once more. Noting that he was looking rosier, Pete charged out the door.

9

Fletcher had left two messages for the itinerant minister, but evidently, they weren't received. As the afternoon wore on, the disinclined host busied himself with chores and reading, anxious to hear Pete's voice on the other end of a phone line rather than on the front stoop. He thought about calling again, but decided against it. Pete's wife didn't like him, but he didn't take it personally. The harried woman didn't seem to like anyone, including Pete.

Sitting at the dining room table, Fletcher was perusing his latest literary acquisition when Oliver galloped in.

"Your food's in there," Fletcher muttered, waving him into the kitchen. The dog galloped first to the kitchen then back through the dining room to the foyer side, where a form appeared in jeans and a faded tee-shirt.

"Well now," the reader closed his book and removed his glasses. "Refreshed?"

"I am, thank you."

"Good. Tea?"

"Yes, thank you."

"Right. Why don't you move some of that mess and sit down?" Fletcher motioned at the books on the table, took a chair from the wall and shoved it toward Tristan. "I'll be just a minute."

While Oliver slopped down his food, Fletcher steeped the tea in a Victorian silver pot and filled the matching sugar and creamer. Arranging a few snacks, he caught the reflection of his denim shirt in the sterling. He mulled over his presentation, then thought, why not? It was a day like no other. He added two linen napkins, lifted the tray and turned the corner into the dining room.

Tristan was still standing, leafing through a biography. "You like Coronado?"

"In a manner of speaking," Fletcher replied, setting the tray on the table.

"Many of the books here are of conquistadores, no? Why?"

"It's a long story. Right now, I'd like to know something about you. Please, sit down."

As Fletcher poured, he sensed Tristan's guardedness. He proceeded with caution. "Do you have work in Spain?"

"At this moment, no. I am here so. . . ."

"What do you do?"

"Pictures."

"Illustrations?"

"Yes, illustrations."

Fletcher smiled. "It doesn't surprise me. Your mother was artistic, a very good artist."

"Yes, she say the same of you."

Fletcher's face flushed. "Any reason to get back right away?"

Tristan put down his cup and eyed his host. "Why?"

"I'll get straight to the point, Tristan. I'd like to get to know you. I thought perhaps you could stay for a bit. I feel, well, you can understand, somewhat. . . ."

"You have no obligation."

"No. No. It's not like that. I'd like to know you better, that's all. Perhaps I can help you in some way."

"I cannot stay."

"Oh." Fletcher's cup clattered back on its saucer. "May I ask why?"

Tristan toyed with his spoon.

"Tristan, you came all this way to see me. Is that all you wanted? Am I *that* disappointing?"

Silence ensued as the Spaniard shifted in his chair and tapped an unlit cigarette on the table. "Is there work I can do here?"

"Oh, I see," Fletcher murmured. "You're short of money. Is that it? Tristan, you'd be my guest. Obviously, if there is a charge to change your plane ticket, I'll take care of it. I'll gladly take care of your expenses. I can manage the car rental. . . ."

"Mr. Lawson. . . ."

"Fletcher, please or Ryan. Actually, call me whatever you want. Even I don't know what to call me."

It was the first time he had acknowledged his other name or his other life to another living soul in twenty years, and it was also the first time he saw Tristan smile. It was a dazzling smile. The same smile that won Fletcher any woman he wanted had been gifted to his son. That smile, he thought. That dangerous smile . . . .

Then it vanished. "I must work to feel . . . with honor. You understand, Fletcher?"

"Yes, I do. But it's not necessary this time. I'll help you as I would truly like to."

Tristan was staring a crack in the mahogany table. "How long?" he finally asked.

"As long as you care to stay."

"I must not be a problem for you."

"You're *not* a problem."

"Perhaps you help me to speak English? I will work. I will do work here if there is nothing."

Fletcher was filled with an unfamiliar rush of joy and realized that what he was actually feeling was pride, respecting this young man in a way that he could never respect himself. Taking a deep breath, Fletcher nodded acknowledgement, blinking away the unexpected saline that threatened to blur the image of his progeny.

10

Pete arrived promptly at six-thirty with Brie, grapes and a baguette. He rang twice and stood at the front door for five minutes, surprised by the uncharacteristic delay. Fletcher greeted him somewhat stiffly, but then, with his usual "Good evening, Friar," ushered him into the study.

"Sorry to keep you waiting." Fletcher poured two drinks from a decanter. "I have a friend in from out-of-town. He wanted to take a walk; I was just showing him the way. Oh, look, what a feast!" Fletcher emptied the contents of Pete's bag as the big man peered out a window.

"Your friend?" Pete motioned out the window to a tall figure accompanied by Oliver strolling west.

Fletcher glanced up. "Yes. I'll fetch some plates."

The card table was already set with ashtrays and two medieval armies ready to charge a checkered battlefield. The room was warmed by a sepia glow via the long, burnt rays of late afternoon. Pete nestled into a burgundy wing-back and nursed his scotch. Oil paintings hung like necklaces along the walls. On either side of the fireplace, built-in bookcases housed leather-bound classics as well as obscure volumes of poetry. The cherry wainscoting constrained the massive room and tied the publications, artwork and antiques together in a rich, luxurious knot. There was something to be said for money, Pete mused. His own executive suite was an open area next to the furnace in the basement defined by piles of dog-eared books surrounding his chipped –as opposed to Chippendale - metal desk. He did have artwork. Tacked on to the unpainted sheetrock, crayoned stick figures with big toothy mouths brightened his windowless, one bulb office. He glanced around the rich man's lair with his glass raised, saluting Fletcher's good taste and good luck as the lord of the manor strolled in with the evening's repast.

"What are you doing?" Fletcher asked, relinquishing a tray to a side table.

"Just saluting your blessings and my own," the pauper replied. "I was also thinking that I might ask for a raise."

"Oh. Well Pete, my good fortune is due to my father-in-law's *obscene* one." The host raised his glass. "May he hate me in peace. Cheers."

After refilling his guest's glass and offering him a cigar, Fletcher took his seat at the table and pondered his opponent's first move.

The big man leaned forward. "So, Fletcher, who's your friend, if I may ask?"

"Help yourself to the spread, Pete." Fletcher tilted his head at the side table and mimicked Pete's move, exposing his queen by moving a pawn up two squares.

"Hmmm. No reply… what could that mean?" Pete murmured, freeing his knight from its line.

Fletcher pushed another pawn and reached for the pate. He fumbled with a couple of napkins, and dropped a slice of bread.

"Well, Mr. Lawson, are you going to reveal the identity of your friend?"

"Actually, he's the son of a friend … just here to see the States."

"Ah," The minister exclaimed, repositioning his knight to within striking distance of the pawn. "A *furrrriner.* Where's he from?"

"Europe."

"*Europe!* Well that narrows it down. Your move, Fletch."

Fletcher inched another pawn from its line.

"*Unlike you,* my man!" Pete replaced his opponent's unguarded pawn with his dark horse and took a victorious drag from his stogy.

Fletcher placed his rook behind the other vulnerable pawn, but realized – too late – that his queen was in jeopardy. Two more moves, and she would be in enemy hands. As Pete maneuvered, Fletcher looked for a way to guard her. He blocked the threat by advancing another pawn, freeing his bishop. Pete paused – momentarily perplexed - and then slowly replaced the white, gothic lady with his villainous cavalryman. Fletcher gasped. How could he make such a stupid mistake? Pete was studying him through a curtain of smoke.

"Fletch - not to state the obvious – but your mind's not on the game."

"No. Sorry. Let me see what I can do to salvage it. Bloody stupid, I must say."

Pete popped a grape in his mouth and said, "Forget it. There's always another game." He leaned back. "Something you want to talk about?"

"No."

Oliver bounded into the room, greeting the reverend with a quick bark and a lick of pate. Pete grabbed the dish as the dirty animal paraded around the room then dashing back into the hallway. Fletcher looked over his shoulder as Tristan tipped his head into the study. "Excuse me. I do not wish to disturb you. I will read now, and see you in the morning. All right?"

"Yes, of course," Fletcher replied, without introducing his chess partner.

But the partner was not to be ignored. Dropping his smoldering stub into the ashtray, Pete rose, extending his sizeable hand. "Pete Peters."

Tristan moved forward and clasped it. "Tristan Velasco. A pleasure." He glanced back at Fletcher. "Well, good night, Gentlemen." Tristan's smile momentarily arrested them from nightfall.

"Good night." The players choired as he disappeared with Oliver.

The good friar took the decanter, refilling Fletcher's glass and his own, while his host dwelled in an alternate state.

"You say he's the son of a friend?" Pete repeated the question. "Fletcher?"

"Oh yes. Yes."

"I take it . . . a close friend." Pete grinned, relighting his cigar. "A *very close* friend."

Fletcher raised his eyebrows.

"He looks like you, Fletch." Pete stoked his stogie with a few shallow inhales. "In fact," he continued, the smoke billowing from his Havana, "with a couple of minor adjustments, I'd say he looks *exactly* like you. You know? Same car, different year."

Fletcher drained his scotch. Slouching back, he let the alcohol wash over him, his eyes resting on the ceiling. The ticking of a mantle clock logged the irreplaceable minutes until finally, he muttered, "I'm not proud of what I've done. I'm not proud of any of it."

Pete sat quietly as his host forayed into the past. It began, not with the story of his troubled youth, nor with the affair that consumed him, but with his marriage to Meredith Drexden Palter.

Any onlooker would have envied the couple that wed in a Vegas chapel that rare rainy evening in May. They were beautiful and loaded. She was heir to the Palter fortune: a conglomeration of blue chip solar systems feeding an ever expanding universe by the name of Drexden International. Only God and the occasional federal warning kept the monstrous corporation from becoming an all consuming hole through which even light would bend, not to mention the world economy. Meredith Palter had never washed a dish in her life nor had she ever known a day without superficial concerns or maid service. Any physical feature that promised to be awkward was fixed by the age of fourteen. She didn't have her own room, but several, from Carmel to Monte Carlo. She was a dutiful dieter and appropriately bored. Strangely, her lavish upbringing did not spawn the usual haughty persona, but rather a naiveté that led her far from the safety of her empty Eden straight into the seductive, opportunistic arms of an English bartender.

Fletcher was pouring drinks at a royalty-wannabe gala when young Meredith escaped the laments of a left-wing filmmaker looking for a comrade, or – more likely – money. All she wanted, she said, was champagne. Fletcher handed her a glass, quickly surmising that that wasn't all on her list. She was an early-twenties old lady of the court, similar to every other lasered smile in the Hamptons with one exception: she was sincere when she thanked him. She also did something quite extraordinary: she asked him about *him*. In Fletcher style, he answered with a double entendre. She got it, and, like every woman he had known since he was sixteen, she was hooked. The only difference this time was that he was not about to let her millions upon millions escape. She adored him; eventually, so did everyone else. Invited to every resplendent function, Fletcher was dazzling and Meredith envied, suiting them both perfectly. His masquerade as the poor but untarnished nobleman remained unchallenged until the first dinner with old man Palter, who made it clear his daughter wasn't *seriously* available to a low-life limey. As Fletcher had lived with that remark in one form or another all his life, he simply smiled and nodded. That same night, he proposed to the thrilled young heiress. They were married the next flight out. Her trust fund seemed intact and there was no prenup, so, admittedly, the new husband enjoyed immense satisfaction when Meredith broke the news to her father three days into the honeymoon. While Ross V. Palter yelled profanities and threats, Meredith's mother properly congratulated them, barely able to conceal her delight. Unfortunately, the lovely lady took her last breath soon afterward, unable to endure another year of chain smoking or her husband's choking grip on her once free spirit. Out of deference to her – and not one to show weakness on any front - Palter was careful to not scorn his daughter publicly or her idiotic choice of husbands. But privately, he hated her for her insurrection and cut her off.

Fletcher and Meredith were invited to fewer and fewer parties. Remaining friends finally distanced themselves, intimidated by Palter's Wall Street fist. Even Hollywood's Left was touched by the tension in a family that convolutedly backed their bigger projects. The message was clear. Socialist ideology was perfectly acceptable as long as it was profitable. Glitzy parties could continue to awe the struggling American. But, Meredith Drexden Palter Lawson was not to be thrown up in the chief benefactor's face. Meredith took her crown jewel and escaped her father's domain, determined to make him miss her. He never did.

The couple bought a remote three hundred acre parcel in Colorado, one accessible to Denver as well as Aspen, should the occasion arise. They giggled over the house design while strolling their newly acquired meadows. But, within a year of the house's completion, Fletcher and Meredith began to squabble over trivialities. He found her youthful conversation a bore and withdrew into books and painting, announcing that his study was off limits to the Mexican housekeeper, the Vietnamese cook and most importantly, his spouse. Barricaded in against his young wife's screams, he spent half his long day in isolation. A social creature, Meredith longed for her amusing husband. She poured over catalogs smoking, spending her half of the day in bed. She tearfully admitted to the staff that home on the range was not suiting her at all until one dreary morning, on a remote sandy intersection, she literally ran into a man pulling a trailer in a red pick-up. As it happened, she was trying to light a stubborn cigarette when suddenly, her freshly acquired groceries splattered across the dash of her pre-celebrity owned, 1989 Mercedes as it plowed unchecked into a rusty rear side panel. Unhurt, she emerged from the car with a dead cellphone and profuse apologies. The other driver simply stepped from his truck and peered in between the slats of the stock trailer. He then examined the truck's twisted wheel well, walked to the back of the trailer, opened the metal door and caught a huge haltered horse as it bolted from its domain. She asked if he had a cellphone. The man shook his head, and handed her the lead rope. He reached back into his truck cab for his jacket, his wallet and the eagle feather dangling from the center mirror. He then retrieved the horse and began walking east with a slight limp along the gravel embankment. To Meredith's surprise, he hadn't asked for her name or even her insurance company. She climbed back into her car, but the impact had done something to prevent it from starting. She turned the key again and again, cursing the cold, the car and her stupidity. She scanned her surroundings; there was no sign of life other than the black hatted figure ambling up the road with a dancing horse. She abandoned the car and raced to catch up with him, startling the creature in tow. It lunged forward, but the man kept a firm grasp on its tether and glanced behind him. She shouted "please" and the man stopped, waiting for her with the kindest eyes and the sweetest smile she had ever seen under the crease of a western fedora. She introduced herself, apologized yet again and asked where the nearest house was. He said that the nearest house was his, a couple of miles down the road. She shivered against the chill. He offered her his jacket. She declined. He gave it to her anyway. She asked his name and about the young horse. The gelding, he said, was from Pueblo, ready for training. His name was Little John.

"Little John?" she repeated, wide-eyed.

He laughed. "The *horse's* name is Little John. Mine is Elan."

She confessed that she was terrified of horses. She fell off one when she was little. Despite her protests, he rested the lead rope in her hand and closed it. The three walked together braced against a bitter wind on a mid-April day, beginning a journey that would end with hot chocolate, a can of sweet feed, a new passion and a lasting friendship.

11

Tristan searched the darkness for the voice that had awakened him. Someone had shouted his name; he distinctly heard it. He called out but no one responded. The clock read 3:04 a.m., making a slight clicking noise as the four rolled into five. He tossed the quilt to one side and lit from the bed. As he moved out into the hallway, he realized the dog wasn't there. He saw a pale glow emanating from the study, but the smoky room appeared deserted. He shuffled east, observed Fletcher's undisturbed blankets, and then returned to the cigar soaked parlor. Through the window, he saw a brief flash of light. He revisited his bedroom long enough to pull a sweatshirt over his pajamas and slip into a pair of loafers. He then exited through the kitchen to face the cold desert air. With only the monochromatic shapes of rock and ponderosa to guide him, he edged his way down a craggy slope toward a flickering yellow beam and a barely audible voice. He hesitated as he saw his host's frame with a glass in his right hand, appearing to toast someone or something unseen in the moonlight. Tristan withdrew into the shadows while Fletcher perched precariously on a boulder, continuing his address. As Tristan inched closer, the keen senses of the Briard betrayed him. Rising from the rocky terrain, Oliver sifted the night air for the familiar scent and found it behind the useless cover of a sapling. The dog yelped in delight which ended Fletcher's diatribe. He dropped his glass and turned his drunken attention to the pursuit of his hound.

"Oliver, you idiot. Get away from that!" Fletcher scrambled up the slope. *"Get away from it!* You'll stink or *you'll have needles in your face!* I'll have to take you to the vets!"

Fletcher stumbled on loose rock and fell to one knee. Trying to right himself, he relied too heavily on his other leg, which buckled as the gravel slid out from under it. He was finally steadied by a large boulder, which he met full force with his chest. As he hollered in pain, Oliver dashed to his rescue while Tristan skidded down the pine needles to him, nearly meeting disaster but for the same boulder that blocked his descent.

"Well that hurts," Fletcher slurred as he rolled onto his back, patting his frantic dog. "At least you don't stink." He looked up at a thin figure kneeling down above his head.

"Jesus!"

"Are you well, Fletcher?"

"Tristan?"

"Yes?"

The fallen man sighed. "Oh, thank God." He slowly sat up. "Yes, I'm sure I'm fine, just a bit . . . you know, undone."

"Too much drink?"

"Yes, probably . . . too much drink." Fletcher chuckled. "What are you doing out here?"

Tristan began to search for an explanation; Fletcher waved him off.

"Never mind. I don't care. Let's go to bed." Ignoring Tristan's outstretched hand, Fletcher struggled to his feet.

"There is no one here but you?" Tristan queried softly.

Fletcher reeled, but regained his stance. "What? Yes. No. Oh, *right!* You saw me talking to myself? Yes, well, only when I'm drunk. I imagine it looks quite ... *bizarre*, but other than that little *idiocy* ... *idiosyncrasy,* I'm pretty normal for out here."

He staggered, aware that the Spaniard was riveted on the dull glow of the flashlight perched over a crevice below them.

Your friend is not here?" Tristan asked.

"*Pete*? No, he left ages ago. Come on, Lad. It's cold. Let's go in."

"What *is* that?"

Fletcher laughed. "Nothing. Come on, old boy. Come on. We'll get a drink inside."

Fletcher tried to steer the meddlesome probe out of the canyon, but the foreign body remained embedded.

"Please, Tristan, let's get out of the chill. It's just a bloody flashlight. It's nothing! *Leave it*, damn it!"

Ignoring him, the lodger clamored down the slope toward the oval object eerily targeted by the flashlight's waning beam. Fletcher watched with fascinated detachment as his guest crouched over the shape and then recoiled, his curious, up-lit countenance transforming to shock. By the time Fletcher joined him, Tristan's eyes were saucers, black with horror. He whorled into the darkness, away from the earthling Englishman, then reappeared with necromantic illumination. In the battery driven glow, the foreigner was a translucent extraterrestrial, trying to communicate with a primitive species.

"*What? What is this? Did you do this?*" the young man spat as he pointed to a skull cresting between the rocks.

Fletcher was unmoved by his guest's reaction. Instead, he stood calmly transfixed by the image in the ebbing light. Then, wearily stooping over the skeletal remains, he began an obviously routine procedure, loosely fitting rocks over the fissure that served as its sarcophagus.

"Who is this?" Tristan demanded. "*Who is this?*"

Fletcher met the accusing glare with a smile. The dog's ranting filled the darkness.

"Hush, Oliver. *Quiet!* Well, Tristan, I'll introduce you." Fletcher took a seat beside the nearly covered cranium. Its large empty eyes followed Fletcher's outstretched hand, its entomber sifting absently through the shale.

"May I present Don Christoval Alcon de Navarre y Marquis."

Tristan took one step closer, staring at the gaping visage. "A man?" he stammered, "From Spain?"

"Given his name, a likely conclusion." Fletcher yawned.

Tristan edged closer. "Did you kill him?" he whispered.

"Did I *what* . . . kill him? Rather unlikely." Fletcher retrieved the flashlight, shaking it for a last glimmer. "Take another look. I may feel five hundred years old, but I assure you I haven't been around that long. He – on the other hand - certainly has."

Tristan was overcome by curiosity. He bent down over the light, fascinated by the ancient countenance.

Fletcher placed the last two pieces of rock over its smooth forehead and stood up, announcing, "I'm going to bed."

"How do you know his name?" Tristan asked as Fletcher began his ascent.

"He wrote it," Fletcher shouted over his shoulder.

"He wrote it?" Tristan gasped.

"He inscribed it in the rock."

Tristan scurried up the outcroppings after his laboring host. "Why? Why here? Why is he here?"

Fletcher paused to catch his breath. "I don't know."

"What happened to him?"

"I don't know, Tristan."

"Why you *talk* to him?" Tristan persisted.

Fletcher stared down at the pile of rock. "He's a good listener."

Not amused, Tristan searched the inebriated eyes. "What is this, Fletcher? Who is this man?"

Fletcher lifted his head to the canopy of stars. "I imagine just another lost soul, Tristan, like me. Maybe like you. 'Lost souls in a New World.'"

12

Pete lay on his back listening to his wife's snoring. Her thick platinum hair was buried in the pillow, looking – in the dim light - like a fluffy, white Persian cat. She snorted, took a long gulp of air, and then resumed her loud purring. *When did she start that*, he wondered. He stared at the gray ceiling trying to still his thoughts but it was futile. The evening with Fletcher kept playing across his mind. The Englishman's confidence was so uncharacteristic that afterward, the poor man was spent. Still, despite the amount of libation, he was careful to edit. Pete knew better than to press the gaps. Instead, he accepted his challenge to one more chess game, and - considering it all – they both played well. It was only when Fletcher checked Pete's king that he said something in Latin so peculiar that Pete had to have its meaning. He rolled out of bed. Stealing down the basement stairs, he whispered it over and over again. He *knew* Latin, so he why didn't he get it? Blame it on the Dewars. He yanked the light chain, fumbled for the dictionary, and then realized that his glasses were still on the nightstand. He groaned, slamming the book on the desk. Then, he remembered. It struck him like a wave from a subconscious sea.

"Yes," Pete murmured. *"In hoc signo vinces."* He closed his eyes. "Under this sign, thou shalt conquer."

The new day arrived at the headboards of two men who let most of the morning tick by without notice. Tristan, on one side of the county, and Pete, on the other, did not stir from their peaceful dreams. But, no matter how he tried to remain in his own, Fletcher was compelled to wrench his aching body and pounding cranium from bed at his usual waking hour: six a.m. The previous night seemed centuries ago, but he remembered it in excruciating detail, trying to think how he could explain his behavior to his newly acquainted son. His divulgence to Pete was embarrassing enough. Tristan, on the other hand, had witnessed something utterly unnerving: his old man talking to a skeleton. He laughed out loud, ruefully preparing himself for his guest's imminent departure, but it never came. Instead, when a showered and shaved Tristan appeared in the hallway at noon, his first words were, "It is strange that a Spaniard should come here long ago. I must learn him."

As Fletcher raised his eyebrows, his occupant added, "I hope to have coffee."

Fletcher handed him his own freshly poured mug and watched his lodger waltz to the dining room research center. Trailing him, Fletcher began to broach the subject of the previous night, but was immediately dismissed with a flick of a long hand. "Not important," was all Tristan said.

The young Spaniard browsed through Fletcher's collection, flipping through pages, scrutinizing paragraphs. He would use his forefinger to hold a line of interest, and then snap each volume shut.

"First," Tristan announced, "I need English. You perhaps to teach me?"

13

"Dad, wake up." Pete felt his shoulder being poked. "Dad, Mom says you have to get up now. Here's your coffee."

Pete's eyes opened to behold his daughter's angelic face, and – at the sight of her – her rude intrusion was immediately forgiven. He received the mug with gratitude, and asked her the time.

"It's after twelve."

Ellen was eighteen and didn't look a thing like him. Then again, she wouldn't, as she wasn't *his* in the physical sense. She was, however, his spiritual and intellectual clone, as he enjoyed saying, if only to himself. She looked a lot like her mother and barely at all like the half-wit father who abandoned her when she was a year old. Pete's adopted was reddish-blonde and fair, with an aquiline nose and long, thick lashes shrouding her smoky amber eyes. She had a cleft in her chin and dimples when she smiled, as she was doing at the moment, smirking at his sinful state.

"Were you boozin' it last night, Mr. Pete?"

"I thought you were working today, Ellen."

"I am, at one. And, guess what?"

"What?"

"Bill's offered me a full-time position until the fall."

"No!"

"He did! Soooo. . . ." Ellen twisted the corner of his sheet around her finger. "I guess I'll need my own car sooner than we thought!"

"Oh."

"See ya, Dad! Good sermon-writing!" She skipped out of the room before he could beg a refill.

She poked her head around the door jamb. "Mom's taking me to work, so you don't have to. Up and at 'em, Reverend!"

Pete bounded out of bed like an over-fed impala, hastily hoisting up his pants and buttoning his wrinkled shirt as he pounded down the stairs. There was no way he was letting his wife take Ellen to work. He'd never hear the end of it.

"I'll do it!" he cried, "I'm coming! Ellen, I'm coming!"

She was waiting for him in the kitchen. "I thought so. . . ." She grinned, having already poured him one for the road.

A gathering of clouds forecasted a quiet afternoon for the private airport where Ellen worked. Pete rubbed his puffy eyes at the empty parking lot; its gooey asphalt shimmering in the heat. The airport manager was Bill Tabor; his SUV was parked in the back. Mechanic Nick Sparta had left his duelly in the hangar. Nevertheless, Pete waited for his petite daughter to emerge from the building with a thumb up before starting his car. She would be a freshman at Metropolitan State this year. With her brains and dedication, she should have been at Harvard. He sighed. It would have been his alma mater had he stayed, but a funny thing happened on the way to his future. He was sitting on a bench in the bitter Boston cold, contemplating a girlfriend's blistering farewell, when a snowflake melted on his hand. Another one floated to him, dissolving on his blue coat and then another one, on his knee. It was fascinating. As the snow gathered in the icy air, Pete used his breath to melt each tiny pristine deposit, knowing that each snowflake was distinct: a unique individual. It was only united that their metamorphosis could form a watery, life-giving membrane along his woolen sleeve. He squinted at the ice covered pond before him. On its furthest side, dark blurs scurried along a slippery sidewalk, rushing to warm havens where beer and lively debate would mix in the glow of candles and fireplaces. But for Pete, the frozen water that distanced him from his contemporaries was an infinite sea, separating a lucrative future from a destiny. That New England evening, physics and theology fused in the mind of a gawky, brilliant science major, and a new life form was born.

A sharp rap on the driver's side so startled Pete that he inadvertently slammed his palm into the horn, sending his perplexed daughter to the glass door.

"Heh, Pete!"

It was Bill Tabor, his Alfred E. Newman smile marred by two stained front teeth.

"Bill, my goodness!" Pete exclaimed. "How are you?"

"Good. Listen, do you think I can get you to move your car? You know? I could hit it if I have an emergency."

Pete scanned the autoless expanse around him, trying to control the involuntary moue that threatened to expose his opinion of the man.

"Of course, Bill. I was just leaving."

"Thanks. Take it easy, O.K?"

Pete threw the car into reverse, trying to grasp how his daughter could tolerate Bill. St. Ellen, he thought. He watched as the airport manager strutted into the building with the kind of smug satisfaction reserved for control freaks or megalomaniacs.

14

He was late: to be expected. Corey rested her aching back against the dowel fence. She had gathered the last of her three year olds into the corral – two fillies and two geldings – with the intention of sending them to Elan for training. Fifty-four and arthritic from injuries, she could no longer train them herself nor could she load them without help, so she was forced to wait. She wouldn't be breeding anymore. Houses were as hard to sell as horses, but at least real estate was easier on her bones. As Elan's truck and two horse trailer grumbled up the drive, she silently commended his wisdom. It would be so much easier to load two into her trailer and two into his, rather than all of them into his stock trailer.

Elan strolled toward her.

"What took you so long?" she snorted.

He ducked under the fence, his smooth ponytail caught by a sudden rush of cool air. Behind him, the sky was darkening. Corey watched as he quietly assessed each horse and murmured assurance. In the sixteen years she had known him, he had not aged at all. When her whole life was horses and her stallion was the darling of the show ring, Elan became her full-time ranch manager. He was the only long-term employee she had ever had, as he was the only one who could withstand her hellish temper. The payoff, though, was that he learned about training in a way that his gentle spirit could embrace. For all her faults, Corey had limitless kindness for horses; he forgave the rest.

"Elan, we better hurry. We're in for rain."

He adjusted a gelding's halter, and then snapped a lead rope on a filly. "We'll start with her. If you can keep him next to her," he pointed to the gelding," he'll do better."

In accord, Corey took charge of the gelding as her former apprentice opened the gate.

Elan grew up in New Mexico, the eldest son of six. Like many young men of his town and era, he was drawn to bull riding and bar fights. The bulls were overwhelmingly victorious, laying waste to most who rode them, and - with eight seconds an eternity - Elan was no exception. The hospital staff knew all the boys' names on arrival, but was particularly fond of the sunny Native American who withstood the agony of internal injuries and broken bones with rare forbearance. Ironically, it was when Elan converted to the relative safety of bronc riding that the real trouble began. No one knows what prompted the firing of a gun that penetrated his pick-up door and shattered his leg, but it put an end to his rodeo career, and ultimately, to his life in his home state.

"That's it." Corey swung the trailer door shut and felt a rush of unseasonably cold air at her back. She climbed into her truck. "Went better than I thought. I'll meet you at your house."

Elan nodded, hopped into his cab and lit a cigarette. His nervous cargo was stomping around the trailer, begging with high pitched pleas for freedom. The diesel engines roared, drowning out the distant thunder. As the trailers fought the ruddy gravel roads for balance and compromise, ever thickening clouds continued to billow at the horizon, plunging the golden grasses into colorless shadow, and sending an ominous message to the west.

15

All night a tempest ebbed and flowed, the plains undulating with the shapes and echoes of an ancient ocean. Fletcher passed on port to retire, leaving his dimly lit study to hum with the staccato of a computer keyboard, just audible above the rhythm of rain.

Tristan was a nocturnal creature, and always had been. It had served him well, especially as a small boy. When the relief of darkness descended on his tiny bedroom, his imagination would take him far from the daily rantings of his grandparents, the drunken vitriol of uncles, and away from the shrill defenses of his cornered mother. Deep into the night, he would draw pictures at his window, the street light illuminating a fanciful world that only he knew: a world of fierce, benevolent creatures protective of their maker, bent on the annihilation of those who would destroy their delicate creator with humiliation and violence. The gory bullfights that his uncles so adored and so sickened the boy would have a far different outcome in his youthful imagination. The tortured beast would be saved from the mob by the lethal sword of a warrior: a hero, a conquistador from another realm. As the cowards goaded the besieged animal, they would be struck down one by one, their hideous faces all the more repulsive as they begged for mercy, a mercy that would not be granted, not ever. Finally, his bloody weapon drawn, the conquistador would turn slowly, searching beyond the arena, beyond the dead for the one left standing: the evil one, the one who inflicted pain in the name of money: the matador. But even through Tristan's dreams, the matador would elude him, evil incarnate escaping into another world, always escaping . . . until now.

Like a first star, the computer screen burned brightly in the clearing night.

Ea, all is well. He's just what you said. A complete fool.

Tristan's thin finger pressed enter; the screen stating "sent" as the operator squashed the life from his cigarette in his father's Edwardian ashtray.

16

That Sunday, after Hymn Number Whatever, Pete took his usual place at the pulpit and announced that he couldn't think of a sermon that week, and, therefore, his congregation was discharged; they could go home . . . unless, of course, they felt like staying to share - for lack of a better definition – an exploration. A collective murmur reverberated across the vaulted ceiling, but no one got up to leave.

Pete cleared his throat and addressed his audience. "In that case, I'd like begin with a quote by a man named Wittgenstein: "To live in the present, is to live in eternity. Now, is that true? To live in the present," he repeated slowly, "is to live in eternity. I've been giving it a great deal of thought lately." Pete nodded at his ushers who picked up piles of stapled papers, and began passing them down the aisles. "And," Pete continued, "I am of the belief that this statement has merit. How can this be? And how does it relate to our conventional vision of heaven? Brothers and Sisters, I have taken the liberty of reprinting excerpts of articles that encapsulate a few theories by some of our great minds: Einstein, David Deutsche and Stephen Hawking among others. Please take a moment to review it."

The grumbling that followed sounded ominously like a rebellion. People rifled through the papers, glancing at each other with confusion and alarm. Pete waved his hands for their attention.

"Let's not worry about the reading material right now. All right. I might be a bit ahead of myself." He tapped on the pulpit. "All right, folks. What I'd like us to explore today is the matter of choice. Our choices: how many choices at any given moment we have and whether or not they affect not only our lives in the here and now, but other lives in other times. Seem simple? Then I ask you: could our choices actually affect *the past* as well as the present and the future? And, if we can determine even the smallest outcome, doesn't that mean we've altered all that is, perhaps was and will be? Doesn't that make us masters – if you will – of not only our own fate, but the fate of all? Doesn't it make us so powerful that we do not need God? Or could there be more to it?"

Ray sat stiffly next to Corey. He had not been to church in over twenty years, and had fully expected something so dull that he had planned a morning nap to counter the night's DT's. But now, he was wide-eyed, watching the fluid figure at the head of the little cathedral. Back lit by the graceful cambers of Art Nouveau stained glass, Pete flashed in and out of a kaleidoscope of color, strolling back and forth with the rise and fall of his baritone until his audience was utterly rapt. He thrust his large hand at each of his awestruck attendees, daring them to see beyond their limited horizons and cloistered lives. His voice in steady crescendo, he cast them into alternate dimensions, into time and space and parallel universes so vast and frightening that it exhilarated them and left them – for the first time that they remembered – truly alive and breathless. Leading them through the Big Bang theory into chaos, past the formation of galaxies, into the dawn of man - for those ethereal moments - Pete was able to share his staggering intellect and burn a simple message into their humbled souls: they counted. Every last one of them counted, supported not only by ancient texts but by far reaching theories that were just beginning to shed light on the meaning of existence, the truth of eternity and the unfathomable power at the tumultuous core of *energy, creation and consciousness: God.* Members of Pete's congregation filed out of the church that glorious morning with seared spirits, but they no longer bled. Pete had branded them with purpose and comradery and the wondrous joy of being children in an integral part of now and forever, Amen.

Ray's hand was the last one to shake. Pete thanked him for attending, discreetly reminding him that the AA meeting was at seven. As the rancher ambled away, Pete noticed the Deutsche/Hawking précis tucked under his arm. Ray had been the only one to take it.

Returning to the church, Pete found it deserted save for a small, platinum-haired woman gathering the volumes of paper left on the benches.

"Well, what did you think, Ruthie?" Pete asked, joining her in her methodical clean-up.

"What did *I* think?"

"Come on, Ruth," he begged. "A little over the top, was it?"

She left a neat stack of papers in the center aisle and sat down on the front pew, motioning him to join her. He did, stretching his spine over the hard wooden back, rolling his eyes with agony in anticipation of an honest answer.

"Pete," she said, "you were incredible. Was it over the top? *Yes.* More to the point, it was risky, and you know it. But you're an amazing man; so amazing, I'm not sure why you married little old me." She winked at him. "I guess I'm a good cook."

Pete draped a satin-robed arm around her. "You underestimate yourself, my dear." He let his head fall back, gazing into the arched ceiling. "You're a great cook."

17

At four o'clock, Ellen burst into the dining room and took her place at the table across from her twin brothers. There was only one thing better than her mother's Sunday dinner: a Sunday flying lesson with Guru Bill Tabor. The family didn't dare ask her about her afternoon until everyone was served, knowing that her exuberant recount might last as long as the flight. Sure enough it did, and no one got a word in edge wise. Finally finished, Ellen took a deep breath and looked around her. To her right, her brother Dillon feigned snoring. Her mother looked pained - as usual - at the mere mention of a flimsy twin engine. Pete continued to sip an espresso and nibble on apple pie. The twins were poking at each other and giggling, until one hazarded a request.

"Ellen, if you crash, can I have your iPod?"

Oblivious, Ellen washed down her dessert with milk and addressed her father beaming. "Dad, guess who has a perfect little runway for tricky take-offs!"

"Who?"

"Your friend, Fletcher Lawson."

"Oh. Yes, well. . . ."

"We flew over it today. It would be perfect for practice! Bill said so. It would be a great place to learn how to land – you know – over tough terrain. Great for competition! It's really pretty there, too. Do you think he'd let us? I mean do you think you might ask...."

"No!" Suddenly alert, Pete surprised everyone – including himself – by a reflexive slap on the table.

Ellen weighed her father's reaction. "Why not? Nobody's using it."

"Ellen, even if I had the *audacity* to ask – which I don't - he's not going to say yes. *Have you lost your mind?* That's where his wife...."

"Oh!" Ruth groaned. "Enough said! Out of the question."

"Oh come on!" Ellen cried. "It was a long time ago."

"Not for him." Pete tossed down the last of his coffee. "I won't ask him, and you're not to, either. Ruth - as usual - that was excellent." He stood, reaching for an empty plate.

Ellen tapped on her dessert dish with her fork. "Heh Dad, that was quite a sermon this morning."

"Did you like it?" He motioned to his boys to help clear the table. "What did you think?"

"What *I* think obviously doesn't matter," she declared. "But, if you get *fired again*, can we finally move to California?"

"*Ellen!*" Ruth shouted.

Dillon choked back a laugh.

"Yeah! California!" the twins squealed.

Pete wheeled to face his daughter. "We'll talk about it tomorrow."

"Tomorrow? Why tomorrow?"

He glowered at her. "We'll have plenty of time to talk on the way to Denver."

"Denver?"

"Yes, you know, *Denver:* where you find snazzy cars for snooty daughters."

Ellen screamed and leapt from the table to bear-hug her absolutely perfect old man.

18

Through ponderosa, the western sun dappled Tristan's pine-needled carpet. Books were open and strewn around him with doodles and questions scribbled in margins, to be dutifully addressed to his father. Picking debris from Oliver's coat, Tristan lazily repeated English phrases to the Briard, but the dog could only assure him that he was loved, not understood. From the bluff above them, Fletcher shouted that dinner was almost ready. Tristan rose and brushed himself off, gathered up his libros and bid farewell to Don Christoval Alcon de Navarre y Marquis.

Trout Almandine was served and not wasted on the only patron, who wolfed down a second helping. He declined a cup of tea, but accepted coffee. With desert on hold, the two exited out through the kitchen to indulge in the chef's other passion: gardening. Not long after his wife's demise, Fletcher had constructed an eight foot walled sanctuary and within it, painstakingly created a microclimate agreeable to the most delicate of perennials and imports. He began with a large central pond, and then –in lieu of his preferred cypress – lined upright juniper along the ivied walls. He then planted fruit trees along the pool's periphery, with English oaks on the water's edge to the east and west. Neither dogwoods nor azaleas would normally survive the climate, but Fletcher managed to coax them into full bloom in the years that followed, and was even witness to the flowering of a decade old Magnolia, its rusty petals still floating on the water's surface. With a never-ending supply of Little John fertilizer, the gardener kept his plot blanketed in acidic warmth throughout the winter; a fountain and heater keeping the pond open and the precious humidity ample. As father and son meandered along a slate path, Fletcher identified the garden's colorful components, interrupted by the scent of his most cherished labors of love. In four enormous Greek urns, orange trees were reaching for the twilight, their branches draped in veils of virgin white. Like sirens, they seduced the men into lingering with their sweet scent. Sinking on to a wrought iron bench, Fletcher whispered, "And these are. . . ."

"Naranjos," Tristan murmured with closed eyes and a smile.

On the way back to the house, the two made a quick detour to Little John's corral. The horse nickered, trotting to the corral fence in anticipation of supper. His soft nostrils blew into Tristan's palm, searching for the alfalfa cube that Fletcher had deposited there before parting for the hay loft. Finding the treat, the animal's large, curious eyes examined the soulful stranger, inviting him to come closer. Tristan tentatively reached for the massive, moonlit shoulder, and for the first time in his life, felt the silky neck and reverential power of equus caballus.

19

Tristan spent much of his time by the side of the lost conquistador or in the enormous walled garden, fondly named the "the fortress" by its British architect and builder. While Fletcher pampered his English roses, the language itself was being practiced loudly and theatrically by his son, hushed only in deference to a hummingbird's trill or a Nighthawk's evening buzz. The creatures of the plains delighted Tristan, but it was Little John that kept him in attendance. As the Iberian assumed the barn chores, the horse warmed to his surrogate keeper, who added a four o'clock brushing and an eight o'clock apple to the routine. When asked if the old horse was trained, Fletcher said that he was, but because he himself was not a rider, it had been a good twelve years since anyone had even saddled the beast. For that reason, he added – warding off the inevitable question – he did not trust the animal with a novice. Tristan's disappointment apparent, Fletcher thought about calling Corey for lessons, but dismissed the idea, fearing an irreversible intrusion into his life. So, for Fletcher, it was both fortuitous and unnerving, when - on an early June morning - the problem solved itself in the form of a man on a gray horse, ponying a red filly as he tracked along the Lawsons' eastern fence line.

Tristan was sketching in the company of Don Christoval and Oliver, when the canine barreled down the embankment and across the air strip, his aggressive alarm frightening the little mare in tow. Desperate to flee, she pitted herself against the rider and a fierce struggle ensued. The horseman tried to calm her as she threw all her strength against him, her rope leveraged against his saddle horn. The lead horse fought for balance, but his rider's skewed weight and the mare's backward thrust caused him to stagger. Charging down the hill to the fence line, Tristan lunged for the dog, furiously demanding silence. The yapping ceased but the mare broke away, snapping her halter and falling on her haunches. Righting herself, she stood trembling and white-eyed as she faced the dog and the stranger. Commanding Oliver to stay, Tristan edged toward her, then slowly picked up the broken halter and line. The rider freed the other end and watched as the Spaniard's quiet words transformed her fear into trust. As Tristan hung the rope over her neck, the cowboy dismounted, knotted the halter together and slipped it over her head. He then reached in his front pocket and withdrew a pack of smokes. Pushing back his hat, he grinned.

"How've you been, Hombre?"

Tristan smiled. "Good. You?"

"Good." Elan lit a cigarette. "Thanks for your help. How do you like the States?"

"I like it. It's good."

"Yeah?" Elan's moon face became rounder with laughter. "Even in the middle of nowhere?"

"Yes."

"So, have you seen any sights? What are doing with yourself?"

"Mostly, I stay here."

"Oh." The cowboy took a short drag. "Sounds exciting." He extinguished his half-smoked cigarette on his heel and put it back in his pocket. "Tryin' to quit. Well, it looks like you know horses. Maybe you wanna go on a round-up next weekend. It's all day, but the food's good; the beer's cold. There's a band at night if you want to hang around."

Tristan confessed that he had never been on a horse, but had plans to learn soon on one named Little John.

"Oh, Little John, sure. I know him," Elan said slowly. "Maybe not a good choice for someone just starting."

Tristan shrugged, turning to pet the filly.

"Tell you what. . . ." Elan pulled his wallet from his back pocket, extracting a worn business card and a half chewed pencil. Drawing a miniature map, he continued, "Why don't you come by – maybe tomorrow if you're not busy - and I'll help you." He handed Tristan the card. "This one's good to learn on," he added, patting his gray gelding.

"You sure?"

"Yeah. How about around four or five, when it's cooler?"

"O.K. Thanks."

Elan put his foot in the stirrup and swung over the horse, pulling the filly closer. With a two-fingered adios flicked off his brim, he turned to head home. Glancing behind him, he caught sight of Tristan dancing up the rocky slope with the mutt jumping all over him, obviously exposed to a cross-species contagion of pure glee.

20

The riding lesson was announced over shrimp scampi. Fletcher stopped chewing and nearly shattered his plate with his fork. "What was doing here?"

Tristan contemplated him before responding. "You do not like him. I'm sorry. I did not know."

Fletcher bit his lip. "Well, you couldn't have known. It doesn't matter. Anyway, enjoy it. It's a grand idea." He picked up his fork and stabbed at a pea.

"Why do you not like him?"

"I'd rather not discuss it."

"How do you know him?"

For the first time, the chef was annoyed by his company's questions and couldn't hide it. His eyes flickered. Tristan changed course.

"Fletcher, I do not know the rules, but I believe I cannot stay much longer. I have only a passport. . . ."

Fletcher's rising temper was suddenly quenched by fear. The idea of losing his son was intolerable. "We'll simply fix it, Tristan. We'll simply explain the situation and get an extension. I'll make some calls first thing in the morning. Don't worry, all right?"

"All right." Tristan popped a shrimp into his mouth. His was jiggling his foot restlessly.

Fletcher abandoned his meal and cleared his throat. "Listen, Tristan, it's occurred to me that I've shown you nothing of the States. Why don't we make a day of it tomorrow? We'll go to the museum, Denver, the mountains, whatever interests you."

Tristan glanced at him uncomfortably.

"Oh yes! Right! Sorry. 'Riding. Then, Friday."

The young man smirked. "It's all right, Fletcher. I'm fine." He resumed eating in silence.

Realizing that the lamentable gulf between them was his fault, and as the errant father, it was his responsibility to bridge it, Fletcher took a deep breath. He grabbed his wine glass and emptied it with an anxious swallow before proceeding.

"Tristan," he muttered softly, "I don't *dislike* Elan, exactly. I was a lousy husband; I knew it. I just.... My wife and he were ... how do I say it? Anyway, it's hard, you know, to...."

"You need say nothing more. I understand." Tristan applied a napkin to his mouth. "May I ask, how your wife, uh, I think the word is...."

"Muerte?" Fletcher poured himself a refill of burgundy and leaned back. "Is that what you mean?"

The guest shook his head affirmatively; his foot resumed its compulsive wiggling.

"She crashed her plane."

"Tristan helped himself to more wine. "What happened?"

"It's hard to say."

"The plane was not right?"

"They found nothing wrong with it."

"The weather, then?"

"Blue sky." Fletcher sniffled and sloshed down his drink. He sighed. "For a long time, they claimed I murdered her; *they* meaning her father, the police, the dirty tabloids. They said that I had everything to gain by killing her, that I never loved her, that I made her life miserable, and that she was the victim of a sociopathic fortune hunter, all of which - by the way - was true."

"But you did not kill her. She was not good flying."

Fletcher cackled. "She was an excellent pilot. She landed in that canyon a thousand times. I had just come home from the post office. . . ."

"You were not even here! She lost control. That is all!"

"Maybe. I wish it were that simple. I don't know. She simply flew right into the canyon wall."

"But, *why*?"

Fletcher shook his head. "Maybe because I *was* there."

Tristan emptied the bottle and pulled a cigarette from his pocket. "Did she hate you?"

"I thought we had an understanding."

"So, that is all?"

"That's all I can tell you."

"So, how could you kill her? How stupid!"

"One theory was that I broke her neck after I pulled her from the wreckage. Another version was that she was going to land, but saw me with a weapon, a gun or something, so she crashed in an *evasive maneuver*. There were all kinds of stories: horrible, lurid stories. Some said that I was furious over her affairs. But, of course, the overriding motive was that I wanted her money: *all of it*. Well, Tristan, all I can tell you - all I can *swear to you* - is that I didn't. . . ."

With an emphatic wave, Tristan cut him off. "Say nothing more, Fletcher. Say nothing more. I believe you. Truly, I believe you. For all your sins, I don't care. I don't care if you *did* kill her. That is all." He stood, lighting a cigarette, shaking the pack at his host. "Join me?"

Fletcher remained seated. "What do you mean, *you don't care*? You don't want a father that's a. . . ."

"I don't care." Tristan interrupted coolly, stuffing the pack back into his shirt pocket. "Really. There are worse things than killing, don't you think?"

Fletcher blinked. "Worse things? No, I don't."

Tristan shrugged. "In war one kills without regret. In war, *losing* is worse than killing."

"We're not talking about war. We're talking about the life of a young woman."

"It's one person, Fletcher. One person that perhaps was cruel to you. Perhaps it was you or her. I don't know. I don't care. I don't believe you killed her, so. . . ."

"Tristan, I don't understand you. *Murder* means nothing to you?"

"Nothing."

"*It's not wrong*?"

"Fletcher. . . ." Tristan shoved his chair under the table and gripped its back rail with both hands, his cigarette smoldering between two fingers. "This much I have learned in life: there is only one side: my side; in your case: your side. There are billions of people, and none of them care what happens to you or to me. And there's no mercy – believe me - if you're in their way. There are, perhaps, ideas of decency, but, really: what serves us – betters our lives — defines what we find morally acceptable. Hm? It's simple. This is politics: the way of the world. When we kill, we say we have no choice, but really we kill because we're greedy in one way or another; we want more or to keep others from taking what we have away. If we're rich, it's because they're poor; better than the other way around. We want God to support our battles, make our desires a holy cause, but it's a sham. Because the truth is: people send their own children to war, to die – not for ideology – but to keep their big houses and cars. No, Fletcher, it's really very simple: it's us or them; you or me: survival. I don't care what happened to your wife. I doubt you killed her. I don't think you have it in you to kill anyone – at least to do it *yourself* - but if you did, you had your reasons, and it's all right with me."

Tristan's eyes were glowing as if lit by an internal inferno. "Well?" He was puffing compulsively. "Would you join me watching television? Hmm? Have you nothing to say?"

The Englishman was drumming his fingers on the table, finally meeting the scorching gaze with his own. "Well, Tristan, I must say, your command of English is nothing short of *astonishing!*"

Tristan's face flushed.

Fletcher erupted out of his chair. "I guess we can drop the language barrier crap! So, who taught you? Well? *Goddamn it! Who taught you?*"

Tristan was poised for attack when a wave of unnatural calm washed over him, mollifying his posture and dulling his eyes. "You taught me, Fletcher: my inspiration, ever since I first learned of you."

"*Really!* And your cynicism, your so called *moral code?* Who taught you that?"

Fletcher," the Iberian purred, "I'm sorry you find it so offensive. But I hardly think you're one to judge. I mean it's a little late for that. Still, maybe I would have been a better person: an *idealistic,* pussy-chasing money-hungry whore like you, if you hadn't *deserted us!*" Tristan stormed down the hallway. Fletcher bolted after him.

"*I didn't know about you, Tristan!*"

The young man spun around furiously. "You did. You had to have known."

"She never told me!"

"You knew!"

"Tristan, please!"

"You fucking knew! *You knew! Don't lie to me!*" Driving his fists into his pockets, the Spaniard clipped down the corridor. With the slam of the door, he charged out into the plains.

For nearly a dozen years, a recluse had barely experienced personal interaction, much less confrontation. It left him traumatized and in retreat to his study.

21

An eerie, electronic glow was seeping under the master bedroom door as Fletcher stood before it. It was nearly eleven o'clock. He knocked lightly. The door splayed open. On the bed, a suitcase was packed. Tristan was zipping it shut.

Fletcher leaned against the door jamb with his arms crossed. "I think I suspected she was pregnant, all right? I'm fairly certain I knew, but I can't be sure. That's the truth. I don't remember anymore. I've blocked it all out. But maybe that's why I ran out on her. Look, I don't blame you for how you feel, but I'm asking you not to leave. I just want to know what happened . . . what you happened to *you*. I know I can't make it right, but I'd like to . . . I don't know. Why didn't you tell me you spoke English? I mean, you're fluent, more than fluent. So why did you . . . ?"

"I didn't know you." Tristan sighed, rubbing his forehead. "I thought that if there was something that you could teach me, something you could give without it costing much, it would make you feel. . . I don't know . . . absolved or something like that. I thought it would be a reason for me to stay."

Fletcher shook his head. "Jesus, lad."

"I'm sorry. I'm sorry for. . . ."

"Tristan, for God's sake, don't. Look, speak any language you like. It's all right. Just unpack your things. I mean, I must say, the conversation will be so much easier. Not so much bloody work. Please. We can have a better go of it now, don't you think?"

He noticed his lap top glowing in the dark, but said nothing. His counterpart, however, noted his observation and turned to retrieve it. "I'll put it back." Tristan blurted. "I just thought. . . ."

"Don't bother. I rarely use it; I told you. Get some rest."

The Spaniard nodded.

"This business is settled then? Will you stay?"

Assured by a smile, Fletcher bid him good night, and shuffled toward the warm embrace of absolution and bed.

That night, a huge phosphorescent moon defied the darkness, flooding Fletcher's bedroom in an albescent glow. His simple English antiques were transformed into the baroque, embellished with ephemeral silver ormolu. Restless, he kicked off the quilt, drawing back the curtains of his memory, unleashing his painful childhood in an effort to find the soul of his son. He tasted his mother's bitterness. He heard the British secret service bursting through the door, the picture of his father thrust at him. He heard his mother's pleas, her protective arms shoving him up the stairs, blocking their pursuit with kicks, screams and denials. He saw her green eyes slowly become hollow with anger, alcohol and age. He heard her endless reproaches and condemnations, her haughty English invectives against the Irish plague. Life's disappointment became an even more iniquitous torment when her son grew into adolescence. She never wanted an *artist*; she wanted an avenger: an upstanding, ambitious Englishman to vanquish their poverty and to bear the cross that her husband so recklessly cast down, leaving them in ruin and shame. She sacrificed *everything* – including a wellborn London family – to live with a race of curs, and now her only child was one of them.

Fletcher's lids squeezed together in agony. He couldn't bear it then, nor could he now. Ryan Egan raced away, breathlessly distancing himself with the passage of decades. He crashed through the membrane of time, into the world of Lawson, scanning the room for signs of the familiar and blessed present, but it wasn't what he found.

Instead, washed in the moonlight, a figure stood before him. Fletcher sat upright, gasping for air. He called Tristan's name, but instantly realized his error. He tried to quiet his adrenaline-driven heart, whispering, "Who are you?"

The intruder's face was cloaked in shadow. His textured clothes were an indiscernible color; a loose shirt hung over his boney shoulders. He was a wiry man of medium stature. His long wavy hair hinted at gold in the ashen gloom; his coarse beard hung like a dagger across his neck.

"Who are you?" Fletcher repeated.

The stranger slowly lifted his right hand and applied it to his chest. "Mi hijo," he murmured, "he perdido mi caballo."

Fletcher shrank back as the man took a step toward him.

"Mi hijo, he perdido mi caballo." The trespasser's voice was barely audible against a nocturnal wind.

"I don't understand you." Fletcher panted. "What do you want?"

"He perdido mi caballo," the intruder persisted, suddenly thundering, "he perdido mi caballo!"

He rushed to Fletcher's side. He was armed with a short sword, his protruding cheekbones a breath away. A huge scar like a bird of prey was visible through his opaque shirt, the ghastly, outstretched wings graven across both clavicles, the open beak seared into his mid chest. The assailant's deep-set eyes were glassy and impenetrable, terrifyingly fixed and furious.

"Oh God! Jesus!" Fletcher screamed. His hand smashed into the night table lamp, sending it to the floor in a trail of sparks and fragments.

Oliver's bark could be heard echoing down the hallway as his master sat frozen in the darkness. The door burst opened; the ceiling fixture suddenly ablaze. Oliver leapt on the bed, pinpointing the scent of blood to Fletcher's fingers. Tristan was squinting in the harsh light, studying his father's crimson palm and the wreckage on the floor.

"Are you all right? What happened?"

"It was nothing, a dream." Fletcher gulped air, the tension in his body giving way to trembling. He withdrew to the bathroom to run cold water over his hand, then splashed his face. The bleeding stopped. He departed for the hall closet.

Tristan was methodically picking up shards when his counterpart - armed with a dustpan and broom – reappeared. "I'll get it, Tristan."

"What were you dreaming?"

"Oh nothing. A stupid dream. Too much wine. 'Better lay off for a while. Go back to bed. Oliver, get out of that! Tristan, please. Take him out."

The help left with the dog, but quickly returned - unescorted - as Fletcher poured the last of the lamp into the trash can.

"Is your hand all right?"

"Yes."

"I brought you some juice."

"Oh, thank you." Fletcher slumped on the bed and downed it in one swallow. Tristan switched on a less obtrusive desk lamp and extinguished the overhead. Fletcher noticed his curious stare and leaned back on his pillow. "What's on your mind?"

"I wondered what you were dreaming."

"Nothing. It was just a dream."

"Oh. Well then, I'll leave you."

"Tristan, before you go. . . ."

"Yes?"

Fletcher cleared his throat. "What does he perdido mean?"

"I have lost." The Castilian cocked his head. "What have you lost, Fletcher?"

"Aside from my mind?" He shook his head. "Mi caballo."

"Your *horse?*" Tristan's laugh was medicinal. "I assure you, you haven't."

Fletcher chuckled, shaking his head at the absurdity.

Nevertheless, an hour later, he rose, tiptoed to his study and peered through the window, reassured by the silhouette of a huge caballo dozing against the dawn.

22

Ray winged another frozen dinner into his shopping cart, counting to make sure that he had at least a month's supply. He hated the supermarket; all the color and commotion made him nauseated. Finding the complete-and-utter-junk-food aisle, he piled several boxes of assorted fatteners atop his entrees. Calling it good, he squeezed past the busty mothers in the bakery section and made a bee-line to the checkout. As he fidgeted behind a coupon fanatic, a hand grabbed his shoulder. Ducking out from under it, he spun around.

It was Bill Tabor, with his own mound of potato chips and candy bars, smiling in between bites of a particularly gooey treat. "Ray! Nick told me he saw you in church! Wow! Now I believe everything!"

Bill's mouth was so gummed up he couldn't chew anymore. All he could do was to wait for the stuff to melt. "So, are you really off the sauce?" he garbled.

Ray blushed and angled a glance at the check-out girl still ringing up discounts. "What of it?"

"Actually," Bill replied with a happy face, "we've been thinking about you! Nick's vacation is coming up. He's taking two weeks next month. And if you really are, you know, not, uh . . ." With an air bottle, Tabor cocked his head back and took a long, dramatic guzzle, "doing *that* all the time, I was wondering if you could sub for him again."

Ray didn't answer. He was too busy trying to figure how long he would serve for clocking old Billy right there, right into the stand of Enquirers and People Magazines. Let's see, he pondered. It had been a long time since he'd been in any real trouble, so maybe. . . . Ray scowled. The truth was he needed the money. "Sure, I'll do it."

"You'll need to come by and spend a few days with Nick. And you can only do the little stuff; nothing major. I know, I know. You can handle the big repairs - everybody knows you can fix anything - but, remember, you're not licensed and you've got that *little problem*. Anyway, we have more planes now, but the routine's the same. Nick will bring you up to speed. You sure you can stay off. . . ?"

"Yeh. Is that it?"

"That's it. Great. Well, Nick will call you, then. I see you like to cook." Bill was smirking, his lower lip smeared with chocolate. If only it was blood, Ray thought.

23

With Ray's truck fixed, Corey was free to schedule errands without him, but found that she missed him. He had given her an excuse to dress up a little and go out to lunch. Now, she had a feeling that her next trip into Denver would be its usual lonely tedium. She glanced at Ray's old wolf, its fearsome head propped on her toes like a puppy. If Ray stayed sober she might have to give him back but she'd hate to. She added rawhide bones to her list and was contemplating a haircut when the phone rang. It was her zillionaire client, Gordon Mackey. He was considering Fletcher's property, but not at the asking. Corey listened to his reasons for low balling: he didn't really need another house; the beauty of the land was appealing, but *awfully* remote, blah, blah, blah. When he finally gave her his price, she countered it with two words: water rights. They were old and deep, making them valuable, and the seller was no fool, implying that she wasn't either. Whether Gordon *needed* another house was of no consequence to Lawson, who, by the way, had no mortgage. In other words: wrong season for a fire sale, all of which Gordon knew. With Colorado's sluggish economy grinding to a halt, he had plenty of time. He thanked her for her candor.

With vast holdings in the western states, magnate Gordon Mackey was an insatiable real estate investor, converting much of his acreage into tax-escaping conservancies, serving the multiple purposes of inflating his wealth, supporting his huge cattle operation, and curtailing development which served to mute his greenie, methane-hating critics. As an investment banking mogul, his profit proliferating cerebrum had seemed invincible, but, along with his empire, the headache plagued CEO was showing signs of unraveling. Somewhere deep within his long, convoluted contracts, Gordon Mackey's emotive persona was resentfully buried and pounding on its would-be coffin. No acquisition would quell it for long, and his pre-emptive business strikes failed to distract it. The ever rising tide of discontent that threatened to expose 58 empty years was drowning him. Worse, his dispassionate façade was having a hard time masking it. Thus, it was strangely fortuitous when a geographic anomaly was discovered by Mackey's aerial mapper along the Lawson side of Wolf canyon. When it was brought to Gordon's attention, his internal rebellion instantly subsided, replaced by pure, focused excitement. The sharp intellect that had tamed Wall Street's greenback was setting his sights on something far more colorful: gold.

24

It was a forgery, Fletcher thought. He watched the clouds waft into an Italian masterpiece: shafts of virgin light striking through Sistine pastels. He sighed. Sunset in Colorado could be as glorious as creation itself. But, he had accounting to do. If he knew Elan at all, Tristan would be home late.

Fletcher fetched his laptop from the master bedroom and set it on his desk. His mother's monthly deposit used to be his only need for the internet, but recently he found it just as easy to tender all his bills that way. Logging on, the home page indicated e-mails. As Tristan had been surfing, Fletcher assumed it was spam and was tempted to disregard it, but curiosity spurred him to take a look, if – for no other reason – than to clear out all the cyber-offal. Indeed, there was plenty of garbage, but two seemingly legitimate missives were directed to Tristan, one with a subject: Ea; the other: Christoval Alcon... too intriguing to ignore. In English, it was from a professor at a Mexican university. It simply stated that there was a mention of a Christoval Alcon de Navarre y Marquis in the colonial record during the requested time frame. This man had applied to the Viceroy, Don Luis de Velasco II for permission to lead an expedition into northern territory. There is no further information other than the request was denied. The year of application was 1595.

Fletcher sat momentarily stunned, then, bolted out of his chair and sprinted to the dining room. It was late for Spanish exploration. He flipped through his notes: they generally concentrated on Coronado's era, off – he realized now – by some fifty years. But there was someone else, someone he hadn't considered because of lack of renown, someone tied to the last years of that sixteenth century. He thumbed through his loose-leaf impatiently, finding nothing until a margin jot leapt off a page: Quivira, with an arrow pointing to 1601, and the name Onate. He scoured his texts, finding a summary of the man. The same viceroy that had dashed the dream of Christoval de Navarre had granted one to Don Juan de Onate in - none other - the year 1595. His subsequent campaign would ford two centuries and the reign of two kings.

Fletcher piled any material pertinent to Juan de Onate in a corner of the dining room table, then - remembering that the computer was on - dashed back to the study. The screen was counting down the minutes to disconnection. The mysterious e-mail with subject Ea was there, tempting him, but it was embarrassing enough that he had already opened *one*, how could open the other? How could he possibly explain his invasion of Tristan's privacy? There was no excuse; clearly, he had breached a trust. Suddenly, Fletcher was reading the second e-mail without a conscious decision to do so. It simply happened, and there it was in English: one sentence. *Password your inbox before 12:00 a.m. Ea.*

"Well now I can see why," Tristan's proclaimed, spanking the back of the spy's chair.

"Jesus! Tristan! Lord! *Oliver!* What's *matter* with you? You're supposed to warn me!"

Stretched beside the desk with a guilty eye on his master, Oliver offered his torso for a belly rub. Tristan obliged.

"I have no excuse, Tristan. A deplorable thing to do. It won't happen again; you have my word."

Tristan sprawled out on the rug next to the dog.

"Well?" Fletcher stared down at the two prostrates. "Have you nothing to say?"

"I'm sore." Tristan hung his calves up over the edge of the coffee table. "And it might be worse tomorrow."

"Possibly. Are you an official cowboy now?"

"No. I am an official cripple. I don't think cowboys feel like this at the end of the day."

"Don't kid yourself. That's why they're always hobbling around with a beer in their hand. Listen, Tristan, I feel like a. . . ."

"The e-mail? Don't worry. It's natural. I looked at yours, too."

"*Did you?*"

"Yes."

"I didn't know I had any."

"Nothing but garbage, but I *looked*. What can I say?" Tristan dropped his legs to the floor, rolled over and groaned.

"Serves you right," Fletcher stepped over him, "for reading my e-mails. I saved you some dinner. By the way, you might check your other message. . . ." He trailed off down the hallway.

25

It was the second day that Ray's primer-gray pick-up was waiting in front of the local library as a hefty Ronnie Dunne was unlocking the front door. He skipped up the front steps.

"Ray!" she exclaimed, exasperatedly. "I told you! It takes a while for those books to come in!"

"I know, but. . . . Well, how long?"

"I don't know." She sighed, attempting to get the stubborn lock to catch. "It could be up to six weeks. I mean, I haven't heard. I don't know if they've been checked out or. . . ."

"Where are you getting them?"

Her eyebrows narrowed as she tried to force the door open. "They're not common books: books on physics and theories and all that stuff. . . ." Her teeth clenched, she was pushing the door with her shoulder while angrily twisting the key in its slot. "I guess most of them would be coming from the Denver Public. . . ."

"You want me to try that?"

She gratefully stepped aside, smoothing her paisley skirt. Ray played the old opener from side to side, listening with an ear cocked to the single bolt. He then applied upward pressure on the key, and the lock responded with an affable click.

"Oh, wow! Thank you, Ray! Honestly, you're a genius. Can you fix that for good?"

"Yea, probably; I'd have to take it apart."

"Can you fix it today? I'll pay you!" She glanced at her watch.

"Maybe this afternoon."

"Good! See you later!"

She rushed into the dark breezeway while Ray sauntered back to his truck, whistling. The magicien mecanique was definitely back in business. He drove straight to the gas station. While filling up, he made a phone call.

"Heh, it's me. Wanna go to Denver?"

"When?"

Corey would be ready in ten minutes. He hung up beaming, scrutinizing his shirt for stains: not bad. She'd probably want to drive; he didn't have a license. He frowned. Still, she had GPS so it'd be easier to find the library. Ah, what the heck.

26

"*It's our caballero! Amazing!*" Tristan was busy disorganizing the Onate records, hurling publications everywhere as he plunked his hot coffee on the mahogany. Fletcher snatched it and repositioned it on a coaster before settling across the dining room table. "What makes you think he was a *caballero*?"

Tristan looked at him stupefied. "He *must* have had a horse, which makes him a caballero!" He reached for his mug, sifting through an encyclopedia.

"Right." Fletcher rubbed his jaw, feeling his uncustomary five o'clock shadow. Too tired to shave, he had been barely able to stomach tea and hadn't showered. "God," he muttered, "what brought him *here*? Assuming he was with Onate, why did he leave his party?"

"Perhaps he didn't like the company," Tristan mused, flipping another page. "Perhaps the Falcon of Navarre preferred to hunt alone."

The ensuing silence prompted Tristan to divert his attention from Volume 8 to his present company, whose pale color and troubled expression prompted him to put down his coffee. "What is it?"

"*What* did you call him?"

"What, the Falcon? His name: Alcon means falcon. Christoval Alcon de Navarre: De Navarre: of. . . ."

"Yes, I know. He or some ancestor was from the province or something of Navarre. But . . . is that usual? I mean, was it? To have a name of a bird: falcon?"

Tristan shrugged. "I don't know. It's just a name. Why? What does it matter? You look strange. Are you all right?"

Fletcher didn't answer, lost in a recent dream.

27

Pete was chauffeured to his chess match by his daughter. Her new, midnight blue Camaro was coated with silt by the time they arrived. To her father's dismay, she revved the motor playfully before parking. As the big man tried to extricate himself from the car, she hopped out and swept her hand across the hood, lamenting its condition.

"California has *paved* roads, Dad."

With one leg in and one leg out, Pete felt wedged between two worlds. He clawed the roof with his right hand and braced his left elbow against the seat, wrestling against his imprisonment. Oliver rounded the corner, broadcasting their arrival with unnerving zeal.

"Oh perfect," Pete moaned, unable to move. "Ellen, could you give me a hand, here. Ellen?"

She didn't respond. Between the dog's decibels and the eyes of an amused, indigo-eyed Adonis, she was lost to her father's appeals.

Taking pity on the trapped apostle, Tristan strolled down the steps, his perfect continental smile twisting into a grimace as he strained against Pete's corpulent six foot five frame. The young man braced his foot against the rocker panel and pulled on Pete's wide arms. Ellen begged her father not to dent the car as she pushed from the driver's side. While Oliver noisily refereed, Tristan jerked hard and the pastor finally hit the ground – bottoms up - along with his Spanish liberator. Ellen rushed to the hero, offering him a hand, but Tristan was laughing so hard he could neither stand nor speak. Chuckling, Fletcher trotted down the stairs to meet his guest, Pete wearing an aggrieved look as he was helped to his feet.

"Well, that calls for a drink!" Fletcher declared, dusting him off. "Perhaps you should allow me to give you a lift home, old boy." Peals of laughter followed.

Taking a deep breath, the minister loomed over his companions, pointing at his host. "Oh! A persifleur! How irritating! I assure you, revenge will be mine tonight." He flicked a bug from his sleeve. "Now, where's that drink?"

Feigning to leverage his weight against Ellen's tiny hand, Tristan hoisted himself up. She blushed and introduced herself.

He studied her. "You have a beautiful car, Ellen."

"Thank you." She looked away, twirling a lock of hair around her finger.

"Ellen, did I forget to say hello?" Fletcher kissed her on the cheek. "By the way, I'm serious. I *will* take your father home."

"Oh, great, Fletcher. Thanks."

"Would you join us for uh, let's see, lemonade or soda? Tea, perhaps?"

"Yes, thank you. Anything. I'd like that."

"Well, come in! Ellen's too *young* to partake legally," Fletcher announced, shooting a glance at his son.

"I *see*," Tristan replied genially. "Well, I'm not, and a beer would taste great!" He helped Ellen with the grocery bags, skipped up the steps and held the door open.

While Tristan and Ellen toured Fletcher's Garden of Eden, the armchair warriors settled comfortably behind their respective armies. Fletcher tipped back his port. "Pretty fancy wheels for your little girl."

"I had to borrow the money from my mother," Pete declared flatly, helping himself to an apple wedge.

Fletcher regarded him critically. "Forgive me for asking, Pete, but. . . ."

"But why – at age fifty- five - am I still borrowing money from my mother?"

"Well, no, not exactly. But, you're possibly the best educated man I've ever met. Naturally, I'm curious. Why are you here, in the middle of . . . nowhere?"

"Well, my dear friend - to put it bluntly - I don't have an optimum employment record."

"In the ministry? How can you have bad resume in the ministry?"

"You've never heard my sermons."

"What about them?"

"Drop in on Sunday. I think you'll get the gist."

Fletcher's eyes felt like they were burning. He put down his glass. "Pete, forgive me, but you could be raking in a six figure income without any problem. Your background alone is worth. . . ."

"Hardly the point."

"All right. Not my affair. I understand."

"No, that's not what I meant."

"Well, then, I can't help but ask, why do you do it? Is it worth it? Do these people really appreciate you?"

Pete lit his cigar and leaned back. "At the moment, I don't know. Is it important? Why do you paint?"

Fletcher rubbed the back of his neck. "Enjoyment, I suppose."

"But you don't. You told me yourself it was agonizing. That's why you dropped it. Yet, lately, you've been thinking about another canvas. So if it isn't for money or attention – which obviously it isn't – why do you do it?"

"I don't know; it's a drive I suppose."

"To what end?"

"None. It serves no purpose."

"That you know of."

"That I know of. All right. I see your point. Sometimes we're just driven to do things."

"No. That's not my point. You want to make it trivial when it's not. Fletch, painting has no bearing on your survival. You know it, rationally. So, I repeat, why do you do it?"

"I suppose there's a part of me. . . ."

"Yes! Yes! Exactly! There is a part of you, *a part of you* that *transcends* your most basic instincts, and what *should* be your most gratifying pursuits: food, sex, security, comfort. . . . If these issues are addressed, why isn't it enough? Why do you paint? Why garden? Why *create*?"

"I, I don't know."

"Creativity is a process, and we all have that drive: to create something from nothing. When you learn simply for the sake of learning, when you make something - something impractical just because you must - you're *reaching* - like a child without reason – to find something nourishing . . . for your *soul*. Art's just a tool to keep you observant, to keep you *reaching*." Pete's mouth was full of cheese. He swallowed. "Fletcher, right now we are in the midst of discoveries so profound that we can't even see them! We are taking a great step in evolution *right now*. We live as physical beings in a physical dimension, but we're transcending it. Our future! It's fantastic, and it's *not* physical! Learning, art and scientific advancement are all a critical part of a spiritual flight. *We have been gifted!* We are *driven to seek*. Now we have to trust that gift and the light of the path and. . . ."

"Heh, Dad!" Ellen burst into the room and reached over the chair, grabbing Pete's startled shoulders. "We're going to the movies. We can catch the eight o'clock."

Where's Tristan?"

"Changing his shirt. The horse gobbed on it. Gotta go! Bye, Dad. Fletch, great garden! Much better up close!"

She tossed her keys up and snatched them mid-air before disappearing.

The chess opponents were in languid contemplation of the board. Fletcher cleared his throat. "Well, Pete, I can see the problem."

"With?"

"Job security."

"Oh. . . yes."

Fletcher rubbed his temples in response to the dull headache he had endured all day. "Do we feel like playing tonight?"

"I guess we don't."

"Let's take a walk. Grab your drink."

The garden was particularly divine that evening. Rich floral patterns were inlayed like fine marquetry around an obsidian pool. Pete was astonished, not only by the beauty, but the degree of hard labor it must have required. The pastor said little, allowing what was left of his friend's foppish repute to retreat with the evening sunlight.

"A lot of work, Fletch."

"I had time."

"You do it all yourself?"

"Yes."

"Why?"

"Why not?"

"It must have been lonely."

"It was my penitentiary duty."

"Really? How's that?"

There was no answer. A white koi suddenly surfaced and disappeared, breaking the stillness of the water in the twilight. The lily pads rearranged themselves. The gardener scanned the pond, monitoring the first starry reflections. "Do you believe in ghosts, Pete?"

"Define ghosts."

"You know: apparitions."

"Oh, you mean literally: the phenomena of seeing someone in a quote unquote paranormal state. Yes."

"You *do*?" You believe in ghosts?"

"Why? Have you seen one?"

"I had a dream. But, it was just a dream."

"Oh."

"Have *you* ever seen one, Pete, or thought you had?"

"No, but it's not out of the realm of possibility: to encounter someone from the past or – for that matter - the future in some form or another. Time as a long, rigid line doesn't make much sense in terms of space. It probably warps, bends, wrinkles, overlaps. There are probably infinite realities, although we happen to be blindly immersed in this one. Given the right circumstances, anything's possible."

"So, you're a sci-fi enthusiast?"

"A student of physics." The big man bent down on one knee, scrutinizing the murky water. "Great minds are pushing the limit of what we know every day. There's no such thing as *no such thing*."

Fletcher inhaled the moist air and sighed. Tomorrow, the baroque flora would be unmercifully exposed to the sun and the striking chroma bleached from the blooms. His sanctuary would be vulnerable to the hostile elements, just as he would be, if he dared to invite this mystical man into his inner sanctum. Yet, the forces that would redefine the world at daybreak were reshaping him, too, and it was inevitable that the question be addressed.

"Pete," Fletcher cleared his throat. "I know it sounds odd, but I was wondering . . . can I trust you? Should I?"

The friar struggled to his feet. "Fletch, no matter what I say, you're the only one who can answer that."

Fletcher studied his confrere, and then beckoned him to follow. Parting the heavy, inveckee doors, they left the enclosure, just as the Milky Way's luminous brushstroke splashed across an amethyst sky.

28

Around midnight, high beams washed the Lawson driveway with an obscene pallor. Spectral insects danced chaotically as Tristan lit from the Camaro with a "wait" sign to the driver, and dashed into the house. Two men were commiserating in the corner of the parlor like eighteenth century plotters, inebriated and energized. Attuned to the level of excitement, the movie-goer deduced that the heavy man was now privy to the existence of Don Christoval, and found himself resenting it.

"Ellen's waiting," he announced stiffly. "She wants to know if you want a ride home."

The discussion that followed culminated with the Pete's s insistence that he accompany his daughter. Pete squeezed himself into the car, kissed Ellen hello and waved goodbye to Fletcher and son.

The big man compressed his legs under the glove compartment. "You smell like smoke, my dear girl."

"He smokes, Dad. *And I'm eighteen*, remember?"

"You have asthma, remember?"

In the dashboard's lime glow, Pete couldn't get a read his daughter's distant delirium. She remained a near stranger until she eased to the last stop sign, when she turned to him with a vitriolic blast. "I can't believe Fletcher! He called Tristan twice during the movie! I mean, *how weird is that?*"

Pete's eyes widened. "That's ridiculous! He was with me the entire night. He didn't make any calls."

"Oh yeah? What about when he went to the bathroom?"

"All right, that's enough!" Pete shifted his weight to one side. "We were outside most of the time, not that this . . . this *crime* warrants a defense. What's gotten into you?"

"Nothing." She exhaled loudly. "Do you know Tristan hasn't met anybody, not one of Fletcher's friends, except you?"

"He doesn't have any. And - for your information - he hates the telephone. He doesn't even have an answering machine. Is that what Tristan said? Did Tristan say it was *Fletcher* on the phone?"

"Not exactly," she crossly conceded.

He motioned her to accelerate. His legs were cramping. "Ellen, a sign of maturity is not jumping to conclusions."

"I know," she grumbled.

So before you. . . ." He squirmed. A charley horse was coming on. "Oh, thank goodness," he exclaimed, "the driveway!"

Ellen parked the car outside the garage and rushed around to help her Dad, but he had already positioned each limb for a successful catapult, alighting almost gracefully. He limped to the front door. Once inside, he extinguished the outside light and plodded irregularly up the stairs. He paused on the landing.

"Ellen?"

"Yes?"

"Just a word of caution. Don't get wrapped up with him, O.K? He's not here for long."

There was no sound save for her door shutting in the darkness.

29

"Why did you tell him?" Tristan demanded.

Fletcher was absently wiping down the coffee table. "I don't know. I guess I wanted his take on it."

"You've known about Don Christoval for ten years! You've told no one. *Why now?*"

Fletcher shrugged. "I didn't tell him much. I just wanted his advice."

"*About what?*"

"Tristan," Fletcher sighed wearily, "as you know, the place is for sale. Our *caballero* has been on my mind, which probably accounts for. . . . Well, anyway, he *is* a Spaniard; I'm sure a Catholic, probably with descendants. Perhaps he should be returned. . . ."

"What did *he* say?"

"Very simply, Pete thinks he deserves a proper burial and that I should make arrangements. I could notify someone and send him back."

"He's here because he didn't want to be in Spain!"

Fletcher blinked at the baseless assertion. "What's the matter with you, Tristan?"

"That night that you cut your hand, you saw him. Yes, *him!* I know you did! He told you he lost his horse. He perdido mi caballo, remember? He talked to you!"

"Oh no. No." Fletcher chuckled. "You can't be serious."

"I *am* serious."

"That's nonsense, Tristan. It was a dream."

"Englishmen don't dream in Spanish!" Tristan retorted, his voice straining, "And neither *do Irishmen!*"

Fletcher dropped the wash cloth. With his sleeve, he wiped the invisible slap from his face, then announced that he was turning in.

30

Unable to sleep, Ray was fighting the urge. Even rubbing alcohol would do. At two o'clock in the morning, his mind was working at warp speed, threatening to permanently shut down if he couldn't.... He groaned and swallowed a third helping of aspirin, watching the clock's second hand crawl around its face. He couldn't stand it. He surfaced from a mountain of library books and crusty dishes and dressed. With keys and a cashless wallet in hand, he hastened through the cool air and started his truck. The hum of the engine was reassuring. As he flattened the accelerator; the old Chevy fish-tailed down the driveway, spinning onto a dirt road going anywhere.

He passed what was left of his herd grazing on the baled pastures. Like charcoal briquettes on a grill, the old cows dotted the striped fields. Slamming on the brakes to avoid a creek-bound raccoon, he nearly ditched his pick-up, a heart thumping reminder to keep his miles per hour and consequently his pulse, at a reasonable rate. He drove on, finally relaxing; the familiar landscape reminding him that life had not left him behind, he simply hadn't been participating. He turned to the east and let the plains unfold around him, a succession of shooting stars heralding his return. He smiled and eased on to the airport road, glad to be employed, even if it was temporary. Lined up like toy soldiers, aircraft were parked wing to wing along the glassy runway, each one distinctive through the gray blur of the chain link fence. Slowing to count them, he noticed that the gate was ajar, which wouldn't have meant much if he hadn't simultaneously seen a bobbing beam aimed at the cockpit of a celestially expensive Mooney. Ray braked, threw the truck in reverse, then braked again. Across from the fence, on the opposite side of the road, a compact rested - nearly hidden - down an embankment. The rancher reached under his seat for a tire iron, put his truck in neutral and coasted to the gate, his bumper tapping it wide open as he rolled into the parking lot.

Cutting his lights, he rested his elbow out the window, guiding his truck toward a cluster of twin-engines. He was about fifty yards from the flashlight sighting when he thought he heard the sound of giggling. He braked. He heard it again. It was a woman, this time followed by a man. Their voices rose and fell in unison, punctuated by laughter. They were singing! Ray exited his idling truck and strutted straight for the noisy duet when suddenly, he heard nothing, save for a crosscurrent catching a plane's wings. He stopped and listened, turning slowly for an audible clue when a forearm lashed across his windpipe. His right arm was wrenched backward, forcing him to drop the tire iron. He fought for air, desperately using both hands to claw at the strangler. He couldn't make a sound. He tried to kick, but was repeatedly twisted away from his mark. He was losing consciousness. He heard a woman screaming.

"Don't! Don't!" Her high pitch was fading from him. "Please! It's Ray Solner! *Please!* Don't hurt him!" Released, Ray sunk to the pavement, gasping. Retching through his tender throat, he lay there irregularly choking on inhales and exhales until his intake normalized. The woman was supporting his head, begging him to be all right. All he could do was nod.

"I'm so sorry, Ray. We thought. . . . Oh God! Are you O.K?" She held his shoulders as he spat bile.

Trembling, Ray wiped saliva from his face and turned to her. Ellen Peters was kneeling beside him, her eyes filled with tears. "I'm so sorry," she whispered. Her tiny fingers were cold as she inspected his neck. "Can you breathe all right?"

"Who . . . who was that?" he wheezed angrily, his question answered by a long-limbed shadow looming over her. Ray focused on the assailant, its head cocked like a lizard, featureless in the dark. It lit a cigarette; the match's flare revealing a cool, predatory countenance. Without sunglasses, its exposed eyes were large and darkly rimmed, frighteningly analytical and smoldering.

"I know you," Ray hissed.

Like a dragon, it blew a plume of smoke through the tepid night, flicking at Ray's runny nostrils.

Ellen helped the rancher to his feet. She barely knew him, but remembered Bill's snide remark, that Ray was a pit bull. Sure enough, still reeling, he staggered to meet his enemy. His heel had conveniently found the end of the tire iron when, just as inconveniently, a police car's search lights found the airport's wide-open security gate.

Ray instinctively ducked. Ellen and the reptile followed suit.

"Ellen, please," Ray hoarsely implored. "Please help me. I don't have a license. I'll do time. . . ."

"What?"

"A driver's license! I don't have one! That's my truck he's looking at!"

A second police car arrived with lights flashing. Two officers joined the first. A radio crackled.

"Shit! Oh, shit!" Ray shrank back. "Ellen, what are you doing here anyway? And who's your creepy friend?"

"My date."

"Wow! *A murderer?* Oh no! Here they come!"

The police were moving slowly and collectively, their high intensity beams skirting the lot. The reptile was crouched under cover of an adjacent Cessna. Ray noticed.

"They're going to find you, you ass. . . ."

Ellen seized Ray's shoulder, whispering authoritatively into his ear. Then, she departed the shadows and walked rigidly toward the blinding lights, waving sheepishly at the officers, leaving Ray to his embarrassment. He rose stiffly, stealing a glance behind him.

Ellen's killer date was nowhere to be found.

31

Fletcher groped for the telephone in the dark. If only he could find it. It was close to four a.m. His tender palm landed a little too hard on the receiver. Cursing, he dragged it to his lips, then mumbled hello. The ensuing inquisition left him vaguely alarmed and instinctively vague. He repeated that he would speak to his interrogator at a *civilized* hour. The caller, Officer Ordell, settled for a ten a.m. appointment. Oliver observed from the bottom of the bed as his master sat up and shoved his feet into slippers.

Through a front window, Fletcher spied Tristan's suspect rental where he had fully expected it to be: in the driveway. He tapped on the master bedroom door, but there was no response. He cracked it just enough to reveal a mirrored image of his son in the demi-jour. The sound of his breathing was muffled in a ravine of pillows. Fletcher shook his head in disbelief. What an outrage! Some stupid cop on the cattle beat! At eight-thirty, he resolved, he would ring his lawyer and put an end to the lunacy right there. Fuming but exhausted, Fletcher fell back into bed with his uninvited dog braced against his spine. It was the first morning in a decade that he slept past eight.

When the phone shrieked again, Fletcher nearly ripped its lifeline from the wall; he had a pounding headache. "Yes, yes, what is it?"

"It's Pete. Is Tristan there?"

"Why?"

"Fletch, we need to talk."

"I need coffee. I'll ring you back."

"You're still in bed? It's nine-thirty!"

"Oh. Right. I'll just be a minute." Fletcher hung up and made for the kitchen. With coffee brewing, he telephoned the firm of Russell and Vicante, the latter deserting a meeting to take the call. Tom Vicante hadn't heard from Lawson in years, save for the annual Christmas card. Still, he had a soft spot for the man. Fletcher bypassed the niceties and got straight to the point. He recounted last night's phone call in his usual concise style, all of the relevant information on the table, including the fact that his son – yes, son - wasn't currently at home. Tom muzzled his astonishment. It's not every day you find out you have a son. Rebounding, he told Fletcher that he had no obligation to speak to the police, especially without an attorney. A car seen on a county road – even if it was the boy's rental –was hardly a crime. He would update him later. Fletcher replaced the receiver. With aspirin taking effect, he reread Tristan's note. It simply said that he was spending the morning riding with Elan.

After a shower, Fletcher opened his PC for the bill paying he had previously abandoned. Tristan had indeed set up his own in-box complete with a password, something Fletcher found mildly disconcerting. He shrugged it off and attended to his mother's deposit. He had not seen her in over thirty years; the last time they spoke was well over twenty, but they did correspond on a regular basis: every year she sent him a birthday card; every year he sent her one. She never inquired about him or her sizable monthly stipend, but he sensed that she depended on it, and in her own miserable way, may have even been grateful.

He processed the rest of the bills and deleted the infinite spam, finishing his third cup of coffee with the predictable onset of jitters. He hadn't checked on Little John, as Tristan's daily care had usurped his role as caretaker. Nevertheless, the former groom thought he should take a look. Before logging off, he glanced once more at his son's mailbox, the password request blinking patiently. Just for fun, he typed in the horse's name. It was rejected. He tried it backward. Nothing. He typed in the name of their conquistador without success. One more, he thought: Oliver. Oh well. The password box was guarding Tristan's temple of confidences like a recalcitrant foo dog and with good reason, Fletcher thought. He closed the laptop just as Oliver's baying announced a visitor at the front door.

Pete strode in angrily. "I thought you were going to call."

"I'm sorry, I forgot." Fletcher was still clinging to the door knob. "I guess I'm in a bit of a fog."

"You mean a dilemma."

"Really? How's that?"

Fletcher directed his surly caller past the study's aura of evening abandon to the morning's more wholesome kitchen. Pete declined coffee and motioned to his fidgeting host to sit. Fletcher complied, asking, "what's all this about?"

"Where's Tristan?"

"Out."

"Do you know where he was last night?"

"You mean after the movie?"

"Yes, *after the movie.*"

"In bed."

"No, he wasn't."

"He *was,* Pete. I saw him."

"If you did, it was after he broke into the airport with my daughter in tow!"

Fletcher's jaw tightened.

"Listen, Fletch, exactly what do you know about Tristan?"

Fletcher didn't answer, icing over as he returned his prober's gaze. After a long night, Pete had the look of a bloodhound: comically droopy but dangerously sharp.

"All right." Pete took a long breath. "Let me tell you what happened. After you, presumably, went to bed – we were both pretty plowed - Tristan left here and picked Ellen up at the end of our driveway: prearranged. She thought they were going for a little drive just to, uh, talk, but as it turned out, Tristan was very interested in her workplace - so interested, in fact - that he broke the lock to make sure he got a grand tour. In the meantime, Ray Solner's out for a drive and sees the open gate. He goes in to investigate and low and behold, dear Tristan nearly kills him: really, nearly *kills him!* Chokes him! The police show up. Ray's license was revoked a long time ago, so Ellen lies for him; lies to the *police! Actually lies!* She tells them that *she* was driving Ray's truck, that he called looking for me and got her instead or some asinine story that no one would believe, that she felt sorry for him, so *her boyfriend dropped* her at Ray's house, so that *Ray* wouldn't be alone, and they took a drive. They *found* the airport gate open, and went in to look around. *Have you ever heard anything so ridiculous?* When the police called at three-thirty this morning, Ruth answered. I was completely out or would have intervened. Ruth drove down to the airport immediately. She was so terrified that Ellen would land in jail for all that lying - not to mention the vandalism - that she actually corroborated the whole *outrageous account!* I'm sure the only reason they're both home this morning is because the police didn't have the heart to arrest dear sweet Ruthie! But here's the best part: during the discussion, a car pulls away: no doubt *Tristan's* car, but nobody can prove it because no one could get the license number. You see, the police didn't actually *see* it until it was already down the road – *with no lights* - so apparently he managed to dodge them. And – evidently - in exchange for Ellen's big whopper, Ray kept his mouth shut about your kid. So, again, I ask you, what do you really know about Tristan?"

"Did Ellen tell you all this?"

"What difference does it make?"

"They have no license number? You're sure?"

"*What's the matter* with you, *Fletcher?*" Pete shouted. "Ellen's never lied to anyone, never mind law enforcement! She just met that boy yesterday and she's already lying for him. My wife's an *accomplice* for fear of her daughter's future, and all you care about is whether your so-called son's B & E is under *wraps*? He ditched my little girl to contend with the police by herself! She convinced Ray Solner to keep his mouth shut about a guy that almost killed him! Now I want to know! *What do you know about him?* Do we even know for certain that *he's yours?*" Pete's face was crimson.

Fletcher remained unruffled, adopting a conciliatory tone. "Calm down, Pete. Calm down. Just listen to me, please. Just hear me out."

Pete pulled himself into a controlled orbit and awaited Fletcher's explanation.

"Let's assume everything you said is true. Let's assume Tristan attacked a man. . . ."

"Ray Solner is his name."

"Right. Was *Ray Solner* armed?"

Pete hesitated. "No. Well, he might have had something, maybe a crowbar."

"So he was probably looking pretty menacing. Just give me a minute, Pete! Please! Now try to put yourself in Tristan's position. He's a young man who just met a very pretty girl. Neither one of them want the evening to end so they agree to meet for a drive when we're asleep. Perfectly natural. *Remember when you were twenty?* There's no place to go at that hour. She loves flying, was probably talking about it, so Tristan - *recklessly*, I grant you - breaks the lock to the airport. He's probably showing off a bit, but he's only twenty-two years old. I mean, nothing was stolen or damaged, was it?"

Glowering, Pete shook his head.

"Right. Then a man shows up, a man in the dark. Tristan's got a young woman - how did you say it - in tow, and the man is skulking around with a crowbar or something. Tristan may have overreacted, but he probably thought he was protecting your daughter."

"So he leaves her in the lurch when the police come?"

"I don't think he meant to, *and* I don't think he did. He's a foreigner in a country that he doesn't know well, a country not well-disposed to aliens right now, legal or otherwise. He panicked. But he waited long enough to make sure she was all right. Obviously, he was watching! He must have seen Ruth and sensed things settling down. I don't know. I don't know the time frame, but I do know him well enough to know that he wouldn't just *leave* Ellen there. I think he simply didn't know what to do. Really, Pete."

A smile crossed Pete's face. "Maybe. It makes sense, Fletch. He was probably scared witless. I'm surprised he didn't phone you."

"Phone me?" Fletcher sensed a trap. "How? And what good would it have done? I was pretty drunk."

"But you did all right when the police called."

"Did I?"

Suggesting Fletcher get more rest – he looked tired - Pete announced his departure. The good bloodhound was on a scent, but too fond of the quarry to pursue. He knew that Fletcher would wriggle back into the safety of his solitude, and when forced to reemerge, would do so in fighting form: faster, keener but no less blindly devoted to the mystery that nearly killed Ray Solner.

32

Fletcher was in his garden, wading through the pond, netting old leaves and shed blooms. He had just spent the last fifteen minutes on the phone with Tom Vicante and was in need of a respite. As promised, Vicante had successfully intimidated the department into paralysis, specifically Officer Ordell, alluding to harassment and gross incompetence – whatever that meant - but failed to completely close the probing bureaucratic eye that threatened Fletcher's precious privacy. In the scorching heat, the groundskeeper was able to drown out the conversation, feeling safe in the cool water, skimming the surface with the back of his hand, fascinated by the scattering of color against the sky's reflective blue. He pondered nineteenth century simplicity, wondering if he was seeing what Monet saw, and what life was like in a time of soft contrasts. He felt the presence of a young Spaniard behind him and slowly rotated. But it wasn't his troubling offspring.

Like an eclipse against the midday sun, his golden hair glowed like white fire around a blackened ember. Standing amid the orange trees, his coarse shirt rippled slightly with a breeze and then stilled, as did the pond. Fletcher was aware of his pounding heart, remembering the specter whose murderous midnight eyes bore into his soul like a talon. Slowly, the visitant's right hand crossed his heart, and his head dropped forward, bowing once formally, as if to apologize for the terrifying intrusion. And then he vanished into the blinding solar haze. Motionless in the middle of a pond, in the middle of the day, Fletcher was aware of his trembling hands and the searing pain in his head. He labored to the pond's edge and collapsed.

※ ※ ※

Tristan was languidly trickling water along his father's chest, letting it swathe him in an evaporative mist. The hydrotherapy coaxed Fletcher's bewildered eyes to blink with recognition. He was in the shade of an English oak. A cold cloth was resting across his forehead, his wet face pillowed by a patch of blue fescue.

"You're not well, Fletcher, hm?" Tristan asked gently.

"It must have been the heat."

"Here." The son handed his father a bottle of spring water, the latter gulping it until he choked.

"Thanks," Fletcher sputtered, sitting up unsteadily. "I'm better now."

"What's wrong?"

"Nothing. Maybe a bit dehydrated."

"Did you have a difficult morning?"

Fletcher delayed his response, searching his son's eyes for an allusion to last night, but found nothing beyond the prosaic question. He stood, brushing leaves from his arms as he brusquely suggested tea.

Tristan retrieved the tee shirt that had served as a cold compress, and held the garden door open.

Fletcher arrived in the kitchen realizing that he hadn't eaten all day. He found croissants, ham and spinach, threw them together and micro-waved lunch for two. He guzzled orange juice and dropped onto a chair. The tea kettle whistled, but Tristan motioned to him to remain seated. Dusty and energized, he smelled the way Meredith did after a long day blazing trails with Little John. The clatter brought her vividly back. Fletcher drove his forehead into his hands to shut her away. Tristan noticed. Steeping Earl Grey while pouring ice coffee for himself, he erupted with an astonishing apology. He said that he had heard the phone last night and feared that he had brought a big problem to his father's door. He wanted to make it right and thought he could go to the police and explain. Relief washed over Fletcher like a warm rain. He waved Tristan away from the idea, explaining that the police had no plate number, and that Ellen had secured Solner's silence. Better to let sleeping dogs lie.

After placing the tea on the table, Tristan dallied at the counter, obviously screwing up his nerve to ask a favor. Fletcher grew impatient, nodding at him to go ahead.

"Elan could work with Little John again. He'd do well with exercise, don't you think?"

"Yes." Fletcher was too tired to wait for the sequent. "And, then, I imagine you could ride him."

"If you would permit me."

The idea of Elan in proximity was not at all appealing to the emotion-weary veteran of western affairs, but, he realized, if Tristan was to stay, he needed an outlet. The horse had probably mellowed with age, and anything was better than a bored European breaking locks with a dear friend's all-American daughter at three in the morning. He consented. In the meantime, Tristan – with a borrowed mount - was joining the horse trainer on a round-up ride tomorrow, and would most likely stay for the après Longhorn foot stomping jamboree. Fletcher yawned. Yippee.

33

The wide-open country sparkled like an amber ocean in the early morning hours. Warmed by handshakes, caffeine and anticipation, twenty riders set out to guide two hundred cow-calf pair to greener pastures. Unshackled from their twenty-first century lives, the executive cowpokes were reborn: the old were young; the sour, sweet; and the cynical, believers. Moved by yips, whistles, and whirling ponies, the bovines found their respective places in the herd and began a unified western push until – from thousands of feet above – they became the rippling scales of a huge dinosaur, lumbering across a shallow, Jurassic sea. A tiny twin-engined pterodactyl containing a flight instructor and his pretty student swooped down for a better look.

Tristan had never before felt the exhilaration of that day. Both integral and subordinate to the power of his mount, he found it intensely freeing. The air was rich with laughter, the smells primal, and the camaraderie spontaneous and strong. The ensuing drive crossed the fields of time, through ancestral reigns, harsh struggles, and nature's galactic force.

The trail boss, Elan, was regrettably riding a trainee: a palomino quarter horse. Strong and rebellious, the colt was initially more than he could handle atop his appointed duties, so Tristan assumed the lead and the role as gatekeeper. By mid-morning, Elan's horse was getting the hang of it, jogging along evenly, backtracking amiably for an occasional calf.

The hours marched on. At one o'clock lunch was served while the livestock rested. It was ninety minutes before the journey resumed, most of it on dirt roads, making it easier to keep the cattle grouped, but more hazardous as wheeled weekend warriors pressed for passing room. On each end of the herd, orange vested knights hastened to slow oncoming vehicles, the hard gravel and relentless heat wearing on both their horses and nerves. Traffic was on the increase. Developments had cropped up everywhere. Riders were retiring at their driveways. By the time their final destination was in sight, relief swept over the remaining cowboys like the winds of change so sadly blowing from Denver's burgeoning suburbs.

The Larsen ranch was one of the last strongholds on the western edge of the county that had neither been gobbled up by developers nor surrendered to Mackey. Randy, Glen and Rita Larsen were fourth generation, college-educated cowpokes. Randy married another native, consolidating his family's three thousand acres with her two sections. But, regardless of the goldmine in real estate, it took a lot of pounds on the hoof to support the tenacious family, their spouses and children. If it was vacant and grew grass, the Larsen's had it leased and grazed to dirt by autumn. The herd escorted that day was part of an organic beef trust, one growing with demand along with bison. As a consequence, several of the shaggy, primordial creatures were snorting beyond a rugged eight foot fence when two hundred tired pair of longhorn cross plodded across the Larsen perimeter. As fresh employees pushed the herd toward water, Elan and company lounged under the shade of a cottonwood, nursing beers. Tethered to horses caked with sweat, they were glad to see the caravan of stock trailers arriving to take them home.

34

Despite her fears, Ellen wasn't sacked. In fact, her employer found the whole so-called *incident* completely overblown. He knew that Solner was innocuous and that Ellen was incapable of mischief, at least criminal. For all he knew, the gate's old lock popped open on its own. Thus, when he spied Officer Ordell's sedan pulling up to the hangar, Tabor ordered Ellen to make haste. He was embarking on a lesson with his blossoming student and had no intention of being delayed. Besides, it was Saturday, technically his day off. The morning crystal clear, he hopped into the Cessna's passenger seat and - with a Mickey Mouse smile - waved goodbye at the deputy racing toward him with a few more questions.

The plane dipped and soared as Ellen ran through a number of exercises. Bill teasingly wagged his finger as she buzzed her house, and then - with his approval – turned east with Tristan very much on her mind. The instructor sipped coffee, seemingly mesmerized by the droning engines and distant geography. Relieved that all was well, Ellen was babbling over the Cessna's din, pointing out different landmarks and asking advice on freshman courses. She was thrilled to finally spot the cattle drive, circling a descent for a better look, when – without warning – Bill dropped his hand on her knee. She clumsily leveled the plane and shifted away from him, but his hand stayed with her, creeping up her thigh while his fingers drummed the inside of her leg. She froze, trying to think clearly. She was inches away from her pilot's license; she barely needed another hour. She thought about how much she needed her job. Then, as his hand edged closer toward her crotch, she tried to think about anything else.

Perspiration forming over her lip, she was gripped by nausea and breathless. "Bill, um, would you move your hand?"

"What?"

"*Your hand!* Please move your hand!"

"Where would you like me to move it?"

"*Don't!* I mean it!" She glared at him.

He grinned. "Oh, come on, sweetheart, you *don't* mean it! You've been flirting with me forever and I've been a good boy. But, you're eighteen now, so it's O.K . . . for both of us. *And*, big girl," his eyes rolled, "we could have a *really* good. . . ."

The plane banked hard and accelerated. It was descending at a precarious speed, nearly a nosedive.

"Ellen!" Bill shouted, grabbing the yoke.

As the plane steadied, he said nothing to her, keeping his mind - and hands - occupied with the business of flying. When the wheels finally met the runway, a sullen Cessna 172 taxied directly to the hangar.

Dillon's curly head was parked in front of the family computer when his sister swept past him. He said hi with no response. She had almost made it to her bedroom when Ruth intercepted her, asking if she had an hour to spare to help her ice cakes. There was a fund-raising dinner and auction at the church tomorrow. Ruth was responsible for dessert, but now there was so much else to do. The decorations weren't up yet, Dillon was trying to figure out the raffle forms, and. . . . Ellen burst into tears. Ruth was struck dumb; her daughter had been fired.

An hour later, laden with shopping bags, Pete barged into the kitchen with the twins on his heels, shrieking over their new water guns. Pete began filling them, simultaneously unpacking Ruth's order when she appeared under the hallway arch, motioning to him soberly. Pete received the news calmly, although he felt his face flush with a spike of blood pressure. He ambled toward Ellen's room, her sobs audible through the door. He knocked persistently until she let him in. Her Raphaelite face was puffy and streaked with tears. Her blouse was wet. She wouldn't look at him. Pete said nothing as she retreated to her bed. Easing down next to her, he reached to unglue a soggy curl from her cheek when she buried her face into his shoulder. She coughed an apology into his shirt, something about screwing everything up. Pete pinched her dimpled chin and lifting it, peered into her red, half-moon eyes.

"It's amazing how well things work out, isn't it?"

Her nose running, she wiped it with a knuckle, suddenly realizing what her father had just said. She stared at him.

Smiling, he continued, "For example, I'm so glad you thought of getting a car *now* instead of waiting. *Now*, you have access to a whole new world, full of lots of airports and lots of jobs and *decent* employers." He handed her a crumpled tissue from his pocket and squeezed her shoulders. "Listen, kid, you'll have your pilot's license in a month. I'll make sure that he records all your flight hours. . . ."

"How?"

He lowered his voice and adopted a Joysey accent. "I can be very *puhsuasive*. Don't worry about it."

She sniffled through a giggle.

Pete's expression became serious. "Listen, Ellen, there's a lot of really good people in this world, more than the not so good, so don't let him throw you. But, there's a lesson here. I know how hard you tried to keep that job; I know all the ego-massaging you did. But men like that can't be reckoned with, no matter what you do. Now I know you're angry. But try not to waste time stewing about it, O.K? Things will get better."

"He's claiming it's because of the other night."

"I know, but he won't say it too loudly. Believe me, he's not going to tangle with us." His long arm squeezed her shoulders.

Ellen's eyes welled up once more, this time with gratitude.

35

Exiting his doublewide, Elan was pressed and polished and ready to go. He rounded the corner, finding Tristan by the corral, murmuring to his mount of the day.

"You ready?" the trainer queried, creasing his ivory Stetson. "You're gonna get dirty again."

Tristan had brought a change of clothes, and was looking extraordinarily well-groomed, considering. But, he was momentarily glued to his mount of the day, stroking his neck, oblivious to the paddock dust. The evening sun filtered through a row of old juniper, casting long shadows across the dry buffalo grass and the pale animal, making him appear zebra-like on a parched Serengeti. Elan whistled impatiently.

"What are you doing, man?"

"I'm thanking him," Tristan replied. "He was very good to me today."

"Come on! Let's go! Steaks on the grill! *It's party-time!*"

Elan pivoted and strode toward his pick-up, his trainee in pursuit.

Tristan climbed into the cab, eyeing Elan's ivory headgear. "Is it true that only the good guys where white hats?"

"Nope." Elan grinned, checking his brim in the mirror. "The bad guys wear 'em, too . . . when their black ones are dirty."

Lowering the window, Tristan laughed as the driver popped a beer. With a quick channel change, Werewolves of London blared from the speakers. Gravel spraying, they peeled away into Saturday night.

The party was being hosted outdoors at Randy Larsen's log home, a four thousand square foot reflection of cowboy culture. His wife, Pat was an ardent entertainer, which bode well for her political aspirations. The actually number of attendees was at least two hundred, with the cattle drivers a minority. Tristan hadn't expected such a crowd when he had invited Ellen to join him. As she wandered anonymously through a sea of pressed jeans and custom boots, she spotted Tristan easily. Tall, handsome and hatless, her date had the scrutiny of every woman in proximity. Ellen felt raw and insecure. She watched him through jealous eyes conversing with a willowy westernaire. Suddenly feeling ill, she decided to leave, stealing a final look at her continental mirage. But he was snaking through the crowd toward her, his dazzling smile directed at her, only her. She was swept away.

The smell of citronella and sizzling beef filled the air. Steamy baked beans were sloshed into stoneware cauldrons while scalding corn cobs were piled onto platters. Aluminum foil was being peeled back from bowls, exposing mountainous fruit and vegetable concoctions. Beer was flowing; wine was plentiful. A chattering line was forming for the feast. As guitars were tuning to a harmonica, the whine of a violin stabbed the smoky air. The drummer took his seat. Suddenly, the guests' rising din was quashed by the onset of a western ballad.

Ellen had no appetite. Tristan held her hand, dragging her toward food. She resisted, mouthing something. Unable to hear, he stooped with his ear to her lips. She said that she didn't feel like eating, but that she would wait for him. He studied her momentarily, and then ushered her beyond the candle lit bash to the relative peace of parked cars. With the bass thumping, Tristan leaned against Elan's pick-up, guiding her in front of him with his fingers folder over hers.

"Something's the matter. What is it?"

"Nothing. I'm just not hungry."

"You're lying," he said grinning, pushing her arm's length away and then pulling her back. "What is it?"

She glanced toward the party, her eyes wet.

"What is it?" he demanded.

"Um, I was fired today, and um, I didn't want to see him, but he's here. I forgot the Larsens have a plane with us, with him."

"Fired? Because we went . . ."

Ellen shook her head. "No, nothing like that."

"So, what happened?"

She didn't answer.

He applied pressure to her fingers, pushing his palms against hers. *"What happened?"*

As if a dam broke, her story rushed out in a torrent. Her untold tolerance of her boss' demeaning comments had been suffered through with good cheer, only to have it end this way, without her pilot's license, without a job and without justice. She apologized for telling him, and hoped that she didn't ruin his party, adding that she should go.

He reached into the truck bed and pulled a beer from Elan's cooler. He put it to her lips, nursing her with the alcohol, feeling her relax through the play in his fingers. He reached for another. She protested; he insisted. Then another.

He played her back and forth with her hand in his. "You must dance with me!"

She felt giddy and burst out laughing. "O.K!"

He dragged her back to the fray. Picking at food in-between beats, they square-danced, not really knowing how, and slow-danced tenderly to the envy of onlookers. Elan joined them, introduced himself to Ellen with a bow, and presented his new lady friend. Claiming that he had to teach Tristan *everything*, he drunkenly partnered with the Spaniard and stumbled through a two-step to the roar of the crowd. When the band took a break, Tristan asked Ellen who her boss was. She didn't care. He was right over there, she said, fingering Bill Tabor, who was eying her surreptitiously while conversing with Randy Larsen.

"And that's the wife?" Tristan jutted his jaw at a tipsy, fortyish-looking blonde being ignored at Bill's elbow.

Ellen nodded. "Dana."

Tristan leaned Ellen's back against him, encircling her with his arms. She melted into him. Nothing else mattered. He whispered a question in her ear and then turned her to face him. She looked at him adoringly, shouting "Both!" in playful response. He guided her to a chair on the periphery of the dance floor, secured a promise that she would stay no matter what, and then he was lost to her. When the band began to play, Tristan reemerged, holding Dana Tabor to a slow waltz.

Ellen was too numb to move. She gripped the chair, sickened as she watched Tristan's nose lift Dana's yellow hair, then nuzzle the side of her neck with his cheek. At first, the pilot's wife seemed flushed and uncertain, but soon didn't muster a token resistance. Tristan pulled her into him, holding her hips lewdly close to his. As his hand dipped below the curve of her spine, people murmured uncomfortably. Dana didn't care. For the first time in twelve dreary years, she felt alive. Drunk and engulfed by irresistible arms, she hardly acknowledged the glittering eyes of her husband as he tapped impatiently on her partner's shoulder. Tristan ignored him and kissed her.

"Heh! You son of a bitch!" Bill Tabor jerked Tristan's arm from his wife, pushing him backward.

The band stopped playing. As the Spaniard staggered, Elan dashed over, catching his friend by the elbow.

"*What are you doing?*" Elan's hushed admonish was clearly not being heard. "*Tristan, look at me.* That's somebody's wife. Knock it off."

Sharp words were being exchanged between Dana and her husband while the novice rider drunkenly appealed to his mentor for forgiveness. The cowboy loosened his hold.

Abruptly, Tristan spun away, swaggered back to Dana, and lifting her hand, kissed her arm. Dana's repudiations were insincere; Bill Tabor was speechless.

Ellen rose, clenching her stomach.

"Your wife," Tristan slurred, "is beautiful."

Tabor's fists were clenched when Randy Larsen intervened. "Come on, Bill. He's drunk."

The flight instructor didn't acknowledge him. His eyes were gleaming. He shoved Tristan hard in the chest. Tristan stumbled to the ground.

Tears clouded Ellen's eyes. The guests gasped.

"*Dana, please,*" Tristan wailed loudly, rocking back on his heels, his hands crossed on his heart. "One more dance, *one more for me.*"

A current of tittering ran through the women while the men tried to stifle their laughter. Pat Larsen raised her eyebrows at Dana, mouthing "Ooh la la."

Tabor's eyes hardened with fury.

Elan seized Tristan under the arm, dragging him away from the amused patrons and the rabid spouse. But Tabor was smelling blood. He dashed across the platform with Randy in pursuit. "Bill, he's just a kid! He's drunk, damn it!" The host grabbed the pilot's shoulder. Tabor angrily shook him off, plowed through Larsen's henchmen, and screamed in Tristan's face. "Listen, you stupid fuck, go back where you came from. *Got it?*"

Tristan nodded obediently.

Ellen covered her face.

"Where do they get these people?" Tabor demanded of his audience, crossing back across the planks, searching for his wife. "They need to tighten the borders."

Livid, Elan dragged Tristan like a rag doll through the parking area. But, nearing the truck, the doll suddenly twisted out from under him and raced back to the party with astonishing speed.

"Dana! Dana!" Tristan bawled as he reached the dance floor. "Come away with me! *You know you want me!*"

It was the truth that sent Tabor into an uncontrollable fury. Three men couldn't hold the irate husband as he broke ranks and ran for the insolent foreigner. Tabor's first punch caught the side of the Iberian jaw, hurtling him to the ground. But the attacker wasn't finished. Spurned by two women that day, the blood coursing through him was poisoned with humiliation and rage. He kicked at the Spaniard, barely missing his groin. Tristan struggled to his knees. As Larsen and his startled men nearly reached them, Tabor was yanking the young man up by the hair, but it was too late. Like a flash from an unknown weapon, a steel fist smashed into the pilot's nose, driving bone and cartilage deep into his skull, dropping him like a stringless marionette; a dark, critical flood streaming across the dance floor.

Ellen buckled, asthmatic by the sight and her sudden, horrifying comprehension. Hot, convulsive tears spilled across her lips as she mouthed Tristan's name.

"Love or justice?" he had whispered. She had wanted both.

36

In his anteroom, Pete had just donned his robe, reviewing marked passages and the selection of hymns. As he poured a glass of ice water, Larry Wheeler peaked around the door.

"Another few minutes, Larry," Pete grumbled, checking his watch.

"Oh. Uh, Pete? I was wondering, are you going to say a few words for Bill?"

Pete swallowed. "Bill? Bill who?"

"Bill Tabor."

Pete parked his glass on the window sill. "What about Bill Tabor?"

"You didn't hear? He's in a coma."

"A coma?"

"Yeah. You didn't know? Some guy at a party last night *really* clocked him. A foreign guy, lives up on the hill with that English nut...."

The rest of Larry's monologue went unheard, including the fact that Bill hardly ever attended. Still....

Pete anxiously searched for an image of his daughter, secure at home. He saw her this morning. Was it this morning? Yes, yes. It was. She was asleep. She was sleeping in. There were unfamiliar butterflies in his stomach. He plowed through his sermon. The last of his flock couldn't leave fast enough.

✳ ✳ ✳

Pete doggedly waited at the front door. As it flew open, it was as predicted. A new Fletcher was ready for him. Taut and suspicious, this one was cold and in fighting form.

"Fletch, sorry. But, you weren't answering your phone."

"*So?* What is it?"

"Is Tristan home?"

"What's this about?"

"I'd like to talk to him, Fletch. Last night. . . ."

"No."

"Please."

"No!"

"Fletcher, listen. Bill Tabor. . . . "

"It was self-defense! Everyone there concurred!"

"Fletcher, please. Listen to me. There's more to it and you know it."

"Go home!" Fletcher tried to close the gateway but Pete caught it, blocking it with his bulk.

"I want ten minutes," the big man demanded.

"No!"

"Ten minutes. *With you*, Fletch. Give me ten minutes and I'll leave you alone. You have my word."

The doorman bristled.

"Strictly confidential, I promise you."

Fletcher snorted. His corpulent caller was firmly planted on the threshold. Pete was brusquely ushered to the study. Fletcher closed the door.

"You're wasting your time, Pete. He defended himself."

"Tabor's in the hospital."

"So?"

"He's a husband and a human being!"

"So that's his defense?"

The minister collapsed on a chair. "Can you answer me a simple question?"

"Depends."

"How do we know Tristan's yours, I mean, aside from the resemblance? What do you know about him?"

Fletcher snatched a jar of aspirin off the table, tossing back three. His jaw flexed. "There's a history that he knows, that no one else could know. But, for your information, Reverend, he came with a letter from his mother."

"Oh? I thought she was. . . ."

"She is. It was written when he was a boy."

"What does it say?"

There was no answer.

"Fletch?" Pete cocked his head. "Well?"

"It was her handwriting . . . an old envelope. It sufficed."

"It sufficed," the counselor echoed. "Sufficed. . . . You didn't read it?" Pete stared at him. *"You didn't read it! Why?"*

"It's none of your business!"

"But why wouldn't you? *Why?*"

"It doesn't matter anymore! She's gone."

"Where is it?"

"I have it."

"May I see it?"

"Why?"

"I want to read it! *Somebody should!*"

"No."

"What are you afraid of, Fletch? That she didn't forgive you? That she did? *What?*"

Fletcher glared at him while Pete marked time, drumming the chair arm until the fragments were forced from Fletcher's heart.

"I can't make it up to her, you see? I lived for years . . . for the hope that. . . . Not knowing that she was. . . .Well, it's done now, isn't it? I can't go back. I can't make it right. I can't save her. I ruined her life. I ruined my own."

Pitching forward like a masthead, Pete relayed his observation softly. "So you think you're responsible. Is that it? You think she killed herself. Why?"

"Because, if *I* had *known* that she was lost to me. . . . Lord." Fletcher began pacing. "We were very close. I know we were young, but what we had was rare. I had no family worth mentioning, and her's was. . . . God, when I think of it. Anyway, I just left . . . without a word. When I married. . . ." Fletcher gripped his head; his eyes squeezed shut. "I don't know . . . I wanted *money!* I wanted to *be someone else!* Look, I was nothing: a nobody with champagne taste. Anyway, it wasn't worth it. I missed her. . . . Everything: that feeling, that time, *her*. But back then . . . I was afraid, afraid she'd find me out . . . that I couldn't give her a decent life."

Pete's hands were joined at his chest, his forefingers tapping together. "You were going back. That's why the house is for sale."

Static electricity sparkled like zircons under Fletcher's soles. He stopped at the desk, extracted a cigarette from a silver case, then promptly dropped it.

"So in walks Tristan," Pete gently continued, "her son . . . your salvation. He delivers the news that she's dead, and becomes your reason to live."

Silence hung over the room like a fog.

"Let me see the letter."

The timepiece ticked convulsively.

"Please, Fletch."

The consignee sighed, drew a key from under the mantle clock and inserted it into the desk drawer. He tossed the envelope to his confessor and returned to the desk, flopping on a chair. Pete carefully tore it open. His eyes narrowed.

"I don't understand."

Fletcher shrugged. "I'm not surprised. It's in Spanish."

"No, Fletch, it isn't." Pete stood and strode to him. "It's very much in English." He dropped the paper on the blotter. "What do you think this means?"

Dashed across crisp, white stationery, three large, jagged words formed one desperate plea:

Save your son.

There was no response. Fletcher sat fused to his chair, his eyes fixed to the words. And then, a drop of saline blotted the blue ink. And then another. And then another. The shoulders trembled. She was alive.

On his way out, Pete caught a glimpse of Tristan through the window. Returning from the barn, his hand was swollen, the welt across his jaw . . . almost convincing.

37

Ellen was reinstated. The call came Sunday afternoon from Nick Sparta. He had just talked to Russ, the owner of the airport. Nick would take over operations, but *had* to have Ellen's administrative help, so all was forgiven. Ray would get started first thing Monday morning. Tabor was stable, but it would be awhile. There was a nine a.m. meeting on Monday. The show would go on.

✳ ✳ ✳

Elan slipped a bridle from a colt and shooed him out to pasture. A late afternoon zephyr ignited an ever darkening sky. The trainer had already seen the red car in his driveway, its sinuous driver leaning on the side fence. Limping slightly, Elan stormed past him.

Tristan fell in step. "I want to apologize to you."

"I'm tired, Tristan."

"Please, one moment."

Elan coiled. *"Or what?"* He resumed his march. "You set that guy up last night. You set me up."

"You said nothing to the police."

Elan stopped in his tracks. "Maybe I should have."

Tristan met his hard stare, but was silent.

Elan withdrew an empty pack from his shirt pocket, then crushing it irritably, turned toward his truck at a faster clip.

Tristan kept up. "He was screwing with Ellen."

Elan paused to spit. He pushed his hat up and faced his pursuer. "A lot of guys are gonna screw with Ellen. You gonna kill 'em all?" He rotated, took two more steps and jerked the truck door open. The seat was bare.

The Spaniard reached into his t-shirt pocket and pulled out a smoke, offering it to the horseman, who – still glowering – accepted. "So, where'd you learn all that, Tristan?"

The visitor shrugged, handing him matches. "Growing up."

"Oh, right." The cowboy nursed burning life into the tobacco. "You're no street fighter. You were trained."

Tristan rolled a stone back and forth with his heel. "You said you could start with Little John tomorrow."

Elan tossed the matches back. "I'll sleep on it." Abandoning his caller, he let the screen door slam behind him.

38

The day had been tortuously long. Now on her way to meet him, Ellen was consumed by the urgency. Pete knew it. He had pleaded with her to stay home. Ruth went a step further, demanding the car keys, but Pete intervened. He knew that any restraint would only earn his daughter's hatred, and her family would never prevail. As he watched her car disappear down the wet road, he understood that she was lost to him that Sunday night. From deep within, he felt something terrible in their midst. Ruth wasn't speaking to him. It hardly mattered.

Ellen found him in an isolated lot, as specified. He was perched on his car, his dark figure glistening in the rain. She pulled up beside him. As she reached for the ignition key, her door was wrenched open. He slammed her back in place and held her wrists, demanding to know if she had missed him. She had. He licked her nose playfully, and then kissed her savagely. Her neck was pressed painfully into the headrest, her heart pounding. He told her to live for him. She did.

The lot belonged to an abandoned meat packing plant, its warped, weathered door padlocked. He shouldered it open and pulled her in behind him. They were immediately engulfed in a cinereous dust. The old planks groaned as they stole through the gloom. He asked her about her day. She said that she had been rehired, eliciting his wry congratulation. He stopped and turned to her. As he feathered through her curls, she caressed his swollen jaw, her face clouding as she begged to know if he truly meant to hurt Tabor that way. He caught her with two fistfuls of hair, nosing the side of her cheek.

"You liked it. Be truthful."

"What if died?"

"He didn't."

"But . . . ."

He slammed her back on her heels with a disaffected bulletin. "Ellen, you have your job back. He's no longer a problem. Hm?"

She reached for his hands. The ceiling was sagging, the air acrid and musty. The plant was alive with vermin.

He looked around critically as if it were a stage set. "Does it matter where we are?"

She said no, unbuttoning his shirt. He seized her shoulders and pushed her away.

"It matters to me."

He steered her outside. They were shrouded in mist. Leaving her in his rental car, he refastened the plant lock and pulled her Camaro behind the building. Returning, he slipped behind the wheel and tossed her keys in the center console.

"Where are we going?" she asked.

He didn't answer, but the journey wasn't long. It ended in Fletcher's driveway.

39

Save your son. Save your son. Oliver was barking. Fletcher restuffed the envelope and shoved it under the blotter just as Tristan peered around the door jamb. Through nausea and a damnable headache, Fletcher felt a flood of relief.

"Tristan, I'd appreciate it if you'd tell me when you're leaving. We have enough problems, don't you think?"

"Sorry."

"Hungry?"

"No. I'm going to bed." Tristan cocked his head. "Maybe you should, too. You don't look right."

"Oh thank you. Listen, Tristan. . . ."

"Yes?"

"Come in." Fletcher motioned him into the study. "Please, if you don't mind."

"Fletcher, I know you want to talk, but if it could wait 'til the morning. . . ." Tristan's voice trailed off as he sailed down the hallway.

He entered the bedroom and found Ellen shrinking behind the door. Shaking his head at her comical posture, he locked the door and extinguished the light. He casually undressed and stretched across the sheets, slapping the mattress for her impatiently. Washed by a voyeuristic moon, his contour was regal, like a resting cheetah. He leaned back into the pillows, assessing her as she shyly shed her clothes. She came to him like a phantom, her skin glistening with a preternatural glow, her thick hair like an ancient silver headdress. Under salacious stars, he was tender and violent.

At four-thirty in the morning, Oliver went into a frenzied alarm. Incandescent light flooded the entry and then the foyer, dominoeing through the house. Loud, argumentative voices traveled down the corridor. The rapping at the door was too urgent to dismiss. Tristan pulled on his jeans and cracked the door slightly. Ellen gasped, gripping the sheets.

"Tristan, I'm sorry to wake you." Fletcher was in sweatpants; his eyes hollow. "Pete's here. Ellen didn't come home last night. Do you have an idea as to where she might be?"

Tristan sniffled, rubbing his eyes against the glare. "Yes."

Fletcher stiffened. Behind him, Pete's voice was menacing. "Where?"

"Here."

Fletcher gasped. "What?"

Pete pushed past him. "What do you mean: *here?*"

"*Here! Right here!*" Tristan flung the door wide open. Naked from the waist up, Ellen had one leg in her jeans. She cried out. Her father yanked the door shut with such velocity that a panel cracked, forcing Tristan into the hallway.

"You bastard!" Pete screamed, the side of his hand slamming the door molding.

Fletcher dodged in front of his son with a hand raised, Pete shouting at him with unprecedented fury. "What have you got here, Fletcher? Who is this. . . ?"

"All right. All right, now, Pete."

The big man trained a wrathful stare into Tristan's venomous eyes. "Who is this son of a. . . ?"

Ellen jerked the door open. She was barefoot, her shirt half-buttoned. "Dad! It's my fault. My fault! I should have called."

Her father was wild-eyed. "Your mother's frantic! How could you? *How could you?*"

"I'm sorry. I fell asleep."

"You fell asleep!" Pete's face was crimson. Turning back to the seducer, his nostrils flared. Fletcher held outstretched fingers against Pete's monstrous pectorals.

"Easy. Calm down, Pete."

The minister's air intake came under control. "Ellen, get your shoes. Where's the phone, Fletcher?"

"The study."

Pete started down the hallway, and then wheeled around, pointing a Herculean digit at the lesser mortal. *"Don't touch her!"*

Tristan stifled a laugh, kissing Ellen on the neck as she slipped past him into the dawn. But with her departure, a stranger had arrived. The day's virgin rays split into shafts of color, zigzagging down the corridor with the propulsion of paneled mirrors, striping his Gaelic features. His white chest heaved with anger; his hair flowed across his deltoids like a violent waterfall. Tristan appraised him thoughtfully. "I'm sorry, Fletcher."

"We'll have that talk now," his father responded coldly.

40

Tristan was sipping coffee, watching Fletcher pace with rabid energy.

"You couldn't have left her alone, Tristan! A good friend's daughter! Are you serious about her? How can you be? *She's barely of age!*"

"It didn't stop you."

Fletcher slammed his hands onto the table. "How dare you!"

Tristan stretched his arms out in mock crucifixion. "Fletcher, if you want me to go, I'll go. But please don't lecture me on noble conduct. What's the problem? She *is* of age."

"You brought her here *without my consent!*"

"So? It was better you didn't know. That way your fat friend can't blame you."

Fletcher leaned across the table. "Do you have any idea what you're doing? You're putting us in a very precarious position! You're putting average citizens in hospitals and screwing with a minister's daughter! *This isn't your country*, Tristan! It isn't mine!"

Tristan patted his pocket for a cigarette. "Why are you so worried, Fletcher? I didn't do anything wrong or at least, unforgivable. But, if it makes you feel better, I'll be more careful. No more parties. You have my word."

"And what about the girl?"

"The girl?"

"Ellen, damn it!"

"Oh. Well, if she's not already pregnant, I'll be more careful about that, too."

"*God damn you, Tristan!*" Fletcher flung his mug across the table. "You don't give a damn about her! You don't give a damn about *anything, do you?*"

Tristan sprung from his chair, shocking Fletcher with depth of his fury. His eyes flashed wildly as he charged into his father's face, his hands curled and his arms coiled tensely into his chest, unstable and steaming with seismic rage.

"*I* don't give a damn?" Tristan's mouth was lathering, his spit reaching Fletcher's cheeks. "*What do you know? Hiding here like a rat, all by yourself! I* don't give a damn? When I got here, you saw no television. There was no radio. Nothing! I asked you! You said you cared nothing for the world!"

Tristan swallowed hard and wiped his mouth. He stared at his father, suddenly reigniting. "You worry about this little girl? You left one worse off than that in Spain, pregnant and poor and you *fucking knew! Do you know what happened to her, Fletcher, huh?* While you were running around with your phony name, your rich wife and *all your stupid shit!* Her father beat her for being a whore. She was a poor whore with an Irish bastard boy. She started hearing voices, people no one could see. And then one night she came to my bed, *with a pillow so I couldn't breathe!* My tio put her someplace. They wouldn't tell me. Then she went into the sea, *probably looking for you, you piece of shit! Don't you fucking tell me about giving a fucking damn!*"

Oliver was barking hysterically as Tristan's hand struck the mirror behind Fletcher's ear, sending a blizzard of shards through the air. They met the floor in sparkling anarchy. As they jingled to a rest, the atmosphere settled with a cataleptic calm. Short of breath, Fletcher slowly lifted his arm to wipe the sweat and saliva from his face, fighting back a surge of tears. Tristan's eyes were wet, his hands trembling as he lit a cigarette. There was a persistent knocking at the back door. Motioning numbly to his son to stay, Fletcher navigated through the shrapnel, pausing to steady himself before answering.

"Oh! Elan."

"Fletcher. Um, sorry it's so early. I thought. . . . Anyway, uh, Tristan said you were all right with. . . ."

"Yes, yes, I am."

"O.K. Well, you know, the horse is over twenty, so I'm not sure. . . ."

"Do as you see fit, Elan. I'm paying you, of course."

"I don't. . . ."

"I insist. You know where he is. The tack's in the barn. I'll tell Tristan you're here."

Fletcher stood at the threshold, not able to grasp the undercurrent of his emotions. He never expected that he would be glad to see Elan's round, timeless face, but he was. Although all the lurid gossip and speculation of a decade ago was gone, the unwavering Native American remained, as tested as truth, and infinitely stronger than the sleazy reporters who couldn't entice him into a single, condemning word about a dead lover's disingenuous husband. In modern society, Elan's brand of honor was interpreted as foolish. He could have capitalized richly on the media frenzy by trading in his dignity and the humiliating indiscretions he was privy to. But he didn't. Not once. Consequently, his vehicle was the same familiar wreck that had parked there a dozen years ago. The only marked difference today was in his beholder. For the first time, Fletcher realized that Elan's integrity made him a truly rich man, and like the Great Plains, he would prevail.

Returning to the dining room, Fletcher found Tristan slouched at the table in a state of resignation. Disheveled and smoking, he was compulsively scribbling on a napkin, certain that their association had not survived an eruption of that magnitude, and he was right. Still, no evacuation was ordered. Unquestionably, the relationship had disintegrated, but out of the rubble, a tentative, new alliance was taking hold. It began with a fresh cup of coffee and a simple request.

"Tristan, you might try calling me Ryan. It is, after all, my name. Oh, and the coffee's for Elan. If I recall, he takes it that way."

41

Fletcher was mesmerized by the ease in which Elan was reacquainting Little John with gait commands. He was showing Tristan the basics of lunging when the phone rang. It was ten o'clock. Tearing himself from the north window, he grabbed the receiver.

"Fletcher, it's Tom. I'm afraid we've got a problem."

"Oh?"

"Obviously, you know what happened."

"Yes."

"The Tabors - to put it bluntly - are looking for a settlement."

"Well that didn't take long! Absurd!"

"*Absurd?* Do you know what happened?"

"It was self-defense! Everyone saw it!"

"Maybe, Fletch, but it's not that simple. The police aren't dropping it. Remember Officer Ordell? He's the rabid kind. He says he's got two witnesses who aren't *sure* what happened. The kid's foreign. They're threatening criminal charges. They're trying to spook us with the F.B.I., Homeland Security. I know it's all saber-rattling for now, but an assault charge could stick."

"That's ridiculous, Tom. First of all, I'm sure there was a background check or he wouldn't be in the country. F.B.I! What do they hope to find? As far as a charge is concerned, he was drunk, flirting with some woman when he was. . . ."

"Listen, Fletch. You're not responsible, so there's an easy way to make this whole thing disappear."

"That would be?"

"Send him back."

"No."

"Just for a while."

"No."

"Fletcher, this kid. . . ."

"*Tristan*, Tom."

"All right, *Tristan*. I'm your lawyer, Fletch. You've been through a lot. *Tristan* – to put it bluntly - is a loose cannon. If he goes now. . . ."

"He's staying."

"Fletcher, just think about it. It doesn't mean for. . . ."

"No!"

"Just listen to me! It's a simple solution to what could be a. . . ."

"Pay them."

"*What?*"

"Settle with them, Tom."

"Fletcher. . . ."

"*I mean it! Pay them!*"

"Do you have any idea? There's reconstructive surgery! No kidding. *Tristan* really clocked this guy! It's a lot of money!"

"Well, you're good at negotiations. Pay them – whatever it takes – but Tristan stays."

"Fletcher, I'm going to level with you. You're not being rational. I haven't heard from you in over ten years, and this is the second time in a week that there's been a problem, this time with six figures attached. What about the next time?"

"Tom, please."

"All right," the attorney sighed. "I'll do my best. But he's *got* to stay out of trouble. I mean, even with a visa, one more incident, he's out anyway. I'll let you know."

Fletcher hung up and returned to the window. Tristan's was holding the lunge line, Da Vinci's horse flashing around him in waves of burnt gold. Most facts arguable, one was indisputable: Little John was magnificent.

42

Fletcher Lawson had to be the worst client anyone could ever have. He rarely answered the phone and was inflexible about showings. With a lousy economy, there were few qualified clients, and most of them were too superstitious to even look. Stupid people, Corey thought, as she scanned her dinky cubicle, but not as stupid as Fletcher, for thinking that a he was going to sell by being firm on the price, uncooperative about showings, and now – rumor had it – living with some guy half his age in God-knows-what capacity. She was actually considering a drive over there to terminate the listing when there he was - miraculously - on line 2.

"Well, I can hardly believe it! Fletcher Lawson!"

"All right, I deserve that."

"What's on your mind? It's so *weird* to hear from you!"

"Nothing really. I just thought I'd check to see if there was any interest, and see what I could do to help."

"Well, you could start by answering the phone, and - in case you can afford one - answering machines start at about six bucks."

"All right. Consider it done."

"I called you three times, Fletcher. Mackey has some interest."

"Good."

"Not so good. He wants it for a song."

"All right. Anyone else?"

"I might be asking *you* that." Corey popped a Kiss in her mouth.

"I'm sorry? Did I miss something?"

"Who's your friend?"

"My friend?"

"Don't be coy!"

"I'm not being coy. You mean the fellow staying with me?"

She was defoiling another Kiss. "Yup!"

"My son."

"Oh!" Corey coughed. "I didn't know you had a son! From England?"

"No, actually. He grew up in Spain. He's here for a visit."

"Oh my God! *Him?* That was *him? I should have known!*"

"What?"

"That was *him,* with the accent! Elan's friend! The one that punched out the airport manager! I saw it happen! I was there!"

"Yes, well, unfortunate but it. . . ."

"Fletcher, *your son* egged that guy on; you should know that. And *that punch* was no accident! I told the police. That one - I think - believed me, but. . . ." She cut herself off.

"But what? What did you say to the police, Corey?"

"Fletch, I didn't *know* he was your son, not that it matters. I told the truth."

"As you saw you it. Well, Corey, I dare say you were wrong."

"I wasn't *wrong.*"

"You were. But, we can discuss it . . . over dinner, on me."

"I'm not that easy, Fletch."

"You name the place and time."

"*I'm not that easy, Fletcher!*"

"All right. You're not that easy."

"You're serious? *Really?*"

"Yes."

"Hmm." She decided to test him with something expensive. "The Brown Palace, Wednesday."

"Done."

"*Really?* Six-thirty?"

"I'll pick you up at five."

He hung up. Corey plunked down the phone. She was eighteen again. With a quick word to a substitute receptionist, she went AWOL from floor duty, racing to Park Meadows for a dress.

43

Monday morning, Russ Belmont concluded his staff meeting and offered to take his employees to lunch. Ellen stole a sidelong glance at Ray. He caught it, reciprocating with a forgiving wink. Nick Sparta suggested the tacky little diner on Main Street. As Russ had to leave directly afterward, he took his own car while Nick, Ray and Ellen piled into Nick's extended cab. Although it seemed unthinkable to leave the airport unmanned, Russ's order was to lock up and leave a note. Given the circumstances, an hour's inconvenience was excusable.

Bill Tabor would be out for at least a month which was worth every minute of Nick's postponed vacation. Driving at breakneck speed, he was laughing at everything, even the birds rushing to get out of the way. An Iraq veteran who served two tours as an aircraft mechanic, the Houston transplant could make just about anything airborne. Although he hated paper work and long-winded talkers, he loved his job, country and Colorado home of six years. The only fly in the ointment to his otherwise ideal life was Bill Tabor, but he wouldn't be buzzing around for a while. *Nirvana!*

"Heh! Lighten up, Ellen! Why so sad? Missing old Billy already?" Nick was steering with one finger.

She forced a laugh. It came out like a sniffle.

"What's the matter with you?" Nick slowed, and then barreled through a stop sign. The cat's away!"

She fidgeted with her pocketbook. "Um, you know he fired me on Saturday."

"So what!"

"Don't you want to know why?"

"I don't care. Do you care, Ray?" Nick shouted over his shoulder.

"No, Sir!" Ray shot back.

"Forget, Ellen." Nick pulled into the diner parking lot. "You're in the money, now, honey! I got you a buck more an hour! And see? *Look!* Today, lunch is on *ooooold Billy!*"

Over burgers, Belmont quietly revealed his plans for an imminent expansion, with the goal a major facility accommodating larger craft. The demand was certainly there. The airport was at full capacity and had a waiting list. Of course, the owner added, there'd be a half a million bureaucratic hoops, but *together*, he smiled, they'd get it done, all of which made Nick more thrilled. He ordered a double sundae. Ray, desperately hoping to keep the job, ordered coffee. Ellen greeted the news with feigned enthusiasm, crest-fallen that she'd be excluded when Tabor returned. She declined anything more. As they rose to leave, Russ - counting out a tip - motioned to Nick to stay behind.

"Nick, just between you and me, I saw Bill on Saturday. He told me he fired that girl. Do you know why?"

"He didn't tell you?"

"He wasn't very clear. Something about something that happened off-hours."

The mechanic shrugged. "I don't know."

"Look, Nick, I understand," Russ said slowly, "but there's a lot happening over the next few weeks, and I don't need any problems. If you *do* know, I'd appreciate you being blunt."

"All right. She's a good kid: responsible, smart. Does her job. Everybody likes her. My guess? It had to do with the way he eyeballed her ass every time she got up."

"Oh!" Russ dropped another dollar on the table. "Um, well, thanks, Nick, for your candor."

44

At six o'clock, dinner was waiting. The chef had fully expected to find the caballero in the barn, but where he was actually discovered was under the pines, asleep by a sepulcher. Weighted by a rock, sketch paper was rustling by his side. A book about the Spanish New World lay closed. It was a beautiful evening. Even Oliver didn't have the heart to shatter the peace. He had fashioned himself a pine needle bed and was napping in it.

Like his father, Tristan had read and reread every available account of Spanish expeditions in the New World, particularly those concerning Onate. Yet, nothing was revelatory regarding the fate of Don Christoval. All that could be gleaned was that – if he was typical of his nation and era - he was an aberration of both of man and nature. During his supremely savage life, he was the essence of civility. Through his most pitiless plunder, he was the embodiment of piety. His insatiable greed was equal only to his excessive generosity to church and king. Moreover, he lived to die, and died to live, driven by God, gold and glory. Paintings suggested that he was pampered, depicted in ostentatious regalia astride dashing stallions. But that image could neither be bought nor won; it had to be bestowed. And it took immeasurable humility, cruelty, sweat, pesos, savvy, vanity and bloodshed to win the ultimate prize: an exalted place in Iberian eternity. The conquistador's intrepid, fissured soul walked this earth embodying all that could be reviled and revered in the polarity of mankind.

A breeze tugged at Oliver's hair and rustled Tristan's paper, revealing sketches on the undersides. Curious, Fletcher inched closer and shagged them. In pencil, the renderings were rough depictions of the canyon's rocky slope and pine. One even contained an armored man in the current setting, no doubt a tribute to the noble remains. But, it was the fourth drawing's sharp contrast in light and shadow that held Fletcher's attention. There was a disturbing incongruity in the landscape. He examined the other drawings. Upon inspection, they all had it to a degree: an odd vertical stripe. Fletcher stumbled to the bottom of the ravine and looked up. What appeared in the drawings as an artificial shadow was actually there: a long, nearly straight perpendicular channel running through the outcroppings.

"Do you like them?" the artist shouted from his perch.

His father scanned the craggy slope. "Tristan, come here!"

The napper rocked to his feet and slid lazily to his side.

"Look here. *Look*. Something's here." Handing Tristan his drawings, his father charged up the unnatural declivity. It was approximately twelve feet wide. Its depth varied considerably, its lowest point more than three feet below the raw surface. Fletcher stood in the hollow, not three yards from Don Christoval's resting place.

Tristan saw it clearly and scrambled up the hill. "What do you think it is?"

"I don't know, but it's odd. Very odd. Worth finding out. What we need is a plan . . . and shovels."

45

A man of his word, Ray never disclosed the truth about the airport incident to anyone. But on his first day, he felt he had no other choice but to drive to work without a license, which appalled his knowing young coworker. During a coffee break, Ellen suggested that she pick him up in the mornings, if he could just find a legal way home. With the emphasis on legal, Ray knew exactly who to call. Given how many times he had fixed old, budget-short squad cars, the least the county could do is shuttle him to his hacienda. It was in the best interests of everyone involved, he said cheerfully, and although Officer Ordell resented the order, his lieutenant was insistent: he was now a taxi service. Tomorrow Ordell would send out another batch of resumes. It had only been six weeks since the last mailing, but, maybe this time, he'd get a bite.

The country life did not suit Glen Ordell, but he had agreed to it to pacify his post-partum wife. Having had just two collars – one for domestic violence and one for drunk driving - his rural career was showing real signs of progress: he now had a mind-numbing night patrol and school crossings during football season. Since the old-timers got the meth labs and no one was retiring, he was ready to take a job anywhere with more than two stop lights and a bar. Admittedly, the events of the last few days had breathed a little life into rustic law enforcement. The Spaniard who had so deftly parted Tabor from his nose was the focus of the policeman's eager scrutiny. There was something about him . . . but there was very little to go on. There was no siren on the national level. The guy was here legally. The whole party saw it as a defending punch, except for the Indian, who wouldn't say anything. Then, of course, there was Corey Martin, the only eye-witness he *really* had, willing to testify that it had been a premeditated assault. But then, an American hyphenate was about to change all that on Wednesday night.

46

As of late, insomnia was the rule for the senior occupant of the Lawson estate. Although, Tristan's nocturnal restlessness was the norm, his father had generally relied on six hours of uninterrupted sleep commencing at midnight. Now, with a persistent headache, nausea and joint pain, he no longer enjoyed the predictable rhythm of his former solitude. Shuffling across the study carpet, he yawned and turned on the light. As the clock tolled two a.m., he grabbed the aspirin bottle and desk key from the mantle.

He withdrew the missive - Ryan Egan - and reread it, wondering how she had done it. He turned the envelope over. There was a trace of glue under the flap. He smiled. She must have written him a letter in Tristan's early years. It's possible that she thought her errant lover would want to reconnect or maybe it was as simple as needing funds: child support. Regardless, without an address, she never posted it, but kept it as some kind of anchor to the past. Tristan must have discovered it and ferreted it away as any desperate boy would. As he told it, his mother battled depression, was even delusional. But, apparently the condition was only episodic in that she was clearly lucid enough to know that her son had been seeking his father and had traced him to the United States. She was aware that Tristan had her old letter. She was in a hurry, as the script shows. Cleverly, she chose three words that would eliminate all doubt as to who he was while simultaneously petitioning help. Then she carefully replaced the old communiqué with the new and resealed the envelope. She expected that Tristan would use the letter as an introduction, and she was right. But, why did Tristan lie about her death? Was it as simple as wanting to hurt him?

Fletcher tapped the envelope on the blotter, the lamp shade casting his name in putrid green. Ryan Egan; *Ryan Lawson Egan,* to be true to the birth certificate. Lawson was his mother's surname. After her husband's rise to felonious stardom, Elizabeth Lawson dumped the name Egan and every trace of him, moving to Dublin but not for long. From there, she crossed the Irish Sea and settled in Manchester, drilling into her son that he was a *Lawson,* an Englishman, and nothing but an Englishman, lest it be known that he was the son of an Irish murderer. Young Ryan was deeply ashamed of his tainted roots. As his mother drank and grew more irascible, his self-loathing manifested itself in petty thievery, vandalism and truancy. At fourteen, he suddenly adopted the name Fletcher, his Anglican grandfather's name - a nice old man he vaguely remembered - believing that his mother would see him more favorably. She didn't. Finally arrested for breaking a church window, he decided the name Egan was good enough for him, escaping the charges, his mother and only family at age fifteen. He drifted to London. A year later, the name Lawson came in handy again, this time when a young Egan was sought for theft of a painting.

What should have been his mother's gifts were good taste and education. But they proved to be more a curse than a blessing for a tender boy who was taught to value both without the means for either. They were always poor. His mother's kin was not moneyed, but intellectual: traditionally schoolmasters. Despite Elizabeth's scandalous elopement, they were hospitable enough until her husband's mug shot became such a reviled daily venue, that the

London Lawsons felt compelled to keep their distance. Her alcoholic rages didn't help and, eventually, her relatives were lost to her.

Fletcher refocused on the pretty script forming his Irish name. He wondered where she was. The Sonsoles of his dreams was no doubt, very different now, as was he. But, it wouldn't matter. What he felt for her was not tied to youth, it was deeper. He wanted to see her, but his only avenue to her was through Tristan, and divulging what he knew now would compromise them all. He reread her plea one more time: *Save Your Son.*

"From what?" he murmured.

Wearily, he locked the envelope away, extinguished the light and made his way down the hallway. Hearing the hiss of the television, he paused by Tristan's room. Fletcher knocked softly. There was no answer. He tapped again, and then cracked the door. "Tristan?"

There was no reply.

The TV's static glow washed the room in cobalt. As Fletcher reached for the remote, he was suddenly aware of the empty bed. He glanced through the open casement; the rental car was gone. Remarkably, he was no longer tired. On the night table, his steely computer sat tight-lipped. He confiscated it and dropped it off at his study. With the coffee maker on, he returned to his desk. He had tried to respect Tristan's privacy. . . . He jerked the laptop open and logged on.

Tristan's mailbox was blinking for a password. Fletcher went through the obvious litany without success. He tried all sorts of names and adjectives, forward and backward, with and without numerical designations. He tried to think the way his son would, knowing he had a taste for irony. He kept at it, through a second cup of coffee, and then a third, Oliver upside down under his chair.

"God, it could be anything," he muttered under his breath. Tristan had a twenty-two year data base of which he knew nothing.

The hacker tried his limited vocabulary of Spanish words and phrases. He typed in provinces and towns. He typed in Ryan:

the peevish winking continued. He typed in Egan. Again, access denied. Then he typed in Ryan Egan. He was right; his son had a taste for irony. He was in.

Everything in Tristan's Sent folder had been erased, but there was an already opened message left in his In-Box. It was short: *Denver Wed. 9 p.m.* The sender was the familiar Ea. Above the dog's snoring, Fletcher thought he heard something.

He slammed down the lid and yanked out the cord. It was after three. He crept down the hall and peered out the front window. Tristan's car had rolled to a stop. Fletcher decided to play it straight. He scurried back to his study.

Oliver woke, his head cocked in alert as he sensed a presence in the corridor. Fletcher was at his desk, the computer glowing. Like a leopard, Tristan prowled into the study, fixing on his father.

"I was with Ellen," he snarled.

"I see."

"What were you doing in my room? I thought you valued privacy, *Ryan*."

"I turned the bloody T.V. off. In the future, you might try using the front door. It works as well as a window, better in fact. In and out in a jiffy."

"The dog barks." Tristan was glued to the computer screen, smoldering. "What are you doing?"

"I thought you valued privacy, Tristan."

The itinerant had no retort. He turned on his heel and stomped out.

When he was assured of solitude, Fletcher re-entered the internet. Relieved that the message was intact, he was about to log off when a new e-mail appeared for Tristan. In bold green letters, it announced itself as unread. Fletcher didn't dare do the honors, but it amazed him. Evidently, no one else required sleep but Fletcher, who - at that moment - was in such dire need that the couch was as far as he could get.

47

As Nick coordinated daily operations, he kept a close eye on Ray who predictably, was up to Mach speed on maintenance and repairs. But then, Nick was accustomed to his assistant's talent, having worked with him off and on in prior years. Ray was a remarkable problem solver, brilliant in fact, as long as he stayed sober, and, to that end, Corey and the big minister were doing a heck of job. Ultimately, though, the battle of the booze was going to be lost or won by Ray, as Nick well knew, having fought it himself. He could only lend his support by urging Ray to consider becoming a licensed aircraft mechanic. Ray said he would think on it. On Tuesday morning, Nick gave him a number to call, and said not to worry about the money. He knew the guy. Ray seemed genuinely pleased by the offer.

A little before noon, Ellen was putting the finishing touches on a mailer when Pete showed up unexpectedly. Delighted, she watched him plow through the glass doors laden with bags of burgers and fries. She greeted him, then skipped out to the hangar and returned with Ray. After finishing a call, Nick joined them. Après lunch, Pete was permitted to borrow his daughter for a ten minute stroll.

"So, little girl. . . ."

"Dad, before you start, I was home before one as we agreed."

Pete rolled his eyes. "True."

"So, what's up?"

"Nothing really." Pete ran his hand across his hair. "Just wanted to see how you were doing."

"Fine. I'm fine."

"Obviously, you were with Tristan last night."

"*Yes.*" Her mouth pursed defensively.

"It's O.K." Pete put his hands up in surrender. "Just conversation. Where'd you go?"

"We rode around, that's all."

"Oh, O.K. Uh, well, you left well after ten, so, I couldn't imagine . . . did you get dinner or . . . ?

"*Why?*"

"Take it easy, Ellen. I'm just making sure you're O.K."

"I'm fine, Dad."

"Do you mind my asking why he can't just come get you at a reasonable hour?"

Ellen's eyes widened. "Because he thinks you hate him! Because Fletcher's after him to keep a *low profile.* That means not coming up *our* driveway or seeing me at a *reasonable hour,* all right?"

"Wrong, Ellen. He's welcome to pick you up at the house."

"Oh yeah? What about Mom?"

"You have my word: she'll be fine. O.K?"

"O.K."

They were passing a huge, corrugated hangar. Pete paused. "Is Ray in there?"

"Probably."

"I need to see him."

"Sure. Thanks, Dad."

Pete watched her scamper away and then stepped into the cavernous shelter.

Ray was sifting through a pile of bolts. Pete cleared his throat.

Glancing up, Ray nodded amicably. "Question, Pete."

"Shoot."

"If matter and antimatter coexist in the same ratio, why aren't we. . . . "

"It doesn't exist in the same ratio, theoretically. It's assumed that if anti-matter exits, matter dominates."

"I read that, Pete, but it makes no sense."

"So, what do you think?"

"I think that anti-matter makes up certain universes, as does matter. The ratio between matter and anti-matter *is* exact, divided by dimensions."

"But then, theoretically, they would still cancel each other out. . . ."

"Not if partitioned by membranes. Well, maybe. Anyway, that's as far as I've gotten with it."

"Thank Goodness!" Pete stretched and twisted his back. "To be continued, when I can keep up. Now – in its simplest form - how are you?"

"Good."

"Lonely?"

"I guess."

"You want a drink?"

Ray laughed. "Every minute."

"Raymond, I'm here because Ruth and I would like you to come for dinner on Sunday. I'll pick you up."

The mechanic frowned and held up a nut for measure. "Don't feel sorry for me, Pete."

"O.K. I won't. Five then?"

"Sunday?"

"I'll pick you up."

"I could probably drive."

"Don't drive, Ray. The hearing on your license is next week. It was hard to get. I'll be there at quarter till on Sunday."

Pete toodled at him before melting back into the summer haze.

48

In the dazzling rays of midafternoon, Fletcher was feeling at peace, the worries of the night fading to fantasy. He was sweeping up around the barn, watching Little John being put through his paces. Tristan was a natural, at least with the lounge line. He had completely tacked the horse, making it clear who was really chomping at the bit, but was too mindful of Elan to do anything more than condition the animal daily. When deemed fit, Little John's first rider in over a decade would no doubt be the native veteran, not the Spanish rookie. From what Fletcher remembered, Meredith got along well with the warmblood: not too many incidents. The glitzy colt was never intended as a trail horse. With his conformation and talent, he was a prospect for top competition, proving his jumping ability by clearing most of his pens. But Meredith's fondness for him changed his destiny. She had paid a premium for the eighteen hand Hanoverian that was never to see a show ring. Instead, his mission became hers: to explore the mysterious canyons, steep buttes and vast grasslands of the west.

That morning, Tristan announced his need for the computer to research *proper* excavation procedure - imitating his father - assuming that it was still available. Of course it was. Fletcher had been insistent that they not dig without some rudimentary know-how. Fletcher also took the moment to announce he had an engagement tomorrow night.

"A *date?*" Tristan teased.

"Something like that," Fletcher muttered.

49

Corey was waiting on the porch Wednesday evening when her escort arrived promptly at five. She was wearing a chiffon evening dress, and looked – quite to Fletcher's astonishment – girlishly lovely. He stood in attendance as she eased herself into the passenger seat.

"Corey, you look divine."

"Thanks, Fletch. I put everything I had into it."

He laughed. "I can see that. By the way, you're free to take your shoes off."

"Oh, thank you! They're. . . ."

"Excruciating, I'm sure. Don't worry. You can hobble into the restaurant on my arm and go barefoot under the table."

Corey flipped the visor down, fluffing her new coif in the mirror. "You're not doing this because of your son, are you?"

"Corey?"

"Well?"

"Corey!"

"It won't work, Fletch."

"Of course it will."

"You *are!* I knew it! You think I'm *that stupid*?"

"No."

"Then what makes you think you can buy me off?"

"I'm not buying you off, Corey. If I wanted to buy you off, I'd write a check."

"So, what *are* you doing?"

The driver sighed. "Having dinner? Enjoying your company . . . if you'd allow me? Is that all right?"

She stared at him, blinking. "I'm sorry."

"I'm not . . . *yet*. Relax. Find something on the radio. We're in no rush. I made reservations. The night's ours if you'll give me half a chance."

Corey leaned back. The air conditioner's cool lambent teased the tension from her face. With a river of traffic, they floated to I-25. There, white clouds stretched across the sky causing solar rays to play hop-scotch across a sea of sluggish trunks and tail fins. It was rush hour's high tide. She opened the sun roof and looked up. She wasn't old; she wasn't young. She wasn't anything. She felt the sun play on her face. The blue sky signaled eternity. She was with Fletcher, that's all.

The mile high city was a Hopper study in contrast. Black, geometric shadows scored white sidewalks and stark, ozone-weary buildings with laser sharpness. Trendy high rises towered over indignant Victorians, dwarfing them with ruthless indifference. The hunger to be a competitive national center was reshaping the once wild frontier town into an extravagant Apple-flavored, California-coated, New Age rehash. Expensive coliseums hosted an endless variety of athletic events, the primary news coverage being the latest gladiatorial review. An art museum had doubled in size; another was on the way. Light rail was whisking commuters from what were once daunting distances into Denver's complex cosmopolitan web. Throughout the city, examples of its uneasy, tangled transition were everywhere, except at its epicenter.

There, old world grandeur wet the nouveau riche appetite with the consummate weave of a silken glove, better known as the Brown Palace.

As planned, Corey hung on an English arm and limped through the soaring 19th century lobby all the way to the dining room, gratefully shedding her heels under the table. Her paramour ordered drinks and kept the conversation focused on her. To his surprise, she had a daughter, albeit estranged. Corey admitted that childrearing had not been a priority during her daughter's formative years. Training horses was a natural path for the natural horsewoman, but it came with a price. The physical injuries were almost as crippling as the heartbreaks, which - after her second drink - she wore on her sleeve with touching candor. He listened with ardent interest, perusing the appetizers. When it came time to order, Corey held the menu at arm's length, feigning indecision. He saved her by insisting on ordering for them both. While he devoured his entrée, she picked at hers nervously through prattle, welcoming coffee and a taste of chocolate afterward. When the subject finally drifted to his offspring, Fletcher carefully crafted a comparison between Corey's travails and his own, interlacing familiar images of her distant daughter with his son's lost and found life. He dangled the hope that given time, Corey might reconcile with her only child, as he had. She was overwhelmed by his sensitive support, his soothing timbre stirring the candle flame with an intimate implication. She blushed. Then, smiling kindly, he offered her a cordial, and rolled his summation into a not so subtle point: that there was no room in his life for anyone adversarial to his family . . . period. As with his timing, his aim was perfect, causing her pulse to spike with a heartfelt stab. She knew she would be seeing Officer Ordell in the morning. She was already in rehearsal with a very different story.

The two left the restaurant with the sun's divided rays still peaking across the Rockies. Fletcher was up for a walk, but remembering Corey's shoes, guided her directly to the Volvo. At her request, they took a sight-seeing tour around the capitol, weaving through downtown. He asked if she would like to catch a movie, perhaps something at an art theater. She was delighted. On Broadway, Fletcher was looking for an opening into the left lane, when he suddenly jammed on the brakes, veered hard to the right, and jumped the curb to the sidewalk. Corey yelled, grabbing the dash. He spun the car into an adjacent parking lot, then lurched to a stop under the shadow of an old brick warehouse.

"Jesus, Fletcher!" She shouted breathlessly. "What the hell are you doing?"

He didn't answer right away. He was riveted on three figures moving along the far side of the avenue. He mumbled an apology and begged her indulgence for a few minutes. She stared at him in bewilderment. He watched as the trio made a diagonal turn, moving toward them across four lanes. They were in a hurry. Fletcher reversed the car, maneuvering quickly out of their direct line of sight. Suddenly, they reappeared within fifty yards, passing in profile. The men were locked in conversation. The paunchy one was carrying a briefcase, his white, wispy hair bouncing with every stride. To his left was a young Arian type in cowboy boots and a fringed shirt. To his right, taller than his counterparts, was Tristan, animated, as if in an argument. A jacket was flung over his arm, a cigarette burning precariously between his fingers.

"Fletcher, what's going on?" Corey was gaping at him. "Why don't you. . . ?"

"Corey, I'll just be a moment." Her date was exiting the vehicle.

"Fletcher! What are you doing? Where. . . ?"

"Wait here!" He commanded, slamming the door.

He trotted across the parking lot, paused at the edge of a graffiti covered two story, and then stepped onto the sidewalk, tracking east behind his quarry. The older man glanced at his watch, and picking up the pace, motioned, presumably, for the conversation's conclusion. Tristan was bent to his ear, looking as if he was driving a point home. They slowed. Fletcher ducked under the shadow of an awning. The street lights were flickering on. The three transited north out of view. Fletcher hastened to the corner, peering across an asphalt set-back into a small office park. Two of them were passing through a doorway. Four windows whitened with a fluorescent glow. The door shut. Tristan's slim silhouette was donning a jacket and . . . heading straight for him.

Fletcher barely made it into a stairwell before his son emerged and stopped, inspecting his surroundings. He was holding something in his jacket pocket. He took one last look around him before bounding across Broadway. Out of sight, his espier raced for his car.

"Corey! I'm so sorry!" He swooped into his seat and turned the key.

"What the hell was that about? *Who are they?*"

The driver was on optimistic alert. "You didn't recognize them?"

"No!"

Any of them?"

"No!"

He was giddy with relief.

"Well?" she demanded.

"Oh. Uh, contractors. I lost their number."

"Are they working on your house?"

"Uh, no. I've changed my mind." He eased out into traffic. "Now let's see about that movie."

50

The following morning, over coffee and an English muffin, Fletcher was reviewing Tristan's notes on the art of archeological forays. Tristan was pacing with a glass of orange juice, repeatedly trying to interpolate while his senior motioned for silence.

Fletcher tossed the notes on the table. "All right, what is it?"

"Let's dig a little today. We'll explore."

"Tristan, there's a lot to it. There's a proper method."

"We don't even know if there's something there!"

"I understand, but if there is, we don't want to destroy it before we even begin. What do you propose? That we just start throwing dirt everywhere?"

Taking a seat, Tristan addressed him earnestly. "If something's there, it survived at least five hundred years. I'm sure, if we're careful, it will survive us. Why not try? You're making it complicated when it's really very simple."

Fletcher was absently tapping a spoon on the table. "I don't know. . . . Oliver would have to stay here. The shovels are in the barn. I suppose if we. . . ."

Tristan's juice trembled with the slap of the screen door.

51

It was ten in the morning and the heat promised to be record-breaking. Officer Ordell was flabbergasted at Corey's new version of the Tabor fight. He pleaded with her to give him the *real* reason for the sudden alteration. She continued to repeat that she had had too much to drink that night, and, in retrospect, felt that she wasn't being entirely fair. He argued with her, swearing that she had not only been reliably sober, but morally courageous, and a pending civil suit might rely on her testimony. With that news, her lips tightened. She snapped that she was not one to be pressured, that it was the last time she would discuss the matter, and, if forced, would tell the whole world that he fed her the original story. He was stunned. As she stormed out, he hurled the file into the Cases Going Nowhere cabinet and kicked it shut . . . several times.

The Fahrenheit past ninety, two amateur archeologists shoveled shale into a trickling mound. It was nowhere near as simple as they thought it would be. They had decided to attack the deepest part of the hollow, which was almost centered on the slope. Not only was the grit fused and hard, but it seemed that as soon as they made a dent, it would rapidly fill in with scree from above. They were straddled awkwardly to either side of the ravine, struggling for footing with every hard-fought shovel-full.

"Tristan, wait a minute. We're not getting anywhere." Fletcher's soaking ascot was in his hand.

Tristan wiped his face with his tee-shirt.

"We need to put some kind of barrier here." Fletcher stabbed his spade into the ground directly above their ditch. "We need a couple of flat rocks to act as a wedge, to keep the dirt from running down into the hole."

Fletcher tucked his shovel under his elbow, perched on a boulder and looked around. He didn't see any flat rocks.

"What about the one you're standing on?" his coworker asked. "It's flat."

Fletcher looked down. "It's also huge. Oh well. Let's see what the bottom looks like."

The two scrambled below it, lying against the declivity, bracing themselves against the slightly exposed underside. With a countdown, they pushed upward. It wouldn't budge.

"Wait." Fletcher snuggled his shoulder against it. "Right. One more time. Ready?"

They pressed against it with face-reddening force. It shifted slightly, sending a stream of gravel under Fletcher's hip, and then a flood under his leg as it angled away from the embankment. The bottom was smooth, convex and absolutely enormous. In a wave, sand and stone slumped forward from above, heeling the rock upward, twisting it away from Fletcher, and sending a torrent of debris into Tristan's eyes, blinding him. He cursed and spat. The boulder's gritty cradle began eroding rapidly, pouring like a waterfall down the ravine. The ominous missile now loomed over the young Samson, threatening to crush him. Tristan had both arms locked against its weight, his palms bleeding from pressure. Fletcher rolled next to him, yelling at him to keep still. Digging his heels into the slippery loess, he held a forearm against craggy giant, but was unable to apply enough tension to relieve his son, who was now groaning under its tonnage. Fletcher scratched frantically into the running sand, hoping to find a wedge. A stone tumbled away. The boulder skidded forward. Tristan yelled. Fletcher curled his arm behind him, pushing from his back with all his strength, using his free hand to grope for a shovel. He felt a handle under the running escarpment but couldn't free it. Gravity was grinding into his shoulders. Tristan's eyes were shut; he was trembling with waning strength. The rock pitched forward again, shadowing Tristan's forehead. Fletcher grappled furiously for the spade. Then someone shouted *"hold on."*

Elan was less than ten yards from them, wading through the fall-out until he was forced to crawl. Fletcher motioned for the shovel. Elan shook his head and scrambled past him. There was a loud pop. The horseman dropped to the excavator's side with a thick branch. Using it as a shim under the massive stone, he shoved it behind the father until it was just shy of the son's right temple. Then, he teased the spade from the sand and leveraged it under the bough. He told Fletcher to keep pushing until they were ready.

"Tristan, on three, you have to let go and roll this way: to me. Fletcher, same thing: to your right! Be fast!"

Tristan grunted. Fletcher hoped he could move; his spine was numb.

"O.K? One, two, three!"

With his wrists locked into a sling, Elan jerked up on the branch, plunging the shovel handle down with his boot. The crusher tipped to Tristan's left as he scuttled from under it. Fletcher grabbed his arm and pulled him across the slope; catapulting him into Elan as the shovel handle broke. The branch split. The cannonball rocked menacingly. Tristan seized his father's shirt and yanked him sideways, forcing them both backward. Deprived of its victim, the angry warhead grazed Tristan's ankle before hurtling down the ravine. A narrow avalanche ensued. Flying artillery skipped across the hill as a river of rubble turned into rapids. The furrow of Tristan's drawings was sinking with a steady flow of pebbles and pine needles. Several saplings rolled like bushy batons to the canyon floor. Boulders collided and shattered before joining the frenzied geologic mob to middle earth. The slope was steaming with dust. The talus simmered to a low hiss.

Elan sat up, scanning the outskirts of the fence. His horse had broken his tie, but was still there, blowing with fear in the willows. The cowboy pulled his hat off and wiped his forehead with his sleeve. "What the hell were you doing, anyway?"

Fletcher propped himself up on his elbows, gripped by a sudden spasmodic giggle. "Digging a hole."

Tristan collapsed backward. He stomped the ground with his foot, his torso curling with silent, convulsive laughter.

"Well, I suppose that's one way to do it," Elan responded, not quite getting it. "Anyway, you've got a hell of a hole, now."

"Thank you, Elan." Fletcher was still sniggering. "I mean it. I can't thank you enough. Would you like some coffee?"

"Later. I've gotta catch a horse." He slapped his giddy student with his hat. "See ya tomorrow."

The knight in shining shale dust slid down the hill sideways until meeting a lower outcropping. From there he picked his way down the rocky terrain until landing on the wide sunny substratum. As he turned back and waved, his shout echoed up the canyon wall. "Yep! That's a *hell* of hole!"

Fletcher followed his line of sight and sobered immediately. He snapped to a stand, and scuttled to the area. Alerted, his collaborator pursued. Their paltry ditch was no longer there. In its place was a deep fissure slashing up the original depression for eight yards. Tristan fell beside it, thrusting his arm into the scar.

Cautioning him, Fletcher descended to a vantage point and stood erect, visually measuring the fracture. At its widest, it was about six feet, tapering slightly to a perpendicular cavity. From there, it closed dramatically - into inches – before meeting shale. Fletcher scrambled up to the chasm's lowest end and peered straight down. It was pitch black. Above him, his accomplice was tossing pebbles, announcing that the crevasse was much deeper than what he could see; he could hear his sounders bouncing off the sides of a subterrane. Now with a myriad of stones to choose from - Fletcher shook his head at the irony - he dropped one into the mysterious lower shaft. There was no sound. He released another, pressing his ear into the abyss. He thought he heard something. He found a fist-sized piece of quartz. Assigning it to the dark domain, he counted. He was up to three before he detected a faint splash.

"Tristan!"

"What?"

"Listen!"

Tristan skidded to his father's perch. Fletcher scooped up a piece of granite and tapped it on the hole's craggy rim. "Put your head here."

As his partner stooped, Fletcher let gravity carry his offer to Hades. Tristan's eyes widened with the sound of its watery receipt. "It's a cave! A cavern!"

"I think so."

Simultaneously, they eyed Don Christoval's jumbled but intact sarcophagus.

"Do you think he was protecting something?" Tristan asked.

"I don't know. I imagine we'll find out. First, though, I think we should cover it. We should camouflage the whole thing right now, before lunch. We'll keep a small gap, something we can access easily."

They hastily concealed their find.

52

Corey had set two showings and was scanning multi-list for more possibilities when Dana, their regular receptionist, appeared from behind the divider. The agent scowled; her computer was operating at a snail's pace. Dana milled around until Corey made eye contact. "Yes?"

Dana smiled. "I was wondering if you want to get some lunch."

Corey reglued herself to the computer screen. "Not today."

"Oh, O.K."

Dana didn't leave. She fussed with the flowers on Corey's cabinet, extracting the browning daisies and rearranging the carnations. Corey exhaled irritably. The florist didn't budge.

"What do you want, Dana?"

"Oh. Well. I just wanted to know. . . ."

"What?"

"Remember the Larsen's party?"

"Yes."

"I wondered what you thought happened, whether you thought. . . ."

"Oh! Let me guess!" Corey's lower lids levitated like a snapping turtle. "Ordell called you!"

"Um, yes. He said. . . ."

"I know what he said."

"Well, Corey, why *did* you change your mind?"

The rapacious reptile flew out of her chair, backing the fearful aide into the next cubicle.

"Why didn't you tell me you were trying to sue *my client?* Fletcher Lawson, right? Thought I'd help you? You want money, Dana? Earn it!" Stomping back to her burrow, Corey snarled, "Like it wasn't your fault! Do you have any idea what you looked like with that kid?"

Dana's eyes reddened. She scurried past the arriving clients and fled into an empty meeting room. Corey greeted the incomers with a great big smile and a pack of new listings. Her buyers of the day were none other than the Mackeys, and she was unusually sugary. But the thrill of victory was short-lived. As she turned back, she watched Dana shamble back to her desk, and Corey felt the familiar byproducts of her temper: guilt and regret.

53

Dropping his pen, Fletcher wiped the moisture from his forehead. He had been making a supply list for the upcoming cave exploration, but with the house gathering degrees all day, it was too muggy to concentrate. Although he rarely used the swamp cooler, he stepped out into the hallway to turn it on. As expected, a cool draft met him when he returned to the study, inducing him to stretch across the sofa to ease his stiffening back. It occurred to him that it was Thursday; he wondered if Pete would show. If he didn't, it would be just as well. The host was worn out and – as usual – his head was throbbing. He closed his eyes. They'd have to scavenge for dinner; groceries were running low. He thought he heard the clock ring five. Was it that late? He glanced at the mantle. He wasn't alone.

The man was standing at the fireplace. The afternoon light rippled through his filigree hair and plated his high cheekbones; his eyes, deeply set, remained in shadow. Fletcher could feel perspiration flood his face as he whispered, "What do you want?"

The visage took a step closer as if he couldn't hear the question. He pressed his right hand to his maimed clavicle and nodded formally.

Fletcher's heart was punching holes through his chest. His back was wet. "What do you want?" he cried hoarsely. *"What do you want?"*

The unnatural guest opened his arms, raising his index finger to his lips before stepping toward the couch's occupant. Fletcher desperately tried to comprehend his gestures. He felt the adrenaline surge through him but his muscles weren't responding; his shoulders were hard and cramped.

"Stay away! Just tell me what you want! *Please!*"

The intruder halted, waving a hand as if in assurance, and then reached his terrified intent in two strides. He seized Fletcher by the forearm; the eyes shining with a familiar, fluid intensity. The hair fell like a blade across his captive's crown as he whispered, "in hoc signo vinces." He repeated it, the manacle tightening as he hissed, *"in hoc signo vinces."*

Fletcher felt pressure on his windpipe; his mouth lathered.

"In hoc signo vinces." The voice was inside him, boring into his subconscious like a wasp. *"In hoc signo vinces!"*

Fletcher rebelled, thrashing for release. It wouldn't let go. It was calling him by name.

"Fletcher!" it thundered, *"in hoc signo vinces! Fletcher!* Wake! Wake up! *Fletcher! Fletcher!* Answer me!"

Fletcher's eyes blinked wildly. His wrist was engulfed by Pete's fingers, checking his pulse against a Timex. Tristan was behind him, the concern etched in his dirty face.

"Are you with us?" Pete's baritone ricocheted through Fletcher's brain until it came to rest with full sentience.

"Yes," Fletcher muttered, nausea seizing him. "What time is it?"

"Six ten," Pete replied. "Just take it easy. Lay back. Tristan said this has happened before. How many times?"

Fletcher struggled to sit up. "What do you mean?"

Pete cleared his throat. "That you passed out and no one could wake you. I think it's a seizure. Your pulse was through the roof. You should see a doctor."

"I'm all right, Pete. Too much sun. Is it really that late?"

"It is."

"Tristan," Fletcher coughed. "Hand me a tissue. Over there. On the desk."

"Are you dizzy?" Pete demanded.

"No." Fletcher lied.

"Are you hungry? I brought the usual fare and then some."

"Sounds great!" He lied again.

Handing Fletcher a Kleenex, Tristan declared, "you were shouting." Pete's "not now" look went completely unheeded. "You were shouting in your sleep."

"Oh? What did I say?" Fletcher blew his nose.

"It was Latin." Tristan jutted his jaw toward Pete. "He knows."

Rummaging through the food bags, the minister clarified. "In hoc signo vinces. Under this sign thou shalt conquer."

"Really!" Fletcher rose. "Gentlemen, I'm going to wash up. Help yourself to a drink, Pete. If it's too hot in the kitchen, we'll eat in here." He left. Tristan stared after him. Pete dropped the baguette back into the sack.

By the time Fletcher's bare feet met the tiles of his bathroom, he could no longer suppress the terror pounding at his core. Tears raged over his cheeks as his nose bled, dripping into the white sink like molten lava. He opened the faucet, trying to douse his fear with cold splashes, but it was no use. It was as if he was forced to confront his worst memories, his meanest deeds and deepest dreads all at once. It was like the moment before passing. He folded to the floor, sickened and sobbing.

Pete knew. Fletcher felt his paternal presence at the threshold. Flicking a towel from a holder, the pastor soaked it with fresh water and stooped to cool Fletcher's sinuses. Tristan rounded the corner, appalled by his father's state.

"Jesus," Fletcher choked, burying his face in the cotton compress. "I'm so sorry."

Pete said nothing, soaking another towel. Tristan dropped next to the fallen man, prying the cloth from his face, examining his nose like a medic.

"Did you get hurt today?"

Fletcher shook his head. "No. I'm sorry. How awful. I'll be all right. Please go."

"Can you stand?" Tristan queried.

"There's no hurry," Pete overruled.

"Did you have another dream? Did you? Did you see him?" Tristan demanded.

There was no answer.

His progeny was not to be ignored. "He spoke to you? Those words: in hoc signo. . . ?"

Fletcher draped the towel around his neck. His nose had stopped bleeding. "Yes, those words."

Pete was reluctant to catch on, not wanting to give the apparition theory precedence over a full checkup. Nevertheless, he was willing to indulge one question.

"Fletch, what does that Latin phrase mean to you?"

Catching the sink like a cragsman, Fletcher hoisted himself up. He doused his head with cold water and dried off. Discarding his shirt, he crossed into his bedroom. There, he changed into a fresh polo and motioned his faithful to follow.

Retracing his steps, he glided through the study and fumbled for the mantle key. He collapsed at the desk chair as he unlocked the center drawer, retrieving - from his most secret repository - his metallurgic soul. As if forged by a supernatural force, the huge medallion hung almost weightlessly from its chain, its jewels prism-like, fracturing the room in a magnificent regeneration of color, humbling the setting sun with shafts from its own golden dawn. Tristan was thunderstruck. Pete's mouth was agape. *In hoc signo vinces* dangled hypnotically in front of its subjects with the charge that glory was a duty, a destiny.

"Good heavens, Fletch!" Pete exclaimed. "I've never seen anything like it! Dare I ask? *Where did you get it?*"

Catching the eye of his father, Tristan spoke softly for him. "The Falcon: Don Christoval. I'm sure it was his."

Tristan reached through the evening haze for the Roman cross of Spanish centuries. Fletcher relinquished it, letting the priceless pendant fall. Like the morning's revelatory landslide, it flowed with the shower of its chain, to be received by a deft Iberian chalice.

✳ ✳ ✳

Fletcher was nibbling at Pete's insistence while Pete gobbled up Brie. Tristan was still pacing the hall with the cordless, spending more than his self-imposed three minute allotment for breaking a date. Through the spans of silence, Pete could hear his daughter's bitter disappointment. Tristan's callous dismissals were within earshot.

"Why doesn't he just invite her over? There's no need to upset her!" Pete slapped the table. "Honestly! Were we all such. . . ?"

"Dogs?" Fletcher chuckled.

Pete growled, though he was secretly rejoicing his daughter's deliverance. Beneath him, Oliver was whimpering plaintively over his stinginess.

The no show hung up and joined them.

"If you'd like to invite her over, Tristan, call her back," his father brokered. "It's fine with me."

"No. Not tonight." Don Cad was smearing his bread with pate. "Tonight we should think. And you need quiet."

"Oh? Did you hear that Oliver?" Fletcher quipped. "*Quiet.*"

Assuming it was a hint directed at him, Pete rolled his eyes, capitulating to the whining cur by handing him a smidgen of chicken. Oliver nearly took his hallowed hand off. "All right!" Pete grimaced, wiping his saliva soaked palm on his pant leg. "That's it for you!"

Satiated, the trio put their feet on the coffee table, encircling the new treasure like planets ensnared by gravity. The medallion's discovery was in no small measure miraculous, thus, Pete was eager for a detailed accounting. But, in order to do so, Fletcher had to revisit the painful aftermath of Meredith's accident. He did so haltingly.

He began by remembering how seemingly insignificant splinters of the aircraft were everywhere and how he felt a need to clean up; but was warned not to meddle with the crash site, not to move an iota of debris or rummage around the area. Nevertheless, in shock and inebriated, he had wandered down to the wreckage around four a.m. the following morning. He waded through the refuse, not knowing what he was looking for, only that he was compelled to do so. The Cessna's nose was rippled and folded into the upper third of the slope as if hinged; the fuselage was tossed over it, upside down. A propeller had disconnected; it was horribly twisted and inserted like a scissor midway on the hill. When Fletcher slipped and fell against the blade, it seemed as if his leg was predestined to become wedged in a peculiar sink hole. Freeing himself, rock by rock, he discovered that he was not alone. He had been trapped in a sepulcher; in it was a skull. Don Christoval's jaw was open as if astonished that someone had finally found him. Fletcher didn't know what drove him to do it, but by the time the investigators arrived that morning, he had exhumed the entire skeleton and entombed it in a hollow approximately seventy feet from the original site, well away from the location of interest. He absconded with the fabulous medallion in case the ancient man was unearthed. But, no one found the conquistador, primarily because Fletcher was perched over the remains daily, watching the investigators comb the canyon under his suspected pathological - and often drunken - eye. When the clean-up terminated and Tom Vicante had restored his client's trampled right to privacy, the conquistador's guardian worked feverishly by moonlight, reinterring Don Christoval in his original grave. But, the fact that Fletcher had disturbed the area coupled with his obsessive monitoring fueled conjecture that he was the nefarious cause of his wife's demise. Meredith's ailing father fanned the flames and sued for a freeze of her trust. Fletcher's picture graced the front page of every rag until finally, under Tom Vicente's dogged fielding, the improbable and, more importantly, improvable murder theory dissolved into a pilot error determination. Nevertheless, it took years for the scandal to fade. Under the auspices of the vindictive Palter, the bulk of Meredith's fortune was permanently withheld - without a fight - from her despondent husband. Tom couldn't talk him into a resistance.

In a strange way, Fletcher considered the nobleman's find recompense for Meredith's loss. His inability to mourn her convinced him that he was an undeserving philanderer; and in truth, he was never in love with her. But, although it was money that had cemented their marriage, somewhere through the years, Fletcher's fondness for her became more than gratuitous. Unable to come to terms with her death, the sole architect and builder of the property's enormous walled garden honored her life with life: in pure floral heraldry. "To Meredith" was carved into the only blooming Magnolia on the high plains desert. From an aerial perspective, the garden's scrolling color was a breathtaking replica of the Spanish medallion's filigree. The sanctuary eventually became a landmark to recreational pilots in the know, which pleased the memorial's creator. He couldn't think of a more fitting tribute to his high-flying companion of ten years.

Pete cleared his throat. "You have no idea what brought him here?"

"Don Christoval? No, I'm sorry to say." Fletcher replied. "He may be linked to a party that made it to Kansas."

"We might know more if you'd listen . . . if you weren't so afraid," Tristan grumbled.

Pete grinned. "You're convinced your father's being haunted?"

"Is it so hard to believe?" Tristan retorted. "This man spoke to him in Spanish; he doesn't *know* Spanish."

"I know a little Spanish," Fletcher countered. "Besides, Tristan, that's patently absurd. It was a dream."

"It's no dream!" Tristan snorted.

"Actually," Pete mused, "An encounter might be entirely possible, if. . . ."

"Oh no," Fletcher groaned.

"Now, hypothetically speaking, let's assume that time exists dimensionally like an invisible CD, recording our universe in a continuously expanding spiral. Then, let's suppose something comes along, something unusual – an energy, a spike in our magnetic field or a cosmic force – something that creates a warp or a fold so that one history simultaneously records the *noise* of another. Or...."

"Or," Fletcher yawned, "how 'bout this? It's just a dream, Pete."

Tristan was rapt. "You're saying that it's possible, that these meetings could be real?"

Pete laughed. "Hypothetically, and I mean *hypothetically*, but it's worth exploring."

Fletcher abruptly rose. "Gentlemen, I hope you understand...."

The reverend stood. "Of course, Fletch. "I should be on my way. I just want to mention that you look, frankly...."

"Thank you, Peters!" Fletcher saluted good-bye and withdrew to his bedroom.

54

The following morning was cool, due to a dense cloud cover. The prairie's flora was empowered by the gray shield; pure color danced chaotically across the hills, celebrating the rout of the sun's sapping rays. Elan's stock trailer echoed the riotous display; every hue imaginable dotted its rusty sides. There was no longer any point in repainting it; it was a Pollock revival, parked as it was in the Lawson driveway. Fletcher was in the kitchen, reviewing his shopping list when a shrill ring demanded a Pavlovian response. Still not well trained, the English retriever hesitated before lifting the receiver.

"Hello."

"Fletch, it's Tom. Gotta minute?"

"Sure."

"They'll settle for sixty-five."

"Sixty-five?"

"Thousand. Sixty-five thousand. Don't ask me how I did it. Let's take it and run."

"Oh, now, wait a minute, Tom."

"What? *Wait a minute?* Sixty-five thousand buys no liabilities, no charges, no investigation, it never happened, the kid stays. The

Tabors go away, *permanently*. They'll sign. I said I'd get back to them today."

"Offer them ten for their trouble, same conditions."

"*What?*"

"Offer ten, Tom, better yet, five: start there. Same conditions: they go away."

"Fletcher, have you. . . ? They'll never take *that!*"

"Given the circumstances, I think we're being generous. Try it."

"Have you gone crazy? I think I should advise you. . . ."

"Tom, please. Five for their trouble. Ten max. I'll ring you later."

"What do you know, Fletcher?"

"I'll call this afternoon. I'm running late."

Fletcher rang off, but was glad of the reminder. He needed to follow-up on his insurance policy. He leafed through his rolodex, pulling Corey's card from the R for Really Lucky file. He dialed the number and waited for his cuddly claims adjuster to pick up: Line Two.

"Hello," she purred.

Fletcher smiled: five thousand max.

He spent a full five minutes on the phone with the no-witness, then grabbed his car keys and dashed to town.

✳ ✳ ✳

Elan led his gray off the trailer as Tristan finished with Little John's lunging. Swapping horses, Elan explained that he would ride Little John around the barn, just the basic gaits. If everything went well, they'd take a tour of the Lawson countryside. Everything did. Neither hurried nor stubborn, the old giant seemed happy to earn a living again. With Elan's signal, Tristan opened the gate. Colorado loomed large under a silver sky.

They spent the first hour following the creek. In the distance, a flock of starlings parted noisily from a thicket. Elan had heard that the English were to blame for the obnoxious immigrants. Tristan laughed, saying that it wouldn't surprise him. "The Spanish," he boasted, "brought canaries."

"It would have been better if the Spanish kept their canaries and stayed home," Elan scoffed, then – noting Tristan's reaction - quickly added that the Spaniards brought horses; not that it was a fair deal, but it was a start.

They splashed across the brook where they found a ribbon of trail that led to the canyon. Elan tugged on the reins. As the big horse halted, Elan scanned the cottonwood canopy.

Tristan joined the search. "What are we looking for?"

"A golden eagle. One used to camp here."

"Ah. When did you last see it?"

Elan pulled a cigarette from his pocket. "Oh, I don't know. Maybe twelve years back."

Tristan offered him a light. "That's a long time. Do they live that long?"

Sporadic raindrops were leaving pearly beads on Little John's neck.

Elan surveyed the sky. "I don't know."

As the wind picked up, the horsemen followed the overgrown path that would circumvent the gorge. They rode in silence, the rain escalating to a monotonous rattle as it met the crusted earth. Tristan tucked his head to his chest, the water trickling down his back bone like an icy massage. A glimmer of lightning creased the muddy sky. Elan motioned for the pines, heeling the big horse for speed as he detoured from the track. Tristan followed, breaking into a gallop as a fiery flash started a drum roll across the teeming plains. By the time they reached cover, the sky had unleashed a torrent of blistering hail. Thunder bugled furiously above their leaky, ponderosa roof; the air sizzled with an electrical snap. Tristan had his arms folded as his horse hung his head in resignation. But Little John was impatiently churning up pine cones, racking around Elan in revolt.

Tristan hollered an offer of help, but his friend shook his head. "He always does this in a storm," Elan yelled back. The Spaniard nodded, watching the horse threaten to run over his handler. Elan stepped to one side, jerking on the reins, keeping the gargantuan circling around him.

"She must have been a good rider," Tristan shouted.

Elan nodded affirmation; water was pouring off his hat in a downspout.

"Did you ride with her a lot?"

"Yeah, I guess." Elan's octave lowered a note as the storm sallied, taking its noisy campaign eastward.

"Was she nice?"

"Sure."

"Pretty?"

"I'm sure he's got pictures of her."

Little John was settling down. With a loud crunch, he sampled bark from his washed out shelter.

Tristan shook his head. "No, no pictures. I've never seen any."

"Oh." Elan had positioned his pawing mount downhill, wiping the saddle with his wet sleeve.

"Um, yeah, she was pretty, very pretty."

A percussion of rain jingled like tiny cymbals through the pines.

Tristan clamped his goose-bumped arms tighter against him. "Do you ever. . . ."

"Come on, let's go," Elan ordered, swinging his leg over his snorting steed. "I don't think we can get any wetter."

They decided to make the most of the miserable ride by making it short. Opting out of a Meredith blazed path, they took the more direct route, aiming directly for the Lawson barn with a high pressure charge. With hoots and hollers, the cavalry raced across the plains with barometric-defying speed.

Elan loaded his horse onto the trailer and pulled a dry sweatshirt and socks from his truck. There was a pale, thin line of cerulean hovering just above the horizon. Figures, he thought. Tristan had promised him a mug of Fletcher's memorable chicory blend - worth the wait - but not in the awkward confines of the house. So, he headed for the barn to receive his pending reward in the tack room. Shutting the door, he collapsed on a couch upholstered in dust, pulled his waterlogged boots off and peeled out of his socks. He drew his sopping shirt over his head. Across from him, a faded tack box with the initials MPL sat under a stiffening English saddle. A long, linear spider web connected the lid with the girth buckle, rippling with his movement as if waving farewell.

The wall clock had stopped working, but many years ago, it was as reliable as a sentry, reminding him of a husband's e.t.a. Back then, the couch was supple leather, the plush rug under his feet vacuumed. There was a stereo, Jamaican rum and a phone, a polished mirror and a warm Navajo blanket.

He must have known, Elan thought sadly. But he was always so nice, so polite.

"Sorry for the wait!" The door was kicked open before Elan could reach it. The waiter was sporting dry flannel, carrying two steaming brews with an expensive aroma. "It took me awhile to find the right one."

Tristan couldn't help but notice the two jagged scars girding Elan's rib cage. His right shoulder was slightly irregular as was his right bicep, looking as if the muscle had at one time been split or punctured. Turning away, Elan scooped up his dry sweatshirt and covered his broad back. Then, receiving his coffee, he squeezed his wet clothes under his arm and elbowed his way out of the past, beckoning Tonto to follow.

The beverage was naturally strong, heating the blood and breath of the two plainsmen. A sunny afternoon was promised by the widening blue.

Leaning on a post, Elan pointed at Tristan's pampered old maven picking through his sweet feed. "Next time, you ride him."

The younger man let his forearms dangle across the top rail, an undecided cigarette hanging loosely between his fingers. Elan was offered one but declined, citing his nicotine exit strategy of "only seven a day."

"Do you worry about dying?" Tristan queried.

"No, not really."

"So if you like to smoke, why stop?"

Elan harrumphed good-humoredly. "Women don't like it."

"I think women like you no matter what."

"Oh yeah? Why's that?"

Tristan lit his cigarette and smiled wickedly. "Women like dangerous men."

Elan considered the idea. "I'm not dangerous. Work maybe, sometimes."

"No. It's not your work, *it's you*."

Elan shook his head.

"That night at the party, I saw you with the police. That one was in your face, asking about me. He was angry, but you said nothing. You stared him down."

Elan skimmed his sole across the bottom rail, leaving a miniature pyramid of mud. "What's your point?"

"Nobody scares you. That's my point."

"Oh." Elan blew on his froth.

"It's what makes you dangerous." Tristan's tone became earnest as he embarked on another topic. "If you could change the world – for your people – would you?"

Elan shot him a quizzical sidelong look. "How do you mean, change the world?"

"I mean the way it was: yours. You and your people free."

"There's no going back, Tristan, if that's what you mean."

"But if you could; if you had the power to make it different, would you?"

Elan's mystified expression prompted Tristan's elaboration.

"What I'm asking is: if you knew you could make the world right, a *fair world* for you and your family, *change the balance of power*; if *you* could do it, would you? Would you fight for it?"

"Fight?"

"War."

"Oh…war." Erasing a smirk, Elan rubbed his chin thoughtfully. "Well, we can't win a war against hundreds of millions of people, Tristan. It couldn't be won when there were a lot less. The only way to a better life now is through politics and money, and since I don't get politics and I sure don't have money, I guess I'm stuck with what I've got, and, uh, my *people* will just have to do the best they can."

"You don't understand." Tristan stomped out his cigarette. "I'm not asking you whether it *could* be done. I'm asking you if you *would*. If you could change *everything*, a new start with all the advantages, *would* you fight for it? *If you could win?*"

Elan turned his back to his post and leaned on it, dropping each elbow across the connecting rail. His spine straightened as he studied Tristan's profile.

"No."

Tristan gasped. "*Why?* Don't you want to live better? Don't you want a better place with your *own* horses? You take all the risk, Elan, so rich people can take all the credit. They turn around and sell the horse *you* trained for thousands. Doesn't it bother you?"

Elan balanced his empty mug on the top of the post. "Guess not. Thanks for the coffee."

Tristan kept pace with his departing company. "I'm sorry. I shouldn't have. . . ."

"It's all right."

"Thanks for riding him today."

"It's O.K."

The Spaniard stopped at the gate. The cowboy slammed the door to his truck, then leaned out the window with an outlawed cigarette, shouting, "I still want to know why you were digging that hole!"

Tristan exhaled with a smile. "You'll have to. . . ."

"Yeah, I know. Ride with you again. See ya Monday. Same time." The colorful trailer rounded the corner and disappeared, the rain having allayed its usual dusty wake.

55

Ellen was trying to decipher Nick's handwriting when her office chair spun around violently. Before she could yelp, Tristan caught her by the knee and put his fingers to her mouth for quiet, kissing her on the forehead. She bolted from her seat, scanning for witnesses.

Exaggerating a covert whisper, Tristan informed her that there was no one there. He fell back into her chair, taking her with him. He roped her to his lap with his arms, asking if she really wanted to call for help, but she was so rigid, he let her escape. She patrolled her work area, straining for a sign of her boss while admonishing him. Her lion's mane bounced with every punctuating stomp, as she recalled – verbatim – last night's awful exchange. Tristan put his feet on the desk, swiveling the chair back and forth, making a manifest point of not listening. Her large feline eyes narrowed. She flounced over to the desk, yanking Nick's note out from under his heel; it ripped. Her face reddened as she hurled the two halves at him. They floated to the floor as he caught her wrist, snapping her toward him.

"That's enough." His tenor was vitriolic.

She tried to wriggle from his grasp, calling him a stupid bastard, her eyes glistening with tears. He jerked her downward and held her there, stooped and off balance, curling her wrist back beyond its range. She gasped in pain.

"I said that's enough."

She clawed at his arm with her free hand. He bent her wrist into an unnatural U. She sunk to her knees, whimpering for him to stop.

"Are you finished?"

She nodded.

He released her. She met his cool gaze with red-eyed outrage.

"I'm sorry," he said softly. "I'm sorry for what I did last night."

She was silent. Her wet lashes sparkled as she rubbed her wrist, her shuddered inhales doubling with fury.

"*What's the matter with you?*" she spat, her nostrils flaring.

He shrugged. "I'm sorry. Really. What more can I say, Ellen?"

"*You hurt me!*"

"No. No, I didn't. I had to make you stop. You were loud. There'd be problems with your job if I was found here."

"Then, why did you *come here?*"

"To tell you I missed you, to ask you to dinner tonight. But, I think I should go." He turned from her, scanning the window for a safe exit.

"No. No, don't." Ellen took his fingers in her hands, playing them with the diffidence of a child. "Really. Don't go."

"Ellen, I should."

"Please, it was my fault. I guess I've been pretty mad."

"Why?" He relaxed into a half-sit on the desk. Her diaphanous digits pressed into his palm like little scouting leeches, testing for tenderness in a warm new terrain.

"I was looking at my log book. I've gone through all the tests: all signed off. I only need two more hours of flight time, and I could go for my license. But, Bill will never. . . ."

"That's all you need?"

"Yes."

"Two hours. You sure?"

"Yes."

"Let me see. Where's the log book?"

She reached across the desk and pulled it out from under a stack of manila files.

She tried to explain it, but he wasn't attentive. He leafed through it impatiently, snatching a pen from a plastic tray. Before she could protest, he inscribed a mark on a particularly busy page, flinging it back on the desk.

"There. Go take your test."

"Tristan, *what did you do?*"

"You have enough hours now. Be a pilot."

She seized the book and scoured it with urgent concentration. She couldn't find his alteration.

"*What did you do?*"

"Ellen, do you *know* how to fly?"

"Yes, of course."

"So? Get your license! Take me flying!"

"But, Tristan, you can't just. . . ."

"Just *what?*" His tone conveyed a brewing annoyance. "What do you want? Is it your fault he did what he did? Is it your fault that you don't have enough hours? No. You paid with hard work and money. You have to take care of yourself; solve your own problems."

"Tristan, I can't! What if Bill. . . ?"

"What can he say, Ellen? Hm? Your boyfriend hit him. He's spiteful. No one will believe him. You're a minister's daughter. Take the test, Ellen. Or stop complaining."

"But what if they find it?" She inspected the middle page nervously.

"They won't! And I have to go."

She suddenly jammed the book in a side drawer, sweeping it shut with her hip. "I'll see you tonight?"

"It depends. Will you take the test?"

She squirmed. "Tristan. . . ."

"Yes or no?"

She groaned. "I'll be too scared. . . ." She touched his hand.

He flicked it away, taking a threatening step backward.

She whined for mercy. "What about my *Dad?*"

"What about him? Don't tell him. You're not a child."

Like a rare and coveted drug, Tristan was standing just outside her moral budget, and he knew it. He was testing her desire for him, measuring her commitment with an irresistible frown.

"All right." She put her hands over her eyes as if to block out her sin. "I will."

He would pick her up at six, he whispered, winking his approval. Her resignation complete, he taxied through the glass doors, his take-off as smooth as his landing.

56

Plastic grocery bags were so rapidly consuming kitchen space that they looked like they were replicating, uniting to form one huge counter clogging super cell. It had taken Fletcher all damned day to get everything. He hated shopping. Over the years, he had learned how to throw eight hours at it and be done for a month. He brought the last of the hardware bags in and assigned them to the floor as he glanced at the oven clock. It was too late to call Tom, but he had a feeling that he would hear from him on Monday. He was wrong. The phone's ring had a lawyerly trill.

"Fletcher! What *did* you do?"

"What's the bottom line, Tom?"

"Five thousand and *that's* charity. So what did you do?"

"Same terms?"

"You bet. Five grand and I think he'd sign his mother away." There was no one more winsome than Tom in triumph. *"Do you want his mother?"*

"I'll pass. I'll send you a check: five thousand along with your fees. Let me know."

"Just do a certified on the five, Fletch. Can you drop it off Monday morning? You can review the papers then."

"Fine."

"Now, are you going to tell me what I had up my sleeve?"

"Sure, on Monday. And you're certain? Tristan's absolutely – *irrevocably* – out of this mess?"

Oliver was under foot as Fletcher hung up and rifled through the groceries, looking for apples. He finally found one and tossed it at the pectin loving pooch. He hadn't realized that Tristan was there, beyond the oak table, braced against the wall with his arms crossed. His hands were raw from chores and the dig, but Fletcher had remembered leather gloves. He had also picked up a few pair of work boots figuring something would fit him, along with a sack of assorted sweatshirts. Tristan's had holes. Merrily humming details through a poisonous silence, Fletcher was finally interrupted by a sound he hadn't heard before: a guttural hiss emanating from the hooded cobra shoring up the corner of his kitchen.

"Five thousand dollars? For what? What did you mean: *Tristan's out of this mess*? What have you fucking done?"

Fletcher fumbled with two cans of olives and slammed them on the counter. "What have I *fucking done*? I kept you in the United States for as long as you want to be. I put the brakes on a criminal investigation. That's what I've fucking done!"

"Why?"

"*Why?*"

"Yes, *why? The question is*: why would you pay that piece of shit five thousand dollars for nothing?"

Fletcher laughed, looking to the ceiling for guidance. "You don't know what it's like to be accused, Tristan. Just accused. Not guilty. Just accused. In the United States, you might as well hang yourself."

"I'll solve my own problems, Ryan. I'll defend myself and *not with your money*. Tell them you won't pay."

The shopper turned back to the groceries, opening cabinet doors and stacking cans. He crossed to the refrigerator with frozen fish, trying to stomach his irritation. "I told you. I've agreed to it. It's done."

"You have time. Call him back."

"What the hell's the matter with you?" Fletcher shouted. "What possible difference could it make to you? It was a problem that needed solving. I solved it!" He kicked freezer door shut.

"Tell them you won't pay!" Tristan's tone was venomous. He stepped away from the wall, skirting the table to cross to the island, trapping his father in a third of the room. "Tell them. No money."

Fletcher flung a head of lettuce into the sink and met Tristan head on at the butcher block. "I said no! *No!* Get out of the way."

Tristan remained steadfast, rage carved into his lineaments. He took a half step sideways, still acting as a blockade, reaching for a sauce jar. He plucked it from the counter, and - glaring at his father – dropped it on the floor. "Tell them."

The tomato puree doused Fletcher's jeans, flooded the tile and oozed down the woodwork with glass mixed in the flow. Fletcher's civilized English sensibilities countermanded a fight or flight instinct in favor of an analytical battle plan. He appraised the disaster if he just arrived on the front, calculating the enemy, assessing his offense, and mostly, the animus if met with resistance. He decided to test it with stepped up harassment.

"*You call yourself a man?* What a stupid thing to do!"

"Tell them you won't pay." Shaking glass from his shoe, Tristan glowered. "You had no right. You should have told me."

From across the line, had Fletcher heard an offer of parley? He seized it. "What difference does it make?"

"You don't understand! You pay them, it makes what I did wrong. He's the asshole! *I wasn't wrong!*"

"That's not the point. I know what he is. But, he can make things difficult. . . ."

"How?"

"By inviting *scrutiny!* It's the one thing I don't want, and either do you!"

Tristan's white flag wasn't showing yet. He fingered his jaw, his lips sharpening. "Don't pay him. Stand with me."

"Tristan, are you mad? Look, I know you didn't mean to, but you could have killed him. You almost did."

The hiss was returning. "If I had known, I would have. . . ."

"*Would have what?* What did you mean by that?"

Tristan raised his hands in mock surrender. Fletcher opted to take it on face value. He returned to the sink, issuing his volatile private towels for floor detail. But he was on high alert. He knew a war crime when he heard one.

57

Port and a cigarette came early. Fletcher wasn't in the mood to either cook or converse, so he was glad to hear about Tristan's dinner date. On his way out, the latter detoured into the executive suite looking remarkably dapper and unfrontiered. He was wearing the suit he had met his maker in, minus the tie. The shirt was pale green, and the London bowler was splendidly roguish. Fletcher couldn't help but laugh.

"My God. Look at you! 'Too much panache for the locals. You must be going to Denver."

"Yes. And I have something to say," Tristan announced. "I want to apologize for what I did today."

Fletcher nodded.

"And I want to thank you."

"It's all right."

"It's not really. I can't pay you back, not for a while."

"Well, Tristan," Fletcher sighed, "I can't pay you back for twenty-two years, can I? So let's just forget it."

The cosmopolite smiled. "Anyway, I'll be back late. I have a favor?"

"Shoot."

"Here's better than a motel, you know?"

"Tristan, you're really pushing the limit. I know what this girl means to you, and it's nowhere near what you mean to her. She's Pete's daughter. And she's very young. I just. . . ."

"Whatever you prefer. . . ."

"Get home late! And I don't want to see her over coffee. In fact, I don't want to see her at all. Understood?"

"Yes. Adios, Ryan Fletcher Lawson Egan. . . ."

"Get out. Have a good time."

As soon as the Prism dipped beyond the driveway, Fletcher stole into the garage and retrieved the lap top from the Volvo's back seat. Tristan's cyber time was generally late at night, so when Fletcher stashed it in the car early that morning, he was fairly sure it wouldn't be missed. Its destination had been a Geek enterprise called P C Barnum, run by – who else – Harvey Barnum, the master hacker of the high plains. Harvey's gifts weren't all that easy to come by; it had taken several phone calls to find the one man who could reboot his conscience after a no-questions-asked foray into a hard drive's personals. He generally worked underground for lawyers and detectives, only popping up occasionally in a flyer, and Harvey was careful. The tropical shirted, rodent-faced cyber miner hadn't been all that enthusiastic about the new English guy, until it was disclosed that the computer's steward had all the necessary passwords, making it legit enough for Harvey and legal enough for anyone. At that point, the hundred dollar bill that doubled on the component cluttered counter met Harvey's drop-everything price tag, which he did with a big bucked tooth smile. As his whiskered lips wrapped around a fistful of sunflower seeds, he inserted a CD into the anonymous P C.

Harvey quickly deduced that his client did not have the best server for invisibly reading e-mails; for future reference he could name a few. But the accent said it wasn't possible to change now, not wanting to risk a new password, blah, blah, blah. Harvey understood. He explained that past communications were probably lost, adding that he would dig around anyway, suggesting wistfully that it might take all morning. As per the agreement, he *would* download his own homegrown form of spyware that would snare every future incoming or outgoing missive, copy it to a guarded location, and no one, save Fletcher and the proud program writer, would ever know: guaranteed. It would just take a while, hinting again that the hovering Brit weirdo come back after errands. But, instinctively cautious, Fletcher had no intention of leaving anything left of Tristan's communiqués stored with a dark minded mole that tunneled into people's electronics. If something came up, he wanted to be able to backfill promptly. So, much to the techy's irritation, Fletcher settled in with a cold cup of coffee, parked behind the rodent on the only other stool in Suite 202, watching the burrowing byter rapidly descend into the bowels of somebody else's life.

Fletcher gazed beyond the liquid crystal display to the pocked, gray wall, needing to reaffirm why he was there. He could barely recall his outing with Corey. In fact he wouldn't have given Wednesday night a second thought had it not been for the triumvirate parading down the Boulevard. Since then, however, the triage had been on relentless replay, running through his mind with exhaustive analyses. His son's interaction with the older chap suggested a quasi-comical business relationship, but one with a disturbing implication: that their bond had been forged long before Tristan's appearance on the Lawson doorstep. All through the movie - a bloody tedium he could vaguely remember – Fletcher had tried to think of ways to address the matter of his son's affiliates, finally settling on his only option: a flat out question. When he rolled into his dark kitchen around twelve that night, Tristan was on a rapacious raid, his balanced features blanched by the refrigerator's fifteen watt filament.

"How was your date?" the forager queried, extracting a slab of Gouda.

"Long." Fletcher tossed his keys on the table.

"Oh. Too bad. Want some?" Tristan was absorbed by the limited choices. He had apples, peanut butter and bread piled on a plate. Relinquishing it to the counter, he continued the plunder.

"No, thanks."

"What did you do?"

"Dinner and a movie. *You?*"

"Nothing." The marauder was deliberating on a slab of smoked salmon.

"*Nothing?* Really?" Fletcher was suddenly a gambler, playing against the odds. "No dates tonight?"

"No."

"Did you go out at all?"

The icebox door shut. "*Why?*" demanded the gloom.

Just as Fletcher had feared, there was no payout; the game had been rigged from the beginning. All he could bank on was his gut feeling, not to fold, not yet. Without doubt there was a duel game in progress, one with higher stakes, confirmed by the stalwart secrecy of the insiders. Fletcher's hand showed very little promise. Still, with *Save Your Son* the mantra of the deck, scripted on every card with urgent issuance, there would be no leaving the table.

"Heh!" Harvey chirped, whipping his client back to the present. "I snagged a couple: yesterday's. Wanna see?"

Fletcher squinted at the screen. "No, not now. Can you put them somewhere?"

"Sure. Where?"

They were copied into a document folder and left unread, much to the annoyance of the prurient varmint who continued his search. "Yeah, that's it. Everything else is gone. I'll fix her up so - from here on out - you'll know whose screwing around . . . with your computer, that is."

Harvey ejected the first disc and inserted another. The whirring of the drive coupled with the lap top's racing verbiage induced a sleep-like state in its consigner. The consignee, however, was busy typing like mad, his tiny black eyes darting around the screen. He retrieved the second CD and then rebooted the device.

"What's your e-mail address again?" Harvey was at his own greasy keyboard.

"Why?"

"I'm gonna test it!"

Fletcher was suddenly unplugging wires. "Don't bother. I'm in a hurry. If it doesn't work, I'll bring it back."

"Wait a minute!" Harvey's eyes were as wide as they could get and the whites still weren't showing. "Don't you want to know how it works?"

"Just give me some notes."

Shaking his head, the cracker scribbled a few instructions, and placed the paper between Fletcher's beckoning fingers. Harvey gave him a quick once over. "Got everything? Listen, thanks for the business. Any problems let me know. . . ." Harvey's hand was out, but Fletcher had already cleared the door, flying down the stairwell.

As the little metallic madam was carried to from the car to the desk, two CD's fell from her slightly open mouth. Fletcher stooped to pick them up, wondering if they had been missed yet. He was ambivalent about their theft, but as his feeling about Harvey couldn't be ignored, he had absconded with everything having touched his now deflowered databank. He would check for infection in due course. First, though, he wanted to see if any new dispatches had arrived. Typing in Tristan's password, he found an e-mail waiting. Fletcher's eyes fell back to Harvey's instructions, followed them precisely and presto. As promised, a copy of the missive's contents appeared in a buried folder with the password *Gotcha,* Harvey's idea of funny. In the same folder, the two prior e-mails were also stored. The first was from *Ea:*

Merodach: Meeting Saturday, 9 p.m. Denver.

The second: *Do not react,* signed *Quixote*

The third had still to be read by Tristan: *Circumstances cannot change. Ea.*

Fletcher checked the dates. The first two were indeed yesterday's, written in the afternoon within minutes of each other. He wondered if the Saturday *meeting* would be at the office complex he had seen. He tried to remember if anything unusual had happened to prompt the second e-mail from the mysterious

Quixote. Pete had been over; Tristan had seen the medallion. But, no, it didn't sound like a fitting reaction to news that big. Besides, Tristan wrote at night, so the e-mail was likely a reply to a correspondence written eight hours earlier. *Do not react.* Fletcher was stumped.

The third was the most provocative. *Circumstances cannot change.* What circumstances? Tristan's current living arrangement? He lit a cigarette. There was nothing more he could do but to close the folder. Any outgoing could be intercepted tomorrow. Checking back at Tristan's mailbox, the latest e-mail appeared unread. Sure enough, seedy Harvey was a genius.

Fletcher logged off and placed one of the pilfered discs in the D tray. After a lot of high octave spinning, the screen came up with something unintelligible to the geekless eye, so Fletcher assumed it was the pirating program. He extracted it, and, then inserted the second CD, not quite expecting that every shred of his personal information, page by page, site by site, account by account would materialize, but it did. It was fascinating: rolling through his would be identity theft. Good old Harvey: the s. o. b. Beyond all of the financials was a cache of browser destinations, only they weren't his; they were Tristan's from the past few days. Fletcher decided to take a look. He revisited the internet, sifting through the addresses. It was numbing. Nearly all of Tristan's research was on twentieth century revolutionaries, their philosophies and tactics, with a few detours into Spanish medieval history. Two sites covering modern weaponry were extensive: all the latest in human annihilating hardware. The last visit was to an aeronautics site with a comparison of small aircraft capabilities. It was an enormous compilation for three nights, and none of it made Fletcher feel any better. He logged off.

An even more troubling issue was Tristan's cash flow. Fletcher had been handling the declared expenses which didn't amount to much: the rental car, dates and cigarettes. But, lately, Tristan was on the road a lot. It seemed likely that the extra gas would be spilling over his estimated budget, yet he asked for nothing more. The new hat was typical of the expensive surprises he would bring home. Last week he had bought a half a dozen dress shirts; Fletcher discovered them arranged across the bed like an Armani patchwork. They weren't stolen; he saw the receipt. Yet when offered extra cash, Tristan refused it. A few days later, when Fletcher remarked on the twenty or so new CD's overflowing the rental console, he was all but ignored. To Tristan's credit, he wasn't lazy. He was Mr. Fix-It if he knew how, and had taken over most of the residential maintenance to make sure his meager salary was earned. But, he wasn't exactly a rich man when he arrived. His sole credit card had been maxed out, the minimum payment met only through his father's insistence. Consequently, when a gleaming pair of Gravati loafers strutted across the kitchen floor two mornings ago, Fletcher couldn't help but beg an explanation. Tristan simply said that he had *resources* – whatever that meant - with a reminder that although his host's charity was appreciated, it wasn't obligatory. In other words: no prying.

Fletcher loathed invasive questions, and was no more inclined to ask them than to answer them. So how was he to know what prompted *Save Your Son?* He drummed the desk and then grabbed the phone.

"Corey?"

"Hello, Fletcher," she responded flatly.

"What's the matter?"

"I was wondering if you'd ever call again."

"How long has it been? A *day?* Gee, darling, I wouldn't want you to play hard to get. Has anyone ever told you that you're honest to a fault?"

"*Everyone.* So what is it?"

"What's your car doing tomorrow night?"

"*My car?*"

"Mmm."

"You want to borrow my car?"

"Only on one condition."

"What?"

"That you have brunch with me on Sunday."

"Wait a minute! You have a *date* on Saturday and you want to borrow *my car?*"

"No. I don't have a date on Saturday, but I *do* want to borrow your car. And since we're being honest, Madam, I could go borrow somebody else's car – or rent one – and be done with you. I don't have to ask you to Sunday brunch, but I am. You're a pain in the ass, Corey, but I'm asking anyway. Yes or no."

"To which? Borrowing the car or Sunday? Or does one depend on the other?"

"I'm not rising to the bait. What's the answer?"

"Yes."

"To?"

"Both."

"Fine. Thank you. I'll pick your car up tomorrow around six and *you*: at ten thirty on Sunday."

"What do you need my car for?"

"I'll tell you over pancakes."

"I bet you won't."

"*It's not a date!* Thank you!"

"You're welcome!"

Fletcher rang off, having no idea who served brunch on Sunday, but he was sure he could find some place suitable. In the meantime, he would use Saturday to dig around on two fronts. Don Christoval's world was a deep, sunless grotto, guarded by a dead knight and centuries of obscurity. Tristan's world was darker still, filled with deceptive signs and troubling strangers. Shedding light on both in one day would be a daunting task. But since that was the plan, real rest was in order. Fletcher paddled to the kitchen for a sleeping pill, pulled a book from his dining room collection, and - with his quasi-faithful dog – retired early.

Groaning at Oliver to stop yapping, Fletcher checked the clock. It was just after one a.m. The tapping on the door ceased as it squeaked ajar, Tristan's incantation soothing the long-haired sentry.

"Ryan? Sorry to wake you."

"It's all right. What is it?"

"I took Ellen home."

"Oh."

"I just wanted to tell you."

"Thank you. Everything else. . .?"

"Everything's fine. See you in the morning."

"Right. Good night."

Oliver escaped with the new arrival as Fletcher shivered against the cold. He pulled the blankets to his neck. He could hear Tristan calling the dog. He closed his eyes. In an unexpected midnight exchange, he found tranquilizing warmth. A snowball might have a chance in hell after all.

58

It was only seven in the morning, but Tristan had already gathered their archeological accoutrements and deposited them at the site. He was on his third cup of coffee, apparent by his ever narrowing pupils. He tracked back and forth across the tiles, waiting for his father to finish a stupid thing called breakfast.

"Tristan, did you eat anything at all?"

"Yes! Yes! But time is wasting. It's cool now. Can we go?"

"Just a minute. Let me just. . . ."

An exasperated exhale trumpeted across the kitchen. Tristan collapsed on a chair and folded his arms, tapping his boot against the table leg to amplify his annoyance. His thick lashes were blinking in milliseconds as he observed his partner ruminate. Fletcher choked on toast and laughter, downing his orange juice in one appeasing gulp.

"All right! Let's go."

They burst onto the morning's brilliance, the air so clear that a mile seemed an arm's length away. White vapor trails faceted the sky into a fine blue sapphire, which, in turn, polished the earth's colors into crystalline perfection. Fletcher watched Tristan forge ahead, realizing that he had changed. He no longer had the marble pallor of his arrival, and - although he had lost his blue-blooded look – his new bronze skin suited him. His hair was just long enough to tie back; its auburn cast now interspersed with gold. As he clambered down the canyon slope, he pointed out footholds for his antecedent's edification, punctuating his remarks with good-natured American slang. Arriving at the site, he skewered the dirt with his shovel and began slinging rubble as his venerable joined in.

For over an hour, they worked together removing debris, peering every few frustrating minutes into the shaft. Finally, two boulders were unearthed about three feet below the escarpment, in answer to why their view had been denied. Fletcher suggested that they rope the higher rock and try hoisting it out. His partner agreed. Fletcher used his pick axe to tilt the rock up slightly, while Tristan threaded cord around it. With several coils lashed together, the latter announced that they were ready. Fletcher tested the line and then threw the open end toward an adjacent Ponderosa. His teammate caught on the fly, and ratcheted it around the trunk. Fletcher hooked his axe under a top knot and, on a count of three . . . nothing happened. Four more attempts yielded no better result.

"Damn. Hold up. Hold up!" Fletcher panted, stooping to examine the dilemma. "All right, let's just pry it out. Leave the rope around it and tie your end to that tree. That way, we can avoid the damn thing running at us. When you're ready, grab a shovel, or actually, another axe would be better."

Tristan brought both, sliding to the pit like a base runner.

"It looks like. . . ." Fletcher knelt down, twisting his head underneath the sandstone. "Yes. It looks like we should both be on the lower right side: here. We'll push it to the left."

Tristan was in the process of shedding his t-shirt, making him temporarily headless. He bowed in accord. Fletcher stood, positioning himself on the hill directly below the impediment, his pick axe rammed under it. Tristan skirted around him, stationing himself slightly to his right, shoving his spade under the ties. With a mutual ready sign, the pair pitted all their strength against the massive barricade. It didn't budge.

"Damn it!" Fletcher ripped his gloves off, kneeling to reassess the problem.

Furious, Tristan hurled his shovel like a javelin. He dove to his stomach, inspecting the duct. "I can't see anything!"

"Patience, Tristan. We'll figure something out. Uh, let's see. Let's try it one more time. I'll stand over here. If we can just tip it on its side, right? Come on. Grab the axe. Ready?"

Once again, they tried to dislodge it, but it stubbornly counteracted their effort, pitching lazily back at every groaning exertion. Fletcher motioned to go the other way, but the obstinate crag held its ground, cementing its position by wedging harder into the crevice. Fletcher shook his head, holding up a hand to stop.

Tristan slammed his axe head into the rubble and then kicked it down the slope. He clambered to the equipment pile and seized a sledge hammer.

"Tristan, calm down. We need to look at. . . ."

Like a thwarted conqueror refusing defeat, Tristan reached his enemy with a huge, two fisted swing, driving steel into the opposition with enough impact to score it. Sparks flew as the maul struck again, exacting dust and shrapnel from the belligerent block.

"Tristan, wait. Wait! You're going to. . . ."

The third blow sent a fifth of the rock bulleting sideways, the fourth split the resistor in two. Three more merciless strokes fractured the halves. The final impact smashed what was left into retreating fragments. Tristan's chest heaved from the exertion, his face and abdomen caked with powder, pasted in sweat. He wiped his mouth, leaving a brown gash around his lips as they formed a clownish curl. He dropped the sledge, fisting the heavens in victory.

Fletcher nodded slowly, flinging his axe aside, letting it skitter down the hillside to join the other.

"Well," he chirped, "So much for that!"

Squatting next to the remnants, Fletcher scooped particulates away with his gloves, whistling a jaunty version of

Rock-A-Bye Baby through sidelong smirks at the bludgeoner. Tristan deliberately disregarded him, humming his own off key tune while triumphantly chucking the larger spoils into the canyon, until - irresistibly infused with his senior's silliness – his chantey crumbled into chortling.

"Keep that hammer handy, Tristan!" Fletcher chuckled. "Here comes round two!"

Tristan protested through spasms of laughter. "I think it's your turn."

"Oh no! I couldn't possibly work myself up enough."

"Sure you can! Just think of someone who really pissed you off! Here!" Tristan flipped the handle toward his father.

Fletcher drew the hammer toward him. "I'm only doing this to keep you from getting hurt."

"Oh of course!" Tristan roared.

The second rock proved less cooperative than the first. Fletcher flailed at it until a hairline crack appeared along the right edge of the stone. Exhausted and slightly dizzy, he wasn't sure if he felt a flux underneath him. He motioned to his partner, sweeping him up the slope with his fingers. Amused, Tristan fell back against a tree trunk, sipping water.

Using the time to catch his breath, Fletcher untangled the line from the first rock's remains and tied it around his waist.

Tristan cocked his head. "What are you doing?"

"Didn't you feel that?"

"Feel what?"

"It felt like the ground shifted."

"No."

"Well, just stay back."

The acolyte's grin was irritating. "Ryan Fletcher," Tristan sang, "I think you're just tired. You better let me."

Fletcher swung the sledge hard against the tiny fissure, a tremor shooting through his ulna. The boulder didn't budge.

From above, the younger Olympian leisurely straightened, ready to pinch hit for poor old Zeus.

"Just stay up there!" His father snapped, and then he vanished.

The earth collapsed like an unchecked elevator, hurtling him into an abyss. The hammer spun away as he fell with terrifying velocity, clenching his lifeline, praying it would hold. He was pummeled by scree; something large scraped his scalp. His shoulder bore the full brunt of an angry missile as sand showered him with scalding retribution. He could hear Tristan shouting his name and could vaguely make out the sound of a landslide's assault on water. Then the rope caught. It tightened, fusing into his skin and riding up under his rib cage; he couldn't breathe for the astrictive pain. He shimmied up the cable, bearing all his weight by his arms. Water was dripping somewhere as he dangled in virgin space, shafts of hazy green light crisscrossed yellow, crusty, fungal-laced walls. The downpour dwindled, giving way to an eerie hush. Squinting through gritty lids, he could make out Tristan's contour above him trying to stabilize the cord; his shouts resonating with opera house clarity as he pleaded for an answer. Fletcher found his voice, rasping reassurance. Tristan hollered at him to hold on, and disappeared from the portal. Silence ensued. Fletcher was swaying with an unnaturally cold breeze; he could smell the dank air rising. The sun was almost directly overhead, filtering through the vault's stale atmosphere, defining its soaring mineral coated flanks. A rainbow arced above his head; colorful strata plastered the glimmering expanse. He dared to look down.

He was only six feet from what appeared to be a balcony. It was moss covered siliceous stone, riddled with lime green pools and molehills of grit. His hammer was resting near the edge. There were small animal bones scattered everywhere, but what struck him was the glitter in the pale light. The ledge jutted across about a third of the vault before giving way to deep yawn. Fletcher assumed that the water was far below, where an acrid odor seemed to be gathering. The rope jerked slightly; Tristan shouted that they were hauling him up. Fletcher asked him to wait a minute. His arms ached, but by hanging on with one hand, he managed to loosen the coil around his torso and slip it under his boot, converting the diaphragm crushing lasso to a more tolerable sling. He tugged on the line, signaling that he was ready. He ascended surprisingly quickly. He used an extended leg to ricochet off the narrowing walls. Tristan caught him under the arm pit while hooking his fingers under his belt, pulling him into a sunny Saturday coffee break.

Fletcher was covered with sandy talc; his hair an electrified Einstein shale bouffant. Tristan was in silent stitches.

"Are you all right, Ryan Fletcher? You look like you've been shot from a cannon."

"I'm glad you find it so funny. How on earth did you. . . Oh! Elan!" Fletcher's eyes widened as if the good warlock of the north was floating toward him. In fact, the moon faced cigarette puffing horseman was pouring water in a coffee cup, approaching him with liquid relief. He was grinning under his broad brim.

Fletcher accepted the drink, raising it in salute." God, Elan, how is it we're so lucky?"

"You're not that lucky, Fletcher. I'm by here most every day."

"A new summer route?"

"About ten years now."

"Oh."

"*Did you see this?*" Tristan was crouching like a winged opinicus at the cavern's edge, ready to spring into the underworld. "*Did you?* It's fantastic! 'Good thing about the rope! It's deep!"

Elan and Fletcher crowded over the shaft, but the trio's collective entrancement blocked the light. Fletcher rose and wobbled to fetch the flashlight. With the high intensity beam, they were able to see to the lagoon that presumably covered the foundation of the fabulous subterrane. Extending beyond their field of vision, the grotto's perimeters were anybody's guess. Fletcher audibly estimated the depth at thirty five feet to concurring grunts. Like Tinkerbelle, the trembling spotlight climbed to the second story, resting on unique geological patterns and sweeping across the sparkling protrusion where the fallen hammer lay. Tristan wanted a slow pan of the tier. Fletcher accommodated him by handing him the flashlight.

"What is that? That shine?" His compadres mumbled ignorance as Tristan leaned forward for a better look, then suddenly reeled from the cave's orifice. "Ugh! *Ugh!* What's that *smell?*"

Fletcher's lids squeezed shut as he turned away. Only Elan remained steadfast, holding his breath while usurping the flashlight.

"Maybe its poison." The cowboy chuckled, twisting around for a gulp of clean air. "Give it a few days." He resumed his study of the abyss. You know... I'm not sure, but I think... I think...." He pulled his hat off, taking one more breath from behind him. "I think that...."

"What?" Tristan held a bunched t-shirt to his mouth and peered back in the hole.

"It could be. Something's written there. Look!" Elan steadied the flashlight just above the tier.

Fletcher rotated back to the portal, crushing Elan's hat under his knee. "Where?"

"Right there. See it?"

"Yes, I see it!" Tristan leapt to his feet, sprinting for the rope.

"No, Tristan," Fletcher sighed, "not right now. We don't know what that stench is. We need a ladder and face masks or something. Don't be an idiot!"

The grotto belched another foul blast and Tristan recoiled, not needing further convincing. Elan mouthed *phew* and retrieved his hat. Tristan and Fletcher traded glances; they hadn't factored in a third party.

Perceiving the awkward tenor, Elan excused himself from further involvement. He said he had to work nonstop during the summer months and just didn't have time for anything else. But, they were welcome to his ladder. He'd find it when he got home. Speaking of which, he scoured the canyon floor for his mount. He didn't see her. Hopefully, she hadn't gotten too far. He started down the slope.

With a circumspect look at Tristan – and Tristan's expressive consent – Fletcher called after the horseman, demanding that he find the time to come help; he was sorely needed, and besides, it was an opportunity – even if absolutely nothing was found – to step back in time. No one had seen the place for hundreds of years. "How did *he* know?" Elan retorted. It was a fair question, Fletcher laughed, one that Tristan could explain while helping to find his filly. Tristan trotted down the hill, slapping the back of his smiling new clansman.

It was solidly noon; Fletcher could tell more by the ache in his stomach than by his watch, which had not escaped unscathed. Like its wearer, Fletcher mused, its face was cracked, but the ticker was still reliable. Its second hand was sweeping through another day; well, not quite just another day. In about an hour it would officially be his birthday. He gathered a number of downed branches, screened the hole, and then ambled up the hill for lunch.

By the time he reached the house, his shoulders were noticeably stiffer. His image in the bathroom mirror was shocking. Every facial crease and pore was filled with white powder, making him look decrepit. Although his hair had been tied back, thick sections had escaped the band. With static electricity wiring it every which way, he looked like a hemophilic Medusa. He wiped his eyes. The years had marred him like a lifeless planet. Cruel impacts and bitter tears had taken their toll, sinking his cheeks and isolating his features with deep trenches. Endless emotional drain had sapped the once potent capillaries, leaving his skin slack and colorless. He leaned over the lavatory, examining his stubbled jaw. Somehow, it had resisted gravitational sagging, probably because his obsessive compulsive nature had kept him out so far out of orbit. Otherwise, his star was definitely fading. He popped open an ale, blinking at his reflection. "Happy birthday, you old fucker." The foam swept down his throat like warm rain. Unbuttoning his shirt, he turned the shower handle, then faced the mirror once more. He ruffled his hair into long, exaggerated Mayan sun rays and waved bye-bye to his freakish mime, just as a shadow crossed behind his shoulder. Fletcher wheeled around;

no one was there. He was ice cold in the tropical humidity. He pivoted back slowly. The mirror was accumulating steam, becoming so wet that no image was distinctive, just an admixture of hues under its liquid coat. Fletcher wiped the glass and stood spellbound before bursting out of the bathroom, nearly colliding with Tristan in the hallway.

"Ryan! Wait! Stop! What happened?"

Fletcher rounded the corner to the study, snatched a piece of paper from the drawer and scrawled something. Tristan was at the doorway, gaping at him. "Ryan Fletcher, are you all right?"

"I'm fine. Just give me a minute. Everything's fine."

"You sure?"

"Yes!"

Tristan edged closer, his voice hushed. "Ryan, listen, I saw the words. I had just enough rope! They're really there!"

"*What?*"

"*I saw the words!* In the cave! I'm sure they're Latin. Here. I'll write it."

Fletcher shoved the paper at him. His hand was trembling. "Would that be it?"

Tristan's smile vanished. "*You saw them?* How? I had to clean it off just to be sure it was writing! So why didn't you say something?"

Fletcher sputtered through an onset of coughing. "Because I didn't see them there, at least not that I remember."

"Then where?"

His eyes were tearing. "On the bathroom mirror. Just now."

"The mirror? I don't understand."

"I don't either. But something's...." Fletcher rubbed his throat and then his temples. "I think I'm losing my mind."

Swallowing the probability with a tactful nod, Tristan fingered the paper. "So, what does it mean?"

"I don't know, but Pete would."

✳ ✳ ✳

"Say it again, Fletch." Pete had the phone tucked under his jowl as Ruth handed him a list with a *you're going to be late* glare. The twins were milling around him, using the kitchen counter as a hockey table, zinging dried toast back and forth with jelly-caked spoons.

"Um, let me think here. Quiet, guys! Um. . . . I know it. I know it. Yes! It's common; well, not that common. I mean Latin isn't that common in. . . ."

"Pete!"

Sorry. *Mors janua vitae.* It means in effect: death is the gate of eternal life."

"Really?"

"Fletcher, it's in my genes to curious. Would you please tell me how you happened . . .? Boys! Quiet! Three minutes! I'm on the phone!"

"It's a long story. . . ."

A crust hit Pete in the chest. "Heh! Knock it off!" Sweeping greasy crumbs off of his shirt, he muttered, "You still there? Look, I'm running late, but I want to hear. See you on Thursday?"

"Or sooner. 'Good of you, Pete."

Fletcher relayed the information to Tristan, who received it as if it were communion.

"So, Tristan. Do you have any plans for tonight?" Fletcher expected a laconic answer and got one. He sniffled. "I take it you found Elan's horse. Did he say anything more about the ladder?"

"He said he'll bring tomorrow, I hope early. Ellen's invited me for dinner."

"Oh! That's nice."

"Well, I'm going to work Little John awhile before I clean up."

"Right. You covered the. . . ?"

"Yes."

"Right, then. I better get in the shower."

Assured that Tristan was tied to the horse, Fletcher absconded with the computer and logged on the internet. There were no new mysterious e-mails, leaving him to conclude that Saturday night's meeting – meaning tonight - was a go. While on line, he quickly reviewed his bank account. The Tabor contribution was going to hurt, but it could have been worse; it could have cost him every cent he had. Fletcher reached for a cigarette. Managing money had never been his forte.

59

With her Wranglered legs planted on firmly on the porch, Corey dangled a Broncos keychain in front of a would-be driver, demanding who he planned to spy on, since he obviously wasn't dressed for dinner. Fletcher responded that his intentions were honorable. That was all he said, waiting for her to drop the keys in his hand. When she didn't, he turned on his heel and stomped back to his car. She caught up to him as he lurched the door open.

"Fletcher, forget it! Here! You can have the car!"

"Corey, obviously you're not comfortable. I don't have time to beg you, so. . . ."

"Just take it!"

Eyeballing her skeptically, he reached for the keys. "You sure?"

"Yes." She slapped them in his hand.

"I don't know when I'll be back; I'll try to be quiet."

"Fine."

He kissed her on the cheek, then slipped into her shiny old Mustang.

✳ ✳ ✳

When he reached Broadway, it was just seven-thirty, leaving him plenty of time to reconnoiter before the nine p.m. attroupement. With a dearth of cars, he had a choice of strategic parking spaces, choosing one a few of spaces east of the office park entrance and void of overhead illumination. Hungry, he noted a cruddy little burger bar across the street. Dutifully locking his transport, he left, returning with a heat-lamped gooey chicken disaster, and two coffees. Depositing everything on the floor of the sedan, he opted for later, securing the auto once more before ducking into the complex.

Still in vivid daylight, the office park consisted of three four unit sooty split levels, each with a limited amount of windows and a maximum amount of fascia rot. There were signs stuck here and there without any uniformity. There was a huge hairdresser and a miniscule bail bondsman. There was a fortune teller in cardboard alongside a carpet cleaner who also sold used vacuums. There was a For Rent sign. Several of the businesses preferred not to hang a shingle out, including the one Tristan's party had patronized three nights ago. Fletcher walked the circumference of the commons: no security cameras. He crisscrossed between the buildings. With the exception of a parched pot of geraniums on a stoop, there was no sign of life; the entire place was forsaken for the weekend. Fletcher skipped up the eight or so stairs to the site of Tristan's Door Number One. Naturally, it was locked. Stretching across the side of the railing, he hoped to catch a glimpse of the interior, but the blinds served their purpose. He scouted around for a hidden key, not expecting to find one, and didn't. The tenant directly below was a massage therapist; hours by appointment. All he could see through the sheers was a bed. The door was secure; again, no key, but with a little dedicated effort, he could probably get in. He checked his watched, and then tracked back to the car under the shadow of two low rises - separated by a urine soaked alley- on the west side of the complex. The city was rosy with evening twilight as he slid into the driver's seat. The chicken something was awful, but the coffee wasn't bad. The street lights were buzzing on. It was still before nine, but one possible attendee was early. An SUV with a New Mexico plate had just docked about six parking meters down from him. A briefcase hung from a plump arm as the rest of the body tumbled out to join it. Wednesday night's Humpty Dumpty was instantly recognizable by his kindergarten gait and quarter head of hair. He was wearing a crumpled linen jacket and a loosened tie. His kewpie doll face was surprisingly youthful, at least ten years younger than Fletcher had thought. Crouched behind the wheel, Fletcher watched him round the corner to Door Number . . . Two. Surprise Number Two: the next door office was also in use.

Another car banked behind the SUV, a late model Cadillac. Fletcher scribbled down the license number. Three men emerged, one being the blonde from the prior soiree. The other two looked Latin, maybe Arab. They were in custom suits and smoking. The taller one had a mustache and a drooping eye, dogging along in navy blue with a large Adam's apple and a stare into nowhere. The other was a smarmy shimmerer in a Bostonian brown silk, his mouth twisting petulantly as he logged every scenic detail with scorching suspicion. Fletcher shrunk down, barely able to see above the dash. The three had come to a puzzling halt, dawdling at the curb about thirty feet away. He spotted the reason why. Through the side view mirror he saw her, her long legs skimming the sidewalk like a water strider in white pumps and a mustard skirt. He inched up the back rest for a better look, quickly flattening as she passed within a yard of the Mustang's rear stabilizer. He heard her very American greeting followed by an assortment of guttural rejoinders. As the voices faded, Fletcher straightened, watching them amble toward the fluorescent filled office. She was crimson-headed and tall with a tattoo on her right shoulder. She slipped through the door while the men stubbed out their cigarettes, pocketing their butts before filing in. Fletcher scoured the avenue; there was still no sign of Tristan.

A half an hour passed, and then an hour, at which point the blonde man emerged, scanning the lot before retreating.

Fletcher cracked the window and slouched against the door, rubbing his eyes without relief as he registered the muffled swish of footsteps. His red sclera widened in alert. Tristan must have passed within inches of the car. Through the windshield, Fletcher saw him floating along at a pretty good clip, his jacket flapping behind him. He trotted around the corner, across the asphalt and up the stairs, then barged through the conference door without a knock. Fletcher waited another five minutes before exiting the vehicle.

Keeping to the shadows, he made his way to the recessed entry directly under Busy Board Room 2. A half story below grade, the peeling veneer of Door Number Four was glowing with a ghostly For Rent sign. The ebbs and flows of conversation drifted from the thin walls above. Fletcher was certain that he could hear every word from inside the unoccupied suite; consequently, he tried to force the single lock. Twice, his shoulder collided with the door; the thuds excruciatingly loud. He listened breathlessly. The pitch of the upstairs meeting remained constant. He gave the door another hard shove, this time using his hip. It burst open. He froze, hearing unintelligible shouting. He leapt onto the carpet, flattening against the wall. The door was gaping almost sixty degrees; he didn't dare shut it. People were clattering around on the outside landing directly above.

Someone rocketed down the steps. There was yelling.

"Tristan! Wait! Wait!"

Fletcher curled to the window.

Through the absent risers, he spied a pair of cowboy boots hurtling down the stairwell. Above him, more shuffling as a voice boomed through the darkness.

"Mathew?"

The din of Denver traffic filled a lull until a southern tenor cried, "I've got him. He's fine. He's right here with me. Bad day is all."

"Tristan?" The second level bellowed.

"Just give us a minute," the drawl pleaded. "Just. . . . If everybody could just take it easy. Everything's all right. We'll be just a minute."

From the upper deck, a heated discussion preceded the verdict. "All right, Mathew, we'll be inside. Please don't be long. Tristan? I don't think I need to say more. . . ."

Fletcher heard clomping across the ceiling and chairs dragging across the floor.

"I don't know, Porter."

Fletcher was right. Holding his breath, he could hear every word.

"He'll be all right."

"So, what's his problem, tonight?"

"It doesn't matter. He's just a hot head. Mathew can handle him."

"And if he can't?"

"Then, we'll have to make other arrangements."

"But how will we know?" It was the girl. "He's dangerous."

"Yes! He is! Of course he is! That's why we need him! Sandy, please. We can't change course now. If there's a problem - a serious problem - we'll address it. For now, let's just stay on track. Now, where were we?"

Fletcher edged to the egress, hating to give up his station, but another dialog was moving in audibly from the asphalt. He slipped soundlessly outside, leaving the door ajar. Crouching in the alcove of Door Number Four, he heard the high octave drawl.

"You know, maybe that middle-a- nowhere thing is gettin' to you."

"I'm all right."

"Tristan, listen. I been thinkin' . . . why don't you stay with me? I got room, you know? You'd be in the city. 'Lots to do."

"I can't. You know that."

"Look, Tristan. . . ." Mathew – the southern blonde - had reached the stairs; Fletcher squeezed into the corner, trying not to breath. "Porter's getting worried. Personally, I think something's goin on with. . . ."

"Nothing's going on."

"Then, come on! Stay with me. Just for a while. Tell the old man you met a girl."

"No."

"Oh, come on! It's not like you can't go back. By then, it'll just be a few weeks more. Look, you're doing great. I'm not saying blow it off. We wouldn't want that. It would just do you good to. . . ."

"I said no."

Mathew ran a palm across the newel posts as if playing a harp.

"I know you, Tristan. Something's wrong. It's not the girl, is it? What's her name? Ellen?" Mathew bent down to pucker the crease in his jeans; on his way up, he caught the rail like a monkey and used it for a back scratch. "Nah. I didn't think so. What about the asshole? It's not him, is it? You're not forgetting what he did, are you?"

Silence.

Mathew sighed. "Look, for now, I think everybody would be happier if you were up here, chillin' out. No big deal."

"No."

"Tristan, I'm not really asking. Everybody's getting nervous. That's not good."

"*No! I said no! How many fucking times do I have to say it?*"

Tristan was tracking back and forth like a steam engine. Mathew derailed.

"So what's goin' on, huh? Are you losin' it, Tristan? *There's no gettin' out, if that's what you're thinking.* You knew that from the beginning. Where's your head, man? Huh? You don't want to tell me? Fine. But if you think that piece a shit down there. . . ."

The engine blew, reaching Mathew in one stride, shoving him hard into the stairs, holding him by the throat. "I want out."

Mathew kept his arms outstretched, his delivery cool. "Tristan, let go. I said let go."

Released, the blonde shifted up a step, a hand braced on the balustrade. "I know you can take me, Tristan, but you're gonna have to work at it, and it's not going to do you any good. I'm telling you to *straighten up.* You're in it now. *You can't get out.* Fuck! *Everybody* told you that, right from the start! *What's happening to you?* This is it! *Remember?* Everything you've wanted! Remember? We're in! It's a goddamned privilege! So no more fucking around! All right? Come on. Just come on. They're waiting for us."

"I'm tired. I'm tired of all of you."

"Tristan, don't. Don't walk away! *Don't you fucking walk away!*" The clip of Italian loafers receded into the night.

Mathew rushed up the steps. Fletcher rocketed out of the recess and ran for the west side of the building. The upstairs door burst open. As three men clattered to street level, Fletcher flattened against the stucco. The pursuers paused and then diverged across the asphalt. The squat man and the tall girl stood on the upper outside deck, so preoccupied with their lost cause that they didn't see his father, a mere twenty feet away. Fletcher inched to the corner, his back scraping the knobby wall. He could still hear them.

"Oh, Sandy, what a nuisance that boy is! Anyway, what's your schedule?"

"I'm leaving for Lisbon tonight. Isn't there anybody else?"

"It would take too long."

Slinking around a gutter, Fletcher stole a last glance at the pair. They were clinging to their widow's walk, anxiously scanning the boulevard. Fletcher bolted for the pee soaked alley, grinding mounds of broken glass as he raced through the narrow corridor, reaching a locked dumpster with burning lungs and a mounting terror. Tristan's smart, he thought. Fletcher's heart tried to beat a measure of assurance. He melted behind the dumpster's cover. *He'll know enough to backtrack.*

Fletcher monitored his watch; ten minutes. . . . He crept to the alley's perimeter, peering at the modular. The conference room was dark; the landing empty. Clinging to the shadow of the warehouse, he moved quickly to the avenue. Safely swallowed up by a street light

- and a stone's throw from the car - he scrutinized the office park once more. It was absolutely quiet; locked up. There was no one; nothing... except . . . except. . . . Fletcher squinted. Door Number Four's For Rent sign was full face. Someone must have shut the door. Someone must have. . . . Fletcher pounded across the tar, completely heedless of "Porter" and his three consequences. He rushed down the stairs into the recess, tapping on the hollow-core. "Tristan," he whispered, "Tristan, are you in there? Come on, lad. If you're. . . ."

The door jerked open. Tristan's eyes were glittering from across the threshold, his expression feral. With a stiff arm, he was pointing a gun straight at Fletcher's head. Fletcher raised his hands. "It's all right. It's me."

"Ryan? *Ryan?* What. . .?"

"I'm alone. It's all right."

Tristan lowered the gun, blinking disbelief.

"Quickly. Come on. I have Corey's car. Blue Mustang parked there. See it?"

Tristan stepped outside.

The two fled in full view, skimming across the lot like geese over an oily swamp. Reaching the car, Fletcher crammed into the driver's side as Tristan landed on the passenger seat. The engine rumbled; Fletcher found drive and squealed away from the curb, just as a late model Cadillac raged backward into his lane, and crashed into the right side panel. A spider web fissured across Tristan's side window as the Mustang spun into oncoming traffic. Fletcher pulled the steering wheel into the skid, sinking the pedal as he u-turned – with angry blasts – toward downtown. He kept to the right lane, barreled into the second side street, making another right, then another, gunning the car behind a closed market before lurching to a halt. Tristan was holding the side of his head, muttering something in Spanish.

"Tristan, you all right?"

"Yes. I just hit my head."

Fletcher leaned across the console. Blood was seeping down Tristan's neck.

"God! You sure? You sure you just hit your head?" Fletcher examined the crazed glass.

"What are you looking for?" Tristan snapped.

"I don't know! Christ!" Fletcher pulled back, clenching the steering wheel, staring through the windshield at a thicket of litter. The night swept by him in blurred images, nothing sensible, just distortions and ugly colors.

"So, you followed me?" Tristan muttered.

"Not exactly. I saw you Wednesday night, by accident."

"How did you know about tonight?"

"E-mail."

"Ah, I see." Tristan groped his jacket for a cigarette. "So what were you hoping to find?"

"Tristan, please don't smoke. There'll be hell to pay if she smells smoke."

Tristan gaped at him. "*Smoke?* You're worried about s*moke?* I can't even get the door open. It's all bashed in." He burst out laughing.

"You think it's funny? Then you don't know women. I can bring this thing back a three wheeled accordion. As long as a mountain of putty can fix it, she'll get over it. But, you bring it back after one stinking *cigarette?* She'll swear it's ruined. Oh, what the hell. Go ahead. We'll just buy the goddamned car."

"You're pretty generous, Ryan Fletcher, considering you're broke."

Fletcher winced, hoisting a knee to the steering column as the last comment settled uncomfortably. "And what makes you think that?"

Tristan stared into the weeds, the low beams brightening as the engine's roar slackened to a grumble.

"I know everything there is to know about you."

"Really!"

"Yes. For example: happy birthday, Ryan. You can go on, you know. They won't follow."

"You know everything about them, too? Good. You can fill me in."

"I will. But right now, do you mind if I close my eyes?"

"Tristan. . . ."

"No doctors, Ryan Fletcher. It'll be all right."

"Is it safe to go home?"

"It's as good a place as any."

As Tristan dozed through a concussion, Fletcher navigated through the highway construction. Although the constricted lanes banked all the wrong way and the on-ramps seemed to promote accidents, a cavalry of vehicles managed to find safe passage into the night. One driver barely noticed. Beyond the Tech Center, the freeway cleared, and – from light years away – stars broke through the halogen haze. There, as his wounded Mustang charged south, a reclusive ruler faced defeat. He had been determined to walk this world unaffected by it, and, to that end, had armored himself well. But, enter a continental invader, and his bastion was no longer his.

An electronic jingle roused him from his thoughts. Tristan stirred. Fletcher groped along the console. A cell phone had been regurgitated from his son's left trouser pocket, wedged into the seat. It was playing La Cucaracha. Fletcher extracted it, and, inspecting the bright little buttons, pushed *receive*. Shouting *"fuck off,"* he pitched it out the window.

Tristan's eyes were still closed as sliver of a smile crept across his face. "I hope it wasn't Ellen," he murmured.

60

Corey was seething: no phone call, no car, and it was now eight o'clock in the morning. She had telephoned twice. Predictably, he didn't answer. She wriggled into her tightest jeans and a new form fitting sweater, then plopped in front of the vanity. What an ass, she thought, applying eyeliner and mascara; green shadow would look nice. She chose a red lipstick, grimacing into the mirror. Her whites were as pearly as ever. She found her favorite pair of Santa Fe earrings. Fluffing her hair, she was ready. She trounced out to Fletcher's Volvo, wrenched the door open, hurled her pocketbook on the floor, and nearly squashed the legal-sized paper left on the seat.

I'm so sorry, Corey. Your Mustang had a minor mishap, but don't worry, I'll return it better than new. Just give me a week. My car is yours for the duration. Thank you for understanding. If you don't mind, do you think you could give me a rain check on brunch? A bit under the weather. Will call. Fletch

She considered the message and then crinkled it into a ball before turning the ignition.

From his ear to his cheek bone, Tristan' right side was a puffy, translucent green. He was asleep. Yanking Oliver off his bed, Fletcher - feeling ill with exhaustion - paddled toward the kitchen. Coffee, he thought. He had to have coffee before feeding the horse. No one expected the knock at the kitchen door, not even the dog who bayed his surprise right through Fletcher's tender nervous system. The rapping resumed. Fletcher jerked the door open.

Corey peered at him through gray mesh. "Since when do you lock a screen door?"

"Since when do you ask questions this early on a Sunday?"

"Since my car had a *mishap*. Where is it?"

"In the garage."

"Well?"

"Well what?"

"I'd like to see it. Open the door."

She swept past him and disappeared into the wreck room. Fletcher wearily pulled a can of Columbian out of the fridge; no gourmet grind today.

As expected, she emerged in red-faced fury. "I thought you said *mishap! That's a mishap?*"

"It was a hit and run."

"It's completely stoved in! *And it smells like smoke!* Were you smoking in there?"

"Corey, I'll buy it. I'll be glad to buy it. Tell me what you want for it."

She crossed behind him, shagging two coffee cups from the corner cabinet, slamming them on the counter. "I hope you're making that for me. Black."

"Of course. Look, I'm very sorry."

"Was someone with you? What happened to the glass?"

"Uh, well, it's a long story. Anyway. . . ."

"Who was with you?"

"My *son*, Corey! I told you I'd pay for the car!"

Fletcher's head was pounding. He interrupted the automatic – taking forever – drip, and drained the carafe's shallow syrup into his cup.

Corey shuddered. "You can let mine finish."

"What do you want for the car, Corey?"

A crescent smirk lifted her chin; her eyes twinkled. "Nothing, Fletch. I have insurance. And, since you got the license plate number. . . ."

"I did?"

"Didn't you? She waved the scrap at him. "This one. This is the one that hit you, right?"

"Oh, uh. . . ."

Sure enough. It was the Cadillac. He could simply lie, just tell her no, wrong car and snatch it away. Or. . . . A delightful prospect dawned on him. Did he dare? He smiled sweetly. *"That's the one!"*

"I'll leave a message today. I'm sure they'll get on it first thing tomorrow. If there's a deductible. . . ."

"I'll pay it. Ah! Coffee's ready!" He was humming as he poured.

"Wow!" Corey's mug plummeted back to the counter. "Speaking of mishaps!"

He cocked his head. "Too strong?"

"No!" She thrust a finger at the dining room. "You sure *did* hit the window!"

Tristan was loitering at the threshold, his eyes swimming.

Fletcher scrambled. "Oh! Corey, have you met? This is Tristan, and yes, he's a little banged up. How do you feel?"

Tristan ambled past his father, holding his eyes with a sidelong stare, extending a hand to Corey.

"Nice to meet you, Tristan." Corey gasped. "Wow! Did you see a doctor?"

The phone was ringing. Fletcher winked at Tristan's flickered warning. "Excuse me. I'll take it in the study."

Fletcher shut the door and crossed to his desk, lifting the receiver without saying hello.

"Fletcher Lawson?"

"Yes."

"I assume you know who I am."

"I wouldn't assume anything."

"Oh. Well, I think we can both safely assume you've had a long night. My name is Porter Eckhart."

Fletcher chose not to respond, forcing Porter to proceed into the void.

"I'll get straight to the point: yesterday's antics weren't appreciated."

"No doubt."

"And Mr. Lawson, you're interfering with an individual who is under strict contract. The. . . ."

"Mr. Eckhart, the individual in question can no longer abide by the terms of your contract."

"I'm afraid that's unacceptable."

"Well, acceptable or not, that's the way it is."

"Mr. Lawson, the ramifications are serious."

"I'm sure we can come to some arrangement. Perhaps compensation."

"Money? Don't be ridiculous."

"Forgive me, Mr. Eckhart, but I've seen your company headquarters. I'm sure a little short term financing. . . ."

No, Mr. Lawson. I don't need financing! Tristan is an integral part of a corporate. . . ."

"Which is?"

"Excuse me?"

"Your corporation?"

"Trans-Origins, Inc."

"And what does Trans-Origins Inc. do?"

"That's irrelevant to you. Please put Tristan on."

"No."

Although you may not believe it, it's in your best interest as well as his. Please put him on the phone."

"No."

"Mr. Lawson, put him on the phone! He's a grown man!"

"Yes he is, but he's not feeling talkative. Apparently, a member of your staff has trouble with the finer art of parallel parking."

Porter's laugh was unexpected and Santa Claus jolly. "Well, I am sorry! May I call you Fletcher?"

"Suit yourself."

"Fletcher, I don't know what notions you have about us, but I'm sure they're unfounded. Tristan can be quite . . . volatile, as you probably know. During the course of his employment, there have been . . . differences. Perhaps he's misrepresented us. Now, his position with us is – for lack of a better word – classified. It's the nature of our business. Nevertheless, his term is up very shortly, and then he's absolutely free to do as he pleases. In the interim, all I am asking you to do is be reasonable and not hamper him until his obligations are fulfilled."

"Or what? Or your able driver runs me over? Look, *Porter*, I don't care what your company does. I'm not even curious, although perhaps certain authorities would be. So, let me be blunt. Tristan's no longer in your employ. That's what he wants and that's final. Sorry! I'm sure you can rely on his discretion, if that's what you're worried about. Now, I've offered you remuneration. You may want to consider it."

"Fletcher, before you go. . . ."

"What?"

"If I'm not mistaken, around thirty years ago, a Lawrence disappeared from a London Gallery. Did you ever read about it?"

"No."

"Valuable, though at the time it was only attributed. Kind of a sloppy theft. Since then, provenance has turned up authenticating it. It's early; important. Of course, it's irrelevant. It's gone. But, the hunt goes on. Everything's so sophisticated now: prints, DNA. You'd think they'd find it! You sure you never heard of it? You're something of an art connoisseur, aren't you?"

Porter measured the silence before motoring on.

"Fletcher, listen, I'm fair. I have no interest in a painting. I'm only concerned with the fulfillment of a contract. Now, he's temporarily off course but I *know* you can straighten him out. I only need him for a short term, after which, he'll be well-off and all yours."

"Porter?"

"And, I'm sure *you* could use a little extra cash!"

"Porter?"

"Yes?"

"You're a dirty little piss."

The phone slammed against the wall. Fletcher fumbled through the desk drawer. He seized the closet key. All the paintings were there, all but one.

✳ ✳ ✳

Corey was recounting some melodrama when Fletcher strode in. He stubbed out her conclusion with a loud rap on the counter.

"Corey, what ever happened to Mackey? Is he interested or not?"

Her mouth dropped open. "That was rude, Fletcher!"

"Yes. Sorry, it was. Well?"

"I told you, he wants it for a song."

"So? Can't we let him hum a few bars? See how it sounds?"

"*What?* What's the big hurry? You don't want to look anxious, not with him, anyway. Are you anxious? What happened? You look . . . strange."

Everyone flinched as Oliver's siren went off. The screen door was a shadow box for a wide-brimmed hat.

Fletcher rolled his eyes, telegraphing his impatience. Tristan wired back his helplessness, inviting Elan in.

"Hi. Oh! Hi, Corey. 'Didn't see your car. I'm sorry, am I interrupting?"

She tilted her head. "What are *you* doing here?"

"Uh, I just came to drop something off. Fletcher, I'll leave it in the barn, O.K?"

"Right, Elan. Coffee?"

The cowboy glanced around the room. "No thanks. Catch you later." He hurried out.

Fletcher flexed his jaw. "Corey, if you don't mind, Tristan and I need a word."

Her chair nearly fell backward as she lurched to her feet. "Are you *dismissing* me, Fletcher?"

"No. No. I just . . . Listen, something's come up. Please, I didn't mean it that way, Corey. I mean, won't you be late for church?"

"What the hell do you care? Give me the keys!"

"Keys?"

"To my car! It's drivable isn't it?"

"Oh! Right. Corey, please, don't look so angry. I'm sorry."

"Just open the garage door! And screw you!"

Kicking up gravel, the Mustang thundered down the drive on the wake of Elan's retreat.

Fletcher immediately whisked Tristan into the study. Once there, he accessed the hidden closet, exposing the cryptic contents with a hard fisted flourish. The Spaniard stood in front of the fireplace with his arms crossed, unruffled as Fletcher's vocal chords neared rupture.

"Well, bravo, lad! *Bravo!* Do you know he's blackmailing me?"

Tristan was mute.

Fletcher punched the panel shut; it reverberated back with the force. "You . . . . When did you take it? You could have warned me, damn it!"

Tristan shook his slowly. "No. No, I couldn't."

"Why? *When you knew!*"

"Because . . . if I had told you, it wouldn't be the same as you understanding – truly understanding - who he is. He's a serious man who can't be bought! It's not what you're used to. Now you know. If I go back, there'll be no more problems. So, I thought it would help you to understand. That way, you could decide."

"Decide *what?* As if there's an option; he's a bloody . . . . So *who is he?*"

Tristan's faced flushed. He began pacing around the periphery of the room, rubbing his fingers along his palms. "He's like a general. An officer in an army."

"An army. You're not making any sense. *Who the fuck is he?*"

Tristan approached the desk, extracting a cigarette from his father's sterling case. "He's a scientist."

"A scientist? Like a chemist, a *drug lord?* What's his company do?"

"I can't, I'm sorry."

"No, you tell me!"

"I can't, Ryan."

"Tristan, listen to me. I don't give a damn what's happened or what he threatens me with. I don't care why you came here. I know it's different now. But those men chasing you weren't playing a bloody game of tag! *So, who is he?*"

"Ryan, if I tell you . . . everything you've known . . . you can never go back. You'll have to run away. And he's very smart. You have a life . . . *I can't.* I thought . . . but I can't."

Fletcher stepped past the desk, striding combatively into Tristan's space, forcing him backward, propelling him into the fireplace.

"Who is he? Who is he, Tristan? What's the company do? *Tell me!*"

"No! I said I can't. Enough."

"*It's too late for that now! You can't go back! There's no more job!* He wants to hurt you and you know it! Now I'm in it, and I'm standing with you, Tristan. Remember? That's what you wanted. I'm standing with you because I want to. *I want to!* Whatever it is, we can fix it. But you're going to have to help me. *So tell me! Who is he?*"

"He's a bio-engineer."

"A bio-engineer. What's the company do?"

"It's more like a religion. A society, devoted to an idea."

"What do they want?"

"They want to change the world order. They want to make things better: no more rich living off the poor. No more pollution; no more injustice; no more cruelty. No wars."

"Noble . . . albeit a bit idealistic. 'Kind of a rough crowd for all that peace and prosperity. So what do they have in mind? What's their solution to the world's problems? And what do they want with you?"

"I'm a courier, that's all."

"A courier. And what do you deliver?"

Fletcher waited; the clock ticked rapidly, almost in rhythm with his pulse. "Tristan? What's your job? Delivering what?" He was wading into a rising dread; his son was licking tears. "What's the matter?" Fletcher's voice cracked. "It couldn't be that bad. Just tell me. *Tell me.*"

Tristan shook his head, coughing phlegm and choking. He put his hands to his face. His soundless sobs swept Fletcher under a wave of terror.

"My God, lad. *Please! Just tell me.* Whatever it is, it'll be all right. I swear it. Please."

Tristan's haunted eyes skipped around the room, searching for an escape. He had almost made it, finding an inner route to a sweeter dimension when Fletcher's explosion rocked him back.

"*Goddamn it!* Answer me! *What would a fucking bio-engineer want with you?*"

The courier collapsed on the couch, retching up the life-threatening secret. It came out with bitter remorse and bile. He was doubled over, twisting the skin of his ribs, the truth's potency wresting his gut and searing his throat, until he was aphasic with saliva and self-loathing. Fletcher closed his eyes, hearing him from afar, the facts so paralyzing that he could feel nothing, just a numbing cold. It was as if all his blood had been sapped and diverted to his soul, that he could bear the horror of such a poisonous confession. He sank beside his son. The clock raced on as they sat motionless. Staring into the incomprehensible, Fletcher finally addressed it in a monotone.

"Well, someone must know. One of those agencies: Homeland Security. C.I.A."

Tristan was serene and self-contained, as if he had been exorcised and finally free. He was awake, breathing his new life, tasting it, and for the first time, wanting it. He slouched against the sofa, his mythic symmetry watching as Fletcher absorbed his suffering. Tristan reached for him. He had come to destroy this monster, this matador, this Phoenix of his dreams, and feared he had. But the shoulder he gripped was strong, the jaw resolute. Along with a son, a father was rising from the ashes.

PART II

61

"Well that won't do, Ruth! *Ray's* coming for dinner! When did she invite *him*, and why didn't anyone tell me? Ellen! Ellen!" In full Sunday regalia, Pete was swishing through the kitchen with a box of lozenges and nasal spray. In between sermons he had rushed home for his remedies; summer allergies were kicking in.

"Ruth, I've got to go. Where is she?"

"She must have left already."

Pete checked his watch, aghast. "I've got to go! If you see her, say something!"

He charged out and plopped into the car. His robe was wedged in the door, flying across the pavement like a wind sock as he lurched into his parking space; one minute and counting. Poor Ray, he thought. He knew darn well Ruth wouldn't intervene. He raced up the steps; the organ had just begun. With a deep breath, he dusted off his robe and adopted a righteous bearing.

He waltzed down the aisle with gentle authority, nodding at his attendees, all the while wondering what he was going to say at four o'clock. "Ray, you remember your assailant, Tristan . . . ."

An hour later, he was shaking hands with his constituents, answering enthusiastic questions under the shade of a huge cottonwood. It was a great sermon, even if he had to say so himself. He had digressed a little – O. K, a lot - into the supposition of parallel universes, but it was the clarity that counted; everyone understood and everyone was impressed. Everyone, that is, but the two church elders waiting on the church steps, fingering him over.

"Pete, if you have some time, we'd like to talk to you, maybe a meeting this week."

"Of course! Whatever's convenient! 'Something wrong?'"

"Well, no, nothing that can't be worked out. How 'bout Tuesday, say 2:00?"

"O.K." Shaking his employers' hands, he spied Ellen standing at his elbow, her large, almond orbs rolling with an affected soliloquy. "California, here we come. . . ."

He scowled. "Before you run off, my dear. . . ."

"Yes?"

"Did you know that Ray was coming to dinner?"

"Yes."

"And you invited Tristan anyway?"

"Yes."

"*Why?*"

"Because, *you said* that conflict is concomitant to ignorance. Or maybe it's the other way around. Anyway, I thought they should get to know each other. Besides, he knows, Dad. I told him."

"You did? He's all right with it?"

"He didn't cancel! And you should trust me!"

"You're right! So now, all we have to do is call Fletcher. Or should we leave him: uninvited and abandoned . . . alone and forgotten . . . depressed and despondent. . . . ."

"Oh come on, Dad! How many times have you invited him? He won't come. He never comes!"

Pete lolled his head to one side, puffing his cheeks and pursing his lips, blowing an invisible don't be tiresome trumpet. "Use my office phone."

With an exaggerated nose wrinkle, she declared the mission a folly, but trotted up the steps.

62

Had it not been for the heightened state of alert, Fletcher would have declined Ellen's invite. But Tristan was adamant that he keep his word, and – for safety's sake - they adhere to mutually agreed upon ground rules. Rule Number One: neither should be isolated for a prolonged or predictable period of time. Since the Peters dinner promised to be both - prolonged and predictable - Fletcher was forced to accept. Gushing thanks to Ellen, he hung up, muttering how he hated these affairs. However, since they weren't expected until four, they had enough time to pick up Tristan's rental – deserted since Wednesday - in Denver. It had been garaged quite a distance from the meeting turned melee, and, in retrospect, wisely so. It was unlikely that it would be found and consequently, rendered brakeless.

Sunday's highway was like the yellow brick road, traversed by hoards of munchkins in SUVs and hybrids, on their way to the Village Inn or Kansas. Fletcher was passing them at eighty. Nothing was familiar. Tristan had been right. Fletcher's yesterdays were a forfeit; Trans-Origins, Inc. had claimed them. Even the car seemed strange, as if the new world order had already taken place instead of weighing heavily on his mind. Tristan had tried to piece it together for him, but there was a lot he didn't know. Fletcher was left to fill in the gaps.

Eckhart was vital to Trans-Origins, Inc., in fact the heart of it. He was one of a dozen or so of its founding scientific crème-de-la-crème convening throughout a new age empire. The company didn't begin as a secret society; in fact, only recently had it been operating as one. Its history was fairly straight-forward. Apparently, in the late seventies, a graduate consortium of radical brainy power houses united under an altruistic eco-banner. The idea was that collectively, they could augment each other's field of expertise, enhancing their ability to solve specific environmental and scientific problems. To that end, they were brilliant, dedicated and – most of all - right. They had slam-dunk strategies to ward off everything from extinction to climate change to viral epidemics. They could resurrect species, predict weather patterns, revitalize wastelands and clean contaminated seas. They had models, inventions and plans; they even had patents. What they didn't have, however, was support. In fact, since most of their long-term solutions required a huge amount of money and drastic materialistic restraint, all they managed to do was rattle the beanstalk of giants like Drexden International. Emerging countries couldn't afford their ideology either, so they were virtually ignored. Gradually, the company's meeker members dropped out, leaving a core of bold, embittered geniuses, tired of greed and a deaf-eared proliferating populace. Trans-Origins set up shop underground, administering to the needs of shadowy clients who paid handsomely for a glimpse of the future and profited surprisingly well by it. In turn, the company's vanguard was able to forge ahead with well-intentioned developments, careful to keep a lid on any diabolical by-products. But the underworld was no place for those raised in the light of reason. The idealistic dozen began to stumble, unable to discern right from wrong as they ventured into the darkness. Watching intently was a charismatic Moroccan-borne vampire named Etienne de Sernet. Wooing them with visions of utopia, the arms dealer turned power broker pledged them light at the end of his tunnel. All they had to do, he instructed, was to follow . . . and fashion him a key to Pandora's Box. What De Sernet didn't know was that there was another bat lurking in the recesses, suspicious and learning the treacherous alleys, one all ready to do business.

Sooner than expected, the promised key was delivered to the ecstatic De Sernet. With great expectations, the clavis was turned, the package opened, and his fate sealed. Within six hours, he, his brothers and every one of his resident mercenaries were found dead: cause unknown. What was left of his horrified troops quickly fell in line, looking around for the new Caesar. But, after judicious review, a clandestine Porter Eckhart selected only one - an eighteen year old peripheral named Tristan - to ride under his tutorage into a deadly new realm. The gates of Trans-Origins, Inc. shut behind them.

Tristan was groomed to be one of the company's elite guards, but there was trouble from the start. He was cajoled through his first months in a kind of paramilitary camp in the Pyrenees, but was too volatile to finish. He spent the latter part of his eighteenth year with a lot of idle time on the Costa del Sol. Kept on a tight leash, he still managed to find an art class, a girl and piece-meal illustration work. Occasionally he was called upon to travel to the Canaries or Morocco carrying God knows what. During the second year of his internship, he was in the constant company of another Porter appointee, a twenty-eight year old blonde American ex-car-thief named Mathew Kraft, who was much closer to Trans Origins, having been Eckhart's pre-annum escort. Matt was more than a fan; he was obsessed with the company tenet which was revolutionary, socialistic, and of course, environmentally sound. Long days and nights were spent indoctrinating his Spanish protégé, as together, they traversed the European continent, smuggling pharmaceuticals and answering calls for the occasional rough-up. But, things didn't go well. Tristan took everything to heart and was frighteningly reactive; more than once Matt had to cover his awfully bloody tracks. Finally deemed too dangerous, the Spaniard was sent home, which at the time, was a suite of laboratories in Madrid. Once there, the paternal Porter stressed the importance of self-discipline in the management of nature and man. But, not sure if Tristan got it and not knowing what else to do, the CEO wrapped him snugly under his protective wing, and took him – as a translator of sorts – throughout South America. Although academic sympathizers rallied to Porter's planet in peril cause, it was clear that the environmentalist himself was apathetic, napping through forums. Then, he began to confide in Tristan, drawing him closer to a larger scheme. But there was a matter to be addressed first. In a hotel room in Buenos Aires, the shy and self-effacing scientist confessed: he had fallen in love with the beautiful Iberian. Stunningly rejected, it was another six months before he approached Tristan again, and this time, the unstable Adonis nearly killed him. It was probably at that point, that Tristan went from an intended keepsake to a programmable casualty in Porter's war against mankind.

Fletcher was still having trouble with Denver. Why Denver? Tristan looked at him as if it were simpler than two plus two.

Tristan was Porter's only variable; the rest of his troop was fail-safe. Although he could operate from anywhere, the company's patriarch had to keep the prodigal son occupied, and so found an errant father to fit the bill. Tristan's full attention could be directed at his mother's miserable deserter, keeping the bigger picture out of focus. But, naturally, Porter needed to be in proximity, so he set up camp in the courier's general neighborhood. Then, things started to go awry. Although Porter had factored in his volatility, what he hadn't counted on was Tristan's raw intelligence, which could on occasion, compensate for his immaturity. Nor had it ever occurred to the mastermind that the superficial, fortune-seeking father would shed his phony English dandihood and become a full blown black Irish threat. Tristan had figured out the plan. He was a doomsday deliverer with a one-way ticket, and for the first time he minded. Not only had Porter's trafficker become balky, he wasn't alone in his variability. Fletcher had become quite a wild card.

✳ ✳ ✳

"Damn!" Fletcher had missed the entrance to the garage, but as there was no traffic, he backed up and nosed in. The bar lifted, trapping them into the minimum payment. The rental car was isolated on the third level; the ticket still on the dash. Tristan unlocked it, and then retrieved a wrapped package from the backseat. He strolled to Fletcher's window with a smile.

"I almost forgot. I bought you a birthday present."

"Oh Lord," Fletcher laughed, opening the door. "Thank you. What is it?"

"Open it."

Fletcher turned it over. His face darkened. "Who wrapped it?"

"The store. Why?"

"Wait here! Don't get in that car!" Fletcher dashed to a trash can and shoved his gift in it, covering it with the accumulated garbage. He rushed back, and jutted his head toward the Volvo. "Let's go."

"But. . . . "

"Leave it!"

The car spiraled to the ground level, leaving the garage with its underbelly scraping the sidewalk. The passenger was staring straight ahead. "I don't believe it! You think. . . ?"

"I don't know, Tristan. I just don't know! You said De Sernet was found about six hours after he died. You said he opened a package. Whatever Eckhart has is damn lethal, but once exposed, the stuff must lose potency or something. I mean, it didn't spread or it would've been headline news. Still, that first wallop wiped out a small army. So we have to be careful of packages, vials, things like that. I'm sorry, Tristan. It's probably my imagination. I just don't want to take any chances. What was it, anyway?"

Tristan lit a cigarette. "An Irish cap."

"Ah. Well, that was good of you. Thank you."

63

Ray and Ellen were on the front porch of the Peters' parsonage when the Lawson party arrived. She dropped off the railing to meet them, gasping at the sight of Tristan's greenish-blue facial. He brushed her off with a hug and no explanation, and walked straight up the steps to the veranda. Fletcher was gathering wines and desserts from the back seat when he noticed the posturing on the deck. He stopped mid-grocery bag. He didn't like it. The sandy-haired guest had his arms crossed, studying Tristan through a locked jaw. Tristan took a step toward him. The man dropped his arms. Ellen stopped talking.

"Well, look who's here!" Pete burst through the front entry, looking like an orca in a blocky black and white polo, waving a big, greasy spatula. "Tristan! 'Nice to. . . . Oh! Well! Look at you! What happened? Or do I dare ask?"

Tristan didn't answer. Instead, he extended a hand toward Ray and said, "Before I stay, I want to tell you that I am very sorry for what I did. And if you can't accept my apology, I'll leave. I don't want to ruin your dinner."

Pete disguised his shock with a cough. Ray stood still, weighing the offer. He averted his eyes, color burning into his cheeks as he searched for reverential guidance. Pete telegraphed neutrality. Ray shrugged and took Tristan's hand. "All right then."

With an exhale, Pete clambered down the stairs to meet Fletcher on the lawn and relieve him of dessert. "Well, miracles abound! I'm so glad you're here!"

"Kind of you, Pete. My pleasure."

From the back gate, Pete's twins scampered over to examine the new arrival. They had huge brown orbs and were giggling, blowing big opalescent bubbles into Fletcher's chest from behind Pete's sturdy trunk.

"All right, thank you! That's enough, boys. Michael, Randy, say hello to Mr. Lawson."

They hung behind Pete until he pushed them forward. "Boys, please." They ventured forth, their skinny arms extended. Fletcher nodded and clasped their fingers. It had never occurred to him that Pete's children were adopted. Ruth was calling them from behind the house. With a sweep of their father's spatula, they ran off.

"They're from Ethiopia, Fletch," Pete said, reading his mind. "They came to us when they were just a year. You'll meet Dillon in a minute. He's from Afghanistan, but now," Pete was in crescendo, "he's an all-American top notch soccer player!" The boy was on his way over.

"Dillon, this is Fletcher Lawson."

Dillon grinned at Fletcher, and then informed the chef that his chicken was burning. Pete rushed off. Fletcher meandered to the veranda. Tristan tossed him a beer and introduced him to Ray. The latter said that they had already met, but it was at least ten years ago, at a bar called Billy Bronco's. Fletcher grimaced while Ray smirked, toasting him with a ginger ale. Tristan had his arm draped across Ellen's shoulders, but was focused on Dillon heeling a soccer ball. Dillon looked up. "You play?"

The Spaniard trotted down the stairs.

Fletcher agreed to be a goal keeper so Ray took the opposite side. Sensing a match, the twins escaped a cleanup, shrieking allegiance to Ellen's new boyfriend. Ray and Ellen teamed up with Dillon, who – as Tristan found out – didn't need them. Pete had salvaged his drumsticks and was back, shoring up Tristan's side. Ruth emerged with appetizers and an embattled look on her face. She shook her head and flopped on a chaise lounge.

For nearly an hour, the teams fought for the ball. There was no such thing as a foul, which meant that any dirty trick was acceptable as long as no one got hurt, and Pete was full of them. At one point, he blocked an intended goal with his belly, shoved the ball under his shirt and raced across the grass with every intention of scoring one all by himself. But a pile of youthful anatomy grounded him mid- field, laughing so hard that no one noticed his wife worming her way into the heap. Grabbing the coveted trophy, she giant stepped - with the twins hanging on to her legs - across the yard to Fletcher's goal post. He stepped aside.

"Madame, I can see I've met my match."

"Don't forget it, Fletcher." She scored.

The call for dinner was actually an order issued by the matriarch, and everyone quickly fell in around the table. As per the family tradition, they held hands for prayer. Fletcher closed his eyes. The last time he had heard grace at supper, he was nine years old. He couldn't remember who said it.

The faire was international and superb. The chicken was lathered with Ruth's incomparable ginger sauce. The salad was Greek; the pasta Italian; the wine French; the vegetables Asian; the conversation: galactic. With Pete presiding, no one was off the hook. He explained theories like the Heisenberg Uncertainty Principle, hammering it in until he was sure his company had a toe-hold, and then demanded feedback. It was a stretch for everyone but Ray, who moved through quantum physics as easily as he did an oil change. Ellen was shocked. Very few could keep up with her father. As the evening wore on, they moved to the back yard. When the conversation ebbed, Ruth rose, signaling to her charges that it was time to clean up. Ellen and the boys gathered china and silverware. Fletcher held on to his plate and followed them into the house. "I'll do the dishes, Ruth."

She began scraping dishes. "No need, Fletcher. We'll have this done in no time."

"Please. I'm quite good at it."

She was a tiny woman, smiling up at him with chocolate on her collar. There was a Golden Elder outside the kitchen window swaying in the fading light, speckling her with the shadow of its lacy blooms. Her hair was so white and full that it looked like an ermine hat. Her eyes were clear and – even in the dim kitchen - piercing. "All right." She took her apron off and offered it to him. "The towels are under the sink. Michael, Randy, time for a bath. Upstairs, please."

Tristan strolled in, taking up his father's cause. He cleared plates along with Ellen and Dillon, dousing them under Fletcher's soapy arms. Pete peered through the screen door, announcing that he was taking Ray home, but he'd just be a few minutes, telegraphing to Fletcher to stick around. Ellen insisted on delivering Ray via her much more fun Camaro. Grabbing Tristan's hand, she winked at her Dad. Detecting the dishwasher's stiffness at the sink, Tristan promised not to be long.

Pete dismissed Dillon from chores and shoved the last of the chocolate cake in the refrigerator. "Don't worry about that, Fletch. Just leave it! The kids will get it later."

"I'm almost done, Pete."

"How 'bout an Irish cream?"

"Sure. Just hand me that pan over there." Fletcher left it to soak and emptied the sink. Pete found a sponge and wiped down the counters and then poured two shots. The two idled out onto the moon washed porch, and eased into plastic chairs. Fletcher complimented Pete on his children, saying they seemed so happy.

"You never cease to amaze me." Fletcher added, "I imagine you. . . ."

"You can't imagine, Fletch. They're going to fire me soon."

Fletcher repositioned his chair closer to Pete. The reverend looked more angular in the lunar glow, as if he had lost weight, but perhaps he had simply hardened with the latest disappointment. Fletcher whistled softly. "What makes you say that?"

"Fletch, I cannot and *will not* separate *science* and the pursuit of knowledge from a divine plan. It can't possibly be an either-or situation. I simply refuse to believe that we've be imbued with extraordinary brain power just to be chained to long term ignorance. I don't understand them! There's no sin in exploring how we evolved, the way the universe is expanding or what the universe is! There's a method to everything! There's nothing wrong with considering life at its most fundamental, and that we might even have some company out there somewhere." Pete jabbed at a star with his fore finger. He jumped up and disappeared into the house, and then quickly reappeared with a bottle in hand. He poured two more shots.

"And, you know, there's nothing wrong with saying 'I don't know.' When people ask me about Adam and Eve: did it really happen *exactly* that way? I tell them I don't know. I tell them it's possible, but we don't know yet. It's beside the point! The story had a greater purpose than its factual dissection. But if you only knew how hard it is for people to grasp that simple concept and live with it, that *we just don't know yet!* That our answers lie in the *future,* not the past! They resent it! They want some artifact to be dug up somewhere that says Noah was here! Or some supernatural event to validate their faith. I try to guide them along a path of learning and kindness: that God is within us, that we can show each other the way. But they want something . . . mean and irrefutable. They want me to stand there and. . . . Oh, it's just so frustrating!"

Fletcher fingered the rim of his shot glass, not really wanting to finish it. The good friar, however, was topping his off again.

"Pete, you have two doctorates, one is in physics or something, isn't it? You could land yourself a good job in any private school. There's not that many theoretical whatevers running around."

"Private schools. Universities. They're not the people that *need* to know."

"But they might be the only ones that *want* to know." Fletcher wished he hadn't said it. He plunked down his glass. "Look, I . . . ."

"It's nothing I haven't been told a hundred times by Ruth, and lately, Ellen."

Fletcher reclaimed his drink and swallowed. "Blast it, Peters; you know you touch a lot of people. I had a great time tonight. I know it sounds ridiculous, but I didn't think I could. And look at Ray. He's a new man largely because of your . . . your faith. So, please don't think I discount what you do. I just think, sometimes, you deserve a wider audience. You have such a remarkable mind, Pete. Lord knows I believe everything you say just because *you* said it. I've never met your equal."

Pete laughed, toasting Fletcher and his appalling charm before sloshing down another.

Fletcher wondered if the oncoming headlights could be Tristan. They passed. His host had his chin tucked into his chest and was at least three to four sheets, which presented Fletcher with an opportunity. If it backfired, Pete may not remember anyway. "Have you ever heard of a man named Porter Eckhart?"

"*Porter?* Sure. How on earth do you know him?"

"How do *you* know him?"

"Went to school with him."

"No!"

"Yeah. He was a grad student while I was at Harvard. Wound up at Berkeley, I think. Maybe MIT. Way out there."

Fletcher leaned forward. "Did you know him well?"

"No."

"What else do you know about him?"

"Not much. Why? Is this a test?" Pete looked up at him, then settled back. "Let's see. Genetics: a clonemeister. Early on, he published some really off the wall papers that sure got a second look about ten years ago. That's the last I heard of him. Why?"

"Have you ever heard of a company called Trans-Origins, Inc.?"

"No. Maybe. I don't know."

"Do you remember anything else about him, what he was like?"

"I told you. I didn't know him very well. We were in chess club. A little guy with a lot of girls. 'Came from a ton of money. Nice enough. Why? Is he moving out here, too? Maybe he's replacing me."

"Did he have any causes? Was he political?"

"I don't know, Fletch. I told you; I didn't know him *that* well. Now that you mention it, I think he was an environmental guy, pretty excited about bio-engineered food. Kind of a turn-off for the mother earth set. *Why?*"

"Pete, have I ever beaten you at chess?"

"*What?* What's that have to do with anything?"

"Have I? I'm asking you: have I *ever* won a chess match against you?"

"No, but, so what? Does it bother you? It never occurred to me that it would. I thought, to *let* you win would be insulting. We don't have to play anymore. I just thought. . . . I didn't think that was the point, to win."

"It's not the point; I enjoy it. Pete, are you sober enough to hear me?"

The big man put down his glass. "As long as you start connecting some dots. What's the matter with you?"

Fletcher bit his lip and took the plunge. "I need you to sort of play chess. I need you to play like your life . . . well, like everything depends on it."

The pastor's nose flattened against his cheeks as he tried to suppress a burp. "What's gotten into you?"

"I need to trust you. And maybe. . . ." Fletcher folded his arms. "Maybe there's a reason for your life that you never dreamed of. 'Something you couldn't imagine."

Pete's heavy slits widened a notch. "Fletcher, maybe we've both had a little too much."

"Did you hear me?"

"Yes." Pete's laughter emanated from the back of his throat, the liquor driving it through his nose into a high pitched whistle. "Yes! I hear you!"

"Well?"

"You're so serious!" Scrutinizing his deck mate, Pete tapered off. "You're not serious, are you Fletch?"

"I am. Really I am. And no one can know."

"A chess match."

"In a manner of speaking."

"All right. I'm in! Who am I playing chess with . . . that no one can know, that the whole world is riding on?"

"Eckhart."

"*Porter?*" Pete's laughter rose to a roar that resonated across the porch. "Well, old boy, I might disappoint you there!"

Headlights were coming from the east, slowing to the driveway. Fletcher stood. "Thank Ruth for me?"

"Yep. So, what's all this about?"

"I have your word. No one can know."

"Of course, that's easy. I have no idea what you're talking about."

Fletcher patted the bewildered man's shoulder and made for the wagon. Tristan walked Ellen to the porch, logged Pete's befuddled stare and then joined Fletcher, slamming the car door.

"You told him! *Have you lost your mind?*"

"Possibly, but listen to me, Tristan. You know who Eckhart is. If we're going to survive him - if anyone is - we're going to need help. So, call it instinct. I have a feeling; Peters is the one man who can beat him."

64

The oval moon had bleached the mystery from the night; the shapes were familiar and welcoming. Fletcher and Tristan stepped onto a silver-studded driveway. After an extensive inspection, the house was declared firmly locked, at which point, Fletcher garaged the car, threw the keys on the counter and let the frantic dog out. His head ached. Tristan's bruise had crept under his eye. They examined every room. All their planted warnings were as they left them. Porter was giving them plenty of rope. Fletcher wondered when he would hear from him. Popping three aspirin, he hoped it wouldn't be tonight. But it was.

The phone rang at precisely ten thirty.

"You didn't like your present?"

Porter waited for a response but got none. "It was completely innocuous, Fletcher. I left you a means to contact me. A cell phone in the box to be exact."

"How thoughtful."

Porter sighed. "Perhaps we should just get down to business."

"There is no business."

"I wouldn't be too hasty."

"Hasty? *Hasty?* You don't really think we can negotiate this one, do you? That I'd actually sacrifice Tristan to some scheme . . . some epidemic! You must be insane."

"An epidemic?" Porter's laugh was rosy and round, like – Fletcher envisioned - his face.

"What do you know of me," the scientist queried, "that you would come to such a conclusion?"

"De Sernet. I know about him."

"Ah. Well, Fletcher, for your information, De Sernet was a gangster. That said, what makes you think I was involved?"

"Well, *Porter.* No one knows what killed him. But, whatever did, wiped out an entire household within hours. Certainly something somebody like you might have concocted."

"I see. Well, if you really believe that, why haven't you contacted the C.D.C or the World Health Organization? The C.I.A? The Secret Service? Don't you think they'd be interested?"

"I have no proof."

"Proof? Shame on you! The fact is you really don't care what killed that man any more than I do. Look, Fletcher, all you care about is you and your genetic derivative. That's it. That's all of it. You referred to an epidemic. To wipe out the human race? Isn't that right? So, there you are, *with all of humanity depending on you,* depending on you to make one phone call. *Just one.* But you won't do it. Why? Because, not only are you *not certain,* but you really don't give a damn. One phone call to save *billions* means that you might do a little time for theft. It means your son might be incarcerated for a few of those Tabors that weren't so fortunate back in Europe. No. We can't have that. Too much sacrifice for the masses."

"Fuck you!"

"There's no need to be angry, Fletcher. I certainly don't blame you. You're no different than anyone else. Ask Tristan. He understands. He'll tell you."

"He's not what you think."

"Oh, but he is! He's just like you! He thinks like you, that the two of you will sail into to some safe harbor while the rest of the world evaporates. Maybe some island. You'll grow your trees, keep a couple of women. You swing that way, don't you Fletcher? Or were they *all* just a means to an end?"

"You son of a. . ."

"None of this is personal to me, although it should be, given your conclusions. But, I'll tell you what. I'm going to give you the opportunity to see what I see, to know what I know. How does that sound? To know what no one else *is willing* to know. I'm going to show you exactly what you're up against. And why your little island doesn't exist. And then, I'm going to show you the only way out and your son's only prayer! All right? Then, you can tell me whether or not the fulfillment of his contract is worth it!"

"You're proposing what?" Fletcher lit a cigarette.

"See me at my office."

"Not alone."

"What choice do you have? Law enforcement?" Porter snickered. "So, when are you available, Mr. Lawson?"

"I want to bring someone else. Someone you can trust. Someone you know."

"I hardly think we travel in the same circles."

"Pete Peters. You went to school with him."

"Peters?"

"I won't come alone."

"Come alone, Fletcher."

"When?"

"Wednesday night. Seven."

"I'm bringing Peters."

"He's a minister, isn't he? Why would you risk him, Lawson? Given what you think of me, why would you do that? Are you really that selfish?"

"According to you, there's nothing to lose."

"Oh, I never said that." There was a click across the telephone line. Porter was gone.

Fletcher watched his cigarette shrink with a spiral of smoke before espying Tristan's wraithlike frame at the threshold.

"I take it you heard." Fletcher stubbed out his cigarette and reached for another.

Tristan paddled over, offering him a light. "I'm going with you."

"No."

"He's dangerous."

"I'll take Pete."

"Be reasonable." Tristan plunked on the couch. "You can't involve him."

"I shouldn't, but I will. Tristan, what's in that office?"

"Nothing, really. Telephones, computers, maybe a fax."

"When are they there?"

"They're in and out but almost always at night."

"I need to go back there, before the meeting."

65

Elan's timing couldn't have been better. He arrived with his poke-a-dotted trailer at eight-thirty a.m., just as Fletcher and son were getting ready to leave for Vicante's office. Fletcher motioned at the window. With an irrepressible smile, Tristan dashed down the hallway to swap his loafers for boots. He had forgotten; it was Monday. While Fletcher shuffled papers, he could be riding through one of his last days on the frontier.

He returned to the kitchen, pulling a tee-shirt over his head. "You'll be all right?"

"I won't be long." Fletcher picked up the keys. "There's some coffee left."

✳ ✳ ✳

Rather than take the previous route, Elan opted to go straight west through the neighbor's pasture and return from the north, following the edge of the Lawson ranch via the dirt road. It was a pretty ride, he declared, and would give his Tristan a new perspective. They set out, ambling for a mile or so through crisp grass until meeting the wire perimeter. Once there,

Tristan motioned to Elan to open the gate, the latter grinning understandably. It was a long reach from the back of Little John.

Elan knew the neighbors well enough. They raised Angus. As the riders crossed their field, the herd scattered, all except a magnificent bull who tracked them through a face full of flies. Elan pointed to their destination - a stretch of gravel o the north - but he wanted Tristan to see something first. As they loped up a ridgeline, the Rocky Mountains rolled into view like a huge broken tidal wave ready to engulf the sunny plains. An abandoned homestead crumbled in the dale to the south. Dried stream beds etched their way to the foot of the great swells. It was rugged, unpredictable country, Elan said. The plains' natives knew enough to keep moving. Very few settlers lasted.

The returning road cut a swathe through a pine laden hill; at one time, it was an old lumber trail. Tristan was completely relaxed on Little John, jogging along the embankment as a few cars passed. Elan was impressed; his student had graduated. Just east of the canyon, Elan asked if there had been any further cave exploration. Tristan said no, but since he had brought it up, why didn't he stay for lunch? They could take another look. The riders passed through the Lawson gate, the heat producing mirage puddles all the way up the gravel drive. Fifteen minutes later – and five thousand dollars lighter - Fletcher pulled up.

He was sifting through envelopes as Tristan scuffled past him with soda and a bag of chips. Fletcher mumbled something about fresh cold cuts. Tristan unloaded the refrigerator, heaped a do-it-yourself on the table and slid a plate in front of Elan, who was sitting quietly nursing a cola.

"Ryan Fletcher," Tristan's mouth was full as he handed Oliver a slice of turkey, "you can do that later."

Fletcher looked up.

"Today, we're going to the cave."

"Oh. All right, then." Fletcher threw the mail on the counter. "I'll change. Make me a sandwich."

66

The sun was blazing as the men trudged to the site dragging the ladder. Surprisingly heavy, it was at least thirty feet long, originally intended to ford a Pueblo rock face. It was wrestled to the cave's entrance and fastened to a tree. With a heave, the ladder dropped straight past the first tier into the inscrutable darkness. Fletcher tugged on it, announcing that they were good to go.

Tristan was the first down, loudly reporting his observations until Fletcher yelled down that it wasn't necessary; they'd be right along. Surveying the watery foundation with his flashlight, Tristan hung quietly while his counterparts eased down the ladder. They bottle-necked just below the balcony. Before venturing further, Fletcher demanded that they utilize their masks. He could smell the dank liquid beneath him. Donning the apparatus, Tristan resumed his descent, tonally relaying that he had – literally - reached the end of his rope. It was several feet short, which wasn't about to stop him. He leapt. Sounding like a gramophone, he conveyed his awe with shouts of "Magnifico!" He was ankle deep in citrine fluid.

Fletcher scaled to the end of the ladder, which was only about five feet shy of the bottom. He landed with a splashy thud next to his son. Elan noiselessly touched down behind them.

Their flashlights fanned the cavern like RKO theater spots. The men could only gasp. The soaring walls were chiseled by water and colorfully layered by time. It appeared as if they were beneath the apex of the cave, their gateway a mere tube of light high above. The grotto wandered off in three directions, bubbling with mineral deposits. A cluster of stone glittered. Elan touched it.

"What is it?" Tristan asked, adjusting his face mask.

"I think it's pyrite. Fool's gold. But, that doesn't mean that the real thing isn't here. In all my life, I've never seen anything like it."

Fletcher meandered to the eastern conduit, his light aimed at the ceiling. He waved the others over, steadying the beam on the overhead. Flattened by the ages, a gnarled branch was embedded in the rock. Now petrified, it spanned across the subterrane, its leafy palm prints singed into the shale. With the collective power of their flashlights, they were able to discern tiny stamped ferns interspersed throughout the moist corridor until it twisted out of view. Intrigued, they waded into the darkness. Small, fossilized fish swam alongside them, seemingly unaware that millions of years had passed since they had once thrived. The explorers began stumbling over heaps of rubble as the channel dried, climbed and tightened. Ducking under an ever lowering arch way, they were engulfed in fine dust. Finally forced into a single file crawl, Fletcher signaled for them to wait. His arms arched. He caught his breath and bellied upward; loose sand swarmed under his shirt like fire ants. The parched fissure abruptly ended as a two foot pile of powdered sandstone and gravel. Disappointed, he tried to rub the spasm out of his neck. Tristan squeezed beside him. With exasperated huffs, he clawed the debris with his gloves.

Fletcher watched beads of frustration drip from his brow. "Take it easy, Tristan. What are you hoping to find?"

The Spaniard crossly shook his head just as his glove struck something hard, smooth and uncannily civilized. Fletcher scooped back more grit. A shape emerged. The two traded looks. They eagerly pawed through the rubble. In the light of their dusty filaments emerged a large box with a metal veneer, the patina suggesting bronze. Fletcher brushed off the last of the sand as Tristan carefully extricated it. It appeared as if it had been locked, but the iron had rusted away, leaving only its impression in burnt red. The hinges had met a similar fate, otherwise the box was intact. Tristan was noticeably shaking. It did not have a treasure chest's likely poundage, but had reckonable weight. Fletcher nodded solemnly. His colleague carefully removed the lid.

Lining the thick wooden container was a rough-textured cloth, amber with age. As Tristan lifted it, it disintegrated into a shower of lint. It had been placed there to protect something valuable, and to that end, had served its purpose, for interred within, was a stack of brittle but well-preserved parchment. Strategically hidden from moisture and light, an epic story had waited over five hundred years to be told. Tristan's eyes blazed with the realization. Before him was the life and last chronicled days of Christoval Alcon de Navarre y Marquis.

Elan tapped on a boot, demanding to know what they had found. Fletcher cleared his throat: it looked like a diary of a sort. He urged Elan into reverse, the claustrophobia becoming unbearable. Tristan replaced the lid and tucked the box under his arm, keeping it sealed between his ribs and his elbow. The trio counter-crawled out of the oppressive space, and then retraced their steps to the cathedral-like lobby. Fletcher said that there was probably some urgency in finding airtight storage. The others agreed, vowing to return later. They clambered quickly up the ladder, anxious for sunny relief.

Bursting into the kitchen, Fletcher immediately assigned the relic to a plastic garbage bag, but continued to scour the house for something more secure, something that could be sealed. The documents were too large for zip-locks. He seized on the solution. With his associates in tow, he dashed down the corridor to his bedroom. The shadow boxes hanging there had been custom made; they were quite large, and there were four of them, exhibiting his English collectibles. He ordered them off the wall and emptied.

Elan examined them. "You sure?"

"Yes! Yes! Absolutely!"

Fletcher was the first to depose one. Prying off the back, he ripped his make-believe family out of its place of honor. The renowned nineteen century faces were now adorning the carpet. He had searched the world over for their related memorabilia, only to have their letters, postcards and possessions litter the floor like so much scrap. These adventurous people, whose smiles and signatures had ushered in the twentieth century and Fletcher into his dreams were no longer needed. There was another story to tell and with it, another history in the making. A Falcon had come to stay.

With the exhibits ousted, the containers were carted to the kitchen for a meticulous cleaning. Fletcher insisted that they wear plastic gloves to handle the parchment, and – since he only had one pair – he did the honors. The receptacles were arranged on the counter, the curtains drawn, and Don Christoval's manuscript brought to light. Tristan and Elan watched spellbound as Fletcher counted out twenty-four thick pages, over half of them illustrated. He allotted six sheets to a box. As per Tristan's request, the first four leafs would be visible under glass; that way they could be read and – presumably - translated in order. Although the title page required no interpretation, its beauty mandated prominence. Bearing the name of the nobleman under a finely rendered coat of arms, Don Christoval's insignia was telling: two dolphins flanked a lion; above them, spread the wings of a falcon in flight. Across the centuries, it spoke stridently about the soul of a daring and insubordinate man.

The ring of the phone catapulted them into a modern Monday. As Tristan sealed the last shadowbox, Fletcher addressed the cordless with a mechanical greeting.

"Lawson?"

"Yes?"

"You have something of mine."

"Oh, right. I'll be right with you."

Clutching the phone, Fletcher dashed to the den and swept the door shut with his foot. "You still there?"

"I want it back, Lawson."

"I'm sure you do. But, it seems to me you almost had something of mine that wasn't part of the deal. I don't share my bank accounts, Harvey, or - for that matter - my personal life with anyone, in case you weren't clear on that."

"Fine. You've got that disc. I just want the program, all right? Just give me back the program."

"You mean program-*za*; I think there's more than one on there. I could probably do that, but I really do need something in the way of compensation."

"What? Money? *You want money?*"

"No, Harvey, not at all. Just a little of your time and expertise."

"What do you want?"

"I need you to find out everything you can about an individual, his associates and his company, but not the usual superficial fact-finding. I'd like you to do one of those in depth analyses that I suspect you're so good at."

"There's no freebees."

"I see. In that case. . . ."

"I'll give you a discount. Just give me the fucking program."

"Program- *za*, and the answer's no, Harvey. I think you owe me one."

"Fine. Screw you. Keep it."

"All right."

"Lawson, *come on!* Just give it to me. I'll give you a break."

"Harvey, I need you to do this one favor for me quickly and discreetly. I need the information by Wednesday."

"Fuck you!"

"All right, then, Harvey. So, write another program, if you can . . . *all by yourself.* You know, I wonder if that's the reason you called me. Could it be that the disc isn't solely your handiwork? Did P.C. pirate from another pirate?"

The rodent was chewing on something crunchy like peanut brittle or maybe – Fletcher mused – that indigestible rock and a hard place.

"O.K." Harvey capitulated with a loud chomp. "Give me the names. But, listen, I can't guarantee anything. I tell everybody that. Sometimes there's nothing I can find. Everybody thinks. . . ."

"I understand, Harvey, but I have faith in you, given your insatiable curiosity."

"Just give me the fuckin' names, Lawson."

Fletcher relayed the particulars with one last question. "One last thing, Harvey. You must know somebody in um, *electronics.*"

"What kind of. . . ? Oh. Now, *that*'s gonna cost you, Lawson."

Fletcher returned to the kitchen, finding Tristan pouring over the Falcon's exposé.

"Where's Elan?"

"He had to go. He said he'd be by later."

"Oh. How was your ride this morning?"

"Great." Tristan peered into the frame. "This is hard to read."

Fletcher examined the calligraphy. Each letter was scribed with a flourish, the lines amazingly delicate. The words were closely clustered, making it difficult to separate one from another. The faded ink and the brown parchment provided little contrast.

"Is it formal: the language?" Fletcher asked.

"Yes, very much so." Tristan turned to him abruptly. "I want to go back today. Now."

"What about Elan?"

"He can come another time."

"Well, I . . . I suppose. Let's put these somewhere safe. The study should do, maybe the wall closet, if you're the *only* one to know about it. Oh, the blasted phone again. I'll be right there."

Tristan stored the shadow boxes while Fletcher tucked the phone under his chin. "Hello."

"Fletch? You got a minute?"

"Sure, Pete."

"Last night, I dreamt you were trying to rope me into something, with – of all people - Porter Eckhart. Was I dreaming?"

"Um, well. . . . No."

"*No?*"

"Listen, can you make it over tonight?"

"Not tonight. Maybe tomorrow, right after my *shape up or ship out* meeting. I'm sure I'll need a drink afterward."

"Well that's good news, then. You're still not sacked."

"Oh, but I am. It's just that it takes three meetings. The next one will be: *now, look, we're warning you,* which will be followed by: *we hate to do this, you have such a lovely family. . . .*"

"Well, you know my opinion. I won't bore you with it again. What time will you be done?"

"I don't know. Probably around four."

"Right, then, I'll have a Scotch waiting."

Fletcher rung off and strolled down the hall to the study, expecting to find his collaborator pouring over the ancient text. As expected, Tristan was engrossed, but not with a sixteenth century manuscript. Rather, he was gazing at the portrait of his mother. It had been recovered from the cache of closeted artwork, and been propped against the desk for a better look. He was stationed away from it, gnawing on the inside of cheek as he processed the image, his face reflecting both her semblance and her torment. Guilt routed Fletcher at the entry.

"Tristan. I. . . ."

"It's quite good. You're very good, Ryan Fletcher. Better than me. Better. . . ."

"No. No. I'm not. Just older. Look, I'm sorry. Let's just go."

"Was she always sad like that?"

"Sad? No, I don't think so. We need to go."

"That's how I remember her. Always sad. I don't ever remember her laughing. I don't remember a smile."

"Tristan. Look, I'm sorry. It was the worst mistake. . . ."

"I don't know. Think of what your life would have been like, someone without a smile. . . ."

"*Stop it!* Christ! Look, she's not to blame! It was my fault, all right? *My fault!*"

Tristan abruptly faced him. "You're right. We should go."

67

A strong western wind was whipping a tower of cumulonimbus into an afternoon eruption. Tristan plunged quickly into the chasm, as if there, he could escape both the unstable stratosphere and a brewing inner storm. Fletcher pursued. The grotto had lost its appeal. A few hours ago, it was magical; now it was oppressive. Fletcher was coated with humidity, wearing it like a vile new skin.

"Well, Tristan. Which way?"

There was no reply. The Spaniard simply forged ahead into the mysterious western conduit. Fletcher trailed wordlessly, knowing that Tristan was lost in an internal labyrinth, one he knew well: a maze of cruel memories. Muffled thunder grumbled above the passageway. The fissure ascended sharply and narrowed. Unlike the other, it was not decorated with Pleistocene prints, and went on seemingly forever. With his head lowered, Tristan trudged along too confidently, tripping over outcroppings and careening around bends until he finally fell. His spotlight skittered across the slimy floor, illuminating its rough, patchy glittering base. Focusing a beam on his impetuous leader, Fletcher saw that Tristan's knee and calf were stained red. He had fallen against something sizeable.

"You all right?" Fletcher offered a hand, but it wasn't taken. "What's all the urgency, anyway?"

Tristan retrieved his flashlight and took a closer look at the impediment to his progress. It was a strange, crusty protrusion, approximately two feet high with stubby arms. He immediately lost interest, directing his ray into the next turn. From far away, there was an angry rumble, a tempest fomenting above them.

"Wait a minute." Fletcher peered at the formation, scraping it with his thumb. Underneath the deposits, scalloped marks were evident. It was wood although its precise shape had been refashioned by the elements. "It's a cross! Tristan, did you hear me? Someone. . . ."

"I know."

Fletcher tried to straighten, nicking the crown of his head. His hands were soaking under his gloves. His source of light was waning, not a comforting sign. "What do you mean, you know? What *exactly* are we looking for, Tristan?"

"I think they're here."

"Who's here?"

"Don Christoval's party."

"His party? What do you mean?"

"On the first page, he writes of soldiers: loyal friends that he would follow to eternity. Something like that."

"Oh no."

"If they're here, they can't be far."

"Tristan, wait a minute. Stop. Let's think about this. I'm not sure we're being . . . respectful, you know?"

Tristan was already pressing further into unchartered territory. Fletcher groaned, tracking behind him, keeping his flashlight pointed at the precarious terrain. The passageway constantly switched back, the confinement nerve racking. Fletcher was shoulder to shoulder with the walls. The ceiling rolled inward. He grazed his scalp. With his fearless leader lost up ahead, Fletcher quickly navigated around a slippery, constrictive turn, and then another, twisting his ankle slightly as he plowed right into a clammy obstruction with a bloody leg and rapid respiration.

"Look, Ryan! Look at this."

They were standing at the edge of a semi-circular vault that dropped three or so feet with its canopy approximately ten feet above them. Fletcher guided Tristan's brighter light across the bourn. It was sooty and airless: an amphitheater void of life, moisture or sound. Directly ahead, appearing like a ghastly white stitch, a large cross had been etched in the wall, and under it, like fresh brands on an ebony hide, three names had been scored into the shale. Fletcher scoured the bedrock. Three dust covered shapes were braced against a natural sill. They were skeletons, each placed on a low rectangular pyre of round and rough rock.

Fletcher fought back a retch. "Tristan, come on. Let's go."

"*Wait!* It's fantastic! Is that a sword? I think they have armor. *Do you see it?*"

"*I don't want to see it.* I don't want to see anymore. Let's go!"

"Wait! We can learn something. They might have gold. Don't panic. You'll be all right."

"This is a crypt! These people are buried here. We're not grave robbers! I mean it. I'm leaving, and your battery's running low, so I suggest you do the same!"

Fletcher wheeled around. His flashlight flickered weakly with every hurried stumble. Tristan was on his heels. Fletcher slid downward, catching himself on a crag, righting himself before the next hurtle.

"You were all right with Don Christoval!" Tristan cried breathlessly from behind him. "He's a skeleton! You *talked* to him! What's the matter with you?"

"I don't know. It's different. He's up there. God, I can barely breathe."

"It's no different, Ryan! Try to think. . . ."

"I can't think! I don't want to think." Fletcher managed to sidestep the guardian cross, accelerating his descent.

"Don't you want to know what happened to them?"

"No! I don't want to know. Where the hell's the end of the damn thing? Oh good. Almost there!"

Fletcher had broken into a jog. His pulse had doubled. His hair was matted against his neck. A thunder clap and a terrible roar reverberated across the steaming cavity. The flashlight nearly exhausted, it illuminated the unmitigated nightmare with its very last flicker. Fletcher was just above the apex, but there was no apex. All he could see was water, churning toward him in a dense prurient wall. From the gates of hell, the torrid wrath was spiraling toward them, a plutonian reprisal for their incursion.

"*Oh Jesus! Get back! Tristan, go back!*" Twisting around, Fletcher shoved him into the darkness.

Tristan charged blindly ahead. The furious hiss was just behind them as they scrambled back up the shaft. Assuming it was a recurring event, Fletcher ripped his gloves off, feeling along the walls for an end to the slime that would mark the water table. Tristan shook his flashlight for one last look and yelled that he was at the cross. By amazing coincidence, it was also the high water mark. The light then vanished. They flailed in the darkness, finding each other as they sat in terrifying blackness; the terminating water gurgling their rout, chiding them from below.

Tristan tapped on his father's shoulder. "You all right?"

"Yes. You?"

"Yes. But I can't see at all. Nothing."

"I know. Can you get anything out of your flashlight?"

The plastic jiggled. "No."

Fletcher sighed. "Well, this is a first. Now I know what it must be like to be some poor creature flushed down a bloody toilet."

Tristan's laughter pealed through the cavity like a bell, ringing in their relief. "How long do you think we'll have to wait?"

"I have no idea. It could be minutes or days. I imagine we'll have to swim out."

"Why not wait? It'll drain."

"Eventually. But, we have no idea how long we could be here."

"It won't take long. Maybe a few hours."

"Tristan?"

"Hm?"

"Let me guess. You can't swim, can you?"

"No."

Fletcher sighed. "Bloody hell. Let me see if I can find where the water is. If it's receding, we'll wait. If not, we'll have to think of something."

"Ryan, I prefer to wait."

"Tristan, we're not staying here all night. We're not joining that party up there because of lack of oxygen. I'll be right back."

"There's lots of air!"

"I said oxygen! *Oxygen!* Look, don't worry. Stay here."

"No."

Fletcher kept his hands to the ceiling, groping his way down the channel with Tristan in close proximity. His mind wandered off into the bizarre; the lack of light was maddening. He stumbled into the water, realizing that it was full of earthen waste and – like his current surroundings – absolutely pitch. He had lost track of where they were in relation to the lobby.

'Tristan, I'm going to see how far we are from the main room, all right?"

"No."

"I'll be right back. Don't worry. I promise. I'll be right back."

"You could drown!"

"No, I can't. I'll just be a minute. Don't worry. I'm a good swimmer."

"Ryan, I can't. I can't. . . . I feel like my mind. . . ."

"I know. I know exactly how you feel. Think about something pleasant. Just hold on. We're going to get out of here. Count to sixty. I'll be back before then."

Fletcher forced himself into the cold water, groping for finger-holds as he submerged into the depths. Up-side down, he paddled along the ceiling like a crustacean, moving as rapidly as possible in descent. He was discharging carbon dioxide at regular intervals, but there were no air pockets at all, and his chest was beginning to compress. He felt the overhang give way. He longed to inhale but didn't dare surface, fearing that he could lose his way back through the egress. He coiled around, his bronchia now burning as he lunged back up the artery. He fought his way through the silt strewn water, jamming his hands and feet in every accessible niche to propel upward. His lungs were in full rebellion when he finally surfaced, gasping to fill his flattened alveoli. Tristan grabbed his sleeve; his fingers twisted around the dripping shirt. Fletcher smiled at his childlike reaction and his own simple realization. They weren't far. They could do it; even a non-swimmer could make it on one inhale.

"We're close." Fletcher panted. "You don't have to swim; you can push off the rock. It's black as pitch so it's easy to panic, but you can't. You'll feel the end of the tunnel, and then you just let yourself go. I'll get a hold of you. Don't fight me and don't get turned around! You'll rise naturally. Then we'll find the ladder. Remember, now. Don't struggle! I can keep you afloat. It's probably not even that deep. All right? So we're off. It'll be easy."

"I hate the water, and it's probably lower than it was."

"Not by much, and we're not staying here all bloody night."

"It might only take a few hours, just to empty the tunnel."

"Tristan, I don't know about you, but I'll go insane. You have to trust me, all right? Get a good fill of air, and you'll be drinking a beer in ten minutes. The hardest part will be keeping your wits about you. *It's not far*. Ready?"

"All right."

"Stay with me, now. Let's go."

With a massive inhale, Fletcher slipped into the water, reaching around in the blackness. Tristan was there. Fletcher yanked on his shirt for good measure and plunged forward, scraping across the upper limits as rapidly as he could. He snaked through the grime, coursing ever deeper, praying that Tristan was keeping up. He hesitated, probing ahead with an outstretched hand; the ceiling was still there. He surged forward, the subway guiding his descent. He fought back a wave of panic as he propelled further into the abyss, relieving his lungs with a torrent of bubbles. Inverted, he clawed against the jagged crown, pushing hard through the blackness, and suddenly felt the overhang give way. With one arm, he braced himself against the ledge, searching through the silt for Tristan. He wasn't there. Fletcher sunk, anxiously groping through the tunnel aperture until his lungs screamed for air. He twisted around, lunging beyond the egress, propelling himself upward, the water paling to an eerie green. He broke the surface gasping, pivoting frantically, choking Tristan's name. He wasn't there. With a desperate inhale, he dove back into the gloom, feeling along the bottom, rushing toward the western duct. He couldn't find the opening, feeling a swell of horror as he forced himself to stay submerged. And then a hand caught him, gripping his lower arm like a vice. Fletcher nodded relief, lunging upward, but there was too much resistance. He tried to find Tristan's shoulder, to reassure him, but was suddenly snapped downward with a terrible force. He plunged sideways to the bottom of the cistern. He fought to free his arm, shouting "no!" and pulled fiercely against the uncanny strength that slammed him into a vertical protrusion, wrenching him through a breach. It was the western tunnel. He surged backward, screaming Tristan's name, pounding on him not to panic, wrestling against the iron claw, but he was out of air and exhausted. He acceded limply, trying to preserve his consciousness as he was towed back up the fissure. Then, he was abruptly released. Weakly probing the water, he felt Tristan's hair swaying flaccidly in the current. He grappled for his shirt and seized him under the arm, his strength returning as adrenaline hijacked every molecule of cellular oxygen to snatch his unconscious progeny from the underworld.

Fletcher shot into the atmosphere coughing up water, choking on the sewage in his lungs, gulping frantically for air. Tristan was draped over his shoulder. The ladder was ten feet away. Gasping, he splashed to it, bracing his son against the rungs, shaking him furiously, shouting in his face to breathe. He searched for a pulse, his eyes filling with tears as Tristan hung lifelessly over the rope: a beautiful, untimely sacrifice in the ethereal light. Fletcher's lungs raged against his deep inhales, a savage fire spreading through his chest as he filled it with oxygen, exhaling into Tristan's mouth like a dragon. Again and again, he breathed for him. Under the water, a finger flinched; a pulse beat wildly. Fletcher redoubled his effort, forcing air down the constricted trachea. Tristan's arms spasmed violently. His head jerked back. He retched up water. Through convulsive coughing, he vomited. Fletcher forced his head down, shouting at him to breathe, no matter what, *breathe*. And he did.

Fletcher clung to the rope, too overcome to speak. Tears touched the verdant water. The color in Tristan's face returned with a tentative ray of sunlight. Fletcher rasped an apology. Tristan was voiceless but alert.

The ladder floated serenely in the murky water. Fletcher looked up, squinting. They were about twenty feet from freedom. Sunlight pierced through the vault; trembling rainbows arced across the natural cathedral like living stained glass. On the first tier, a familiar presence was standing: his golden hair threading across his rough open shirt, his high cheekbones metallic in the solar haze. For the first time, Fletcher was not afraid, acknowledging the figure as it disappeared into the white corona.

68

Tristan was lounging on the sofa, nursing tea. Fletcher was on line. Predictably, Tristan was no longer getting e-mails, although his past correspondence was still stored. Fletcher ran through the missives one more time.

"Tristan, out of curiosity, why does Porter sign his name Ea?"

"It's a god: Babylonian. The god of inner earth or something like that."

"I see. I notice he never addressed you by name. He calls you Merodach. Who's that?"

"The son of Ea, the one that carries out Ea's plan."

"Oh. And why didn't he buy you a computer of your own?"

"He's cautious. If the account belongs to you - another person - it's better. He never texts and tries not to use a cellphone for more than a minute. And they're never under his name."

"Ah. So, apparently he's been investigated."

"Naturally. He's a scientist. He works in foreign countries. Someone - some official - told him once that he was photographed with De Sernet. He didn't like it. After that, he was really careful."

"So . . ." Fletcher gnawed on his lip. "Someone may be on to him."

Tristan was watching him. "Isn't that good?"

Fletcher logged off. "Yes, but, if *he's* been watched, then - well let's put it this way - I'd just as soon you stay out of sight."

Tristan stretched, depositing his cup on the coffee table. "May I ask you a question?"

"Sure."

"The painting. Was it the only thing you ever stole?"

Fletcher leaned back and drained his port. "No."

"So, were you a thief back in England?"

Fletcher reached for a cigarette and tapped it. "I suppose I was."

"What else did you steal?"

"I don't know." Fletcher's lighter wasn't working. He opened his right drawer, searching for matches. "Things I liked. Rare things."

"What happened to them?"

"I sold them . . . to get enough money to come to the States."

"Did you ever steal anything here?"

Fletcher shut the drawer, having discovered matches on the lamp base. He struck one, smiling. "Only a heart."

"Oh. A Don Juan."

"Hardly. I think that title's reserved for you. Speaking of which, how goes it with poor Ellen? Tired of her already?"

"No. It's not that. It's just not fair. I don't know what will happen here, and she's not part of the plan anymore, so. . . ."

"The plan? What plan?"

Tristan rose, ambling over to the desk for a cigarette. "You knew I was a courier."

"Yes, but. . . . My God! You mean the plane. She was to *fly you somewhere? Where?*"

Tristan shrugged.

"And what was supposed to happen to her, the eighteen year old girl?"

"I don't know, Ryan. Does it matter? I'm not going."

Fletcher smashed his cigarette out. "Tristan, what could have possessed you? I mean, what could have driven you to even *think* of doing something so, so . . . horrid?"

Tristan stood stock still. He was peering down at his judge with his jaw flexing. "I believed in what I was doing, you know? Like war . . . it's a cause I believed in. But how could you possibly understand that? All I have to do is look around here to know that you've never once thought about anything besides yourself."

"Oh, Tristan. I'm too tired for this. Yes, I'm a selfish S.O.B. But, just to set the record straight, I knew where to draw the line, even at your age."

"Yes, you did, Ryan. You knew how to draw a line between yourself and any inconvenience, like a poor pregnant girl and a life of luxury. Right? That line was very clear."

Fletcher's eyes widened. His voice trembled. "Get this straight, Tristan, once and for all. I can't go back. I can't change it, and you know it. Now you have to decide whether you can live with that, because all I can do is try to right it from here on out. So, can you live with that? *Can you?*"

Tristan regarded him and then returned to the couch. "You know, I came here to kill you."

"No doubt. A family tradition."

Tristan put his hands together as if praying. He leaned forward, monitoring Fletcher's face. "You said you can't change it, you know: the past. I *know* you can't. But I can't either, Ryan. All I can do is try to do better, hm? Be a better man . . . from now on, like you. So, the question is, can *you* live with that? Because I've done things, things that you're going to know about: terrible things. You weren't there, so you can't imagine. And now, I can't change it."

The admission sent blood to Fletcher's face. "Lad, I can live with anything you've done. In a way, your deeds are mine, because I *wasn't* there."

"I've killed, Ryan. At the time I thought the cause was just."

"And now?"

"And, now, I just want to be. Now, I want to be small. Now there's only our side."

Fletcher tilted his head and smiled. "Agreed. Our side." He reached for the decanter. "So, tell me something. How did Eckhart convince you to join his . . . holy war?"

"He'll tell you, I'm sure. You think it will be easy, but it won't. Then, you'll have to decide."

The clock was chiming seven. Tristan rolled on to the carpet, running his hand through Oliver's coat with his eyes closed. Fletcher shuffled into the kitchen. He'd throw together a seafood salad for dinner. He'd use up the spinach and escarole. He had some melon. They'd turn in early. Just for a few minutes, he'd do the usual on a most unusual day.

69

Corey walked into the office with Tuesday's posted schedule glaring back at her: Corey Martin: floor duty, 10:00 – 4:00. Dana was looking at her strangely.

"What?" Corey snapped. "I know I'm late! Any calls?"

"No."

"So? What's the matter?"

"You'll see."

Corey eyed her suspiciously, and then rounded the partition and gasped. On her desk weren't a dozen long-stem roses, but two: all red. She approached them cautiously as if they were a mirage, albeit the envelope perched amid the blooms looked real enough. She donned her glasses and opened it.

Sorry about the car and my abysmal behavior. I'll make it up to you. Fletch

She reread it three times before tossing it in the basket. The man was a torment. She decided to wait until the afternoon to call him, musing whether she'd even mention the flowers. She moved the bouquet to her filing cabinet, realizing that Dana must have put them in water, as the huge vase was the one usually parked on the front desk. Corey peered around the corner.

"Dana!"

"What?"

"Thanks, and I'm sorry about the other day."

There was a pause. "Who are they from?"

"You don't want to know," Corey giggled.

"Oh," Dana responded. "In that case, they must be from *Fletchah Loowson.*"

70

While Tristan rustled up some music for the journey, Fletcher was feeling the effects of another bout of guilt. Guilt was his least favorite affliction, and, like an allergy, it seemed to flare-up every time he went near a woman. Corey was the latest provocation. Against his better judgment, he ordered roses for her, knowing it was a salve at best. Fletcher was accustomed to accusations of using people. He also knew when he didn't deserve it. In Corey's case – he had to admit - it was a gray area: murky gray.

It was just eleven when he stopped at the local bank and withdrew a fistful of twenties. He handed some cash to his son. He was a daily reminder of his mother. Of course, his mother had been so different from anyone. He wondered at what point he could approach Tristan about the truth: that she was alive. He sighed. Not today.

Once in Denver, Fletcher pulled up to a used electronics store and dashed in. He reappeared within minutes. It was another twenty minutes to Porter's empty executive suite. Passing it slowly, he parked a block east. Tristan had already opened the bags containing the two recorders and remotes, simpering at the sight of them.

"Ryan Fletcher, you don't really think. . . ."

"Yes, I do. Put the batteries in. Make sure they work."

Tristan played with the buttons. "They do, but they're antiques!"

Wait a minute." Fletcher exited with the remotes and backed away from the car door until Tristan signaled that he was out of range. "Just enough!" Fletcher announced.

Tristan lit from the seat. "This is *absurd!* They'll find them! Believe me!"

"We have to make this quick. Come on."

Fletcher felt reasonably safe in broad daylight, especially since Porter's office park was bustling. While Tristan stood guard out of sight below the stairs, Fletcher trotted briskly up to Door Number One and knocked loudly. There was no answer. He pounded on Number Two with the same result. He clattered downstairs to the rental. The landlord had replaced the lock, predictably, with the cheapest one he could find. Fletcher had three old skeleton keys in his pocket. The first one worked.

He ducked into the unit and scaled to the drop ceiling via the window sill. He slid a panel back and deposited the recorder. He tested the remote from the floor. It was working. With the so called acoustic tile replaced, he exited. Gaining entry next door was even easier. The massage therapist had left the door open. He climbed on to the bed, hid the second recorder in the ceiling and left quickly. He signaled to Tristan.

"That's it?" Tristan was incredulous.

"That's it. Come on."

They walked briskly to the car. Tristan shut the door and turned to his father. "You can hear voices from below?"

"If it's quiet. Porter might have guessed, which is why your meetings have been held over the unoccupied office. But, it really doesn't matter. They won't have the inclination to check every single ceiling panel. And what they'd sweep for isn't something like this: something you'd use for music or shopping lists."

"Still. . . ."

"Look, Tristan, I'm not the C.I.A. It's the best I can do, given the circumstances. If they find them, so be it. Hungry?"

They ate Mexican and were back at the house by two. Tristan revisited Don Christoval's cave, returning with the news that it had drained considerably. He wanted to go riding, but said he would stay close. Fletcher was concentrating on the internet, sending him off with a thumb up and a last minute directive.

"Take the dog!"

Public information about Trans-Origins, Inc. was scant. Information about Porter was scarce, too. He was on a pharmaceutical board: scary enough. Fletcher managed to find him referenced in a few articles about cloning and one about genetically modified crops. Pete was right; Porter was a visionary. He was talking in practical terms about human cloning and gene manipulation when it was still, essentially, science fiction. Fletcher could find nothing authored by the man in the last ten years. He was either so fed up or so far ahead of his colleagues that he found them a bore; maybe both. Fletcher logged off. He hoped Harvey would have better luck.

Pete would be another hour, so Fletcher decided to clean up a bit. He wrestled the vacuum out of the hall closet and dragged it into the study, knowing he wouldn't be able to hear himself think which seemed idyllic. He wondered why Corey hadn't called. With a flick of the switch, the machine roared across the Orientals, slurping up Oliver hair under the desk. Fletcher shifted to the coffee table, then shoved the sofa back to be thorough. He was whistling over the din when the vacuum whimpered to a halt. He looked at the outlet. The plug was out, trapped under an Oxford shoe.

Fletcher recognized him: one of Porter's attendees. He was tall and had a drooping eye. The two recorders were under his arm. The man dropped them on the floor and took a step toward the housecleaner. Fletcher opened his mouth, but the man put a cautionary finger to his lips.

"Mr. Lawson, I have a message." He was soft spoken and European. "You have an appointment. You are to come alone." He pause, then added, "It's important for you to understand that I am here as a courtesy. Do you understand?"

Fletcher's breath was shallow. "Yes."

"Are you sure that you understand *why* it's a courtesy?"

"Yes."

"Good." The intruder turned to the door, glancing at Fletcher over his shoulder. As he stepped into the hallway, he was slammed into the door jamb. Tristan was holding him by his jacket. A gun was parked against the man's temple. Tristan slipped his hand under the intruder's lapel and extracted a pistol.

Fletcher's mouth was so dry he could barely speak. "All right. He was leaving. It was the recorders, that's all."

Tristan had an unrecognizable stare. His lips were white. He was spitting into the man's ear.

"Claude, you will leave *as a courtesy*, you understand?"

The man's nod was barely detectable.

"Are you sure you understand *why it's a courtesy?*" Tristan twisted the gun into the man's hair.

Claude said nothing.

Fletcher inched forward. "All right, let him go. Please. It was a warning, that's all. Please, Tristan, let him leave!"

Tristan shadowed Claude beyond the front door to the crest of the driveway, then watched the trespasser rush down the gravel to his car. He waited until the car disappeared. Trudging back toward the house, he met Fletcher at the entryway. He pushed past him.

"*I told you, didn't I?* Claude! That French fool!"

Fletcher trailed him. "God, you scared the hell out of me."

Tristan wheeled around, keeping both guns aimed at the floor. "Well, perhaps now you'll be – what is it you English say – sensible? *How could you think something so stupid would work?*"

Fletcher leaned into Tristan's ear and whispered, "Actually, old boy, I think it did."

71

With Oliver beside him, an English bartender was sitting on the front stoop with a fresh scotch on the rocks. Pete had just arrived, wearing a gray suit. He plucked the drink from Fletcher's hand, took two sips and strolled into the house. Fletcher tracked after him into the half vacuumed study. The friar eased onto the sofa, already through most of his Dewars.

"Hmm, that is good, Fletch!" He offered his glass for a refill.

"How did it go, today?"

"As expected. The congregation loves me. The church elders think I'm too radical. I still don't know what that means."

"And?"

"And I'm not fired yet, if that's you mean. I told you how that works. But, I'm not here to talk about me. What's going on?"

"Well, actually, Pete, I've been giving it some thought. I'm not sure I can involve you."

"Oh, come on, Fletcher!"

"Pete, listen, I'm serious. It's not what you think. These people could hurt you . . . hurt your family."

"Let me guess: Tristan. He's involved with hoodlums."

"No."

"Well then?"

"Worse."

"What's worse? Murderers? Terrorists?"

"Have another drink."

The bloodhound's eyes followed his host to the bottle. "Fletcher, the other night you were asking about Eckhart. How do you know him? Does this have to do with him?"

Fletcher handed his friend another scotch. "Pete, you can't utter a word about this, not to anyone at all. Tristan's life depends on it and so does mine."

"Here we go again. *What?* What's going on?"

"If I tell you, it's only because I'm selfish. They could hurt your family. I mean it."

Pete put down his drink, looking more sober than when he arrived. "Fletcher, what on earth are you involved in?"

"I'm not sure."

"Just start from the beginning. It'll be all right. I'm a big boy."

The story of Tristan and Eckhart unfolded as impartially as a troubled father could tell it. For the duration, Pete sat motionless, listening intently through the folds of his long face. He didn't touch his drink. He would occasionally ask a question, but was more inclined to let Fletcher fill in the blanks later, as – he had learned - was his habit. The narrator finally poured himself his own scotch, concluding that he had a meeting scheduled tomorrow night. Pete took a deep breath, rubbing his forehead.

"You're not going to like this, but you *know* you're way over your head. It's a matter for the authorities. They have to be told. If there's a grain of truth to this. . . ."

"They can't be told, Pete."

"Fletcher, be reasonable. We're not talking about *just you or Tristan*. We're talking about - maybe - some kind of plot. Look, it's probably not that serious, maybe it's nothing, but we still need to. . . ."

"No! You listen to me, Pete. They'll lock Tristan away. I know how it works. He's not what he was! He was a troubled boy and *used!* But a beaurocracy's not forgiving. It's full of nasty, petty little. . . . *I know what I'm talking about!* The answer's no. I would never do that."

"Fletcher. . . ."

"No!"

"Look, I agree with you to a certain extent, but deals can be. . . ."

"I asked you for your help, Pete! You're the one that said that it's easy to love your own children; it's loving other people's that's hard. Well, I'm asking you to love mine! I don't care what they do to me, but Tristan has a shot at a life. What if there's nothing to this, as you said? Then his is wasted and so is mine!"

"And if there is something to it?"

"Then, we'll do whatever we can to change it. But, no authorities, Pete."

Pete sighed. "So, how do you think I can help, Fletch?"

"If I get you information, get his data or something, can you tell me if what he's planning is scientifically feasible?"

"Oh I don't know. Really, Fletcher, this sounds crazy. And what if whatever it is – assuming there's something at all - *is* feasible?"

"Then, and only then, can you make that phone call. But, I want a running start with Tristan."

Pete reached for his scotch and closed his eyes. "Well, Fletch, all right, then. But you shouldn't go alone tomorrow. I'll go with you."

"No, Pete."

"I said I'll go. You already told Eckhart."

"I know but I was warned."

"Oh for heaven's sake. *Warned!* Look, don't worry. He'll put up with me."

"And your family?"

"It just so happens they're leaving for my mother's on Friday. They'll be in Maine for a couple of weeks."

"And Ellen?"

"Her, too. Tabor's coming back early, and she's nursing a broken heart, *as we all know.*" Pete's nostrils flared as he cleared his throat. "Better she gets away."

"Pete, maybe it's not what you think; maybe he really does care for her."

"Oh sure. In the meantime, would you give him this?" Pete withdrew Ellen's log book from his jacket pocket, and tossed it on the coffee table. "Ask him to undo whatever he did, not that it really matters. I'm just making a point."

Tristan was at the doorway. "She told you?"

Pete eyed him over the back rest and then pulled himself up from the sofa. "So what time tomorrow?"

72

It was after six when Corey called. Fletcher asked her to hold on. Tristan had decided to try his luck at riding again, saying he would circle the house. He gave his father Claude's gun, demanding that he keep it by him at all times. Fletcher immediately assigned it to a kitchen drawer when Tristan left. He returned to the phone.

"Corey, I was beginning to wonder. . . ."

"Wonder what? Whether I'd mention the flowers?"

"Ah. But you couldn't help yourself. How are you, Corey?"

"Worn out. Anyway, thank you. They're beautiful. You busy?"

"Making supper. It's all right."

"O.K. So, Fletch, you want the good news or the bad?"

"Let's start out with the good news. I could use some."

"Mackey wants to go to contract, but he wants to meet with you personally about the terms."

"Really? Why?"

"Oh, he always does that," she scoffed. "He likes to meet with the *principals*."

"When?"

"Next week. I'll find out."

"And the other news? The car, I take it."

"Yup. It'll cost roughly three thousand to fix. My deductible's a thousand."

"All right."

"The license plate you gave me? "The car's a company lease."

"What company?"

"I think Ziffon, Inc."

"Ziffon? Where is it? Denver? Local?"

"Who cares?"

"Just curious."

"So, back to the flowers. What's on your mind, Fletcher?"

"I just . . . I wanted you to know that I'm not a complete ass." Fletcher tucked the phone under his chin and pulled the phone book out. He opened it to Z in the business section. "Well, yes I am, but I wanted to compensate for it somehow."

"And?"

"Um . . . and . . . nothing! Nothing, Corey. I just don't want you to be angry with me."

"That's it?"

"Yes." There was no listing for Ziffon, Inc. "Is that so bad?"

"You know, Fletcher, I've know you for a *long* time. I met you when you were still married."

"Has it been that long?"

"Uh huh. I was probably the first to meet you. I'm your closest neighbor, even if I am a mile away. And maybe you don't know, Fletch, how I feel. . . ."

"Hold on, Corey! I'm burning something." Fletcher dropped the phone by the microwave, leaving it there for a full minute before retrieving it. "All right, I'm back."

Banking on her impatience, he still felt strangely awful when she wasn't there. He'd call her later. He dialed information. There was indeed a phone number for Zephon – with an *e* and a *ph* – Inc., and - according to the area code – it was around Denver somewhere. He hurried to the computer and logged on. Zephon, Inc. had an address, but it wasn't familiar. Mapquest showed it as a big lemon star in a virtual alley north of I-70. He jotted down the directions.

* * *

Fletcher was finishing a salad when Tristan swaggered in smelling like his hobby. A five o'clock shadow was peeking through at seven p.m. Fletcher pointed to an omelet still on the stove. Tristan helped himself and pulled up to the table with a glass of wine.

"Where's the gun?"

Fletcher dabbed his mouth with a napkin. "In the drawer."

Tristan sipped his cabernet. "What good is it in there?"

"How's your dinner?"

"I asked you a question, Ryan."

"I'm not a gunslinger, Tristan." Fletcher rose and shagged the wine from the counter.

"Have you ever fired one?"

"No."

"Then, I'll teach you."

"I have no interest."

Tristan buttered a piece of bread. "You better have an interest. You need to defend yourself. Like today."

"I didn't even hear that man. If he had wanted to kill me, he would have."

"But if you had a gun. . . ."

"Look, I don't want one, all right? I'll keep it by the bed as promised. But, the truth is I'd like to get through my life without shooting anybody. Is that too much to ask?"

"Maybe."

Fletcher topped off Tristan's glass and filled his own. "I know you're fascinated with weaponry. I saw the websites. I can only hope that from here on out, you understand that nothing good comes of it."

"You're wrong, Ryan. You may not like the idea, but protecting yourself is important. If you can't protect yourself, you can't defend your family, your friends, or *anything else* that matters to you. At some time, everybody has enemies. Now you have enemies. You need to be their equal. It's the way of life."

"So, what's the *anything else* that matters to you, Tristan? What's worth someone's life?"

Tristan was munching on lettuce. "I don't know. Freedom."

"Ah. Freedom! Yes, well, it seems everyone has a different idea of what that is. Personally, I don't think it exists. But, for whatever its worth, your grandfather would be proud of you. He believed in freedom. He certainly did." Fletcher emptied his glass with one swallow.

Tristan put down his fork. "Do you remember him?"

"No."

"Do you know anything about him?"

"Let's see. He was twenty-three when I was born. A year later he blew the arms off a young English soldier – younger than you – with a bomb. Noble, don't you think? And he shot two more: one in the chest, and the other in the leg while the poor bloat was running away. They survived, but a third one was killed trying to arrest him somewhere on the coast. He left a wife and a baby with no support, all in the name of freedom. That's it. That's all I know, other than you could do better than to be like him."

"Do you ever wonder if that's true? Do you ever wonder about him?"

"No."

"And are you sure he. . . ?"

"It was all over the newspapers, Tristan. I looked it up when I got older."

Tristan declared himself stuffed. He put his dish in the sink, found an ashtray in the cabinet, and returned to the table with a cigarette. "What about your mother?"

"What about her?"

"What was she like?"

"A drunk. Probably still is." Fletcher rose abruptly and went to the sink. Tristan cracked a window, letting his smoke spiral outside.

"Ryan, have you decided what you want to do when this house sells?"

Fletcher stooped to give the omelet pan to Oliver. "Yes. Leave."

"Where?"

"I used to think Spain. Lately I'd settle for any place where nobody's looking. That, to me, is freedom."

"How will you leave?"

"How will *we* leave, I think, is what you mean." Fletcher applied himself to the dirty pots and pans. "I don't know. Get on a plane and go."

"What if I can't?"

Fletcher dropped a sponge and pivoted. "Why can't you get on a plane?"

"I came on a false passport."

"What do you mean?

"A false passport!"

So, you got here with it, you can leave with it."

"No, I can't."

"Why not?"

"Because I don't have it."

Fletcher folded his arms. "Eckhart's got it."

"Yes."

"So that's what Claude was *really* doing here."

"It seems so."

Fletcher closed his eyes, summoning his strength. "Well, Tristan, all I can tell you is that if we can't get it back, you'll have to learn how to swim. So much for *the French fool.*"

Tristan spent the remainder of the evening in front of Don Christoval's journal. With a notepad and pen, he was deciphering the text when Fletcher turned in. But the Falcon of Navarre was not confined to his script that night. Twice he slipped into Fletcher's dreams. He was standing on the ridge above the cave, ankle deep in snow, murmuring softly. His hair was brushed with ice, his skin white, his breath a blue vapor. Behind him stood Little John. Pale and frost covered, the horse silently pawed the tundra. The conquistador was beckoning to the dreamer, but the dreamer would not oblige him. Early in the morning, the Falcon reappeared with the horse, motioning Fletcher toward the animal, but again, Fletcher refused to go near. The ancient Iberian was trying to send him forth, but Fletcher was afraid, lest he never see his raptor again.

73

The dawn arrived with the salutation of bluebirds. A pair had been nesting outside the window, in a cedar house installed there many years ago. Fletcher shuffled down the corridor to check on Tristan. His door was open. The television was still on. Fletcher shut it off. Tristan groaned and went back to sleep while the Englishman carried on. With Oliver discharged, Fletcher set about making coffee as he done for decades even though the day was like no other: Porter Eckhart was waiting at the other end of it.

Fletcher had hoped to hear from Harvey prior to the last minute, but Harvey had deliberately cut it close. When the phone rang, Fletcher seized it. Harvey was smug; one ring.

"Lawson? I have your information."

"Shoot."

"Not until I see my disc, then you can have the whole three pages."

"That's it?"

"That's it. I told you. And, who knows, *you* might find it fascinating."

"I went to see your friend, Harvey. Your friend told me that *you* have the other half of what I paid for. I do hope that's the case."

"Yeah, I got it, ready to go. I just want a square deal."

"Then, how's six, Harvey?"

"That'll work."

"See you then."

"Don't forget anything, Lawson."

74

Pete's Wednesday afternoon was usually booked through six, so when he arrived home before five, Ruth knew something was up. She demanded to know what. He was vague about his evening plans, something about accompanying a friend on personal business. She was hunched over, scouring the kitchen floor for a button that had just fallen off Dillon's jeans. Nabbing it, she shot up, demanding to know what *friend* that would be. When it turned out to be Fletcher, her eyes narrowed.

"You know, Pete, the boys could use your time. You only have tonight and tomorrow night, and then we leave for two weeks."

"I know. But, I told him I would go, so. . . ."

"What *kind* of personal business, that he can't take care of it by himself?"

"Ruth, you know I can't divulge a confidence, even to you."

"Did you see what he did to Corey's car?"

"It was an accident!"

"Well, Pete, you have three sons and a daughter here that would like to make an appointment to see you, and since Fletcher isn't even a member. . . ."

"Ruth, please don't. I'll be home tomorrow night."

"Oh? And what happened to chess night? Isn't that tomorrow?"

"I won't go. I'll stay home."

"He's using you, Pete!"

"Ruth, that's unfair!"

"It's not unfair! *I know it!* Look at Corey's car! That's what he does to everybody."

"Ruth, I promise, I'll stay home tomorrow night."

"Oh, stop acting like you're doing us a big favor! This is your family, *remember?*"

She slammed the button on the kitchen table, snatched her purse from the back of a chair and headed for the door.

Pete trailed after her. "Where are you going?"

She wheeled around and glared at him. "To pick up the boys, remember? From day camp? *Now that you have something better to do!*"

He clapped his forehead. He had completely forgotten. As she sped away, he glanced at his watch. Fletcher would be there any minute.

✳ ✳ ✳

Tristan was stretched across the rear seat like a happy python while Pete was squeezed in like an ointment tube in the front. Fletcher was driving straight into the late afternoon glare. The dirty windshield was blinding. The visors didn't seem to help.

"You comfortable, Pete? The seat might go back."

"I'm fine. There's not a car in the world designed for anyone over six foot four."

"I can pull over. You can trade places with Tristan."

"No, no. I'm fine, Fletch. I have air and the pleasure of not having to drive."

"All right. Listen, I have a stop to make. I'll only be a few minutes. Keep it running."

Fletcher pulled into a parking space and departed. Tristan looked up from his notes.

Pete glanced back. "What are you up to, Tristan?"

"Translating."

"Oh? Anything interesting?"

"I just started."

"Oh." Pete closed his eyes. The air conditioner was blowing gently in his face. He wondered what California was like this time of year. Maybe Ruth would be happier there. Maybe she'd be happier without him.

The news was softly droning on: natural disasters, terrorist threats, war, dirty politics. Pete punched the channel changer and found a jazz station. Tristan was oblivious, absorbed in his scrawl. His father appeared at the back window with a knock and an ebony box. Tristan received it along with a blast of afternoon heat.

Fletcher slid into the driver's seat. "We're off! Just enough time to grab a bite and settle in. Here, Pete. Have a look at this." He dumped a three page printout onto Pete's lap.

The first page was all about Porter Eckhart, including the fact that he had gone through a daunting personal fortune to keep Trans-Origins, Inc. afloat. About six years ago, that all changed. Porter was able to stop spending and start grossing. He was now Trans-Origin's emperor, although prior to his sole appointment, his rule was shared with a high profile environmentalist named Georgia Russell. Pete remembered her. She was a knock-out that visited campus regularly. Porter was an only child, the son of a couple who had parlayed a mining company into a real estate empire. They were killed in a car accident when Porter was in high school. His inheritance was held in trust until he was twenty-five. At that point, he took the helm of his financial future, and his family assets sailed smoothly into a few hundred million and recently to billions.

His personal wealth was common knowledge, but what wasn't, was that he had married. It had only lasted a year. His ex-wife was Georgia. She got a bundle out of it, but so did he, in the form of a daughter, Sandra. Porter was sixty years old. His offspring was twenty-nine. She was named Trans-Origin's Managing Vice President, but - if it was the same girl Fletcher had seen that night - it had to be in name only. She seemed too vapid for the job.

Ex-wife Georgia was still a prominent member of the team. With the exception of three Europeans, the core staff was all American and star-studded, at least, as far as Pete was concerned. He rattled off their names and disciplines –climatology, paleontology, geology, biology, astronomy, etc. - with a well-known geek rounding out the list. They were once poor, loud-mouth radicals, but - as of late - were enjoying accolades and monumental salaries; they deserved it. They had been devoted to the company throughout its long nonprofit tenure right into its recent income-producing blitz. Although he was rarely credited, there was little doubt that Porter was a genius. Pete was citing his degrees when Fletcher interrupted him.

"Skip over all that, Pete."

"Intimidated?"

"I'm more interested in, uh, you know. . . ."

"Dirt."

"Yes."

Pete scanned the page. "Sorry, Fletch, the rest of it's patent holdings and so on. He's on the board of a pharmaceutical company. His assets are listed. Let's see. His headquarters used to be in Massachusetts, then he moved his ops to Europe. He has three company addresses actually: one in Belgium, one in Switzerland and one in Spain."

"Anything on who he deals with? Trade, anything?"

"Nope. Sorry."

"Anything on Zephon, Inc.?"

"On what?"

"A company named Zephon, Inc."

Pete chuckled. "Strange name: *Paradise Lost*. Yes, it's mentioned here. Just some satellite."

"How about his clients?"

"Sorry. Fletch. Oh! But, here's something I never would've guessed. It would explain his interest in genetics."

"What?"

"He's a hemophiliac."

✳ ✳ ✳

On Broadway, Fletcher found a side street, parked and went over the plan. Nobody liked it, but nobody had a better one, so he would go in alone. He had already planted a tiny transmitter in the molding joint of Door Number One and, likewise, in Door Number Two. That afternoon, Harvey had issued the rest of the package: a battery operated receiver with duel recording capabilities. It would work as long as they were within a reasonable range, and because the listening devices were highly sensitive, the transmissions should be loud and clear. That said, all the equipment was stolen and black market stuff. Pete rolled his eyes.

Fletcher handed them each a cell phone with pre-paid minutes. He told them to stay together and *keep a low profile*. If the recorder didn't work, he ordered them to get out of there. Harvey's information was worthless so it's not like there would be any other leverage with Porter.

At the appointed hour, Fletcher left the Volvo and walked four blocks west to the office park. Tristan took the wheel, drove south and then turned east behind Porter's suites. Fletcher had instructed him to park in a driveway next to a transmission repair shop, being reasonably sure that the car would be overlooked.

Fletcher reached the fringe of the lot with platinum Mathew falling in step beside him. He came out of nowhere, holding out his hand and introducing himself. He directed Fletcher underneath the steps where Claude was waiting. Mathew apologized for the pat down, citing procedure. Fletcher ascended the stairs with his escorts trailing. Waiting on the balcony of Unit Two, Porter was wearing a light suit, a loose tie and dark rim glasses. What was left of his silver hair was sprinkled with blonde and blowing in the wind. Porter extended his hand. Fletcher shook it and then stepped into the humble bureau. The office was comprised of a long formica table and eight chairs, two metal desks – one covered with papers - and a couple of computers tied to a laser printer. There was no wall fluff. The floor was scuffed linoleum.

"Please sit down, Fletcher. Anywhere. It's quite a shock seeing the original. Tristan looks so much like you. Can I get you anything?"

"No thanks." Fletcher remained standing.

Claude and Mathew took seats near the door. Fletcher noticed two large battered briefcases on the floor. Porter hoisted one up on a chair, peering at Fletcher over his glasses. "Please, Fletcher, sit down. Make yourself comfortable. I have quite a bit to show you."

The guest eased into a chair near his host. Porter was sorting through heaps of charts and reports, piling them on the table. He extracted three bound notebooks and arranged them in front of his company. He swept the rest aside.

"Fletcher, what I am about to show you is quite upsetting. But, so you know, what I'm showing you has been issued to every industrialized nation's government and completely dismissed. Of course, we stand by it and can prove it. Now, before I begin, I assume you are aware of global warming, or to be politically correct: *climate change*?"

"Yes."

"And you understand the underlying causes?"

"Only what I've read: fossil fuels, emissions. I haven't been paying much attention."

Porter chuckled. "Well, you're not alone. But you do accept it as fact?"

"Yes, I think so."

"Good. Because it is fact, and, although global fluctuations are normal, this particular episode is unprecedented in terms of the breadth of time and the degree of the increase."

"Yes, I've read some dire predictions, that by the end of the century. . . ."

"Ah. Not quite, Fletcher. Not by the end of the century. Let me explain. You see, people of today don't see themselves living a hundred years. Consequently, they are content to live with an imminent catastrophe, as long as it's not *too imminent*. A century's a comfortable margin, so that's the time-frame projected. They're happy to let another generation deal with it."

"Yes, but it is being fixed. Hydrogen cars along with curbs on emissions. . . ."

"There's no time for that anymore, Fletcher. It would take twenty years to put all the SUV drivers into hydrogen cars, not to mention developing a clean energy source for billions, even if I were to be optimistic. But it's all moot, anyway. The reality is: we're out of time."

"I beg your pardon?"

"To be precise, we have less than twenty-four months to diffuse a ticking bomb. The bomb is global warming, but there's no *long* century to its detonation. We have exactly thirty-three years before the very last man walks this planet. Most mammalian and amphibious life will be extinct within that time frame. In fact, all of life as we know it will cease to exist, with the exception of a few hardy microbes and maybe the die-hard cockroaches."

Fletcher gaped at the cherub-face. The little man sat back. "How old would Tristan be? Let's see, in his fifties I would think, assuming he lasts 'til the bitter end."

"That's ridiculous. You can't be right." Fletcher fingered an unopened notebook. "How can that be possible?"

"That's why you're here. I'm going to show you." Porter shoved a large folded diagram toward his visitor. "We'll start with Exhibit A: the one no one wants to see. The earth's substratum is heating up. Heat causes. . . . ?"

"Expansion."

"Good! Take a look."

Pete and Tristan were barely breathing, glued to the receiver. As promised, the conversation was pitch perfect. The only part of Fletcher's strategy that hadn't worked was the car's assignment. As it turned out, there was no signal from the ordained parking space. Consequently, the two eavesdroppers were crouched beside a dumpster, in the middle of a stinking alley, listening to the chronicle of their ruin, all from an innocuous gray box. Porter was explaining the problem in layman's terms, and, although the cause was theoretical, it had a sickening ring of truth. Trans-Origins, Inc. had been monitoring tectonic movement, noticing unnerving shifts. They were not dramatic, just more frequent and in peculiar areas, not along the usual plate seams. Thermal monitoring from along the sea floor led the staff to theorize that magma was swelling at an unusual rate, but couldn't confirm the findings without comparative readings in key areas around the world. It took several years. Porter had depended on temperature and chemical readouts, underlying volcanic activity, glacial movement and the rise of mountains as evidence. But the seabed was the critical factor. Three areas in the Pacific and four in the Atlantic had shown a marked increase in temperature. About six years ago, they went off the charts.

Essentially, the earth's exhaust valve wasn't functioning, due in large part to an atmosphere so clogged with particulates that it couldn't shed excessive heat. Human actions created more warmth and, consequently, the earth required a better exhaust system. As Porter explained it, the earth could have supported life as we know it for another million years had it not been for a dramatic increase in the effecting population and a drastic reduction in the resources that tempered the effects. What very few realized was that the ramifications were running deep into the earth's layers, and the conventional figures were wrong. Glacial melt-off was already exceeding the accepted projections because the earth's crust was warming faster than anticipated. Although its core was cooling, the globe's mantle was overheating like an engine, its underlying fluid critically expanding because the mitigating atmospheric release was no longer there. If nothing was done, it would eventually right itself with a few massive eruptions and major tectonic shifts to discharge the pressure. Although the planet would probably survive it, its swarming multitudes would not. Pete had been right. Fletcher was over his head.

Porter asked Mathew to get some water. Fletcher examined the spreadsheets and reports. He flipped through a particularly lengthy notebook and then folded his arms.

"I really don't know what I'm looking at. I can only assume that there's some kind of mistake. How could something like this happen so quickly?"

"Actually, it's been going on for quite a while; we just haven't had the means – until recently – to pay close enough attention."

"So, assuming that your data is correct, what's your solution? You must have one or I wouldn't be sitting here."

Porter straightened his shoulders, receiving his water politely. Fletcher contemplated him. It all seemed so normal: a conference in a dingy complex on a Wednesday evening to discuss an imminent apocalypse. It was no different than a meeting to discuss the latest sales figures. Fletcher shifted his gaze to his glass. It was a simple container of water with a couple of chunks of ice. It wouldn't exist in thirty-three years. It was unfathomable. Porter cleared his throat.

"You're not going to like it, any more than I do. Yet, I'm grateful there is potentially one. Unfortunately, it requires a hard decision and sacrifice."

"Go on."

"As you must know, my specialty is bio-engineering . . . genetic manipulation. Without going into detail, I have a substance that can effectively solve the problem."

"Yes?"

"Well, Fletcher, in order to halt the current trend, it must be done *now*. It requires an immediate and fundamental change in how we function. It means eradicating a good portion of that which is exacerbating the problem. That said, it would only buy us time. But, we think that we could slow the increase, given a *radically* friendlier infrastructure, an opportune invention and a reduction in – how shall put this – the contributors to the problem."

"The contributors to the problem. . . . The contributors are people, are they not?"

"A select group."

"*My God!* You actually mean it! You can't be serious!"

"There's no alternative unless you want to lose the entire human race and every other. . . ."

"That's preposterous!"

"Fletcher, calm down. It's *not* preposterous! What I'm talking about is real. Do you think I like it?"

"Notify somebody then!"

"We have! I told you."

"And?"

"And, whether or not you want to believe it, the majority of governments are not run by far-sighted, caring, responsible individuals! Governments are run by power-mongers and idiots: politicians! Politicians are concerned with elections, not bad news. Even those that have acknowledged the facts think that somehow, they will be exempt."

"So *who is* exempt?"

"*No one* if the current trend continues! No human will survive a series of super volcanoes coupled with massive quakes! Islands will disappear; land masses will be unrecognizable. No food source will be available, not that it would matter. The air will be too toxic for mammalian life, anyway. So, given what you now know, what would you do?"

"I'd make them listen to me!"

"Ah! Well they won't! And even if they did, governments are not set up to affect timely change. It would take thirty years just to argue policy. So, tell me, Fletcher, do we all go down with the ship, or do we manage to preserve a good portion of the passengers? It's Noah's Ark, you know. We can hold on to life as we know it or we can abolish it all. What would you do?"

"It can't be true."

"Now you sound like every other recipient of our report. Fletcher, let me put it bluntly. I can save you. Tristan would have a fighting chance. . . ."

"What do you mean: *a fighting chance?*" What do you need him for?"

"He's a courier."

"Why do you need *him?* Get somebody else. Isn't it some paramilitary thug you're looking for?"

"No. No one's like him."

"Why?"

"To be effective, key packages have to be opened."

"What packages? What are you talking about?"

"You know damn well what I mean. Tristan's immune."

"Immune? *How do you know?*"

"He didn't tell you then."

"Tell me what?"

Porter pulled a handkerchief from his pocket and dabbed his upper lip. "He's the one that delivered the package to De Sernet."

Fletcher hung on Porter's words while Pete watched Tristan crush glass with his heel. Through an interminable silence, he never met Pete's gaze. Porter had told the truth.

Had it not been for Fletcher's safety, Pete would have stormed the symposium at the first mention of the solution. But Tristan's sharp reminder served as restraint. Claude and Mathew were most certainly armed, and Fletcher had been adamant: it was up to him to broker a deal. In the event that he failed, Tristan would intervene, but only outside the building, where the openness would give him an advantage. Pete was about to address him when Tristan held up his hand. Fletcher was muttering something.

"Porter, I think it's only fair that I'm able to review the documents."

"You have all night, Fletcher. I'm here to answer any questions."

"I mean, with someone knowledgeable. I'm not. . . ."

"As I said, I'm here to explain it. The data's all there. Take as long as you need. Would you like dinner?"

"No, thank you."

"Mathew, would you be so kind to pick up some Chinese around the corner there? Nothing too spicy. For four. Oh, and coffee if that shop's still open."

Mathew acknowledged the request by exiting. Fletcher fiddled with a graph. "You said a select group?"

"An industrialized group."

"And so, how would that. . . ."

"Governments would destabilize. The old guard would be immediately replaced."

"I see. So, it's politics."

"I have no interest in politics, Fletcher. But, obviously, it has to be addressed."

"No, it *is* all about politics, Porter. Politics and power. You must have quite a following."

Porter removed his glasses and rubbed the bridge of his nose. He shut his eyes; he was perspiring slightly.

Fletcher flexed his jaw. "I can't understand how this plan could possibly affect global temperature to such an extent that. . . ."

"It won't. We're not solving the problem, Fletcher. We're simply *stemming the tide*. We're *buying time*, that's all, and not a lot of it, but perhaps a permanent solution can be found."

"How much time are you buying?"

"It's hard to say. Hopefully enough."

"How will you know?"

"We have bench marks. The first one's in South America. It's classified as a super volcano that – if we are not successful – will erupt by 2020."

"In other words – despite the solution – you're not sure."

"Fletcher, all we can do – at this point – is take our foot off the accelerator, which is considerably better than doing nothing at all! That doesn't mean that we're not still out of control and careening toward the cliff. But with *immediate* modifications, we might have time to come up with a solution. You understand?"

"Porter, that's an awful lot of lives predicated on a maybe."

"Fletcher! *What's the matter with you? Have I not made myself clear?* They have no future anyway! In fact, *it's highly unlikely any of us would make it past the first eruption!* Read the damned data, Fletcher. It's all there. Right in front of you."

"But what if we do – as you say – all go down with the ship? Isn't that natural, isn't that. . . ."

"There's nothing natural about it! We're responsible for our own demise. Look, I'm not about to sit idly by, assigning us all to a mass extinction."

"But what you're doing, Porter, is. . . ."

"I can live with what I'm doing, if it's for the greater good, *and it is.* I can see that you have no interest in the facts. Claude, would you gather up the papers. Apparently, Fletcher's finished."

Claude rose, as did the guest. Porter stiffened; Claude immediately put one hand in his jacket.

"Sit down, Fletcher."

"No."

"I went to a great deal of effort to prepare this for you. I invited you here, expecting an intelligent discourse and an amicable conclusion to our business, only to have you. . . ."

"There's no business."

"I'm offering you *life*, Mr. Lawson, and Tristan. . . . "

"You offer Tristan nothing! You don't really think I would support something so monstrous! And what of Tristan? What does he get? *A fighting chance;* isn't that what you said? What the hell does that mean? It means that you think he'll either be shot or not survive the repeated exposure."

Porter stared at Fletcher. He stood abruptly, his right hand clutching a pen. He tapped it furiously on the table. "Fletcher, *he* is part of a plan to save lives: s*ave them!* You - of all people - talk about ethics, as if it's your strong suit. I'm talking about *humanity!* I'm talking about *life: all of it, as we know it!* Yes, there's a certain risk for Tristan. . . ."

"*A certain risk?* And what of the others? The other couriers with no immunity at all? You're murdering them, throwing their lives away!"

"*They'd do it anyway!* They think they're doing it for Al Qaeda or some other fanatical group! Look, Fletcher, Tristan's invaluable."

"Because he can make multiple deliveries?"

"For God's sake, I can make you a thousand Tristans! *What I cannot do is create another planet!*"

Fletcher lunged across the table, but a forearm caught him across the windpipe, pitching him backward to the floor. As he fell, he glimpsed the horrified genius from the corner of his eye. Claude's gun was leveled at Fletcher's temple, but Porter waved it away, crouching next to the gasping man.

"Fletcher, please. I don't want to hurt you. Try to be reasonable. Tristan would listen to you."

"There's only one Tristan, Porter."

"You're right, and it's his decision. Let me talk to him. He has a right."

"No. You'll only leverage my life against his."

"Fletcher, *there'll be nothing left.* Try to be magnanimous. *Try to think.* Even if Tristan doesn't survive, think of what his sacrifice would mean."

"*No!*"

"The issue at hand concerns the fate of every species on earth! Surely you can see that! Wouldn't you give his life – even your life - to save it all, to save *mankind?*"

From somewhere deep within, Fletcher found his diaphragm and drew from it all his resolve. He struggled to his elbow and smiled. "You're on your own."

Porter braced a hand against the table and pulled himself to his feet. He shook his head. Finding his glasses, he wearily cleaned them on his shirt sleeve. His eyes were bulging.

You know I can't let you leave."

"I don't know that you have much choice."

"Actually, I do. And, whether or not you realize this, you – yourself – may be quite valuable to me. Now, needless to say, with or without your cooperation, Tristan. . . ."

"Tristan won't be found. But what will be is this conversation, in the form of a CD. It will be put in the hands of some official, or perhaps dropped on someone's desk."

Porter's forehead lifted like a Venetian blind. "What are you talking about? Claude? You swept the offices, didn't you? Were you thorough?"

"Yes."

"What a pathetic attempt, Fletcher! I gave you more credit!"

Fletcher lurched to his feet. "I wouldn't expect you to take my word for it. You have a working phone? I suggest you call."

Fletcher plucked Porter's pen from the table and scrawled a large, insolent number over a particularly complicated chart. Porter glared at it and strode to the desk. "Fletcher, I hope for your sake, you haven't done something *irrevocably stupid!*" He dialed the number.

Pete's cell rang. He pulled it from his pocket and grappled with the keys in the dark. Tristan snatched it away, pushed the proper button, and handed it back.

"Hello."

"And this is?"

"Pete Peters. Hello Porter."

"Is it really you, Peters?"

"In the flesh."

"How would I know?"

"Georgia. Thanks to you, she'd have nothing to do with me."

"Well, then, Peters, it is you. Don't take it personally. She only wasted her time on fat wallets. It's been a long time. So why am I calling you?"

"I want a look at your data, Mr. Eckhart. I want to see what you see."

"What data would that be?"

"The same data that gives us roughly thirty-three years."

"Where are you?"

"All in good time, Porter."

"You know, I'm very upset, Peters. He's a damned fool, and so are you, to put yourself in this position."

"Oh, I don't know. Somebody had to. Anyway, there's a solution to everything. Let's solve the problem at hand. I have something you want; you have something I want. I'm for a chivalrous trade. What say you, Eckhart?"

"And why would I trust you, Peters?"

"You have my word, which has been good all my life. But, just for you, I'll swear on it."

"Ah yes! The minister! Well, that's very noble. You're a little out of your element, though, aren't you, Reverend?"

"Not at all. By the way, your theory is fascinating."

"Theory? I hate to disappoint you. It's neither a theory nor entirely mine."

"Regardless, Porter. You're willing to act on it. That makes you the owner of the consequences, right or wrong."

"Where are you, Peters?"

"Send Fletcher out alone."

"Where are you?"

"Send him and you'll have your recording: the only one. I'll swear to it."

"And you?"

"I told you. I want a look at your data."

"And what makes you think you'll go home to a warm, safe bed?"

"Well, Porter, I dare say, you've sent such a chill down my spine that I doubt I'll ever recover, warm bed or not."

Porter chuckled. "You're a good man, Peters. Always were. You wasted your education, but. . . ."

"That's yet to be seen. Send Fletcher out. I'll come in his stead."

"Where are you?"

"I'll be there. I assure you."

"How long will it take you?"

"Let him go."

Tristan snatched the phone and hung it up. "No more," he commanded.

Porter replaced the receiver, turning to Claude with a glower. "Claude. . . ."

"There's nothing here, Porter! I can show you."

"There's something somewhere. Where is it, Lawson? Don't waste my time."

"I'll be glad to let you know once we're safely on our way."

"Peters wants a look," Porter snarled, "so you'll be leaving without him."

"That's not what I had in mind."

"It's his option! Now, where's the. . . ?"

Mathew burst in. "Something's up," he shouted. "There's guys in the alley!"

Porter threw up his hands. Mathew flew out the door with Claude trailing but they were too late. The quarry was gone.

Twenty minutes later, Fletcher was released. The disc was handed over, and a larger than life apostle waited alone in the moonlight for entry into a seedy little office complex in Denver. But he was never admitted, his host disappearing into the darkness with a telephone call.

"I just don't have the heart, Peters. Not you, not tonight. Go home."

75

Fletcher was driving too fast, his face blank. Pete shifted uncomfortably, trying not to air brake at the approaching tail lights.

"Fletcher, take it easy; I think they're stopping."

"I see them!" Fletcher shot back. "What's the matter with you anyway? What could have possessed you to make such an offer?"

"Fletcher, slow down. I was concerned for you."

"The disc was sufficient! Why would you *meet* with him? Just what I need! *You* on my conscience! Have you gone mad?"

"No! And I might ask the same of you! I thought that was the point: to assess the data. I noticed you didn't give it a second look!"

"Why would I? What difference does it make? The man wants to annihilate a third of the population. Who cares *why*?"

"And what if he's right? Did you ever think of that?"

Fletcher slammed on the brake. Pete's seatbelt was so snug that he didn't move but his eyes popped open. The traffic had slowed to a crawl. Tristan rapped on the back of the driver's seat, warning the chauffer to pay more attention.

Fletcher rolled down his window. "Well, Pete, if he *is right*, what the hell can we do about it? Nothing!"

Pete shrugged. "We'll see. Right now, it's paramount that we listen."

"Listen? What a good idea. The last thing we'll ever hear."

"Not necessarily, Fletcher. He's not a psychotic."

"How do you know?"

"Because I'm sitting here and so are you." Pete jabbed a thumb at the air behind him. "And so is he."

Police lights were pulsating far ahead. Reds and blues skittered across windshields, slashing the night. Columns of cars were at a complete standstill. Fletcher threw up his hands. He had a million questions for Tristan, but not in front of Pete. He eyed the minister who was grinning like Mona Lisa. It was annoying.

"What are you smiling at? We're dealing with the epitome of evil here, Reverend."

Peter turned to him, his smile erased. "Evil? What's your definition?"

Fletcher craned his head out the window, looking for any sign of merciful movement. There was none, cornering him into a response.

"Evil. It's a lack of decency I suppose. A lack of common human decency."

"Decency. And what's that?"

"I don't know, Pete! You tell me! Is that an exit over there?"

"No. And decency, Fletch, is a matter of interpretation. The standard isn't universal."

"So?"

"So, then the same applies for what we consider evil."

"What are you saying, that Porter's a damn good fellow?"

"No, but he's not *evil*, Fletch. It's a term vastly overused, and frankly, counterproductive. Porter does, however, have a radically different point of view, and although it seems incomprehensible. . . ."

"Oh come on!"

"Hear me out, Fletch. You're less likely to excuse Porter because you don't love him as you do your own. But, it's important that you don't judge him. He doesn't see himself as malevolent, anymore that you see yourself as such . . . or Tristan." Pete glanced behind him and spoke slowly. "And yet, we've all done brutal, expedient things and felt justified at the time. Fear is driving him now. In his mind, he's altruistic; he's making a sacrifice. My advice to you is to stop arguing about his motives and offer him something compelling."

"*Like what?*"

"Like faith."

"Faith? *Faith? That's it?*"

Cars were merging into one lane. A mangled wreck was up ahead. A policeman was directing traffic. Flashing strobes were piercing retinas. Fletcher veered to the left, trying not to look. Pete rolled down his window.

"Listen, Fletch, I heard him tonight. He's a troubled man, and nowhere near as sure of himself as you think."

A van darted in front of them. Fletcher pounced on the brake, making a fist at the car. He looked around at his passengers, feeling his stomach tighten.

"Well, I must say, you're both taking this very well! No one's terribly alarmed! You must know something I don't! Wasn't it yesterday, Pete, that *you* wanted to run to the authorities? And what about you, Tristan? It seems to me that you intercepted an armed thug in the house or did I dream that?" Anger constricted his throat, raising his pitch. "*What's the matter with you? Here I was, about to agree with you, Pete: that I was wrong; it's too much for us! We need to report it!*"

The traffic lurched forward. Fletcher pressed the accelerator. Pete was staring ahead, deliberating. "Well, Fletch," he said slowly, "I dare say – at this stage in the game – it wouldn't do any good."

"*And what's that supposed to mean?*"

"Well, I think we have to be realistic: Porter's background for openers. He's wealthy and very well connected. I suspect – in fact I'm sure – that a lot of powerful people - maybe even some in the government - are privy to *the plan,* otherwise, he couldn't have gotten this far. I imagine he's already covered his bases regarding us; otherwise, we wouldn't be out and about. Clearly, he wants Tristan's participation, but I have a feeling that's only because it's more practical than Plan B; but there is – without a doubt – a Plan B."

Fletcher glanced in the rear view mirror, catching Tristan's tacit agreement.

"So, where are you going with this, Pete? What are you saying? We're safe? He's done with us?"

"No. But he said he didn't want to hurt you; I think you can take him at his word. Look, Fletcher, we have an enormous responsibility here; we can alter his course."

"How?"

"I don't know yet. But, I know this much. He seems to want something from you, beyond just Tristan, and I think you know it. I'm sure he'll contact you again. This time, you've got to be receptive. Ultimately, it may be up to you to change his mind."

"What? I'm not a scientist. I don't know anything about it. I'm not going change his mind about anything. And what if he *is* right?"

"Then, there's no one more qualified to save us – *all of us* – than Porter Eckhart. Look, Fletcher. . . ."

"You've got the wrong man, Pete."

"Faith, Fletch. We'll see."

Pete waved goodbye at his doorstep. It was another twenty minutes before Fletcher found himself at his own, so lost in thought that he didn't remember getting there. Tristan left the car, checking the perimeters of the house before entering through the front door. Despite his son's instructions, Fletcher rolled into the garage and shuffled into the kitchen. With his habitual key toss, he greeted Oliver and turned on the lights. Tristan emerged from the dining room.

"I told you to stay in the car!"

"I'm not a child, Tristan. If he wants to kill me, he can get it over with." Fletcher was studying the contents of a cabinet, finally pulling out a bottle of gin, a bottle of vermouth and a jar.

Tristan let the dog out, then slumped in a chair, relinquishing his gun to the table. "What are you doing?"

"Making a martini. Haven't had one in years. Want one?"

Fletcher didn't wait for a response. He grabbed another glass and filled it with ice and alcohol. "Right, then, a couple of Spanish olives and there you go!" He handed the cocktail to his son, clanked his glass with his own, then tasting it, smiled approvingly.

Tristan sipped it and grimaced. "You didn't ask for my passport."

"As if it would do any good. Look, Pete's right. He's got us covered. I'm sure by now you're Tristan the Terrible, or Tristan the Terrorist. We'll have to think of something else."

The terrorist let the dog in. "Do you still want to leave?"

"More than ever." Fletcher filled the dog's bowl from a bag in the pantry.

"*Why?* It's not as if we can escape."

"Oh no? Look, lad - for as many years as we have left - I intend we spend them in peace."

Fletcher put the dog bowl on the floor, then swiped his martini from the counter and finished it in one long swallow.

Tristan studied him. "You don't want to help?"

"What do you mean *help?* Help how?"

"Pete told you. He said that Porter. . . ."

"Oh right! That old Porter likes me! Well, I've got news for you, Tristan. Pete's naïve; I'm not going to talk that son of a bitch out of anything. I'm not gonna screw him either, if that's what he wants. All we can do now is find ourselves a nice remote bunker to hunker down in."

Fletcher turned to the counter, pouring more gin over his melting ice. Tristan reached him in three strides, snatching his airborne olives.

"So you don't care what happens? What about your friends? What about Pete?"

Fletcher faced him. "Pete's a grown man. He'll do what he needs to do."

"And what of everyone else?"

"Everyone else? Look, they can fend for themselves! God knows I had to and so did you. Are you going to eat those or do they go in my drink?"

"So you're serious! You don't care!" Tristan flung the olives into Fletcher's glass. Gin splattered across the counter.

Fletcher took a deep breath and grabbed Tristan's shoulders. "Lad, listen to me. You don't really think that anyone's going the change that man's mind, do you? What do you expect me to say to him . . . a genius? I'll tell you what I think. We're damned lucky to be alive right now. I'm bloody grateful! So, we're going to take full advantage of it and get the hell out."

"Then you go ahead!" Tristan struck his father's hands away. "Go ahead! Run! You live with that!"

Fletcher gaped at him. "What do you want, Tristan? You want me to tangle with that man? To what end? Don't you understand? We can't change it! And we're not among his privileged either! He'll kill me and come for you!"

Tristan tipped back his drink, swallowing ice. "When will you learn, hmm? There're worse things than death, I told you!"

"Good. Because that's all we'd be doing: throwing our lives away."

Tristan slammed his glass on the counter. His faced Fletcher as his mouth curled into a sneer. "Your father would be so proud of you."

Fletcher's eyes widened. He shoved Tristan into the refrigerator. *"What do you know? What the fuck do you know about anything?"* He caught his breath and quickly put his hands up. "No more, Tristan. No more for tonight. That's enough."

He grabbed his cocktail and blazed down the hallway, Tristan on his heels.

"He wouldn't run!"

Fletcher marched ahead, not looking back. "He spent his whole fucking life running!"

"He believed in something, Ryan! He thought greater than himself!"

The Englishman reeled. *"He did? I'm so glad you told me that, Tristan, because I thought all he cared about was himself!* That's why I thought he left a wife and a baby and blew the arms off some poor sot! You should've seen the pictures! All these years! *How could I have been so fucking wrong?"* He stomped through the study door.

Tristan caught up. *"You were!* That's not what happened!"

Fletcher about-faced, physically guarding the entrance to his refuge. His drink spilled. His voice trembled. "And how would you know, Tristan? Hm? What great wisdom can your twenty-two years impart about a man you *don't even know?"*

Tristan searched his eyes, telegraphing a terrible apprehension and a genuine plea. Fletcher's mouth dropped open. He staggered backward.

"Oh Christ!"

"Ryan, listen, please! I wanted to tell you!"

"Not now. I can't. *Not now! Get out!"* Fletcher jerked on the door.

Tristan blocked it. "I know how you feel; he's not what you think! *Wait!* Let me. . . ."

"No! *Go on! Get out!* Goddammit! Get out! *Get out! Leave me alone!"*

The door slammed shut. Fletcher couldn't swallow. His head was spinning. It was hard to breathe. He found the mantle clock through blurred vision and extracted the hidden key. He lowered himself on the desk chair, shaking as he inserted it into the desk drawer where he retrieved the note. He fought for control, that he could focus - one last time - on the writing that had held him to so much promise. *Save your son.* The envelope was hers but the missive wasn't. He knew that now. Tristan had not lied. The scrawl before him was not rendered by a lost love, nor was it a note to imply forgiveness. Rather, it was an appeal for such. For somewhere, from a blacker time, in a universe full of irony and lament, a hardened soul went searching and found his only begotten son.

✳ ✳ ✳

The clock chimed two. Fletcher was stretched on the couch in a womb of darkness, save for a small orange glow in an ashtray. The door cracked open.

"Ryan? May I?"

"No lights."

Tristan crept in and shut the door behind him. Feeling for the coffee table; he knelt down. His father's face wasn't discernible, but close. The smell of scotch was strong.

They rested in silence for a while. Tristan could be heard fumbling for a lighter. Fletcher tossed one toward him. It clattered across the table top.

"So, Tristan," Fletcher rasped, "how did you come to know him?"

"He came for me, you know, after my mother. . . ."

"And how did he know about you?"

Tristan took a deep breath, taking a moment to find the beginning.

His mother had been a fragile, artistic woman. She was born of parents that had neither money nor education, but what they did have was a deep and abiding commitment to an archaic Catholic tradition, thus, an intractable version of right and wrong. Her pregnancy was a disgrace. She bore her child to the scorn of her family. Despite her mother's embarrassment, she was at her daughter's side throughout the long labor, planning on the baby's immediate adoption. But, upon Tristan's first cries, Sonsoles refused to relinquish him, threatening the staff when they tried to take him away. The doctors were sympathetic; her family mortified. They brought her and the infant home. However, financial hardship coupled with shame made life under her parent's rule insufferable, and Tristan's formative years were tainted with rejection and rebukes. While his grandmother went to mass every day praying for her daughter's soul, his mother grew more distant, hearing messages from angels. She would feed her son sporadically and often leave him filthy, but would scream unmercifully if anyone tried to commandeer her duties. One night, she hovered over Tristan's alcove bed, telling him that God loved him, and that paradise was waiting for her all too perfect child. She tried to smother him, but her brother heard Tristan's muffled screams and wrenched the pillow away. She was gone for almost two years. When she returned, she was quiet and dutiful, but secretly divulged to her six year old that his father really wanted them but couldn't find them. Determined to locate their redeemer, she only had one avenue: the Irish murderer that had sired him and – by brief account – was hiding somewhere in Spain. Tristan was around seven when Sonsoles began taking him on bus rides to northern coastal towns. She knew that felons, particularly foreign ones, worked with guarded anonymity on the docks or on fishing vessels. Port after port, she made inquiries about a man named Ryan Nolan Egan, but was met with nothing but rebuffs. She left letters and photos of Tristan anyway, eventually abandoning hope and another measure of her sanity. But then, nearly fifteen months after her last foray, an envelope was delivered to her. She was working as a cleaning woman at a Madrid hotel, and was intercepted on her way home by a man who claimed to know nothing of the envelope's contents or its origin, only that it was for her. It contained money, a lot of it.

From that point on, she received a dependable, monthly stipend, lifting her from desperation, even enabling her to entertain the idea of a flat of her own. But as her father had come to rely on her financial contribution, he rejected the idea. Two of her brothers were at home, one with a serious alcohol problem, the other with a failed business. Her help was needed. She suggested she go back to school, maybe even college. She loved art. Her family was outraged at the notion, and began bullying her, demanding to know the source of her funds. Unable to reveal it, she was accused of being a whore in a violent, midnight explosion. She never did enroll in school but did take a flat. She did her best to take care of Tristan. She sold watercolors to tourists. Her final break-down came two weeks before her son's tenth birthday.

While painting in the park, she had come to know an older man who was kind to her. He would meet her on a daily basis, sharing wine and fruit with her, even bringing her roses, her passion. She would cheerfully talk about him to Tristan over dinner. His name was Miguel. After several weeks, he asked her out dancing. She accepted. Tristan didn't t know what happened, but when she returned early in the morning, her dress was torn and a shoe was missing. She had a strange stare and for three days wouldn't leave her bed, her son persuading her to drink water and finally, eat. She never visited the park again, but sat at the apartment window for hours at a time, watching the pedestrians in silence. It went on that way for a couple of weeks until she declared a need for a vacation. Tristan was delighted, thinking her doldrums had passed and that, naturally, they would go together. But, it didn't happen that way. He left for school that morning with a smudge of lipstick on his cheek and never saw her again.

For five days, Tristan came home to an empty apartment before his abuela came to get him. The news of his mother left him numb. His grandmother did the best she could to for him but was tired. Her husband's persistent denigration had worn her into premature old age. It wasn't long before Tristan became the target of family derision. His uncles were employed but were loud and unhappy drunks, arguing all hours about everything from football to bullfights. His grandfather was increasingly forgetful and often violent. During the next few months, Sonsoles' son continued to attend his classes, but was alarmingly thin and showed signs of abuse. Although the nuns were concerned, they were helpless as Tristan would say nothing. At the end of every school day, he would loiter by himself, waiting for another world to arrive, fearing that – like his mother's – it would never come. But, it did, wearing a Donegal cap. It was a wiry figure with a handsome face and a scar under the right eye. He approached Tristan slowly, speaking Spanish with an accent, asking him if he was the son of a particular lady. He took the boy to a restaurant and ordered him exactly what he wanted. He came to the escuela every day for nearly two weeks, waiting with folded arms at the iron gates across the street. He treated the youth to amusements and a museum, asking him about a mark on his forehead and the redness on his arm. But when Tristan met him sporting a bruise across his mouth, the world transformed. It smiled at him with warm indigo eyes, a gold filling and a chipped tooth, taking him by the hand and under an Irish wing, into a rusty Fiat, and out of his childhood purgatory forever.

R. Nolan Egan kept Tristan close to him, tucking him into his bunk every evening while his Portuguese trawler swept the Atlantic. The boat named Tigre de la Noche would rock the boy to sleep and would awaken him to the sun's sparkle, the smell of fish and salt air. While his grandfather dozed, the youth would clean decks and repair nets. By the time he was twelve, he was working alongside the nocturnal crew, learning the constellations. He was treated affectionately by Egan's partner and first mate, Luis, and was doted on by the deck hands and their women when in port. They nicknamed him El Guapo. Egan taught him English and did his best to give him a rudimentary education, hiring all kinds of motley tutors to school him in writing, math and science. He gave him classical literature, making him read three chapters every day out loud, not caring whether it was in English, Spanish or Portuguese. He noticed Tristan's affinity for art and furnished him with sketch pads, paints and canvasses, and took him on tours of coastal galleries. He taught him the harmonica and kept him safe from the authorities. The boy rarely spoke of his mother, her drowning a distant memory. But, despite Egan's best efforts, the adolescent would not learn how to swim, fearing that she would be angry at him for not missing her, and come from the depths to snatch him away. Egan did his best to overcome the boy's anxieties, waking him from nightmares and soothing him with Irish ballads. During storms, he lashed Tristan to him and sang bawdy songs until the terrified youth would giggle. The child grew tall and confident. They were the happiest days of Tristan's life, and they lasted nearly six years.

But, Egan had a darker side, one he tried to keep from his grandson. Occasionally, the boat would make a long trip, but it had little to do with fishing. Egan would not take his usual deckhands, replacing them with a sinister duo. They would pass the straits of Gibraltar, Madeira or the Canaries, so laden with crated cargo that they would have to forfeit their bunks. They would not dock, but tie alongside other vessels in the black of night, loading or unloading freight without a word or illumination. Luis would be paid with a fistful of American dollars; Egan was careful to keep his face obscured. The crewmen never called each other by name. Egan was always referred to as El Marino. Tristan was forbidden on deck.

It was during one of these episodes, that a life-altering incident occurred, and the boy known as El Guapo was propelled into manhood. The Tigre had rendezvoused with a yacht named the Niger. In a matter of hours, the cargo had been transferred, and Tristan was anxious to get under way. He was sixteen, in the galley with a fillet knife, peeling an avocado in the dark when he heard shouts and the sounds of a struggle above. There was a rapping noise and Luis cried out. The youth climbed the ladder, recognizing the Portuguese fisherman crumpled on the starboard side with two men over him; one kicking him in the groin. He could see his grandfather at the stern, and heard the menacing murmur of a gunman next to him, silhouetted against a curtain of stars. With Luis the closest, Tristan crept aft and sprang silently at his assailants, knocking one into the rail as he plunged his knife into the neck of the other. The first man rebounded, diving for the dropped pistol, but Tristan beat him to it, firing his very first shot into the man's abdomen. At the stern, the startled gunman briefly diverted his attention from the captain. Egan seized the opportunity and lunged for the gun. As the two grappled, Tristan reached them, jammed his pistol against the marauder's chest and pulled the trigger. It was one of Egan's crewmen; he only lived for minutes. Egan dashed to the other mutineer, who was trailing blood as he crawled toward the other vessel. The Irishman reached him just in time, covering his mouth as the captain of the Niger called out. Egan held a gun to the man's head, telling him to answer, to say that he had the money and was coming. The man complied. He was then knocked unconscious.

There were three left on the pirate yacht: its Tunisian captain and two crew. Egan checked his gun for ammunition and then Tristan's. He whispered to his grandson to stay there and start releasing lines, but Tristan wouldn't hear of it. Egan had no time to argue. He climbed silently aboard the Niger with his descendant tracking him. He stole behind the first crewman and hit him as hard as he could with the butt of his gun, but the man didn't go down, forcing Egan to shoot him. The other crewman fared better. Hearing the shot, he raced straight into Tristan's deadly aim and surrendered. From the helm's room, the captain unloaded his pistol into the darkness, but to no avail. As Egan approached, the Tunisian begged for his life, insisting that it wasn't his idea. He said it was De Sernet, but Egan just smiled. Then, the captain offered him all the money on board and showed him an impressive stash of American and Swiss currency. Egan shot him. The dead were pitched overboard and the Niger scuttled. Before she went down, her cargo was lifted, her two living bound and gagged, and her cash secured in the hard belly of the Tigre.

Luis had been Egan's partner and friend for twenty-two years. He endured his injuries with typical good nature. He suffered broken ribs, a thirty-two caliber bullet in his shoulder, and a horribly swollen groin. Egan was afraid for him, setting a course for Madeira, but it was Luis – ever practical – that insisted that they first requisition the Niger's freight. With the cargo on board and the Niger sunk, Luis then begged to return to Lisbon, terrified of any attention in an unknown port. The captain fed him pain killers and reluctantly laid a course for Portugal. By dawn, Luis' condition worsened. His lung had collapsed, and he was in agony. Tristan spent the morning listening to his moans and scrubbing the blood from everywhere. Luis asked for a cross and became delirious. Egan panicked. At noon, he radioed for help, but not just any help. Realizing his position, there was only one god he could pray to, and his prayer was heard in Tangiers. Etienne de Sernet immediately rounded up a physician and supplies and – at considerable expense - choppered to his closest interceptor: a yacht named the Afrika. By midnight, Luis had a clean bed, a transfusion and morphine; de Sernet had two captive Tunisians; and Egan had a lot of explaining to do.

He was interrogated for sixty hours without sleep aboard the Moroccan's vessel. All he could do was tell the truth - that the Niger captain had betrayed them all - and in the end, De Sernet believed him. The two Tunisians were likely executed; the commandeered Tigre returned. Before Tristan disembarked, De Sernet gave him his grandfather's payment wrapped with a slip of paper. A phone number was written on it. Tristan was told that – should he ever need employment – to look no further. For three days, the defiant young man had been grilled, and – for three days – had not uttered a word. Etienne was impressed.

Tristan stubbed out a cigarette. The ashtray was full. Fletcher stared out the window, seeing nothing but the desert sky teeming with stars. He wondered what the sky looked like from Egan's vantage, somewhere out on the Atlantic. No doubt, it was blue by now. He heard Tristan yawn and marveled at his own cowardice, that he could have left someone so vulnerable to the fates. And then he wondered about his own father, if he ever felt the same. It didn't matter. Fletcher silently thanked him for a chance to save his son. And yes, he'd take it from there.

It was after four in the morning when the phone rang; Fletcher was wide awake when he answered. As Porter expressed his *profound* disappointment, Fletcher cut him off and said he had given it some thought, and that he'd like to meet again, this time with an open mind. There was a momentary silence as Porter digested the transmission. He said only that he would consider it and hung up.

76

Tristan slipped through the door with coffee in hand. It was almost eleven, an unheard of hour for Fletcher's first stirring. Tristan put the cup on the night stand.

"Corey Martin is here."

Fletcher stretched. "Oh. Thank you. I'll be there in a minute."

To Corey's amazement, Fletcher hadn't bothered to shave, paddling past her with bare feet, wet hair and a damp shirt. He headed directly for the coffee pot. With a refill, he took the seat opposite her. Tristan excused himself and departed for the barn. Corey noted the deep circles under her host's eyes.

"Are you smoking a lot, Fletch?"

He was sniffling. "How are you, Corey?"

"Better than you. Oh, and before I forget, thanks for hanging up on me. So, Fletch, long night?"

"They always are, aren't they? And I didn't mean to hang up on you. So, what brings you here, Ms. Martin?"

"Mackey. He wants to see you. Tomorrow at ten. I was afraid you wouldn't pick up, so. . . ."

"Where?"

"Well, he'd like to see the property, so here. And then we'd go out to lunch, I guess, to discuss it."

"All right. If I spend today cleaning, tomorrow'll be fine."

"Fletcher, I've seen you look better. You sure you're all right?"

He pondered the question. He wasn't hung-over, so the answer was yes, he was well enough.

She was wearing a bright yellow blouse with a fitted linen jacket and pearl earrings. She had lost weight or something and was looking sunny and splendid. Whether it was the caffeine, the potential of a deal, or the pretty woman across from him, Fletcher brightened. He offered her more coffee. She declined, rising to leave, but to her astonishment, he insisted she stay for breakfast. She looked at her watch. Oh well, he meant lunch. She regarded him critically, asking if he really felt like cooking. He said of course. But as soon as he started to rise, she said that if he pointed her at a pan, she'd do the honors. He fell back with a smile, aiming his finger at a lower cabinet.

She shed her jacket and pulled every vegetable out of the refrigerator, keeping up a monologue of absolute trivia which he found remarkably soothing. When she turned to see if he was listening, he acknowledged her with glazed eyes and a grin. She plunked a glass of orange juice in front of him and commanded him to drink. He obeyed. Then she set the table with his worst china. The omelet was great. He could only eat half.

For some reason his face was burning and he felt giddy. She offered to clean-up, but he said no and meant it. He hadn't budged for over an hour, watching her move through a tight skirt. She put the dishes in the sink and faced him, beaming as she reached for her jacket.

"Wow, Fletch! You look alive again! Maybe all you really need is a mother."

He lurched to his feet and doddered into her, wrapping his arm around her neck. "Corey, my dear, the last thing I need is a mother."

She blushed and fumbled for her pocketbook, then turned toward the kitchen exit. He caught her by the arm.

"You're going the wrong way."

"What?"

"That's not the way, Corey. I'll show you."

"Fletcher, what are you. . .?"

"Shhh. You don't know where you're going. Believe me. Come with me."

She blinked at him, allowing herself to be led down the corridor. She was chattering nervously, something about the house needing more light. He paid no attention. When he arrived at his bedroom door, he whispered, "See?" and loosened her scarf.

77

At four forty-five, Corey was sipping ice tea at the kitchen table while Fletcher was hunched over it, scribbling something. Tristan walked in silently, absconded with a beer and exited. Fletcher handed Corey a check for a thousand dollars and escorted her to her car. The damage was much worse than he remembered. She said it was going to the shop on Monday. He bobbed his head and quickly retreated to the kitchen.

Tristan was back, too, pilfering chips, this time grinning from ear to ear.

"Don't say anything, Tristan. I mean it. I don't want to hear a word."

The caballero burst out laughing. "Why would I say anything? I'm so relieved!" His beer fizzled over as his hysteria mounted. "You have no idea! I was beginning to wonder!" He doubled over.

"Wonder what? You're here, aren't you?" Fletcher rubbed his forehead and stared at the floor, trying to not to succumb but it couldn't be helped. His son's laughter was contagious. He erupted. The two of them were in stitches for a full three minutes.

"All right, that's it." Fletcher leaned on a chair with both hands, trying to catch his breath. "I'm exhausted."

Tristan collapsed on the floor, still whimpering. "I'm sure!" Oliver skidded over, licking the tears from his face.

"Well, Ryan Fletcher," Tristan panted, fluffing the dog's hair, "I'm sure you understand if I see Ellen tonight."

Fletcher instantly sobered. "Tristan, I would consider it a personal favor if you would leave that girl alone."

"I can't." Tristan struggled to his feet. "I promised I would say goodbye."

"You called her?" Fletcher's irritation lodged in his throat.

"Look, she's leaving tomorrow. She'll be here at six. We're just going out to dinner. I was hoping that you'd leave the house. I was hoping you'd go to Pete's. I'd prefer you not be alone."

"Well, that's quite out of the question. I'm tired and I didn't know. . . ."

"Please."

"No!" Fletcher snapped, rubbing his temples. His headache was back. "Just go ahead. I'll be all right."

"Please. We can drop you at Pete's."

"No." Fletcher felt another surge of outrage. "Look, I can't help but wonder, with everything we're facing. . . ."

"Because she doesn't understand, and I don't want her feeling bad, you know? I don't want to be. . . ."

"Like me."

Tristan averted his eyes. "Ryan, please. You can't stay here. I'll worry about you."

Fletcher sighed and shook his head. "No. You have a cell phone. I'll ring you if there's any problem, but I shouldn't expect any. It's all right, Tristan. I'll lock the doors. I have Oliver. I need to clean up around here, anyway."

It used to be that Fletcher found cleaning a bore but gratifying. Now, not only was it a bore, but a grueling, arduous, thankless bore. He hadn't realized how long it had been since he had dusted; it seemed to take forever. Reluctant to follow-up with the noisy vacuum, he decided to spend what was left of his energy on gardening. With Oliver in attendance, he entered the sanctuary, astonished at its neglect. It was in dire need of water and pruning. Even the pond required topping off. He turned the sprinklers on, dragged hoses here and there and attended to the potted trees. He picked at a few spent flowers and observed the weeds in dismay. He stuck a hose in the pond and slumped on a bench. The whole business was overwhelming. He tried to remember why it had ever been important.

Twenty years, he thought. He had married her twenty years ago. He had been there for the duration, and for some reason, it seemed as if he had just woken from a coma, not able to recognize himself or anything of those years. The sprinklers were spraying him regularly with cold water, sending a chill through his arms; it felt good. A tiny frog began a shrill proclamation. Others vied with him. Twilight had turned the firmament to silver blue, and the little amphibians got raucous. He had never brought the frogs here, but they had – by some miracle – found his pool in the middle of nowhere. Now they thrived. They were in their element. But, nothing was more evident than the fact that Fletcher was not in his. Like the frogs, he had to make a protracted journey and risk everything to find his proper place. But, at least for that night - in an artificial setting - he was comfortable in his own skin, for the first time that he could remember.

On his way back to the house, he stopped to pet Little John. The big horse was wearing an imprint of a saddle. He had lost his hay belly and was looking surreally beautiful. His old groom was extra generous with treats, and was also reminded that he needed to find for a new home for the old boy.

Oliver was under foot as Fletcher walked into a kitchen striped with moonlight. He was tempted to have a drink but thought the better of it, taking pity on his liver. It was nine-thirty. He thought about Don Christoval, wondering how to handle that issue should Mackey want to close quickly. And then he heard a click. The dog rushed into the dining room, barking hysterically. Fletcher wrenched the kitchen drawer open and seized the gun. A French accent addressed him over the dog's objections.

"Put it down where I can see it. And if he bites, I'll kill him."

Claude was standing at the doorway. Fletcher placed the gun on the counter. "Please. He won't bite. Quiet! *Quiet, Oliver!*" The dog was finally still. Fletcher took a deep breath. "What do you want?"

"Porter will see you now."

Fletcher tried to stall. He said he needed to change his shirt; he was soaking wet. But the Frenchman was determined to propel him out the door – wet or not – and into the memorable Cadillac. Mathew was at the wheel.

The captive was thrust into the back seat. Claude crawled in behind him. Mathew studied them through the rear view mirror, rabidly chewing gum.

"Hi there, Fletcher. Fasten your seat belt!" He blew a bubble. It popped.

Fletcher didn't move. "I assume I'll be returning."

The car pitched forward and began racing down the hill. Mathew licked gum off his lips. "Not up to me. Want a cigarette?" His southern heritage was particularly apparent that evening.

"No. Well, maybe. ..."

"Claude, give him a cigarette. Me, too!" Mathew pulled the gum out of his mouth and squished it in the ashtray. He was reaching for a lighter when he yelled, "*What the . . .?*"

He jammed on the brakes. Fletcher was thrown frontward. Straddled across the end of the driveway like a white, pockmarked elephant was a stock trailer, barricading the exit. It was attached to a rusty pick-up. There was no driver, nor was there an easy way around it. Mathew scoured the environs. They would either have to move it or charge through the boulders and barbed wire flanking both sides of the gate.

"Do you see anybody?" Mathew shouted at the back seat.

Claude answered no, cracking his door.

"Don't get out! Who did that, Fletcher? *Huh?*" Mathew's eyes were glowing in the mirror.

He threw the car into reverse and fired up the driveway, and then slammed on the brakes. He aimed the vehicle at the fence-line, shifted into drive and jammed the pedal. The engine roared. There was a loud pop. The Cadillac careened into a mountain of yuccas. Mathew tried reverse, but the car spun itself into the sandy embankment. He lowered his window. The problem was obvious. The front tire had blown out.

Claude burst out of the car. Mathew pulled a handgun from the glove compartment, twisted around and aimed it at Fletcher. Perspiration sparkled like a mask across his face.

"Who's out there?"

Fletcher deliberated. Mathew pointed the gun directly at his forehead.

"Open your window!"

Fletcher's hands were cold. He pushed the button. The window descended.

"Tell whoever the hell it is out there that we're going to take his truck," Mathew demanded. "Tell him to get over there and unhitch that thing, or it'll be the last he sees of you, you. . . ! *Do it! Yell out the window!*"

Mathew's eyes were darting back and forth. His breath was short. He seemed to be panting. Fletcher tried to find enough spit to rasp "Elan," but couldn't make a sound. Claude leaned in Fletcher's window.

"I don't see anybody. I don't think anybody's here."

"No? Then what happened to the fuckin' tire?"

"He laid something across there. Like farm equipment."

"I'm going to kill that fucker!" Mathew brandished his gun in Fletcher's face. Claude redirected his aim and addressed him in French.

Mathew exhaled angrily and eyed the truck. "I don't suppose the keys are. . . . No, of course not. I'll have to hot wire it. He could be anywhere. Watch for me. Stay here, Fletcher. Any problems, I'll kill you. I swear it."

He exited the car, keeping his arms rigid, the revolver in both hands, aiming at every stirring blade of grass. Claude was posted in the middle of the driveway, scanning the endless prairie for activity. There was none, nor was there a sound, save for the whistling of a nocturnal breeze.

Mathew hoisted himself into the truck. After a minute, he slid out and raised the hood.

"*That son of a bitch!*" he blasted. "Well this ain't goin anywhere!"

"Matt!"

Mathew spun to Claude's voice. "*What?*"

"Why don't we take *his* car?" Claude cocked his head in Fletcher's direction. "It's in the garage."

"For Christ sake, *why didn't you say something?* I thought Tristan had it." He marched back to the sedan, grumbling. "We'll cut the wire. Hope his car's four wheel drive. Come on, Fletcher. Come on. Get out. *Get out!*"

Fletcher lit from the car and started up the gravel knoll as slowly as he dared. Mathew didn't seem to mind. He was trailing behind him, chattering like a sparrow, losing track of his stories, all the while aiming his gun at every shadow. Claude hastened them on. Fletcher scanned the waves of grass, knowing that Elan was out there somewhere. He prayed he wouldn't do something stupid. In fact, he was praying that he wouldn't do anything at all. The flaxen-haired hood seemed oddly unhinged. The house loomed into view. At the garage, Fletcher explained that the keys were in the kitchen, on the counter to be precise. Mathew surveyed the house. He told Claude to go in, get the damned keys and pull the car out. They'd wait right there. Claude disappeared into the front foyer.

The two waited outside for a full five minutes. Mathew grew testier, threatening Fletcher with all kinds of artistic torment if his associate didn't appear. He couldn't stand still. Fletcher could smell him.

"*Where the fuck is he?*" Mathew whined.

The garage door rose fitfully with an uncharacteristic, earsplitting screech. The wagon backed out leisurely, pausing at the pair. Mathew accessed the rear door and shoved Fletcher in. His boot was on a rocker panel when from behind him, a low voice told him to put his gun on the seat. He hesitated. There was a thud and he slumped across the rear bench, his firearm clattering to the floor. Fletcher grabbed the door handle.

"Stay there!" the driver commanded. His moon face grew fuller as it turned all the way around. "You all right?"

"Elan!"

"You owe 'em money or something?" Elan pointed at Mathew's revolver. "Better get that."

Fletcher snatched it. "*Is he alive?*"

Tristan had gathered up Mathew's legs and was pushing him the rest of the way in. "He's all right." He climbed into the front. "Here." He handed Fletcher a rag. "Put this under his head."

The car rolled back into the garage, the door descending with the same horrific shriek.

"*What's wrong with that?*" Fletcher demanded, wrenching his door open. "And how did you know they were here?"

Tristan popped over the luggage rack, and yanked something out of the door track. "You didn't answer the phone!"

"He never does," Elan muttered as he slid out of the car.

"I was in the garden. . . ." Fletcher suddenly turned to Elan. "How would *you* know?"

Elan shrugged. "So! What's all this about? Why couldn't we call the police?"

"I called you *three times, Ryan!*" Tristan spouted. "I had to call Elan!"

"I see that!" Fletcher snapped. "Wait. Where's the other one?"

"You're about to step on him."

Fletcher glanced behind him and hopped forward. Claude was lying on his side semi-conscious. His nose was misshapen and bleeding, his drooping eye tissue thick and blue. His arms and legs were lashed together with an excessive amount of baling twine. A terry strip was tied tightly between his teeth. He looked miserable, wheezing through the gag.

"I hit him with a board," Elan confessed flatly.

"Is he all right?" Fletcher asked.

"You care?" Tristan replied, dragging Mathew from the car. The southerner limply hit the cement. Tristan tied him with such an inordinate amount of hay string that by the time he was finished, Porter's employee looked like a mummy. Mathew groaned. Tristan took the rag from the back seat and stuffed it in his mouth, then rolled him on his back with his heel.

"Let's go in. We'll make a phone call."

Fletcher gaped at him. "What about. . . ?"

"They're going back tonight! *He* can worry about them."

"Who's *he?*" Elan demanded.

Fletcher held up his hand. "Just a minute, Elan. Tristan. . . ."

Tristan charged at him. "Why are they here, Ryan? This is very odd. Did you talk to him? *Did you?*"

"Yes."

"*When?*"

"Early this morning. I said I'd meet with him."

"*Why didn't you didn't tell me?*"

"I don't know! It didn't occur to me. . . . I forgot! "

"*Forgot?* How could you *forget?* What bullshit! I told you! You can't trust him, Ryan! And you can't trust *them* either! Mathew's full of blow! And *that* one," Tristan jabbed a toe at Claude, "is a killer! You understand?"

"Right. I understand."

"You don't *just have a meeting*, Ryan, not with him! We have to plan it!"

Elan hurled the keys at Fletcher and kicked the car door shut. "I've got a lot of questions, and I better hear some answers or I'm calling the police! I mean it! I just hit a guy. That's assault! There better be a reason!"

Tristan extracted a cigarette from his pocket. "You're right, Elan. Let's go inside. I'll tell you about it in there."

Fuming, Elan deliberated, then followed him through the side door into the pantry. Fletcher lingered, examining the vanquished.

They didn't *look* capable of a rally. He sighed, plucked his keys from the floor and withdrew. The garage lights automatically expired, leaving the spoils to languish in the dark.

Much to Fletcher's dismay, Tristan had three consecutive cervezas, pouring out their full and unedited travails without the slightest concern as to their impact. He began with Elan's first inquiry, cheerfully disclosing why he called Fletcher "*Ryan,*" although *Egan* - thankfully - was left out of the narrative. Then he moved right into Trans Origins, Inc., its mission and *his* involvement. At first, the cowboy took it calmly, but, as the story wore on, there was a marked change in his deportment. He no longer wanted to sit, preferring to stand in the shadow near the sink. He left his second beer half full, crossed his arms and hardened with every disturbing detail. When Tristan paused for questions, Elan didn't have any. Instead, he stormed over to the story teller and loomed over the table.

"Either this is bullshit, or you're screwing up big time. If this is true, you call somebody: the F.B.I. or somebody. If it's not true. . . ."

"He told you the truth, Elan," Fletcher ruefully admitted, "at least as much as we know of it."

"Then, tell somebody!" Elan ordered. "Call the police!"

"Why don't *you*, Elan?" Tristan shouted. Fletcher objected, but Tristan persisted. "*You* call somebody."

The horseman glared at him. The Spaniard lurched out of his chair, face to face with him. "Go ahead. Call whoever you like! See what they say! They'll ask a lot of questions, but you know who they'll finally come for? *You!* Maybe for something that happened before, huh? I *saw* you with the police, Elan."

Tristan blasted through Fletcher's protests. "You know why I hit that man: Tabor? Because I knew - *no matter what I did* - it would be all right! Porter would fix it. I was on *the right side!* But not now! And neither are you! *You never were!* But you go ahead, Elan. You trust them! Here's the fucking phone! Call the F.B.I.!" Tristan seized the cordless, bequeathing it to Elan by shoving it in his chest.

Fletcher grabbed his arm. *"Stop it! That's enough!"*

The handset clattered to the floor. Elan's hands curled into fists. "How could you drag me into this? *You son of a bitch!*"

"Because you said you had to know! I promised I'd tell you *so you'd help him!*" Tristan thrust a finger at his father. *"Right?* That's what you said when I called. You said you had to have a reason! It better be good! So now you know! *Was it a good enough reason?"*

Elan struck, missing the intended jaw as Tristan dodged. Fletcher barged between them. Elan pressed hard but Fletcher stayed with him, blocking him until he could see a flicker of reason in his eyes, imploring him to sit down. Instead, Elan shoved him aside, stormed into the garage and ripped the gag out of a now conscious Mathew. Fletcher hastened after him, and then thought the better of it. He returned to the kitchen and shut the door.

"Smart," he said dryly.

Tristan said nothing. He shagged the phone off the floor and dialed. He said no more than a dozen words and hung up. "Tomas is coming. He'll be here in about an hour. We've got to move the trailer."

It was another fifteen minutes before Elan emerged. He slapped a rare mosquito off his arm and leaned against the wall. His round face had sagged to oval. Tristan handed him the rest of his Dos Equis. He received it without a word, mesmerized by a tuft of dog hair floating across the floor. With a long swill, he emptied the bottle. Then he cleared the phlegm from his throat and murmured "So, what now?"

Elan's rig was long gone by the time Tomas arrived. There was blood on the garage floor and dirt everywhere, but Fletcher didn't care. All he could think about was sleep. He'd tackle it early tomorrow.

78

Gordon Mackey was a whole four minutes late, meeting Corey at the front entrance with an apology. She rang the doorbell, the two standing there like newlyweds when Fletcher answered. Mackey had a vigorous handshake and a disarming smile. Corey was unrecognizably demure. Fletcher told them to look around and make themselves at home. As they did, he tried to make himself scarce, but Mackey kept finding him, more interested in the antiques than the room dimensions or for that matter, the house at all. What he really wanted was a tour of the acreage and a ballpark on the furniture, should the seller want to leave it. Fletcher was receptive. Gordon liked that.

Tristan was about to mount up when Fletcher caught him and asked him to keep Corey company while he showed her client around. Her heels, Fletcher began to explain, but Tristan waved him off, nodding that he understood. Fletcher showed Gordon the barn and then the garden, to Gordon's expressed admiration. Then, they ambled north, following the stream bed. The buyer wanted to know the exact issue of water rights, any noxious weed problems, grazing, game, etc. Fletcher was precise in his responses, avoiding the game question by acting as though he didn't hear it. Then, half way to the western property line, Gordon curtailed the expedition. His only other interest, he said, was the canyon. Fletcher redirected him east, thinking that they'd take a casual peek, but as they approached, Gordon's enthusiasm picked up along with his pace. Reaching the rock ledge, he said he couldn't wait to have a *really* good look. Fletcher abruptly ended the tour, mumbling something about terrain instability and a time constraint. Astonished, Gordon couldn't hide his irritation.

Marching back to the house, Gordon's first question regarded mineral rights, and whether Fletcher *was sure* he owned them all. With the answer yes, Gordon brusquely stated that any contract would have to include them *all*. The follow up was a little trickier. Had Fletcher ever probed the canyon, and found anything worth extracting? *Extracting?* The seller considered it, and then said no. The last question was the impossible one: would Fletcher allow someone – a geologist, for example – into the area for a superficial study? Fletcher said nothing, his expression making it clear: nonnegotiable. Gordon nodded amicably; he was no longer put off. He had suddenly remembered the wife's accident and the notorious canyon, so Lawson's odd behavior seemed explicable.

Corey greeted them at the kitchen entrance, surprised that they were back so soon. Fletcher excused himself, saying that he needed a minute. Rounding up Tristan, he retreated into the study, closing the door.

"Tristan, I need to know what those documents say."

"The documents? You mean Don Christoval. . . . ?"

"Yes."

"I haven't had enough time!"

"I know, but. . . ."

"What's the matter? What's wrong?"

"Nothing. I just. . . I just got the distinct impression that. . . . I don't know. I can't explain it. I can't sell the place. Well, I can't without knowing more . . . knowing what his wishes were. I know it doesn't make any sense."

"It's all right. I understand. Is this man interested?"

"Very."

"Can you delay him?"

"I *can*. I certainly don't want to! How long will it take?"

"I'm not sure. What about. . .?"

"I know. Eckhart. I told you I'd do my part and I will. But - if we *do* make it through this - even if the world only muddles on for another *twenty* years. . . ." Fletcher rubbed his forehead.

"*What?*"

"I'm nearly broke, Tristan, as you so astutely pointed out. For however long we've got, I don't really want to be - you know – piss poor."

For a moment, the younger man just stood there with his mouth agape. Then he burst out laughing. Fletcher fired a look at the door, urgently pressing a finger to his lips. Tristan disguised his chuckles as coughs and shook his head.

"You're worried about *that?*" he whispered. "If it helps you sleep, Ryan, our chances over the next *week* aren't very good. But, just in case we *do* get through this . . ." Tristan put his mouth close to Fletcher's ear, "I can find a job. You can do gardens. We'll eat paella every Sunday. We'll pick naranjas. Hm?"

Fletcher's sheepish grin was countered by his son's broad smile. Then Fletcher remembered Pete's advice: faith, and took it at face value, along with Mackey's invitation to lunch. A contract was forwarded to Vicante for review. The price was good.

79

Amid happy squeaks, Pete's family departed for Maine. His mother had a cottage there, on a lake with such a long name that he couldn't remember it: it started with a P. Ruth was a pack rat, consequently the car looked like something out of the Grapes of Wrath, teetering down the road as the kids waved goodbye out the window. Ellen hadn't wanted to go, and too late, Pete realized, she shouldn't have been roped into it. She was miserable. She had seen Tristan last night, was home early, and spent the rest of the evening teary. Prior to her date, though, everything had seemed fine. Last week, her father had seen to the restoration of her log book. She completed her final two hours of flight time, took her last tests and soared into her pilot's license. Tuesday night, the family celebrated, surprising her with an aviator's jacket: the one she had always wanted. Yesterday, the inveterate swollen-nosed airport manager had asked her to stay on, no doubt under pressure from above. But Ellen had already applied for other jobs - one looking very promising – so she didn't commit. Nick – God bless him – had made a compelling case to keep Ray. Not only was the mechanic on the wagon, but – as of Tuesday – would have a license to drive it back and forth to work. In addition, he was on track to get his accreditation, which would certify his already requisite role at the airport. So, on the whole, everything was looking up, except for the small matter of a pending Armageddon. It was that affair that planted Pete in Fletcher's cozy digs at the appointed hour of five. Thankfully, the bar was open. He was nursing a scotch while Fletcher concluded a phone call somewhere else.

Tristan popped his head in the study door. "Ellen leave all right?"

"Yes," Pete replied tersely.

"If you don't mind, Pete, we thought we'd sit outside."

Pete bristled. "It's hot, Tristan."

"Yes, but. . . ."

"Oh, of course. In case we have *listeners*."

Pete hated to leave. He liked that chair and was cool and settled. But, then, he had heard about last night. It *was* quite a coincidence that Fletcher was alone when they showed up. He supposed it was possible that the phone was tapped or there was a listening device, although the possibility seemed *remote*. He sighed, topping off his drink before heading for the garden. The whole thing seemed ludicrous. When he reached the garden, he was pleasantly surprised. Even at eighty-seven degrees, it was enchanting. Another surprise was the presence of a local named Elan, who was clearly ill at ease. Tristan introduced him.

As there was no agenda, Fletcher, Pete and Tristan alternately recounted what they knew in an effort to paint a clearer picture, augmenting each other's narratives with clarifications, elaborations, small details and plenty of suppositions. However, it was Tristan that imparted the most surprising, pertinent and disturbing information, which he had yet to disclose until that night.

Trans-Origins, Inc. was precisely what Tristan had dubbed it: a secret society with a roster of powerful and prosperous. All of the members were keen on Porter's agenda. That said, they didn't know *exactly* what the agenda was, other than they were out of harm's way, having secured an exalted place in a new world order . . . should the order come to pass. Essentially, membership in the clandestine club was an expensive insurance policy with dire consequences for the loose-lipped. And because environmental health was the objective, it meant all those seeking post-annihilation prominence had better be emerald greenies. Since most weren't, they pretended to be and swore they would assume their autocratic duties as good stewards of the planet once the mysterious plan went into effect. Industrial powers would be brought to their knees, and what was left of the ignorant, polluting, disposable masses would have to submit. It seemed utterly silly and terribly drastic, but not entirely without merit. Porter's ark didn't have room for the whole six billion and counting. In fact, it wouldn't float at all unless a very large, *select group* made up the sea on which it would drift. What else could be done? Like rain, those people would fall with a viral deluge that would eventually slow the earth's overheating by virtue of their transformation into nonexistence.

Porter claimed no interest in politics which was an absolute lie, even if he couldn't see it. He was obscenely wealthy, but his disdain for self-indulgence, income inequality and materialism made him the perfect guru for the rich, hollow effete. He saw money only as a means to an end - to arm his principles - and was so unpretentious that he was charismatic. Six years ago, Trans-Origins, Inc. – save for a bio-engineer's nurturing - was on the verge of extinction. Its sudden evolutionary leap into a mega-moneyed mammoth was an irony, even for Porter. His covert initial offering to certain investors went so smoothly the rest of his sought after candidates became aspirants banging on the door to get in. Porter secured their future with their pledge of absolute allegiance, even as he found their self-interest contemptible.

Fletcher blushed, recalling his ridiculous offer during their first exchange. But then, he had known so little and thought Porter was average. He wasn't. Eckhart was an altruistic genius, motivated - in his mind - not by hatred, but by love. He saw himself as earth's white knight, ready to assail her enemies should they threaten her beautiful biodiversity. And she was indeed, being threatened. Porter was in the unenviable position of having to fix it, but fix it, he would. He would not let his beloved earth become a barren effigy to the folly of mankind.

Porter had appointed Tristan his premier angel of death – or salvation – depending on the point of view. Of course, at the time, the troubled lad had full faith in Porter and the sanctity of the plan, believing that he could selflessly, gloriously save humanity by sacrificing a nasty fraction of it. The actual tactic or time was never disclosed, just assumed. At the appointed hour, the courier would sequester a small aircraft and deliver a lethal concoction to specified locations. Tristan said he felt like a super star. Although there were hundreds of carriers, *he* was the prodigal son: loyal, deadly, and – as it turned out - immune. Consequently, he had the preeminent route right into D.C.

And then, something changed, something, Pete theorized, that compelled the scientist to rethink his plan. In an unlikely place, Porter found somebody who couldn't be acquired: Ryan Fletcher Lawson Egan, a nobody. The nobody made it clear; there was no price tag for Tristan and put it all on the line to prove it. Gradually, there was a shift in Porter's attention, finding Fletcher even more intriguing, or perhaps – as a scientist might put it – *useful*.

Pete reiterated his need to see Porter's data. Elan said nothing, stirring the pool with a twig as the others watched the ripples in contemplative silence. Tristan was stretched out in the shade, munching on an apple. Pete homed in on him. "Tristan, how did you come to be immune?"

Adam took another bite of his apple. "I don't know."

"What exactly happened with De Sernet, when you went to see him?"

"Who cares, Pete?" Fletcher demanded.

Pete considered him for a moment, and then said quietly. "You don't think it's important to know everything we can about that episode? You don't think the details would give us any valuable insight?"

"No, I don't. *He's not an expert!* He knows what *we* know: it's lethal. He survived it. Probably just lucky. There's nothing more he can tell us."

Pete stood, his curvilinear cheeks already glazed with sunburn. "What exactly is it that you *don't* want to know, Fletch, if you don't mind my asking?"

"That's not the point. It's painful!"

"It doesn't matter," Elan retorted. "We need to hear it."

"No! We're not going to. . . ."

An apple core hit Fletcher squarely in the chest, diverting his attention to the pitcher. Tristan sat up and draped his elbows over his knees, the sun condensing his eyes into a thicket of lashes. He peered at his mark.

"I didn't know, Ryan. I didn't know what it *was*, if that makes you feel better. But I knew it wasn't good. I knew it would hurt him. I've done things; I told you."

Fletcher squatted, gazing into the depths of the pond. Elan watched him, wondering what he was feeling as Tristan detailed the moments to De Sernet's ruin.

Etienne's staff was familiar enough with Tristan that when he arrived at the Cadiz domicile, he was ushered in without delay. Etienne liked luxury but, for good reason, shunned the spotlight, preferring modest addresses tucked away on working class streets. Outwardly, the Cadiz abode fit the bill. Inside, however, it was a different world, exotic and posh: Arabian lavishness garnished with French art. Once an apartment building, the Cadiz house had been restored to its original intent: a Moorish villa, and, as fulsome as he was ruthless, Etienne knew how to entertain. He had installed an interior courtyard pool which he was enjoying at the time, along with a loud stereo, family and friends. He immediately provided his young envoy with bathing trunks and ordered him a late dasayuno. Knowing that the delivery was from Trans-Origins, Inc., he was elated, awarding a generous tip for Tristan's alacrity.

De Sernet had two parrots: African Grays that he carted everywhere. They were old, multi-lingual birds that never failed to delight. They were in a cage near a fountain by the towels, chipping away at bone meal. Etienne knew Tristan's fondness for the birds, so he thought nothing of it when the Spaniard put one on either shoulder and disappeared up the stairwell. Too late he thought it odd. By that time he had no feeling in his legs.

On his lounge chair, De Sernet had opened the package, thinking it was the ultimate in techno-weaponry, and so it was, although it wasn't hardware. It was a Napoleon III gilt wood box. Porter had chosen well, knowing that his intended would find it irresistible. With his adoring in attendance, Etienne pulled the lid off, and found nothing but a damp rag. Tristan was watching from the second balcony. Having assumed it was a bomb, he was relieved when it didn't detonate; Etienne deserved punishment, not obliteration. The young bystander took a deep breath, about to descend the stairs, when the first signs of trouble glued him to his post. Etienne was trembling and thrashing, as were the others. A maid wandered into the courtyard with Tristan's repast, so aghast that she dropped the tray. She raced for her station, but fell without a cry. Two of Etienne's brothers drowned, catapulted into the pool by seizures; the remaining lay still. When Etienne's militia rushed in, they shared the same fate, although – as the seconds wore on – each took longer. The last man clung to life for nearly a quarter of an hour, so stricken that he couldn't use the cell phone clamped in his hand. There was no one else. Everyone in the household had perished within minutes, everyone, that is, except the horrified courier. At that point, he too, was so ill that he was certain he was next. He flung the two old parrots to the sky, hoping that they would find freedom across the Straits of Gibraltar. It was his last coherent thought. He was told that he was found wandering, but didn't remember. He awoke in the care of Eckhart, recalling vivid dreams but nothing of the interim seven days.

Pete had one last question: had the messenger ever received any shots. The answer was no.

Fletcher glanced at the young chronicler through glassy eyes, hating himself as much as he did Eckhart. Pete was rocking back and forth with his eyes shut, as if he had just heard something as remarkable as the soup of the day. And then Elan grunted, as if he had just found a missing sock. Fletcher felt like punching someone, and the horseman sensed it. Not a moment too soon, he murmured, "Well, maybe now we know why he's so interested in you."

Fletcher snorted that he had no idea what he was talking about. Pete opened his puffy slits long enough to murmur "breeding."

"Excuse me?"

"Breeding, Fletch, breeding. Tristan was never given a vaccine, but survived what – evidently - no one else has."

"Well, that doesn't mean anything. Maybe he wasn't close enough."

"Porter's thorough. I'm sure he looked at the environmental factors. And in doing so, concluded that Tristan should have been a fatality, but wasn't. And. . . ." Pete eyed Fletcher sideways.

"*And?*"

"And I doubt Porter has a vaccine."

"So?"

"Well, he doesn't know how to stop this thing in case it's unleashed in the wrong place, like his office. He's vulnerable. Naturally, he'd rather have a measure of protection. Right now, all he has is one young man with immunity, and. . . ." Pete cleared his throat.

"*And?*"

Pete faced Fletcher. "And his father. Genetics. He suspects that Tristan's immunity is natural. But, even for Porter, it would take years, *decades,* to isolate the component that gives Tristan resistance: countless permutations to see what he has that no one else has, assuming his immunity *is* genetic. Then, maybe when he saw you - or maybe even before he saw you - he thought you might share the trait. With the two of you, he'd have much better odds of hitting the jackpot: extracting *the factor* that kept Tristan alive.

And Porter's better at it than anybody else in the world. With *you*, a solution could be timely. See what I mean?"

Fletcher shook his head. "Yes, but, wouldn't he have to expose me to it to know?"

Elan frowned. "It would seem that way."

Pete plunged into his analytical conserve, sifting through every word of Porter's exchange that evening. To risk Fletcher's life would have been practical and easily done. But Porter didn't want to hurt him and said as much. In fact, he had been solicitous of Fletcher's support and had gone to great lengths to impress him, even court him. Why? Maybe he didn't want to lose Tristan. Pete shut his eyes. Nah, that wasn't it. He barely mentioned Tristan that night. Why would he curry Fletcher's favor? Why would such a powerful man make the investment intellectually, emotionally . . . unless . . . unless . . . . Pete rocketed up.

"Unless he already has!"

"*What?*"

"*Unless you've already been exposed, Fletcher!*"

"Pete, you can't be. . . ."

"Yes! I am!"

A white koi somersaulted out of the pool. Fletcher was suddenly aware of the center fountain. Did it just go on? The spray seemed vibrant and noisy, like hail on an icy sea. Tristan leapt to his feet, pacing madly as he absorbed Pete's reckoning.

"Fletcher. Listen! Why else would Porter engage you? Why would a man so powerful, as *occupied* as Porter Eckhart waste time on *you?*"

"Gee, thanks, Pete."

"I mean it! Why would he want your approval, to solicit your *friendship?*"

"I have no idea. Why?"

"*Because he can't afford not to!* You didn't die! And it's urgent that you be acquired! *You're vital!* You're immune . . . *to him!* Porter's human, Fletcher. He's a genius without parallel but that makes him a very lonely man. At some point, he set this thing loose and you didn't succumb! It was *your* genetics that saved Tristan! You fought off something Porter thought was infallible! With Tristan, there was a question mark - he couldn't be sure - but with you, he's certain! In the mind of a bio-engineer: you're practically divine!"

"He's right, Ryan. I'm sure he is." Tristan had come to a halt. Standing directly in front of the fountain, he looked like a winged messenger, radiant in the commanding light. "You were very sick. I saw you. Pete saw you. You had visions, like me. But you were stronger."

Fletcher rubbed his knees as he straightened. "If that's true, then *how,* Tristan? How did it get here? If we're the only ones. . . ." And then he was seized by the unthinkable and visibly stricken.

Tristan grabbed his shoulders and searched his eyes. "I've always told you the truth, Ryan. Even when you didn't want to hear it! I always said the truth! Now, I'm telling you, *I swear to you, on my soul, my life,* I didn't know! If I brought this to your house, *I didn't know!*"

Elan and Pete exchanged looks, but neither could offer the other a hint of comfort. All they could do is watch as Fletcher transcended the trauma. Privately, their sentiments were akin, that Fletcher's trial was unjustified and the envoy of his pain suspicious. But just when they thought Fletcher's hard expression might support their view, he threw an arm around the courier, assuring him with a rare show of affection.

Elan departed. Pete left around nine o'clock. He told Fletcher he'd check in tomorrow. He ambled down the corridor, and then paused to address the continental door man.

"Tristan, you might think about joining us on Sunday."

"Thank you, but you're not Catholic."

"True. But, you should come anyway." The Reverend leaned over, keeping his tone low. "At this point, I wouldn't be too fussy."

80

There was no phone call that night, nor was there one the following night. Fletcher slept fitfully. Sunday morning appeared out of a mist. Fearing for his family's financial security, Pete kept his sermon traditional, so traditional that he could hardly stand himself. His parishioners were mystified and audibly disappointed. The check-signing elders, however, were elated, cramping Pete's fingers with handshakes.

Tristan had spent the past two nights interpreting the ancient chronicle. He had copious notes, but his lack of sleep was beginning to show. He wandered in the kitchen around nine-thirty a.m., complained about the coffee and said he wasn't hungry. He had a cigarette with orange juice and exploded when Fletcher suggested that he give it break for the day.

"*You're the one* that said you had to have it!"

"I know, Tristan, but you need sleep. Look at you."

"I don't need sleep! When do we need to get out?"

"I don't know, yet. We haven't set a closing date. Look, I'm sorry. I didn't mean to put you under so much pressure."

"I have to go feed the horse now."

"I already have."

"*Why?* You didn't think I'd do it?"

"No, I was up early. I thought you'd sleep in this morning."

"I don't have time. I told you!"

"Then, at least, take a break. You might want to ride. . . ."

"*I don't have time!*" Tristan stormed out of the kitchen and down the hall.

81

By Sunday night, Pete was worried. Fletcher hadn't heard from Porter. Ruth called, having finally made it to Maine, declaring it their last trip there. Of course, she said that every year. The twins fought the whole time; Ellen was sick; Dillon's ipad wasn't working, *and* he'd forgotten his cellphone. It was also cold and rainy. All Pete could do was make ill received suggestions, cheer his kids up with jokes, and thank his mother for her unassailable fortitude.

It was seven p.m. when he hung up, feeling the isolation. He decided to mosey down to the church and finish some paperwork. He could write next week's sermon he supposed sourly, a sequel to today's big turn off. It was a pleasant evening so he walked. The road side cottonwoods were alive with finches. Someone passed him and honked. Sprinklers were on. Little patches of grass were green. He could hear TVs through open windows and smell barbeques from back yards. He rounded the corner, forded the parking lot and skipped up the church stairs.

The door to the chapel was open. He advanced up the aisle smelling furniture polish. Everything was tidy and the floor had been washed. He stepped into the hallway, pulled the keys from his pocket and unlocked his office door. His desk was heaped with paper. He had a myriad of projects he had wanted to pursue but had put on hold pending the Porter affair. As it was provisionally out of his hands, he resolved to pick up where he left off: writing a few letters of recommendation and two grant proposals. He found his schedule book. The week looked hectic. He poured a glass of water.

By ten thirty, he was spent. The proposals were pretty well drafted; he would edit them later. He had tackled all the urgent communiqués, sealing them for tomorrow's mail. He called the house for messages; there were none. He called Ray just to say hello. Yawning, he shut off the computer and locked his office. He entered the chapel with the floor creaking under his weight. The moon had elongated the stain glass images and cast them in tinctured chaos across the rows. He let his eyes adjust. He could still smell lemon oil. Someone was sitting in the second pew.

Pete trained on the shape, asking how he could help.

"To be honest with you, Peters, I wasn't too impressed this morning."

Pete caught his breath, scanning the room for more signs of life. "No, I wasn't either. It's not my usual fare."

"Really? And what *is* your usual fare?"

"A bit more . . . expansive I suppose."

"I see. So, why didn't I hear . . . *expansive?*"

"Because I can't afford to antagonize my employers."

"Ah. Can you afford to placate them?"

"I don't know."

"You won't have this job long, Peters. You'll open your smart trap again, and that'll be the end of it."

"You've been following my career."

"As of late. You're kind of a big frog in a small puddle, aren't you? Does it suit you?"

"For as long as it lasts."

"I see. Well, jobs are like lovers, I suppose. For a while, change is exciting . . . preferable. But as you get older, the glamour wears off; your options . . . limited. You're looking used up."

"Gosh, Porter. You're not here to give me a face lift, are you?"

"I was thinking of something a little more lasting."

"Said like a true bio-engineer. Could we discuss it in my office?"

"No. It's peaceful here. I like it: God's house. Have a seat, Peters. I barely recognized you. You were so gangling back then."

Pete sat at the end of same pew. The two stared straight ahead, past the altar at the large, luminous circular window. Pete thought he heard someone cough. He glanced behind him.

"Mathew," Porter said. "He's outside."

"Oh? How's he feeling?"

"Like an idiot, I imagine."

"Yes, well...." Pete cleared his throat. "Do you mind my asking...?"

"Why did I send them?"

"Yes."

"Because your friend was too eager to see me. I didn't know what he was up to. He's usually so predictable."

"So why do you think...?"

"I'm sitting next to *why*, Peters. He'd rather have nothing to do with me. Take his son and take his chances; that's what he wants, so it had to be you behind the new tune. I'm impressed. He obviously thinks a great deal of you, to put himself out that way. How did you do it?"

"I didn't."

"Sure you did. But, we'll chalk that up to Christian humility. Let's try again. What do you want, Peters?"

"To see your data."

"Why?"

"Why not? Maybe I can help."

Porter's laughter filled the chapel. It was sweet, like a major scale alternating between two octaves. "Oh, Peters. Help? What do you think? That we haven't looked at every possible alternative? That the data's faulty? That we're making it up? How can you help?"

"I don't know until I see it."

"Why should I waste my time?"

"You don't have to waste it on me. You can make your case to Fletcher: convince him. That's what you want, isn't it? Just out of curiosity, why?"

"I have my reasons."

"All right. So, make your arrangements, Porter. I'll just tag along."

"Just like that? That was easy. And here I was ready to make you an offer."

"I want your word he won't be harmed."

"You have my word."

"His son either."

"Oh. Well, that's a tall order, Reverend. I can't roll up every cliff, you know."

Pete crossed his arms, deliberating his next move. His palms were wet. There was a faint breeze moving through the aisles. He took a deep breath. "How'd you do it?"

He felt the bench shift. Porter exhaled quietly. "Do what?"

"Fletcher. The delivery. I was over there a lot. I didn't feel any effects."

"Did he?"

"I think so. To a degree."

"How so?"

"Your turn. How did you do it?"

Porter's head was tilted forward, his glasses were off. He was rocking slightly. "It would suffice to say he's a smoker."

Pete kept his tone impassive. "He's not really. And you have a shelf life, don't you? A short one. Too arbitrary."

"Not at all. As I said, he's predictable."

"Still . . . no one else was infected."

"You mean like you. A smoker's easy. The delivery can be precise. There's no residue; it burns up."

"You've honed it then."

"It can be modified, if that's what you mean."

"So, it *can* be handled. It's not hazardous."

"I wouldn't say that."

"So, then, why this agent, Porter? Why not something . . . conventional?"

Porter rubbed his neck and made a soft, whistling sound. "The meek should inherit the earth, don't you think?"

It took Pete a minute. "Oh yes, the cross-species issue . . . the parrots flew away."

Porter chuckled. "I like parrots."

The bench shuddered. Porter's glasses were on.

"Did Tristan know about Fletcher's exposure?" Pete fired quickly. "Did he bring it?"

"Why don't you ask him?"

"He denies it."

"So you don't believe him? Where's your faith, Reverend?" The scientist rose, pulled his shoulders back and rotated them. "Do people really sit here for an *entire hour?*"

"Porter, I have to know."

"Well, then, just for you, Peters: yes, he brought it."

"Then, he *knew*," Pete exclaimed. "He lied! He gave a poisonous cigarette to his own father!"

"I didn't say that. You disappoint me, again." Porter was edging toward freedom. "I said he *brought* it."

"But then he had to have known."

Porter's shoes clicked down the aisle. "I didn't say who smoked it, Peters. Learn to listen! Things aren't always as they seem. Good night."

✳ ✳ ✳

Pete sat in the darkness, consigning every precious sentence to memory. He leaned forward to relieve his tailbone. The pieces were falling into place.

Porter reveled in sleight of hand. The whole exchange about the cigarette revealed his fondness for concealing facts to elicit the wrong conclusion. Now, Pete was absolutely certain of what he had formerly suspected: Porter had intentionally kept Trans-Origins, Inc. out of mainstream approval. For years, Eckhart had personally propped up the company and its research, able to assume absolute control while basking in international rejection. Publicly, he and his staff were frustrated and ignored. Privately Porter couldn't have been happier.

If Pete was right, the company's team had projected a global crisis as much as thirty years ago. But, just in case there was no reasonable solution, an unreasonable one would do. Porter lackadaisically appealed for international support but as he didn't really want any, didn't get any, which quickly justified his other track. He didn't worry much about government investigation or interference. By the late nineties, he was considered a rich, brilliant, innocuous weirdo, worth a number of favors simply because of his campaign contributions, but professionally - as a scientist and geneticist - he was considered too outrageous to be taken seriously. His baby, Trans-Origins, Inc., was written off as an eccentric indulgence. However, Pete was sure it was subterfuge. Porter had done more than just speculate. The geneticist had gone well beyond his own fantastic theories to accomplish stunning breakthroughs that were never disclosed. He looked ten years younger than he should have, and no doubt, had fixed his hemophilia. And, he had managed to create an unparalleled destroyer in the form of a virus, one that he had hypothesized about - to peer ridicule - just a dozen years ago.

Pete returned to his office to use the phone.

"Fletcher, you awake?"

"Pete?"

"That computer print-out, you still have it?"

"Yes."

"I'm coming over."

82

Fletcher was waiting just outside the front door as Pete waddled up the stairs toward him. "Wait 'til I tell you what happened!"

Fletcher caught him by the arm. "Not in there. Tell me here."

In bare feet and sweatpants, Tristan stepped out to join them. He was about to light a cigarette when Pete snatched it from his fingers and hurled it into the night air. Tristan's mouth dropped open.

"Son, I'm sorry," Pete professed, "and I'm even sorrier for what I thought. Let me explain." He then eased down on a step and recounted the night's events.

By the time the three withdrew to the study, moths had discovered the open front door and were fluttering along the ceiling like homeless dryads. Pete was parked in his favorite chair, nursing bottled water while he perused Harvey's print-outs.

"This company, Fletch," Pete said, tapping on the paper, lowering his voice at Fletcher's warning. "This one here. . . ."

It was Zephon, Inc. Fletcher signaled to him to wait as he rose from the couch. He fetched the company's address from his desk and tossed it on Pete's lap. Pete caught him by the shoulder and whispered in his ear. "Let's round up Tristan and go have a look-see."

✳ ✳ ✳

Just north of I-70 was a conglomeration of warehouses, each one taking up a half acre of space, separated by narrow, flood-lit alleys and one-way streets. The hum of loaders could be heard in some of the facilities, while others sat in derelict silence. Tristan had never heard of Zephon, Inc., and signs were scarce so it was well after two a.m. when they found it.

There was no exterior designation, just a placard tacked on a door. It was a concrete garrison with a dearth of windows. It had a security system with plenty of warnings stuck all over the place. The only landscaping was a four foot wide strip of grass flanking the building. There was a loading dock and garage access, but everything was locked up. A grand total of eight frosted windows were barred.

"What do you think?" Pete whispered.

They were standing in the shadow of the front entrance. Tristan reached for the door knob, but Fletcher barked a warning. The security system looked real enough.

"I wish we could see in," Pete muttered.

"Well, we're not going to see anything tonight." Fletcher turned back toward the car.

"This has got to be it, Fletch," Pete whispered. "His headquarters . . . his storage facility."

"Here?" Tristan posed skeptically.

"It's perfect," Pete countered. "The ideal subterfuge: right here in the middle of the country. By Porter's own admission, it's *risky* to handle. But if he got it to you and you to Fletcher, it had to be local. No one in his right mind is going to fly around with it. . . . Well," Pete rolled his eyes, "almost no one. Look. He could store his entire arsenal. We have to find a way in."

"Not tonight," Fletcher clucked. "Let's think on it."

He hurried them into the car and turned the key. Nothing happened. Again, he tried. Nothing. He rattled the ignition switch and tried again but all he could generate was whirring and finally, a clicking noise. The smell of gasoline permeated the wagon. Fletcher knew nothing about cars. Neither did Pete, but they both agreed with Tristan. They needed to get out and walk away. Something was wrong.

It was almost three in the morning. They started east toward an open diner they had seen a couple of miles back. Pete's feet hurt, making it hard to keep up. At his height, it should have been easy, but over the years his stride had shortened to compensate for his weight and now his heels were taking the brunt. He was about to suggest a breather when the journey was expediently cut short, routed by a drawl in the shadows.

"Car trouble, boys?"

Fletcher spun around. Tristan shoved a hand in his jacket pocket. Pete stood still.

"Hi, fellas." Mathew was perched on the hood of an ancient Dodge. "Figured you'd head this way."

He had something in his hand. Placing it beside him, he bent over to straighten his boot. "Tristan, you shouldn't carry that thing around. This is the Denver. New laws, you know? What if they catch you with that? *Especially you.*"

The southerner shimmied down to the bumper, smiling. He tossed a cylinder up in the air and caught it. "A little trick I picked up in bumfuck somewhere. By the way, thanks for not killing me." He tossed the car part at Fletcher. "But I still get dizzy. Tristan, I mean it. You're making me nervous." Mathew threw his hands up in the air and started laughing. "I give up!"

"So what do you want?" Fletcher snapped.

"What do *I* want? I think the question is: what do *you* want? Skulkin' around here at all hours . . . 'talkin' about breakin' in." Mathew bowed slightly, an eye on Pete. "You want a tour? Isn't that what you want, big fella? A tour? Come on. I'll show you around."

"No!" Fletcher ordered.

"Why not?" Mathew chuckled.

"Yes," Pete announced. "I would. I'd like to see."

Fletcher glared at him; Pete responded in kind. "It's important."

"Well, come on then." Mathew hopped off the bumper, focusing on Pete's disinclined comrades. "You comin'?"

They fell in. Mathew led the way, countermarching while thrusting his hand out to Pete. "My name's Mathew. You can call me Matt." Pete raised an eyebrow as he grasped his hand.

"Weren't you at the church tonight?"

"Yeah, that was me! It's a hell of a drive down there. You know some dickhead gave me a ticket? I mean, there's nothin' out there! Not a car on the road! But he came out of nowhere – a friggin cow field - and gave me a ticket! For speeding! Can you believe it?"

Pete smiled. "Officer Ordell."

"Yeah, that sounds right. By the way, I'm a Baptist."

"Oh. That's nice. A Baptist. Well, Matt, forgive my curiosity, but as a Baptist, why would you involve yourself in this, uh. . . ."

"What do you mean: *involve myself*? It's my job."

"Yes, I know. But, it seems to me that your *job* – as it stands – may have certain inherent risks."

"Nah. Not really. Look, Pete, you don't know how big this thing is. You don't know how big *he* is. You're lucky. I think he likes you."

"Mathew, at some point, people are going to realize what he's doing. The authorities will be involved. This whole thing'll blow up. Someone will say something."

"Yeah, people have done that before. So what? You know what happens? *Nothin'*. No one believes them. There's no proof of anything. *Never has been*. Like UFOs or Big Foot."

"And what if *I* report it?" Pete stopped, looking at him squarely.

"You can try." Mathew halted, rubbing his neck. "But, then, you know . . . things can happen. No offense but you're fat: a prime target for a heart attack. And then your family's in Maine - you know - back country roads. . . ."

Pete suddenly seized Mathew by the collar and twisted it like a tourniquet. Fletcher and Tristan gaped in amazement until Mathew's maroon face and flailing fists catapulted them into reality. Fletcher leapt on Pete's back, shouting at him to stop. Tristan managed to sandwich between the pastor and his victim, absorbing a couple of Matt's punches before prying the heavy figures loose, using his boot to shove the big man away. Pete and Fletcher fell backward on the cement.

"Christ!" Matt croaked, feeling his larynx. "You son of. . . . *You're supposed to be a minister!*"

Pete's face was bright red. He sat up shaking. "You keep my family out of this!"

Mathew loomed over him like a wary vulture. "I don't have any control over *that!* Didn't Tristan tell you? Didn't he warn you? You *didn't understand?* I thought you were smart! Did you think you could just stick your nose in? Did you think he'd tell you just so you could. . . ? *Do you think we're all stupid?*"

Fletcher lurched to his feet and offered Pete a hand. "Come on, Pete."

"That's right! Take fatso here and go home!" Matt hollered. "Oh, and, Tristan, just a word of advice. Next time you point a gun at me, *so help me God. . . .*"

Mathew spat and abruptly deserted them without the benefit of his automotive expertise. As a result, it took another hour to reinstate whatever that thing was before the car fired up.

Fletcher had never seen Pete so distraught. On the return, the clergyman rode in the back seat, his legs wedged into the upholstery, a sleeve on his lacerated lip. He vowed to destroy Porter's plan, then moaned that he had recklessly put Ruth and his children at risk. He proclaimed that he had debased himself and everything he stood for by assaulting Mathew that way. He said he wasn't thinking clearly which made his assistance was worthless. Here he was, one of the few privy to a matter of real consequence, and he was nothing but burden, a liability. Fletcher told him that his reaction was understandable, that he was just tired and that he'd be all right. But after thirty minutes, Tristan had heard enough. He coiled around and blasted the poor passenger, telling him that - priest or not - he was just a *man,* no better than anybody else. Strangely, Pete seemed to find some solace in that and grew quiet. To make sure it lasted, Tristan knobbed through the radio channels until he found a hard rock station and kept it on near earsplitting for the duration of the trip.

Upon arriving home, Fletcher let the dog out and quickly issued Pete a scotch. That's all it took. The big brawler passed out on the study couch before he could be steered to better quarters. Fletcher took the glass off his chest and threw a blanket over him. It was after five; dawn was peeking through the window like a pearl in an opening shell. Tristan had already retired. With a full glass of port, Fletcher shuffled to his bed and kicked his shoes off. Oliver was being a nuisance, parading around with a sock until he realized that no one cared. The onset of Fletcher's snoring was not only immediate; it was unrelenting through the ring of the phone and the dripping of port on the floor.

Pete must have made a half dozen calls in the fifteen minutes that he was awake. He was standing at the desk as Fletcher shut the study door. In the corridor, Tristan asked how he was. Fletcher grimaced. Mathew had landed some good ones; Pete probably hadn't seen a mirror.

In between Pete's outgoings was an incoming, so Fletcher took it in the kitchen. It was Tom. Mackey wanted Fletcher out in thirty days. He'd close in fifteen. There were no conditions. Fletcher hung up and babbled the news to Tristan, who received it as if it were a sentence.

"What about Don Christoval? You said you couldn't leave!"

"There's still time."

"Fifteen days!"

"Thirty. Tristan, be reasonable. The man's been there for centuries. I'll do what I can, but. . . ."

"It meant everything yesterday. You didn't want to leave him until you were sure of what he wanted! And what about Porter? Or doesn't that matter anymore?"

"Tristan, please! *What the hell do you want from me?* What the hell can I do about it? I'll try to talk him out of it, but if I can't, I can't."

Suddenly cautious, Fletcher propelled his son out the back door. There was no breeze, making the noon hour suffocating.

"Look, we're out of our league and you know it. There's no one we can turn to. We're a couple of criminals if we move against him . . . or worse. All I can do is talk to him. I said I'd do it and I will. But that's all! If he decides to go ahead with his plan, all we can do is to get out of here and find someplace to lay low."

"We could kill him."

"*What?*"

"Ryan, if we can find the virus, we're the only ones. . . ."

"That's a *big if,* Tristan. And even if we find it, we can't keep risking exposure! What if the immunity doesn't last?"

"I have to do something."

"*There's nothing you can do.*"

"You don't understand! I was *wrong!*" Tristan stabbed at himself with a finger. "What I did for him was wrong! And I have to make it right!"

"You want absolution, is that it? You think that if you stop him – *even murder him* - you're absolved?"

"I don't know."

"Lad, look, if there's a God worth a prayer, you're forgiven."

"No, Ryan. I have to make it right."

Fletcher slumped against the house.

"Tristan, I'm begging you. Listen to me. I hate the man because of what he did to you. But this is war. You said it yourself. That's what it is to him. He can justify anything - do anything - just like thousands before him, because wars – just like this one - have gone on since the beginning of time, and *everybody* thinks their right! *He* thinks he's preserving and protecting; now *you* think *you* are by destroying *him*. But you won't. If anybody's going to live on, he will, Tristan. Men like that always do. It's the fools around them that lose. They're duped into all the dirty work with words like love and honor and patriotism and duty and all that bull. The annals of history are filled with the names of rich bastards with big ideas who used nameless farm boys for cannon fodder. You want to be another one of those poor lads who suffered for nothing? *They're* not remembered! The farm boys are fertilizer while the rich bastards – win *or* lose –are in Westminster Abbey! Think about it, Tristan. Tyrants live on, but nobody remembers the poor chaps that took up arms to fight for *or* against their causes. So if you really want to win, avoid the whole affair."

"Maybe you can, but I can't."

"Tristan, whether we like it or not, maybe he's needed! To solve a big problem! Do you want to prevent that?"

Tristan shifted, putting his back to the sun, shielding Fletcher with his shadow. "Ryan, if we're all doomed, so be it. I told you, there are things worse than death. But, I think we'll make it - all of us - without his help. For once, let's keep another tyrant from becoming tyrant. Like Pete said, you know, have some faith. Is it worth living to live under *him?* Because that's what it really means. So I'm asking, will you stand with me?"

Fletcher deliberated, weighing his son's desperate need for redemption. He sighed. "I must be a damned fool."

The screen door slammed. Pete strode toward them. "Do you believe my face?" He was beaming, his lip bright purple in the white sunlight. He pointed at his swollen eyes. "Look at me!" Putting his hands behind his head, he wiggled back and forth as if he had a hula hoop, singing *Ain't I Tough Enough* to sidesplitting laughter.

After a long round of applause, Pete disclosed that had just signed on a pal to monitor Zephon, Inc. Fletcher threw his hands up. In retort, Pete wagged Dillon's forgotten cell phone at him, assuring him he had made the call from his car while searching the trunk for clean clothes. Obviously, he didn't find any, so he was on his way home, and then he'd be off on appointments, bruised face and all. Back on the subject, Fletcher wanted to know *who the pal was*, but Pete wouldn't say, only that if anyone could get them *in* there, this guy could, and that he was trustworthy. Unfortunately, Pete lamented, the spy had a day job, so he could only spy at night. The Reverend's parting words were to call *immediately* if anything came up. He recited his cell phone number.

Despite the heat, Tristan decided to clean the corral and - if there was time - take a ride around the house, if only to clear his head. Fletcher watched him from the window, suddenly saddened at the prospect of leaving his only livestock. The sentiment triggered a call to Corey, who said she was wondering if she would ever hear from him again. He received her reproach patiently and then asked her – point blank – if she'd be willing to board his horse for a while. She laughed.

"So *that's* what you planned to do with him! *Pawn him off on me!*"

"Well, actually, Corey, I just hadn't expected. . . ."

"I know," she giggled, "to close so soon. I'll tell you, Fletch, I really don't need another mouth to feed."

"Obviously, I'll pay you."

"How much?"

"Oh. Well. How much do you want?"

"A thousand a month."

"*What?*"

She laughed again. He was over a barrel, and she loved that position. "All right. I'll do it for four fifty, as long as you take care of *all* the vet bills, trims, everything. *Aaaannd,* I'll need an address and phone number! So don't plan on disappearing without a trace or he can live on the highway."

"Corey, thank you."

"Thank *you*, Fletch. And since I'm doing O.K. on your house, I can even take *you* out to dinner!"

"Thanks. After the closing . . . if I can find the time."

He hadn't known how to tell her, so he let his callous riposte sink in with all that it implied, letting the painful silence settle the matter. There was no point in pretending. He was already off and running, well beyond her sweet western rainbow.

Fletcher was twirling a globe with his eyes closed, letting his index finger determine his destiny. Burnt and dusty, Tristan was watching him from the doorway, taking a loud slurp of juice for attention. Fletcher's eyes popped open. His finger was near Easter Island.

"You're getting close to the equator." Tristan drained the carton. His stubble was glistening with pulp.

"Good. I hate the cold." Fletcher spun the globe. "How was your ride?"

"Fine. I need a shower. Then would you like to hear what I've translated?"

"Absolutely! I'll put dinner on. Take your time."

The oven was preheating when there was a tap at the door. Fletcher let Elan in, shoved a casserole in the oven and offered him a beer. The cowboy accepted, explaining that he hadn't heard anything so he thought he had better stop by. Fletcher insisted he stay for a bite. The horseman hung his hat and sat down. Dinner smelled great.

Fletcher tossed a salad and poured them both a glass of wine. He grabbed a couple of chairs and ushered his guest outside, explaining his concern about a listening device somewhere. In the shade of cottonwoods, he filled Elan in on the latest, although there wasn't a lot to tell. It was cat and mouse with Porter, but, thanks to Tristan and his *faith*, they were going see it through. Elan said he had been giving it a lot of thought lately, and felt much the same way. Fletcher asked him if he really understood the risk. Elan nodded, absorbed by a group of Magpies heckling each other on the roof.

Cleaned up, Tristan surfaced, genuinely glad to see his friend. They talked horses, mostly Elan's latest projects. As they rose for to eat, a mountain of a man with a purple lip and impeccable timing rounded the corner. He said he had been thumping on the front door for five minutes, handing Fletcher a bottle of Dewars and a cheesecake.

After dinner, the group gathered in the study to hear the translation. Tristan warned them that it wouldn't be verbatim; there were words that were indecipherable and some phrases he could only guess at. He organized his notes, reminding them that he wasn't even close to done, either. Until dinner, Pete hadn't known about a manuscript. Now, in his usual chair, he sat purple-lipped and fascinated. Elan was stretched on the floor, chewing a toothpick. Fletcher found Tristan's nervousness amusing. He looked like a schoolboy as he began.

Born in 1550, Christoval Alcon de Navarre y Marquis was the youngest of four children but the only one to reach adulthood. He received his full inheritance in 1577, already with a wife, two sons and a daughter. Strangely, that was all Christoval wrote of his early years, shifting immediately to the subject of his first born. Sevastian turned twenty while serving with the famous Armada, although he would never return. The passage mourning him was so poignant that it caused an uncomfortable stir in the room. *Mi hijo valoros - my brave son - mi nino mas querido. Me perdona. May God forgive me as I can never forgive myself for letting you go.*

Christoval's youngest, Alexandre had accompanied him to New Spain, as it was to him that Christoval had hoped to entrust his letters. *My son, I pray you find safety in Mexico. I pray the Viceroy sees the truth in your heart and redeems us. I pray for your return.* But, Don Christoval - a realist - suggested that his words may be a legacy to one – *of fair mind* - in the future. He had lost his horse. He had lost his friends. With the last of his strength, he would tell their story. It was January; the year was sixteen hundred and three. Don Christoval was fifty-two years old and a traitor. He was one of five to abandon the myth of Quivira and desert his pugnacious leader, Juan de Onate. Now, he was alone.

It was the mythic riches of Quivira that lured the conquistadors from Mexico to the Kansas prairie. But the vast plains held no promise of wealth, and its hostile inhabitants proved nothing more than an exhausting trial. Onate's men, numbering seventy, were in constant thirst and became hungrier daily. The wild cows – or bison - had migrated to better forage, and the indigenous people refused to assist them. Christoval was a seasoned captain but ill favored by his leader. Regardless, he was the one chosen by the men to petition Onate for withdrawal. It was rejected. Onate was convinced that gold and a northern sea lay just beyond the horizon. Thus, he pushed onward, despite the discontent. And then, under cover of night came the first desertion. Three men stole horses and provisions, only to be overtaken six hours later and dragged back. Christoval's son desperately pleaded for their clemency. One of the condemned, Arias de Rio, was a dear friend his age, whose bravery and past loyalty had been exemplary. Onate was unmoved and ordered Arias beheaded. Horrified, Alexandre foiled the executioner's swing. Onate slashed the young man's jaw. Christoval drew his sword. Onate ordered them both arrested, and would have likely killed them on the spot, had it not been for a sudden warning by a scout. The Quivirans – native warriors – were fast approaching. Onate could not spare a minute, or so he thought. Christoval saw the attack as a sign from God. In the heat of a skirmish that lasted less than an hour, Christoval escaped with his son and Arias in a frenzied gallop west. The other two deserters, Mateo de Aguirre and Jean Lopez, stole horses and pursued. After five grueling years and nothing to show for it, Christoval was ready to prove his worth, determined to buy forgiveness and present his king with what Onate had yet to proffer: gold.

Christoval admitted to a restless spirit, one that had driven him far from home. But if he regretted it, he didn't say. He had indeed found gold, only to send it with Alexandre to buy a fair hearing. If his son could be restored to the sovereign's graces, he wrote, he would be at peace, even in this lonely place.

Tristan put down his notes.

Long after everyone left, Fletcher received the much anticipated phone call.

"Fletcher, I'll get straight to the point." Porter's voice was muffled. "You've been to the warehouse. Three tomorrow. I'd prefer you come alone."

Fletcher hung up.

Tristan materialized in the moonlight and leaned on the door jamb. "What time?"

"Three. Alone."

"He knows better. He's expecting me."

"Tristan. . . ."

"I'm going. That's all."

83

Fletcher had lost track of the days; was it Monday or Tuesday? Tuesday, Tristan said. They were almost to Tom's office. By eleven o'clock, the property was officially under contract. On the return, Fletcher deliberated on calling Pete but decided against it, not that it mattered. He arrived home to the relentless ringing of the bloodhound demanding to know if anything was up. Fletcher confessed. Pete said he'd be there in an hour. Porter could host three.

The sky's patchy fabric had turned to a sheet of gray when they arrived at Zephon, Inc. Parked directly in front, Pete and Tristan watched from the car as Fletcher knocked on the door. Porter answered unattended. He surveyed Fletcher's faithful through the dirty windshield, but said nothing. Holding the door for Fletcher, he closed it pointedly on his onrushing retinue.

He was surprisingly casual, wearing a rumpled white shirt and jeans. He looked thinner and younger; perhaps it was his clothes. They were in a spacious office, much better appointed than the run-down suites of the Boulevard. Inset lights punctuated the room into thirds. On one side, there were three desks, each with a computer and telephone. Arranged conversationally on the other side were two couches, a coffee table and two arm chairs, all neutral and new. The walls were bare; the carpet was spotless. A side table supported a printer and a well-worn chess set. The focal point of the room was a floor-standing globe, so massive that it looked like it belonged in the lobby of an airport. Porter offered Fletcher a soda, who declined with an apology.

"I know I said I'd come alone."

"Actually you didn't. I told you I'd prefer it. You didn't say a word."

"So, are they invited?"

"No." Porter unlocked an inside door, his key ring jingling. He looked like a janitor. He paused and pushed the slab open. "This way. I have something to show you."

"Uh, I have to let them know."

"Use any of those phones."

Fletcher rang a furious Tristan, assuring him that he would call again in another fifteen minutes and hung up. Porter waited patiently and then shuffled into the next room. On his heels, Fletcher snapped to a halt. His mouth fell open.

Before him was a colossal map of the earth glowing in magnificent, gigahertzed detail. It was over twenty feet long and fifteen feet high, charged with electronic indicators of every color, blinking and pulsating like a cauldron of microbic life. Ocean currents eddied in a translucent blue as multihued continents twinkled with population centers. Aqua rivers wormed through canyons while mountains and strata were layered in iridescent gradients so fine that the topography seemed tangible. It was no wonder that Porter felt like a god. With the world at his beckoning, he could easily make that mistake. Fletcher glanced around. The warehouse was a vacant cosmos washed in the planet's blue light. There was a long ebony counter with no fewer than twelve flat panel screens and key boards. All the seats were empty and the screens dark except one.

"Fletcher, what you are seeing is the current state of your planet."

"How current?"

"Within minutes."

"My God!"

Porter sat down at the one active screen. "You're looking at our life work. Let me show you. What would you like to know? Global temperatures?" Porter punched a few keys. Temperatures materialized across the map. They were in centigrade, at six inch intervals, altering with every fractional fluctuation. "Obviously, these are surface. I'll take you to volcanic activity."

Porter tapped again. Dormant volcanoes smoldered in deep crimson. Eruptions were in glaring orange, mostly on the seabed. Fletcher gasped. The technology seemed impossible, and yet he was witness to it.

"Can you see everything? What about earthquakes?"

Porter commanded it, and so it was done. Fault lines and earth shifts shimmered in an unnatural ginger. There were hundreds of them rippling across land and sea.

Fletcher focused on the Pacific. Porter anticipated his question before he could ask. "I'll give you a three-dimensional look."

The pale blue ocean disintegrated into taupe. A topographical map of the sea floor emerged, integrated with depth measurements.

"My God, Porter! This is incredible! You must be the only one on earth. . . ."

"Not really. We've simply taken it a few steps further. Now, I'll give you some *subsurface* readings. Because they can fluctuate dramatically, the data issued is in a range over the last twenty-four hours."

Porter was typing again. The geologic features receded. The map turned into a carnival of color. Without a legend, Fletcher couldn't interpret it. Porter was a step ahead of him. "I'll isolate the highest temperatures in what's called the asthenosphere."

Pounding the keyboard, Porter sequestered the hottest areas on the planet. It was strange to see scarlet shimmering in the middle of the north Atlantic. These, Porter explained, were vicinities of rising magma.

"Now I'll overlay a comp of twenty years ago." The overlay was in pale gray contrasted by ochre rather than red, the hot areas smaller and fewer. "As you can see, many of these hotspots weren't even there. It was a dramatically different story then." He let Fletcher digest the information and then continue. "This one here," with his finger, he circled an Arctic Circle red zone, "will completely halt the deep water conveyer that drives the Gulf Stream. We estimate nine years, although it could be as early as eight. The crust is liquefying at an accelerated rate. Now I'll show you a thirty year *projection*, assuming the current trend continues."

Even Porter was not immune to the prospects. He twisted in his seat as the new earth materialized. Fletcher gazed at the inhospitable future. The red zones had expanded; the earthquakes spectacular. Yellowstone National Park had become an inferno. Vesuvius had already erupted. The Canaries were gone. Two volcanoes in South America had altered the Andes Mountains into something unrecognizable. Land masses had shrunk. What was left of permafrost had receded to the very tips of the globe. The climate projections were staggering.

"Porter, what are those lines?"

"Magnetic shift. We still don't know the full impact."

"I see." Fletcher chewed on his lip. "So, we're dinosaurs?"

Porter laughed. "Hardly. At least they had a few million years."

A long, loud buzzer sounded. "That must be your boy, Tristan." Porter punched up something on the flat panel. "Of course! Impatient, so unlike him. He's at the door with your minister. Here, why don't you enlighten them while I step out for a few minutes? Don't touch anything. I can trust you, can't I?"

"You'll let them in?"

"I just did. I'll be back momentarily." Porter was traipsing across the huge chamber. "I mean it, Fletcher. Tell them to behave. I'd hate to have anything unpleasant happen."

Porter exited through a far door. Seconds later, Tristan and Pete burst in. They were as thunderstruck as their counterpart had been, riveted on the new world with their mouths agape. Striped in technochroma, Fletcher stood before them, recapping the global crisis. Tristan had heard it, only it was different this time. With the visuals, the scope of the catastrophe resonated at the deepest level. Porter's gamble had had the desired effect.

Tristan plunked down at the keyboard trying to resist an urge to play. Fletcher growled a warning. Pete stood in front of the huge screen with his arms folded, his face washed in blue. "I'd love to see what he has to back this up."

"It's all here!" Porter boomed, using his foot to shut the door behind him. He was balancing a stack of thick notebooks with rolls of paper tucked under his arms. "Good for you, Peters, a skeptic! Here it is, everything that's ever been recorded: every measurement, reading, forecast, and calibration." Porter dropped the heap on the counter next to Tristan. "This is seismic activity here and, let's see, this one is the first in a series of human effects on the environment. It's several volumes, so it might make matters easier if I bring the comparative data up on the computer. Tristan, if you don't mind getting up."

Tristan rose.

"Nice to see you," Porter said, taking his seat. "Gentlemen, I'll start with available records from, say, nineteen twenty. The twenties records are sparse but that should prove a good reference point. It gets better as we go on."

Porter rolled through the twentieth century with a staggering amount of statistics: temperature read-outs, pollution measurements, fuel consumption, conservation efforts, extinctions, deforestation rates, solar effects, nuclear explosions, polar ice composition, water sources, wars, life-expectancy, inventions and population growth. It was a remarkably detailed reconstruction of the human factor, and the impact was shocking. Then came the last decade, but he didn't need to say much more. It was obvious that the planet was overburdened, and the problem – simply put – was a lack of human restraint. Mother Earth was running a fever, trying to extinguish a proliferating germ.

Porter removed his glasses, cleaned them on his sleeve and reapplied them to his nose. He sounded hoarse. "So, Peters, where have we fouled up? Thus far, everything we've forecasted has been realized. But, you tell me. What do you know that we don't?"

"Nothing, Porter, except that it's hard to support the assertion that a population reduction could solve the problem at this late date."

"It can't, but it might buy us time. We need a radical new approach, and we need it now. There're certainly no guarantees, but it's worth a try. We can shut down the aggravating factors."

"What if you're wrong?"

"Look, Peters, we've been over this. There's the data. You can sit here for days. I invite you! In fact, I beg you: tell me where we're wrong."

"I doubt you are."

"Well, then, tell me what we have to lose."

"Lives, Porter! Lives! A significant percent of the industrialized world!"

"*What?*" Porter laughed. "I didn't say that! I was quite specific."

"Porter, I distinctly remember."

"Obviously you don't. I said the *contributors to the problem!*"

"You said industrialized!"

"They are indeed part of the industrialized world, but I said *a select group*. Lord, why can't anybody listen!"

"Well, then *who?*" Fletcher barked.

Suddenly, Pete rocked backwards, smacked by an invisible eureka. His mouth formed an *oh* . . . while he his hands slapped his face. He was gaping at Porter as if he were seeing the creature for the first time. *Things are not always as they seem,* Porter had said. *The meek should inherit the earth, don't you think?* And finally, Pete comprehended not only the plan, but Eckhart himself. He groped for words.

"The select group. *The select group:* the rich, the powerful, the greedy, the elite, the politicians and power brokers running us into ruin. The select group is your *investors*, the very ones who think their lives will be spared!"

In a dark, vaulted universe, a small, unassuming master was illuminated by the colors of a fragile planet. His half smile was barely visible through the primaries of the life that he intended, above all, to preserve.

84

In the front office, four men convened with the earth's globe a centerpiece. The room was uncluttered and peaceful, soothing to the high-tension mind of its administrator. As he stifled a yawn, his company sat mute, Pete finally breaking the silence with a question: how did Porter come to make his choice.

The scientist pondered him, and then replied that certain criteria had to be met. Political and corporate heavy weights were first on his list, and as expected, were the first to jump in. But, Pete asked, didn't the participants understand the actual *geophysical* emergency? Porter smiled, stating that they did to a degree, but were skeptical about the time frame, so weren't too worried. In fact, he said, his enrollees were far more concerned about his nebulous bio-epidemic than solving the environmental crisis. They knew that any environmental solution enacted by Porter would be drastic, which might force them to live within the confines of - God forbid - a commoner. *So what?* Pete was incredulous. Weren't they willing trade privilege for the future their children?

Divinity is hereditary, Porter quipped, explaining that money and power tend to blind people to their own excesses, and over time make them think that they really are impervious to disaster, as if divine. The powerful mingle with the powerful, feeding off each other in board rooms and dinner parties, becoming more callous and corrupt, while the masses – out of economic necessity – are forced to collaborate. Porter cited fossil fuels as an example. The public is aware of the harm and alternatives exist, but oil continues to flow along with its huge profit into a few exclusive pockets. The economy's top predators are on a feeding frenzy, and it's never enough. They proliferate; they pollute, not realizing that. . . . Porter frowned, shaking his head in frustration. Despite a planet in full revolt, they aren't prepared to consider that they *aren't* exempt from the consequences. Somehow, he sighed, the Ferrari will outrun a pyroclastic flow. Of course, ultimately, it won't fare any better than a bicycle.

Porter admitted he had all but abandoned his eco-awareness program years ago, citing the futility, preferring instead to spend his energy on a solution. He stumbled on it while studying an odd little microbe that fed on sewage. He didn't elaborate other than to say that it carried a virus that mutated in his lab monkeys, specifically the ones carrying an innocuous version of Ebola. What resulted didn't kill the apes, just his lab assistants, instantly. He saw their bodies through the windowed door and immediately sealed the room. At first he was aghast, then he got creative. Instead of trying to buy the planet more time by peddling proof of doomsday, he could peddle something simpler: an insurance policy. A lethal virus existed; he could prove it and eventually did, much to the alarm of his prospective privileged. But to his amazement, his affluent investors –well over a million now - were not only complacent but receptive, even flattered to belong to his club as long as *they* were guaranteed "scourge proof" and the victims - should the plan come to pass - were, well: *other people.* Each grateful inductee understood that the plan was a last resort intended to alleviate enough pressure on the eco-system to afford each policy holder an extended stay in the new frontier. How extended was to be determined. Naturally, part of the price tag was absolute secrecy, and it was harshly enforced. Collective thinking might lead to second guessing, hence the members had to remain completely unknown to each other, and they were. It worked out well. As a result, the shareholders couldn't have known that - by eliminating *them* and their contingent – Trans Origins would achieve a much more desirable effect. Their demise would usher in a new dawn and give the meek a shot at salvation, under a whole other *select group* waiting in the wings. Of course there would be collateral damage which Porter regretted, but if the plan worked, it would mean an egalitarian utopia with an urgent mandate, one that might be realized with the full cooperation of the human race. But it had to happen soon.

"Well, Porter, I must say: it all sounds so practical. And if I didn't know better, I'd think you were a saint, bent on destroying the evil empire. A last resort? I doubt it. You would have sent an unwitting boy to his death with that virus of yours, just to eliminate an embarrassment in Cadiz."

Porter was expressionless while considering Fletcher's rebuke. His eyes shifted to Tristan. "What did I tell you that day, Tristan? What did I tell you to do?"

The Spaniard leaned back, addressing the ceiling, "To leave the package. Not to stay."

"Did I tell you it was dangerous? Did I tell you that *your life was at stake?*"

"Yes."

"So, why didn't you leave?"

"I wanted to see."

"Morbid curiosity." Porter sighed, rubbing the bridge of his nose. "Mea culpa. Fletcher. I should have known."

Tristan said nothing. He was fidgety.

"Why don't step you outside and have a smoke?" It was all but an order by his former employer. With a glance at Fletcher, Tristan complied. He slipped through the front door, but kept it ajar with his foot, much to Porter's irritation.

"Fletcher," Porter whispered, "it would behoove you to know that when I brought Tristan in, I did so with great reservation. He was borderline psychotic. He was so violent. . . ."

"So why did you *bring him in?*"

"It was a favor. Obviously, he couldn't keep a conventional job and was in trouble with the police. I thought he was smart and. . . ."

"*Pretty!*" Fletcher sneered.

"Worth the investment!" Porter sniped back. He swallowed hard and cleared his throat. "He eventually improved, but it was hardly worth the price. Now that he's found you - much to my amazement - he seems to be on an even keel. But, whether it lasts remains to be seen."

Fletcher leaned over the coffee table. "*You* taught him how to be a murderer!"

Porter recoiled." I did no such thing! You have your own genetics to blame for that!"

When Tristan returned, Porter seemed sapped. He rolled down his sleeves, and then rolled them up again, staring at the globe. Pete suspected that he was weighing the resistance, specifically Fletcher's. He was right. The CEO abruptly adjourned the meeting. Fletcher had been spoiling for a fight. Porter was not about to oblige him. The host removed his glasses and stood, thanking them for coming.

"That's it? That's *all?*" Fletcher demanded.

Porter's eyebrows lifted, observing him like a lab rat. "Yes."

"I thought you wanted DNA or blood for a vaccine!"

"Not today."

"So, what did we come here for?"

"I thought to listen. I told you I wanted to present my case. I did. Think about it. If you decide that I'm justified. . . ."

"*Justified!*"

Porter exhaled exasperation. "I'll be in touch, or you can reach me at this number." He offered his card. Pete snatched it before Fletcher could snub him. The minister nodded his thanks.

85

"You know he lied to those people." Fletcher was stirring egg drop soup; it was scalding. He licked the side of his mouth. They were seated at his favorite Vietnamese restaurant.

Pete regarded him thoughtfully. "Lied to them? I doubt it. He just let them come to their own conclusions."

"All right, he *misled* them. Rich or not, do you think they deserve it? It sounds like you're defending him!"

Pete looked forlornly at his bowl. His hot and sour was practically boiling. "I didn't say that. Of course they don't deserve it, but I can understand his position. He bought these people, Fletcher. *Bought them!* They're perfectly willing to look the other way while - for all they know – millions are killed."

"How do *you* know? You don't know what he said. How do you know that he didn't present it as either- or: blackmail? And let me ask you this: if there was a vaccine or some way out, wouldn't *you want it*? Wouldn't you want it for your family? And let me ask you something else, Pete. What do you think happened to the people that *did* object, that tried to go public?"

Pete conceded the point.

Fletcher dropped his spoon. His soup was still blistering. "That's what I mean. Who knows what to believe? And how can he even do it? Can you imagine the logistics?"

"He's been at it for a long time, Fletch. And - for the most part - people are easy to control; you know that. I'm betting his would-be *allies* will run in the millions, motivated by all kinds of reasons: communism, idealism, radical Islam, the Third Reich . . . who knows? They just don't know who they're really working for. Look, all he needs is chaos. He's a rich man. I'm sure he's got fingers in all kinds of revolutionary pies. He's got couriers. Ultimately, he's depending on temporary *chaos* to get control. I'm sure very few know the real plan."

"O.K. Let's assume he pulls it off. He annihilates the power base. He sets all the revolutionaries loose at once. How does he rein *them* in?"

"Guess," Tristan replied dryly.

Fletcher grimaced. "Well then, let's assume we have a new world order. What are the odds humanity makes it through the first real *cataclysmic event?* I'm sure we're in for at least one. Based on what I saw today, it's hardly worth his effort."

"In that case, we should let him do whatever he wants," Tristan snorted.

"What's that supposed to mean?" Fletcher shoved his soup to one side. "Make up your mind! Now we *shouldn't* care? Fine!"

"We should care!" Tristan retorted. "But you're acting as if it's hopeless!"

"I didn't say *hopeless!* But let's face it, it looks pretty bad. You saw the data, Tristan! What do *you* think?"

"I think we have a chance without *him*." Tristan's shrimp had just arrived. He dove in.

Pete smiled, blowing on a spoonful of hot and sour. "Faith. Fletch. In the meantime, you know what we really need? A vaccine."

Fletcher rolled his eyes and tested his soup again; it was hot but tolerable.

And," Pete continued, "I know just the man who can make one with a little help from a friend."

"I don't want to help him, Pete."

"It's not for *him*, Fletch." Pete smirked. "Think of all those rich, selfish slobs you could be saving."

86

That evening found Fletcher in his garden, milling around the pond. The Shasta daisies were in full bloom, mirrored in the water like a new galaxy. The flanking carnations were being fought over by a group of humming birds. The grounds keeper plucked a few premature oranges from his potted grove and tossed sections to the fish. Oliver was lounging under the magnolia, intimidating the peepers into silence. The first stars sprinkled across the cobalt sky. With renewed dedication to his plot, the gardener sipped sangria, wondering if he would enjoy such splendor again.

Tristan wandered in with a beer. He drained his bottle and nodded approvingly.

"You'll miss it."

"I suppose."

The two stood in silence. A koi skimmed across the pool, found an orange section and shredded it like a little shark. Tristan forded a patch of pearl delphiniums to squat near the water's edge. Fletcher took a seat on a bench and yanked at a dandelion.

Tristan addressed him softly. "What did Porter say about me?"

Fletcher sneezed. "Nothing worth mentioning."

"Please. What did he say?"

"Tristan, forget it."

"No."

Fletcher straightened his back and cracked his knuckles. "All right. He said you were prone to violence. Nothing I didn't know. But, since we're on the subject, I have a question for you, and I'd like a straight answer."

"All right."

"Did Egan ever tell you to kill anyone?"

"No."

"Did he teach you how?"

"Only to defend myself."

"You know what I mean. Did he encourage you to be violent, Tristan? Did he ever *use you* that way, to rough somebody up?"

"No!"

"Then, can you explain to me what happened? What happened to you?"

Tristan pulled a cigarette from his pocket and lit it. The smell was grating against the floral aroma, but Fletcher didn't budge. Tristan lay back, addressing the stars as he smoked.

Not long after the Niger affair, the captain came clean to his grandson. He was a smuggler, nothing Tristan hadn't known since he was twelve. But Egan was anxious to impart that it hadn't always been that way. When the fish got scarce, the odd jobs for De Sernet kept them afloat. Unfortunately, *scarce* had become the norm. Commercial fleets were gobbling up what little the ocean could spare, and the Tigre had to make do with what the mightier nets might leave her. Tristan knew because Luis had spent many a day decrying the commercial flotillas.

After Luis recovered, he returned to the Tigre, but nothing was the same. His wife was terrified and demanded he stop smuggling. He did, despite Egan's pleas to continue. The money was running low and, for obvious reasons, Egan couldn't rely on anybody else. Luis held firm. As a result, the Irishman was forced to go it alone, depending on his grandson as deck hand and sentry, something he had never wanted. It was nerve-racking duty for the teen. Egan blamed Luis, fueling several vicious exchanges. And the Niger affair had had another side-effect. The nightmares of Tristan's childhood returned. He would wake up screaming and would go days without sleep. After six months, the tension between Luis and Egan erupted in blows. With what little money he had, Egan bought him out. The boat had always been owned jointly but registered to Luis. Upon the transfer, Egan signed the only name he could think of: Marino.

By now Tristan was sixteen and difficult to control. He enjoyed a lot of female attention at port. He was out until all hours. Bar fights became the norm. Many a jealous lover was goaded into battle and left a bloody heap, as if Tristan needed the violent release. Egan tried to rein him in, but it wasn't easy, and he had other problems. De Sernet's cargo was different; Egan didn't like it. They were traveling further and further south, along the African coast, transporting what looked like drugs to Europe. After three trips, the Irishman said no more. De Sernet assured him that it was purely medicinal: no narcotics. The Moroccan claimed the secrecy was due to pharmaceutical R. and D., adding that the client was a good one, doubling Egan's money. The captain reluctantly continued.

And then, a final incident changed the situation forever. The Tigre was just west of Dakar, tied to a fishing boat named The Impala. It was pitch, but the sea was calm. Tristan had taken the last few crates aboard, working by flashlight. Egan had words with the Impala's captain about the number of containers - they were short by two - but he finally to decided let it go and was tying off when he slipped. His leg was caught between the two hulls when he cried out. An Impala deck hand grabbed his arm in an attempt to help him, but in the obfuscated night and the darkness of his mind, Tristan saw it differently. He dashed to the sound of the fracas with a fully loaded .45, and shot the man as well as the only other member of the Impala's crew. With a trapped leg, all Egan could do was yell, but Tristan was deaf to him. The Impala's skipper rushed to his crew's aid only to be killed instantly. Egan scuttled The Impala and headed north. Tristan tried to apologize, but Egan wouldn't listen. Eyes glistening, he snatched the gun from Tristan's pant waist and hurled it over board.

Once in Lisbon, he set his grandson ashore and found him a room near the docks. He paid for his lodging and ordered him to lie low for a while, until things could be sorted out. The captain then traveled north with the Tigre and delivered the cargo alone. He quickly regretted leaving Tristan, and hastily returned for him with the idea of an extended holiday, maybe to Brazil. But he was too late. By the time he arrived, the teenager was gone. All he could find was De Sernet's cell number scratched on an empty matchbook.

The truth was that no sooner had Egan left him, Tristan called De Sernet with a full disclosure of what happened on the Impala. He did it to protect his grandfather, knowing De Sernet was not likely to pardon the Irish captain twice. Etienne was intrigued by the young Spaniard, remembering him well after the Niger episode. For the second time, Tristan impressed him, this time with his selfless confession. The Moroccan told him not to fear, that Egan wouldn't be held accountable. He would take care of the Impala mess and send a car for him, so he could do his penance in De Sernet's employ. Four hours later, a Citroen arrived, and Egan's vacation plans were dashed on a road to Cadiz.

Tristan became De Sernet's errand boy and sometime body guard. He was the darling of Etienne's set, but that came with a price. Six months into his indentured servitude, at a drunken party in Casablanca, Tristan was brutally raped by three of De Sernet's militia. Etienne witnessed it but was too intoxicated to intervene. The following morning he was truly sorry. The teen had been seriously hurt. De Sernet ordered round the clock care for him until he was well, but the recovery was only physical; Tristan was fighting for sanity and filled with a vengeance. Knowing that if he was insubordinate, Etienne would retaliate against Egan, Tristan bided his time. One by one, he stalked his attackers, and one by one, they fell. If De Sernet suspected, he looked the other way, not realizing who else might be in Tristan's sights. Etienne's time would come, and so it did, with the help of an amiable little fellow in a lab coat.

Tristan was acting as De Sernet's courier when he met the Trans Origins bio-engineer. The scientist was kind to the delivery boy, almost fatherly. Upon each delivery, Porter would never fail to stop what he was doing and chat with him. Sensing the young man's despair, Porter encouraged him to paint as a kind of therapy, and eventually offered him unlimited access to his home: a pretty villa just outside Madrid. Tristan met Mathew there, who was outgoing and warm. As they grew closer, Mathew hinted that Etienne was cause for concern. Porter's telephone calls to and from De Sernet were long, angry, and always within earshot of Tristan. After one such exchange that the scientist slammed down the receiver, composed himself, and told the Spaniard that he hoped he could stay for the weekend. Sandy, his daughter, would be arriving the next day. Tristan felt truly like family. That evening, over drinks on the veranda, he told Porter that he detested De Sernet and offered his services should they ever be needed. It was exactly what Porter had waited six months to hear. Champagne was served.

Fletcher rubbed his forehead. "Do you nightmare, now, Tristan?"

"No."

The nightmares stopped after the De Sernet massacre, specifically after Tristan's exposure had made him so sick. It seemed in that way, his demons were exorcised.

87

At two-thirty in the morning, Fletcher gave up on sleep and ambled down the hallway barefoot. The study light was on. He peered around the door jamb. Don Christoval's manuscript was arranged like a crossword across the carpet. Tristan was at the computer, tapping away at the keyboard. Fletcher turned toward the kitchen, but instinct arrested him. He turned back. He was right. Tristan was e-mailing someone.

He stood there - momentarily at a loss - and then journeyed to the kitchen. By moonlight, he poured a glass of juice and found aspirin, trying to quell his rising apprehension. Then, a wave of relief washed over him. Of course, Tristan was doing research. No doubt it was an inquiry about Alexandre's return to Mexico. He refilled his glass and returned to the study.

Tristan heard him and looked up. "If you're up for a while, I'll pick up where I left off."

Fletcher nodded and settled into an arm chair.

Don Christoval had joined Onate's expedition – not by invitation – but by order of the Viceroy of New Spain. Christoval was to monitor Onate's actions and report back his every transgression. As with most ambitious men, Onate knew Christoval's purpose and didn't need testimonials leaked back to Spain. Thus, the deserting Falcon fully expected a vengeful chase and got one. A desperate Onate, assuming Christoval was headed for an audience with the Viceroy, sent six men after him. For two days, Christoval and his company were relentlessly pursued before stumbling upon unlikely help: a band of natives tracking a bison herd westward. The Spaniards traded jewelry for their lives and asked to join them, accompanying them for a full day before parting. The tribe turned back as the fugitives continued west. Christoval suspected that Onate's scouts encountered the natives and probably traded coins for the deserters' heading, but the Indians misdirected them. Thus, after three days, the Spanish posse returned to their anxious leader, but without the elusive Falcon as a prize.

Christoval's text was full of scathing commentary against those countrymen that defied God and His Majesty by maltreating Indians, devoting a particularly derisive page to Onate. To the Spanish authorities, Christoval's compassion may have been viewed as a weakness, which could have explained why - despite comparable resources - Onate's petition was chosen over his. Nevertheless, the Viceroy was shrewd enough to know that there was a certain advantage in having a contender in Onate's ranks. He suggested that Christoval could be handsomely rewarded with a far-reaching commission of his own, should he agree to join Onate's assemblage. Thus, in the company of Alexandre, and despite Onate's vociferous objection, he joined the expedition in 1596. The mission's objective was to establish a lasting Spanish settlement in the northern frontier, deliver heathens to the grace of God, and deliver riches to their sovereign king. Onate failed on all counts.

Of his fellow deserters, Christoval wrote, all were justified. His good friend, Mateo de Aguirre was a miner, and, like so many others, had hoped to forge a better future in the new world. He was thirty-two with a wife and four children when he left San Sebastian, planning to send for them once established in the New World. But the six years that separated him from his family were full of hardship with neither gold nor glory forthcoming. Plagued by an arrow wound, the infection only contributed to his despair.

Jcan Lopez left his family in Mexico City. Originally, his wife was to accompany him, but with his children infants, he thought the better of it. At twenty-eight, Jcan was a skilled fighter and a superb horseman, but he was also an illegitimate child, destined to live without stature unless striking it rich in the frontier. It took several years for him to realize that he was not going to accomplish it with Onate. When deserting for the second time, he had the foresight to steal a pack horse along with his mount: a vital decision. The animal was able to carry their armor and what food they could forage, making escape a surety.

Arias de Rio originally accompanied his father, but the latter disappeared without explanation sometime during the journey. At that point, Arias - simply called Rio – drew closer to Alexandre. They could have been mistaken for brothers; both fair with a penchant for practical jokes. Arias had a sister who had been left behind in Onate's dismal New Mexican settlement of San Juan. When her only brother departed, she was inconsolable. He pledged to restore her to civilization when he returned, which was exactly what he intended to do when he initially deserted. Unable to dissuade him, all Alexandre could do was save him from an executioner's sword. Rio never forgot his friend's devotion. Five months later, he gave his life for the young Navarre on the very ridge where Fletcher sat quietly, listening to their story.

Having safely escaped Onate, the Iberian outlaws traversed the Great Plains for several days until they first glimpsed the Rockies. Although still a distance, Mateo knew that the mountains held far more promise for precious ore than the flat prairie. In fact, the rising peaks were the next best thing to Montezuma's city. As they approached, they began to find sparkling creeks. Game became abundant. Their horses were nourished on virgin grass. Jcan brought down a deer with a hand fashioned bow to the wild cheers of his friends. Under a dazzling blanket of stars, the five dined on roasted venison and drained their only flask of pilfered wine. They were giddy and rejuvenated. That late summer night, their future seemed as bright as the Milky Way, reigning over them like a boundless vein of Spanish silver.

Tristan put down his notes and rubbed his eyes. Fletcher suggested they pick it up tomorrow.

88

The wretched phone woke Fletcher at ten thirty a.m. It was Pete warbling in the new day. He had good news. Fletcher cut him off, grunting that he'd call back. He trudged to the kitchen and found coffee ready, somewhat brightening his mood. He squinted out the window. Tristan was in the corral, cleaning up. Elan was out there, too, holding his own horse while sitting on a rail. Fletcher drained the pot, snagged his new, prepaid cell phone and stepped outside punching buttons. Pete was jubilant. According to his *spy*, there had been no activity at Zephon, Inc. for the last two evenings – at least until midnight - and *the spy* may have a *way in*. Fletcher grumbled that they should meet. They decided on five o'clock.

Fletcher spent the day rummaging through boxes of personal effects and papers. After hours of sorting and indecision, he finally resolved to throw most of it out. He loaded up garbage bags and deposited them in the garage. By the time he was done, it was nearly four. With an hour to spare, he decided to log on. He strolled to the study and opened a window, feeling a dusty breeze swirl through the room. It was then that he noticed Tristan asleep on the sofa. Fletcher soundlessly retrieved his laptop and settled in the kitchen.

There was the usual assortment of spam to delete and bills to pay, and of course, there was the real reason to log on: to read Tristan's e-mail. As expected, he had changed the password. Fletcher looked over his shoulder, examining the hallway for signs of activity. All quiet, he checked Harvey's copied files. Tristan's e-mails were certainly there: all ten of them. There was only one problem, they were pure driveling nonsense. Maybe a code? Fletcher felt a swell of familiar apprehension. Then he heard Oliver clicking down the corridor, a sure sign that someone was awake. Fletcher quickly logged off. Apparently, Pete was early. Tristan was escorting him to the kitchen along with a friend.

Pete's spy was Ray Solner. The mechanic had put on weight and was sporting a pair of glasses, looking almost nerdy. He shook Fletcher's hand. Elan had ridden a horse to the house for the second time that day. He could be seen putting the mare in with Little John before he strode into the kitchen. He confessed that he was having truck trouble.

"Why didn't you ask for a ride?" Tristan asked.

Elan laughed, saying he had all kinds of rides, just none with wheels.

It was apparent that Ray and Elan were well acquainted, chatting as they ambled to the garden. Once through the huge doors, Ray whistled and exclaimed that he had never seen anything like it. He couldn't settle down, examining the pond, the rare plants and the irrigation system. He was full of questions. But as everyone was anxious for Ray's report, Pete urged him to begin.

The one thing Ray knew how to do was act like a drunk, so the first night at Zephon, Inc., he lounged around the parking lot with as fifth of Jack Daniels, lamenting the fact that it was nothing more than ice tea. He was there from seven p.m. 'til midnight and was so bored, he nearly fell asleep. But at least he got a hard look at the utilities and security system. For sure, there was a not–so–well-hidden camera at the front door, and another at the docking area. Everything was wired, he said, to the teeth.

There wasn't any action the second night either, until he was getting ready to leave, around twelve. Then, a blonde guy approached him, a southern fellow. He came out of nowhere, telling Ray that he couldn't hang around there. Ray was obedient and left, teetering around the corner with an eye on the front door. The guy never went in.

Ray surmised that the security system would fail momentarily with a power outage, and had a good idea of where the main line ran into the building. Naturally, it was underground. Since no one seemed to be there between seven and eleven, they would have plenty of time to dig it up and cut it, although, he admitted, it would be kind of tricky with the voltage. Elan asked if he had seen a generator anywhere. The answer was no, but Ray was betting that there was one. Still, it would take a few minutes before a sensor would kick it on. But, Elan queried, if the power went out, wouldn't there be a back-up – like a battery - with enough juice to set off the alarm? Possibly, Ray said. He wasn't an expert, but again, none of those systems are reliable, especially if they aren't serviced, and they usually aren't. It wasn't without risk, he admitted. Still, if it were up to him, he'd cut the power and slip in during that the few minutes of down time. What if it *were* up to him? Would he know how to do that? Rays eyes widened. Sure, he answered slowly, but it was illegal. Pete said absolutely not; he had already done enough. All they needed was the location of the line. Elan wasn't so sure. Ray was the only one among them who would know how to cut it without getting electrocuted. Ray crossed his arms. From everything Pete had said – which wasn't much - he supposed he could help out. Pete said no. Ray said yes.

The second problem was how to know if anyone was inside the building. According to Tristan, Matt was a great shot. And then, there were the others.

"Whoa, wait a minute," Ray blurted. What do you mean *great shot?* What's going on?"

Pete sighed. "Well, if you want to help, we owe it to you to tell you the whole story. Then you can make an informed decision."

Fletcher and Tristan returned to the house as Pete relayed their travails to Ray. When the two Egans returned, they were armed with turkey subs and an ice cold pitcher. Ray was prowling through the flowers, his freckled brow furrowed into a single knot. Pete was quiet, watching a robin wrestle a worm from the mulch. Elan had a honeysuckle bloom in his hand, twisting it in front of Rufous hummingbird. Out of deference to Ray, iced tea was served. The regulars suffered through it, but it was just as well. In short order, the five – with a quick stop at Ray's – were on their way to Zephon, Inc.

89

Under the glare of street lights, the warehouse's empty parking lot glistened with a thin coat of drizzle. Fletcher walked alone to the building's front entrance and knocked loudly. No answer. He pounded against the siding and hollered. Still, all was quiet. He circled the warehouse twice. Not intercepted, he reversed and jogged to the east side of the building. Elan and Ray had just arrived from the car with two shovels, a post-hole digger and a pick-axe. Tristan trotted to them from the north. He told them that Pete would be there in a minute. From his pocket, he withdrew Ray's donated BB gun and shot out the only two halogens within range. Elan whistled at his accuracy and began digging up a narrow strip of turf. When he paused for breath, Fletcher took over and then Ray, who reminded them to keep the dirt pile contained. Pete arrived and wearily deposited some rubberized contraption. The mist had given way to a clear night. Tristan and Pete stationed themselves on either side of the building as lookouts. At a quarter to eleven, the ditch was over five feet deep when Elan hit something. The cable, Ray announced proudly. The phone line was there, too. Perfect. Ray immediately sliced it and called for the device Pete had toted. Something of a Rube Goldberg contraption, he had rigged it in an hour. It was nothing more than a jumbo chain cutter coated in tire rubber, operated by a pair of attached, tire-clad wrenches, which were then attached to two pairs of oversized insulated pliers. He wasn't taking any chances. Donning his safety glasses, he told everybody to stand back, just as Pete strode forward and insisted on doing the honors. Ray handed him his glasses and told him that he didn't have to hack all the way through, which was a good thing, because it took all Pete's strength to cut a sliver. Although sparks flew, the good friar was unharmed. As Pete struggled out of the ditch, Ray slipped in, stuffing pieces of tire around the split. He said he'd give them a cell phone buzz when their time was up. Then he blinked up at them in disbelief, asking why they were still there.

Pete remained outside as look-out. Fletcher's skeleton keys didn't work so Tristan and Elan had to shoulder through the front entry. Once in, they ransacked the reception room looking for keys but didn't find any. Consequently, they had to force the next door which wasn't so easy. It took all three of them to break through it. Suddenly they were in Porter's empty universe; the map of his planet a lifeless, ebony slate. They paused to appraise the huge expanse around them. Above them, steel trusses supported the rooftop, but there was no motion on the catwalks. They listened for noise. It was silent save for their breathing. Fletcher pulled a tiny flashlight from his pocket and aimed it to where he had seen Porter materialize the other day. The door was locked in triplicate. They rushed to it, quickly surmising that the ingress was too secure to muscle through. Tristan would have to shoot it open. Fletcher trained the flashlight on the door. Tristan stood back and – with what he declared was a real gun – fired five rounds into the locks. Fletcher barked at them to hurry; they didn't have much time. They jimmied the door open. Again, they paused to listen, but there was no sound. Fletcher's narrow light scouted the room. It was a windowless square, about eighteen feet across, with a low, unfinished ceiling. The beam skipped across three metal desks piled high with papers. Trash was overflowing. There were two cots along the east wall with jumbled blankets. Straight ahead were three blank monitors. The entire west wall was glinting in stainless steel. They gasped. It was either an enormous vault or a refrigerator, or –as Tristan whispered – both. They knew what they had found.

Fletcher's cell phone suddenly buzzed. The three spun around and stumbled through the door, then flew across the mammoth control room. The room was humming, the screen flickering in color. A deafening ring ensued. The office lights were blinking on. A large figure filled the entry. *Hurry!* Pete trumpeted.

They dashed out the front. The Volvo was parallel to the wall, Ray at the wheel. They scrambled aboard as rushing headlights zeroed in. Ray reversed, nearly crashing the car into the building before lurching forward. He jumped the curb and ripped over a gravel incline into a southern parking lot. He pounced on the pedal. The car reached seventy as it catapulted over the next curb and fishtailed down a steep embankment. Fletcher could see weed barrier airborne like a scarf; shrubs were flying everywhere. His head snapped right as Ray veered left, skirting the next parking lot, barreling into a delivery alley. He aimed for the end and skidded into a side street. The tires squealed as Ray made a nearly catastrophic right hand turn, nicking a parked tractor trailer as he careened onto a larger road, leveling at eighty before bouncing onto a four lane causeway. He took the first exit onto I-70 west, and then the first exit off, immediately roaring back onto the highway, this time eastbound. He moved quickly through traffic, smoothly exited onto to a frontage road, and then adopted a humbler speed. Fletcher knuckles were glowing against the dash. He turned around. Pete was ashen. Tristan was searching his shirt pocket for a cigarette. Elan was lock-jawed, his arms crossed. Next to Fletcher, Racer Ray was giddy, laughing like a maniac.

"Yessir!" Ray hooted, slapping the steering wheel.

Pete pulled a tissue from his pocket and dabbed his forehead. His color was returning. "So, gentlemen," he chirped, scanning the infiltrators, "What did you see?"

"A big refrigerator," Tristan responded.

"You're kidding! *You found it?*" Pete exclaimed.

Fletcher twisted around. "Think so. It's enormous."

"So, what do we do now?" Ray chortled, still reliving his getaway.

"Get rid of the stuff, I imagine," Fletcher replied.

Elan dropped his head back. "That should be easy."

"Whatever we do, we should do it soon," Tristan announced. "They know it was us."

"And," Pete added. "I think we can safely say the gloves are off."

"Oh, I don't know," Ray ruminated. "I mean, this guy should've taken you out a long time ago. Let's face it, it's not like he couldn't. I get the immunity part, but it still doesn't add up, right? I mean dead or alive, he could still get some blood, right? And what if you tell somebody?"

"I think there's a kind of a tacit understanding, Ray," Fletcher interposed, rubbing his temples. "It wouldn't do us any good to tell anyone. You either. By the time we found somebody who might actually listen, we'd be arrested or worse. But, you've got a point. Maybe he's hoping that by giving us time, we'll see things his way."

"Nah!" Ray's lips corkscrewed. "I don't buy it. Sorry! You've got something on him. That's the only reason you're still around." Ray measured the silence, eyeing the trio through the rearview. "Pete, you want to stay at my place? Elan, what about you?"

"Thanks but I'm going home," Elan muttered. "I don't think they know me."

Pete took Raymond up on his offer. "Fletch, what about you?"

"No, Pete, you go on. We'll talk tomorrow. Noon or so."

The Volvo bounded up the hill and stopped in the Lawson driveway. It was drizzling. As Ray, Elan and Pete regrouped into Pete's car, Ray's reedy voice piped through the darkness. "Heh Fletcher, I *know* you've got somethin' on that guy."

90

"Tristan, a word."

Tristan was perched on the side of the bed, pulling off his boots. He assessed his father quietly, and then plucked a sweatshirt from the floor and wrestled it over his head. He used prehensile toes to slide his loafers within reach. He jammed them on and then pressed past Fletcher into the hallway. They shuffled through the kitchen and exited into the damp night air. Tristan struck a match, his surly demeanor revealed as he nursed a cigarette. "So, what is it Ryan? What do you want?"

"I think our boys are having second thoughts."

"So?"

"They think we're not telling them the whole truth."

"So?"

"We need them."

"No we don't. Is that all?"

No, *that's not all*. I don't like the feeling I have, Tristan, that there's something you're not telling me."

"It's late, Ryan."

"*Who are you e-mailing?*"

"Oh, so that's it." Tristan's cigarette's ember danced like a firefly and suddenly dove to the ground. "It doesn't concern you."

"*It doesn't concern me?* Are you *bloody joking?*"

"No, I'm not! What do you think you're doing? *Reading my e-mails! Who the fuck do you think you are?*"

"That won't work, Tristan! What's going on? *What the hell's going on?*"

The surrounding mist was oppressive and cold. Tristan's barely discernible sweatshirt was threateningly still.

"Come on, Tristan," Fletcher implored softly. Ray's right. It doesn't make sense. So. . . ."

"So, *nothing!* What do you want to know, Ryan? Why we're still alive? For you to understand that, you can't think like you do. You have to think like Porter! You have to make hard choices, find weakness! You can't worry about money or plans or what's right or civilized or even about your own life. It has to mean *that* much to you! *Winning! With your whole heart!* Then you can take on Porter or the whole fucking world. So, you really want to know why we're alive? You sure you're ready?"

It was starting to rain. Icy drops stabbed at Fletcher's chest and stung his arms and shoulders. Tristan's gray torso darkened as water beat the ground. Fletcher couldn't think; he was beyond thinking. All he could do was feel: feel the cold, the revulsion, the bitterness. He could taste it yet couldn't stammer the name. So Tristan helped him, shouting it in defiance, shouting how his father must somehow find a way to forgive, find a way to embrace the very reason that he and his only son were standing there in the blackness, breathing against the storm: *Egan.*

Fletcher lifted his face to the sky, letting the deluge wash through his hair, his eyes, down his chest and fingers. He wanted to be so numb that he couldn't hate anyone anymore: not Eckhart, not Egan, not himself. He stood there for minutes, letting the chill soak through him, freeze him, so he could always feel nothing, but Tristan wouldn't let him go. He yanked on his arm, yelling his name over the tempest, dragging him toward the door. Lightening flashed. The downpour pounded across the earth. Fletcher reeled and pushed him away, shouting over the din. *"What did he do? What did the bastard do?"*

Tristan yelled back over the torrent, water streaming down his face. "Eckhart's daughter, Sandy! He's got her, you understand? He sent a message! Anything happens to us – *anything* - he'll kill her. They can't get near him! He'll blow up the boat!" Tristan wiped his eyes. "Ryan, come on! Please! Let's go in! I'll tell you inside! Come on!"

Tristan propelled him forward and yanked the screen door open. They sloshed across the porch, through the entry and onto the kitchen floor. Fletcher was a water fall standing in a tiled river. He was shivering violently, but made no effort to move. Tristan dashed down the hallway and returned with towels, dry shirts and sweat pants. His father was pouring a scotch.

"Ryan, here." Tristan slapped the clothes on the counter. "Come on. You'll get sick."

Fletcher knocked back half his drink before setting his glass down. As if just waking, he rubbed his face and hair, and peeled out of his shirt and jeans. Tristan tossed him a bath towel. Fletcher ignored it and shimmied into sweatpants. He didn't bother with the shirt and snatched his drink from the counter. He held his glass up.

"Well, son, here's to my dear old dad! Is there *anything* he won't do? Any crime he won't commit? I can't think of any, can you?" Fletcher emptied the glass and refilled it immediately.

Tristan was in dry clothes, toweling off his hair. "You don't know him. You don't know him at all, Ryan. You're being an ass. We're alive because of him." He dropped his towel on a puddle of water, jerked the refrigerator door open and netted a beer.

"How about that! What a fucking hero! So when did all this happen?" Fletcher collapsed on a chair, slapping the table with his palm. "Come on! Fill me in. It's only three in the morning, your finest hour! Come on, Tristan, sit down. I want to hear all about it. Tell me what goes on while I'm tucked in bed. I want to know how many phantoms are skulking around here."

Tristan set his beer on the table, biting his lip. "Is that your last drink?"

"What difference does it make?"

"Because if I'm going to bother. . . ."

"Go ahead, dammit! I'm not drunk!"

Tristan studied him skeptically and then took a seat. He squeezed his forehead with his palms. "All right, but I'm tired. I don't want to argue. I don't want to defend him."

"Fair enough. I won't say a word."

Right before the Niger episode, Luis' fascination for techno-gadgets prompted him to buy a computer for the Tigre, and, although Tristan didn't have access to it for long, he was hooked. When Luis departed, so did Tristan's only real outlet. Although financially strapped, Egan was determined to restore some semblance of joy to his ship. So, on a dismal December day, he went shopping in Lisbon and paid cash for the very best laptop he could find. He surprised Tristan with it on Christmas. From then on, every time they docked, Tristan would log on, spending hours in virtual space. He finally convinced his disinclined grandfather to learn, which proved fortuitous. For the first few months of Tristan's tenure with De Sernet, Egan didn't hear from him. Then, a waitress at the Irishman's favorite bar handed him an e-mail address. To his immense relief, he knew exactly who it was from, and - with her help - established contact. From then on, the captain and his grandson were in regular communication.

When Tristan first disappeared, Egan was so furious that he refused to work for De Sernet. He demanded the teen be returned, the Moroccan unable to convince him that his grandson's departure was voluntary. Egan threatened to kill him, even as he was being tendered photos of a happy Tristan aboard yachts. Eventually, though, it was Tristan himself, through e-mails, that persuaded his grandfather to pick up where he left off. He explained that he was fine, that the shipments that Egan had been handling were essential to a client, that client being a very good friend and ally. The captain read between the lines and resumed his work. Eight weeks later, the arms dealer stopped calling . . . permanently. Tristan then wrote that he had a new employer, *the client,* and that someone would be in touch regarding money for Egan's *contribution.* Sure enough, someone was sent, but a wary Egan found the blonde envoy unacceptable. He wanted to meet the principal. Porter capitulated and negotiated the terms personally, knowing that captain's experience made him indispensable. Still, Egan drove a hard bargain. He wouldn't deliver to strangers. He wanted to see the same face every time, one connected intimately to the contractor or he would simply sail away. On a summer night, over white linen and mariscos, it was settled. They were in Lisbon. Porter was sitting next to his daughter when she suggested it. She could get a pied a terre; she loved Portugal. Porter mulled it over and consented, as long as it was *oversight* only. She was never to board Egan's boat. Little did Porter know that as they toasted, Sandy Eckhart's qualifying presence would prove her father's undoing.

Sandy left early that night, leaving Porter alone to broach the subject of a certain grandson. Egan was eager for news, but not the news he heard. Bluntly put, Tristan was unstable and sometimes violent. He also didn't want to go back to the boat. The captain was contemplative, wondering out loud if there was still a niche for Tristan in Porter's employ. It was Porter's turn to set the terms. He said he could use Tristan's talents, place him in a certain – unspecified - position and try to mollify his temper. But, if he failed, Tristan would be a serious liability. Egan should know that – should it become necessary –*the liability* would have to be dealt with accordingly. The seaman didn't like it. He tried to persuade Tristan to come back, but the young man wouldn't hear of it, entrenched now with his new family, a glamorous lifestyle and an all-consuming ideology. Egan kept close tabs, but there was little else he could do. He tried not to worry, but there was something about Tristan's communiqués, something disturbing and fatalistic. . . .

Fletcher leaned back, locking his fingers together as he popped his knuckles. "How do you know all of this?"

"He told me not too long ago."

"The coded e-mails."

Tristan raised his eyebrows. "Yes."

Fletcher smiled. "And here I thought you were working on Christoval's text."

"I was . . . most of the time."

"When did you last see him? Egan that is."

"Right before I got here." Tristan sounded hoarse. "Just long enough for him to switch the letter."

"Ah." Fletcher tipped his head back, opened wide and let ice clink across his teeth. "So he told you about that, too."

"Yes."

Fletcher yawned and plunked down his glass. "Let's turn in. I'll get the lights."

As Tristan trudged down the hall, Fletcher leaned his chair back and reached behind him for the switch. In the darkness, it occurred to him how odd it was to have lived without a single memory of his father, not knowing him as anything but a felon. He was suddenly aware of how it had shaped him, how the shame had plagued him. Growing up, he kept the family secret, but every day he was aware of it, that he was somehow impure and unworthy of love. On that basis, he dutifully deserted anyone who cared for him except Meredith, who was easy enough to cast off. He squeezed his eyes shut, recalling her last tearful reach for him. She was so angry, screaming at him, hurling books at him and finally her drink, glass and all. He just stood there at the fireplace mute, despising her for needing him. He recalled how he inspected the mess at his feet, dripping in her gin. She declared she was pregnant. She told him about her affairs, about Elan. She confessed all that he already knew. And then, she threatened to kill him, or was it herself, or was it both . . . finally begging him, pleading with him to say something, *anything,* so he did. He said that he hoped she was having a good time. That was it; that was all.

He might as well have crashed the plane himself into the canyon wall. He closed his eyes, still seeing himself standing there on the ridge, his arms outstretched, baiting her. But at the last minute she spared him, either loving or hating him so much that he could spend the next ten years tortured by her clemency.

He realized that his eyes were wet. He rose slowly, weighed by fatigue and melancholia. He saw a figure beyond the table in the dining room.

"Tristan?"

It was gone.

91

It was almost noon when Fletcher woke, reconciled to the fact that the phone had now converted to an alarm clock. He croaked good morning, assuming he knew who it was, but, he was wrong.

"I'm sorry, did I wake you? I had no idea you'd be asleep at this hour."

Fletcher held the receiver away while he sneezed.

"Are you ill, Fletcher or merely indolent?"

"Neither. I waited until dawn for your call. I was disappointed."

"I'm flattered. Did you enjoy yourself last night?"

"Not really. It was stressful."

"I can imagine. Stress comes from pushing our limits, Fletcher. And you don't want to push yours, believe me. So let me help by defining your parameters, lest you be tempted again. You won't be breaking into my business or Reverend Peters won't be showing up for Sunday service. I'm still undecided about the Indian. Do you understand?"

Fletcher sniffled. "What do you mean?"

"Perhaps I should call back when you're conscious."

Fletcher shot up. "I'm listening."

"Ah! So I *do* have your attention! Your friend is with us. He'll remain with us until you and I can come to terms, which I'm sure will be soon. In the meantime, he was hoping that someone could feed his horses. Oh, and his cat. Would you see to it, please, until further notice?"

"You *fuck!* I'll go to the police! There's a limit to what you can do!"

"You go right ahead! Be my guest! Now that you mention it, it would solve a lot of problems, having you and Tristan rounded up. Of course, he'll be deported, probably serve life, not to mention you, you thief! But by all means, go ahead! Why didn't *I* think of that?"

"Your *daughter!*"

Porter's raging silence was followed by a soft spoken rejoinder. "So he finally told you. I was wondering if he would. Not sure you had the stomach for it, eh? Old Egan. Funny, you're named after him, though you don't have his guts. So are you going by your real name these days? Ryan, isn't it?"

"What do you want?"

"Your cooperation. I told you that from the beginning."

"Specifically."

"I want you here. I want blood. I want a fresh sample from Tristan. I want a picture of you both with a newspaper dated today. And when the time comes, I want you to run an errand."

So that's it. You fucker."

"Don't! There's no point. You're strong, Fletcher. Stronger. And smarter, rational. You'll live through it. I told you, I can give you a new life, a very long one. Tristan, too. Now, about my daughter. . . ."

"No deal, Porter. No errand, no daughter. She's insurance. I want Elan. I'll come. . . ."

There was a click on the other end. Fletcher sat there, running a hand through his hair. He dropped the receiver in the cradle, catching sight of Tristan hovering at the doorway. "Elan?"

"Oh Christ." Fletcher dropped his head in his hands. "Will they hurt him?"

Tristan studied him. "Get dressed." He turned and strode down the hallway.

Pete called Fletcher from a diner and immediately sensed something was wrong. He was seated at the counter next to Ray, barely able to hear over the clattering of dishes and the gurgling of French fries. He gulped down the last of his soda and told the rancher that he was off, landing at the Lawson residence within minutes. Once there, he was bluntly advised that Eckhart was no longer amicable. But what else did he say? What else did he want? Pete cornered Fletcher in the kitchen, demanding answers. Fletcher was evasive while Tristan paced, clearly preoccupied, not acknowledging Pete's questions unless they were repeated a few times, and then – vexingly – responding in monosyllables. Tristan finally withdrew to his bedroom and shut the door. Fletcher nodded at Pete to wait. He traipsed down the hallway and rapped on Tristan's door. There was no answer. He leaned on the wall and waited, and then resumed knocking, calling Tristan out. It was only when he heard the car racing down the driveway that he realized what his son had done. Fletcher burst through the door, seeing the open window and the note on the blanket. *Trust me.* The message was weighted by a revolver. He quickly shoved it under a pillow as Pete crossed into the room.

"Where's he going?" Pete asked. "Is he insane? What's he doing?"

Fletcher slumped on the bed. In a barely audible voice, he replied, "Pete, you have to leave. Stay with Ray. Stick together. They probably don't know about him. For God's sake, don't be alone. Delay your family. Tell them to stay up there with your mother. I'm sorry. I'm so sorry I involved you in the whole bloody mess. Please. Don't go home."

Pete stared at him. "What's going on, Fletcher? Where's Tristan gone?"

Fletcher whispered, "Elan."

"What do you mean?" Then Pete's turned gray. "Oh my God. You mean? But, how?"

Pete tried to absorb this new world, one made in black and white, one far removed from Bingo and raffle tickets, one where only the stakes were in ruthless red. "What about you, Fletch? Don't you think. . . ?"

"Shhh. I'll be fine, Pete. I'll keep the cell with me. You should too. We'll keep in touch."

Pete nodded slowly and left reluctantly, as he couldn't convince his friend to leave with him. Once Fletcher heard his car clear the drive, he seized the cell phone from his pocket and dashed outside to dial Corey's number. She wasn't home. He tried her office. She was on a showing. He thought he was stranded, but within minutes Corey crackled back to him. He said he needed her car. Through the static, she told him to rent one. He said it would take too long. She told him that he had colossal nerve since it was all fixed, but fine, she'd loan it to him. If he wrecked it this time, her commission would be double. He said he couldn't come for it and needed it now. She replied that she'd be over in a couple of hours, as long as he could run her home. *A couple of hours?* Yes! That was the best she could do! Well, in the meantime, could she tell him how to feed Elan's horses? She asked why, *was he on a toot?* He said nothing. She sighed and said that she'd take care of that, too, as long as he could tack on another fifteen minutes. He told her it was urgent, begging her to be as quick as possible. He thought he heard an obscenity as she rang off.

92

Tristan was certain that Elan wouldn't be at the Zephon warehouse. Porter kept messes at a distance. So, as the Iberian sped north on I-25, he took his best guess. He exited on Yale West. Mathew loved the mountains. If he couldn't live in them, he'd live in their shadow. He also liked the heart of downtown. His apartment was central to both. Tristan remembered it well. He lit a cigarette, traveled a few miles until he recognized a laundry mat, and then parked on a side street. It was a Latin neighborhood. Salsa was playing from a boom box. He pulled his revolver from under the seat, released the barrel and examined it. It was an old .45 automatic. He took a deep breath and locked the car. Matt was dedicated. They had been fast friends for years and knew the stakes almost as well as they knew each other. Now, as it had always been, the winner would take all.

Mathew's second floor apartment spanned the northwest corner of an old four-story Masonite wedge. Approaching from the east, Tristan hastened down the dandelion-dotted sidewalk, noting the building's red fire escape. Dangling above a litter-strewn parking lot, its platforms were decorated with pots of fake flowers. Ragged shrubs brushed his shoulder. It was just two o'clock. The front door was glass and faced the noisy avenue. He was last there five months ago for an all-night party, something Matt lived for, along with Hispanic girls. At that time, the shrubs were bare and the entry lock was broken, but not now. Tristan backed into the street between two parked cars, scouring the facade. All the blinds were drawn, all except one, on the western side of the second floor. He smiled. The door unexpectedly buzzed, welcoming him to perdition. Tristan dashed for it, and held it ajar as he peered into the lobby. By now Mathew was in the hallway, probably on the stairs, coming for him. Someone else would be with Elan. Tristan slipped into the foyer, forced a tissue in between the door and its frame, and flattened himself against the wall next to the steps. It was a black hole; Matt had seen to it. He heard his sing-song drawl taunting him from above. Tristan jingled his keys and listened. The whole place was carpeted . . . soundless, but he could feel Mathew creeping toward him down the stairwell. He would have a silencer. Tristan didn't dare look. The southerner was fast and an uncanny shot but he had a weakness. He was cautious and would take just a little too long. Tristan was motionless, counting steadily to a hundred before bolting into the street.

He dashed to the fire escape, leapt for the first rung and hoisted himself up. Clattering up the metal steps, he reached the second story staging, snatched a pot and sent it crashing through the window, cutting his hand as he dove in after it. He landed in the shards of a vacant apartment. He was lucky, really lucky; the door was unlocked. He charged into the corridor, running full speed toward the staircase. Mathew would know now and could have beaten him into the hallway, but didn't. For sure, he'd be on the second floor, but just behind the exit door because he'd be too fucking cautious. He'd figure Tristan for the apartment, but he'd be wrong. Breathlessly, Tristan seized the stairwell door handle, jerked it open and somersaulted across the aperture as a revolver clicked; two bullets whistled just above his back. Landing on his stomach, he curled and jammed his foot into the closing door's gap, simultaneously blasting four shots into the darkness. Then he was on his feet again, racing for Mathew's apartment, not wasting a second on the southerner's status. If he was alive, he'd be too wary to make a move. Tristan slammed through Matt's apartment door at full speed. He dove behind the kitchen wall just as a startled Tomas fired from the living room. Tristan had two shots left and didn't dare reload. He remembered the layout well enough. He gambled that Tomas would retreat into the hall bathroom, the one connected to the bedroom where Elan probably was. Tomas would guard his hostage from there. So with a deep breath, Tristan boldly left the kitchen and was relieved to find that he was right. He stationed himself in the living room, diagonally across the bathroom door, calling Tomas by name. He answered. Tristan said that all he wanted was Elan. If he agreed, they could all live. Tomas didn't reply. Tristan picked up a magazine and stole to one side of the bathroom egress. He rattled the pages along the floor. Two bullets pierced the hollow core. Tristan lunged across the doorway, a bullet searing the back of his neck as he burst into the back bedroom, wheeled around and fired both shots into the open lavatory. Tomas' face was frozen in shock as he fell across the white sink and then onto the blue linoleum floor, the navy pattern purpling with a red torrent.

Behind Tristan, Elan was stirring face down on a vomit-soaked mattress. Hands shaking, Tristan reloaded, shouting Elan's name. There was no answer. Tristan snapped the gun barrel back in position, and then turned Elan over and slapped him. There was no reaction. Tristan hit him again. The hostage threw a wild punch. Tristan seized the horseman's belt and yanked him off the bed, hoping that the fall would revive him. It did; Elan blinked in recognition but said he couldn't walk. Tristan told him to wait while he checked the corridor. It was quiet. With Elan balanced against him, Tristan dragged him toward the stairwell. He braced him against the wall as he slowly splayed the door. Mathew's hair was shimmering on the landing floor. Tristan kicked the gun from his hand and knelt down. He put two fingers on his neck, then pulled the cell phone from the immobile man's pocket and dialed 911. He rose, grasped Elan around the waist and told him to watch his step. They stumbled down the stairs, hurried out the glass entry and through the parking lot, then crashed through the bushes to the south. Minutes later the first police car arrived. Elan was ill, nearly fainting twice. They negotiated curbs and asphalt like drunks, staggered past taco smelling tenements and avoided commercial areas that might have cameras or curious clerks, moving as fast as Elan's unsteady legs would allow. They finally reached the car; it was suffocatingly hot. Soaking and out of breath, Tristan turned up the air conditioner and drove south, keeping to the speed limits, using nothing but side streets as he crossed major thoroughfares, weaving steadily southeast until accessing an I-25 ramp. He kept an anxious eye on Elan, gratified that he seemed better. It was just three-thirty. He picked up his phone and reached Fletcher in one ring. He said that he was on his way and hung up. Elan watched the driver through sharpening vision, surprised to the see tears striping the sweat-streaked face.

Corey was feeding horses when their keeper arrived. Before Elan could slink into the house, she headed him off in the middle of the baking driveway, shoved a grain can into his stomach and, sniffing the air, declared that he smelled horrible and that he ought to be ashamed himself. He was over forty for cryin' out loud! Time to grow up! She was dressed in the prettiest rhinestone studded jeans he had ever seen, but he was too sick to say a word. All he could do was sway with her scolding. Shaking her head in disgust, she stomped to her car and yelled that she had fed everything in the corral and that he could take care of his pastured colts *himself!* As Tristan emerged from the parked wagon, she paused and suddenly spun around, marching back to her former employee.

"How old is he, twenty? You're on a tear with a *twenty year old? What's the matter with you?*" She retraced her steps, plopped into her Mustang and left him, braking at Tristan's scruffy contour. "I suppose your father doesn't need my car anymore. Nice of you to bring *his* back! *Look at you!* You two are really a mess!" She scowled, checked the mirror, and then careened around the mailbox en route to the Lawson estate.

Grinning at Tristan, Elan shrugged and passed out.

Thirty minutes later, Fletcher heard the garage door open and intercepted his son with audible relief. Grasping the back of his the neck, he felt sticky hair while spotting Elan asleep in the car. Tristan said that he didn't know what else to do. He was afraid to leave him alone, thinking they'd be back. He was overwrought, proclaiming that they had to leave *now,* while they still had time. Fletcher inspected Elan through the windshield and then whisked Tristan through the kitchen, past an astonished Corey, down the hallway and into the master bath. Sloshing peroxide over Tristan's grazed vertebrae, he realized how lucky he had been: a question of a millimeter.

He left Tristan to clean up and dashed back into the kitchen. Corey was standing, straightening her vest, clearly affronted, and – in her host's eyes – prematurely ready to run off. He begged her to come outside and to sit with him, pouring her a highball's glass of wine while apologizing profusely. He steered her out of the kitchen to the garden. Corey remained standing with folded her arms but finally sat, cajoled by Fletcher's mysterious sincerity. When he finally broached the favor, she was so incredulous that she shot off the chair and grabbed her purse. Fletcher leapt up, seized her by the shoulders and begged her to listen. Elan wasn't drunk, he whispered. Please, he implored. Please. He had something to tell her.

93

Clutching a revolver, Tristan was stretched on his bed when Fletcher appeared. It was six-thirty. The gunman murmured a salutation. Fletcher whispered in his ear that Corey had taken Elan and gone home. Tristan nodded and closed his eyes. By seven, he was up and about, checking every window and door. Everything was locked, Fletcher affirmed, adding that the horse was fed and the alarm was on. He was in the kitchen with a pistol on the counter, having just garnished a couple of bowls of spaghetti. He presented one to his roommate. They ate in silence and then stepped outside. Fletcher proposed a hotel for the night, but Tristan was reluctant, feeling safer in familiar surroundings. Fletcher concurred, thinking they probably had a few hours to go before Porter unleashed his hounds. They'd pack what they would need, sleep in the study and leave early. In the meantime, what about Egan? Tristan replied that – as of an hour ago - all was well. Had Fletcher talked to Pete? Yes, late that afternoon, relieved to hear that Elan was all right. He'd check in again later.

The evening passed with Fletcher prepaying bills, stuffing a suitcase and filling boxes. For some reason, he had a fanatical interest in sorting through what was left of his personal effects.

Items that he wanted stored and shipped to him were boxed and stacked neatly along the wall, accumulating impractically by the hour. He rummaged through drawers and cabinets until he was satisfied that there wasn't one unaccounted-for scrap, filling another jumbo garbage bag. Then he started dusting, which Tristan found incredibly weird, glancing up from Don Christoval's pages. Fletcher looked back at him and explained that there would be an inspection before closing; everything had to be in order. Tristan grumbled something. The conquistador's gleaming medallion was hanging from his neck. He had a fresh cup of coffee and copious notes on the desk. Determined to finish the manuscript that night, he growled to the cleaning service to *please* not vacuum.

As promised, Pete rang Fletcher's cell for a ten o'clock update. He was at Ray's as promised. Fletcher relayed that the most they dared hope for was one more peaceful night and thanked Pete for everything. Pete didn't like his tone. Fletcher apologized but said that unfortunately, he wasn't quite finished. He added that he'd never known a better friend or a more decent man, and that he would always be indebted. Then he clicked off.

Having wiped down every feasible corner of the house, the janitor ran out of nervous energy and collapsed on the couch, watching his issue scribbling on a note pad. The desk lamp cast the room in sea green shadows. Only Tristan's face was illuminated brightly, gleaming like phosphorus as the medallion sent shafts of gold upward across his features. Bent over the ancient chronicle, he looked like a scribe to one of its pages.

Fletcher must have dozed off because Tristan was standing over him, barking his name with such urgency that Fletcher snapped to his feet. "*What? What is it?*" He looked around wildly.

"Ryan, listen to me," Tristan whispered. "They have to go home."

"*What?*" Fletcher eyes were watering. "*Who?*"

"Don Christoval's men. It's what they wanted and what he wanted for them."

"Home?"

"Spain."

Fletcher fell back on the sofa and moaned. "Well, we can't. Not now."

"There must be a way."

"Oh, come on, Tristan! There's nothing we can do!"

"We have to get them home. It's a final request, Ryan. We can't refuse."

"Are you mad? How? I don't have the means. We probably won't get out with our own skins! At least they're buried somewhere."

"Don Christoval only asks for his friends. He expects nothing for himself."

"Why not? What's the difference between three and four? He doesn't want to go back?"

"He prays only for his horse to return," Tristan replied quietly, fingering the gold pendant. "Remember?"

Fletcher massaged his temples. "Oh Lord."

"Think, Ryan. I'm sure there's a way."

Fletcher studied him, unconvinced. "What time is it?"

"After two."

"Get some sleep, Tristan. You're going to need it. Go ahead. I'm wide awake. Get some sleep."

Tristan couldn't refuse. He placed two loaded revolvers on the coffee table and fell on the couch with a groan of gratitude. Fletcher dropped into Pete's favorite chair and put his feet up. Oliver was snoring next to him like the utterly worthless guard dog that he was.

94

E arly the following morning, Officer Glen Ordell - in jeans and a tee-shirt - stopped by the station to make a few quick copies. He had taken yesterday off for an interview and felt his sanity depended on the outcome. His wife had been sullen all week. The most he could do was pretend to care. Extracting the last photocopy, the officer caught sight of his lieutenant, Roy Faller, as he moseyed into the room. Ordell snatched the original from the printer and held the precious letter of recommendation to his chest.

"Oh! Glen! What timing!" Faller was beaming.

"Sir."

"You must be chomping at the bit!"

Ordell blushed. *Chomping? How did he know?* "Well, sort of. I mean, it's an opportunity, I suppose."

"An *opportunity?* Well, that's one way to put it." Faller chuckled. He was an ex-marine, in remarkable shape for his age. "You should be proud. Your instincts were right."

Instincts? What the hell was he talking about? "Maybe. I mean I hope so," Ordell sputtered.

"So here you are, saving me a phone call! Who told you, anyway? *I* only got the news an hour ago."

"News?" Ordell felt perspiration on his lip. "Yeah. Sure was quick."

"Well, it's your baby! Why aren't you in uniform?"

"Baby? Uniform? Sir? I'm not on until four . . . this afternoon."

"You don't think we're going to wait *that* long, do you?" Faller snarled. "Suit up! When Interpol calls. . . ."

"*Interpol?*"

"Don't you want the collar, Ordell? What's the matter with you?" Faller stared at him. "Do you have any idea what I'm talking about?"

"Sir? Uh, maybe not, Sir."

"Your Spaniard, Deputy! He's wanted for questioning! Murder! In Europe!"

Ordell's mouth dropped open. "No shit! I'll be right there!"

95

It was just after eight a.m. Fletcher rinsed the last dish and put his suitcase in the car. Corey would pick up Little John around midday. Tristan had left most of his clothes in the dryer, packing only the essentials: his underwear, his arsenal, and the medallion. His notes and Don Christoval's letters were wrapped in cellophane and sandwiched in cardboard at the bottom of his suitcase, which was now resting open on the rear seat. The computer and cord were on top, pillowed in a pair of jeans. Fletcher checked his watch. It was getting late. He returned to the kitchen, spying Tristan out the window. He was at the corral fence. Fletcher's cell phone trilled in his pocket. While Tristan sadly palmed his last carrot, he was shocked to see his father running to him yelling. Fletcher raced past him into the barn and reappeared, hurling a saddle and bridle over the fence.

"Tristan, you have to get out! Now! The police are coming! Hurry up!" Fletcher unhooked the gate.

"*Now!* Go! *Get on!* Hurry! *Go to Corey's!*"

"*What?* I can't. . . ."

"Yes you can! *I can handle them! Please!* Don't argue with me! Don't take the road! Hurry, damn it! They're almost here!"

Fletcher threw the saddle on the startled horse and jerked the bridle over his head.

"Ryan, what about. . . ?"

"You have to go *now*, Lad! *Now! Across the valley!*"

"Ryan, this is crazy! How will I know. . . ?"

Fletcher fumbled with the girth. "That way! Just do it! *Now!*" He stepped behind Tristan and gave him a leg up. "Stay out of sight! Stay to the north! In the trees! *Go on!*" Fletcher bounded to the west gate and lurched it open.

Trapped in the house, Oliver's frenzied yapping announced the first set of tires skidding across the gravel drive. His heart pounding, Fletcher paused just long enough to see the huge horse thunder over the northern embankment and vanish from sight. He raced into the kitchen and locked the door behind him just as two policemen ambled to the rear yard, antagonizing the dog by peeping in windows. Fletcher ducked into the garage and wrestled the luggage from the back seat. He threw his own on the cement floor, then jammed Tristan's suitcase in the wagon's hidden rear storage compartment, shutting it firmly. He opened the glove compartment, making sure it was completely exposed and locked the car. Then he walked briskly into the kitchen. With feigned surprise he acknowledged the two officers standing at the screen. Oliver continued to yelp. Fletcher snapped a leash on him and ordered him to be still.

Two more policemen pounded on the front door, one of them being Officer Ordell. He had a search warrant as well as an arrest warrant for Tristan, demanding to know where he was. Fletcher said nothing, marching defiantly down the corridor. Ordell scurried after him. In the study, Fletcher grabbed the phone and dialed Vicante's cell phone number. Ordell had the audacity to trip over the phone cord but too late. The lawyer was on his way. More police arrived. Having surmised that Fletcher wasn't the obliging type, Ordell ordered them to ransack the house. Fletcher was escorted to a chair and commanded to sit. His mind raced through details. Tristan's sheets had been washed; his bed was made. His room was at least dusted and his bathroom was spotless. For all they knew, he hadn't been there for days, except, maybe, for the clothes in the dryer. But then, they could just as easily be Fletcher's.

"Planning on leaving, Mr. Lawson?" Ordell was rifling through a desk drawer. "Sure looks like it. All that stuff in the hall there. Where're you running off to?"

Fletcher ignored him, eyeballing a yellow jacket hovering near the ceiling.

"Mr. Lawson, where's your son?"

Fletcher sighed. Ordell was a pugnacious pisshead.

"You've got big problems, Mr. Lawson." Ordell moved behind Fletcher's chair. "You're in big trouble if you're harboring a criminal. He's wanted for murder. Do you have any idea what could to happen to you?"

Fletcher coughed. He could hear police clomping down the hallway. They strode past the door with plastic gloves. By now, he was sure the house was a wreck. Maybe Mackey would understand. Ordell was nosing around the fireplace with his back to him. Soundlessly, Fletcher pulled the keys from his pocket. He cautiously detached the car key from the ring, and - waiting for the opportune moment - slipped it in his shoe. He noiselessly deposited the rest on the coffee table.

"Glen!" A police woman strode in.

"Yeah."

"I don't see any horses, but there's got to be one."

"Really! Where's the horse, Lawson?"

"Sold." Fletcher closed his eyes. He wondered how long it would take Tom to get there and – with a spasm of panic – where Tristan was by now.

For the last hour, Corey had been doing chores in her usual green gym shorts and work boots. It was already hot, but she was almost done. She plunged a hose in her stallion's tank, and - waiting for it to fill - was picking burrs from his mane when his head rocketed up. He scented the air, circled and snorted. She followed his line of sight to observe what looked like an auburn whirlwind flashing through the tree line. She climbed on the fence for a better look. From the northwest, it was heading her way at eye-popping speed. She heard the porch door slam as Elan dashed down the stairs. She called to him, opening her mouth to point it out, but he seemed to know about it, monitoring the copper giant that was now charging east through the open prairie at an incredible speed.

"Come on, John," he prayed.

He watched for another minute and then rushed to the corral, seized a lead shank off the fence and roped one of her geldings. "Corey, give me a halter! Hurry up! He's too old! He won't to make it!" He didn't wait for her, snatching a halter from the ground.

Corey stared out into the valley. "Oh my God! Is that Fletcher's. . . ?"

"I need a bridle!"

Corey dashed to the shed and emerged with one, thrusting it at him in shock.

"Is that Fletcher?"

"Open the gate!"

"Is that *Fletcher?*"

"*No!* And don't answer the phone!" Elan slipped the headstall on the horse. Stepping off a rail, he swung on bareback. He had a mare in tow. He pushed past the gate and hurtled down the slope, driving the horses westward toward a fallen charger.

Little John's sides were heaving; he was covered in lather. He was at a standstill in the middle of a grassy basin a half mile from Corey's ranch. The old Trojan couldn't take another step, threatening to collapse, but Tristan held his head up, fearing that if he went down once more he'd never rise. Elan pulled up, hopped to the ground and scanned the western cliff. He was well aware that anyone sharp-eyed on the Lawson bluff would see them. Tristan had untacked the big horse, but had left the reins around his neck. Elan ran a hand along the gelding's flanks. There was no doubt that the animal was in dire straits, but there was nothing they could do. He ordered the Spaniard to hold the haltered mare while he removed the reins from Little John. Tristan shook his head. Elan explained that they had no choice. They'd come back for him later, he said softly, but right now they had to get out of sight. Tristan wouldn't budge. Elan shouted at him, demanding that he think. Then, to his relief, he saw Corey astride her old stallion approaching at a lope. She stopped and dismounted, assuring Tristan that she'd stay with the old giraffe and bring him along when he was ready, but right now he had to go. Elan threw Little John's slathered, ill-fitting saddle on the mare, and boosted Tristan to her back. He hung the bridle on Tristan's shoulder and said not to worry, that the mare would just follow in a halter, adding quickly that Little John's leathers had to disappear with them. Elan launched onto his gelding and slapped Tristan's mare. They galloped toward Corey's, snaking under the pines that stepped like a pyramid to the butte supporting her home. They turned north and out of sight of the Lawson estate, emerging fifteen minutes later to the east side of Corey's wrap-around porch. Elan slid off, handed Tristan his reins and told him to stay put. He hurried through the scattered trees to the edge of her southwest pasture. From there, he could see how the big horse was faring. It was as expected. Corey was on her way back. Elan turned away, opting to say nothing. She'd be better at it, he thought.

Elan fell in step with Tristan as he led the horses to the barn. Tristan paused, appraised him, and then shifted his gaze to the ground. Elan took the reins and watched as the Spaniard wandered westward under a stark blue sky and then fold against an outcropping. Staring across the eternal grasslands, he was focused on the motionless shape of a deeply cherished companion.

Her stallion in tow, Corey hobbled to Elan. "Well, that's that," she muttered, glancing beyond the field to Tristan's stricken profile. "Let him be for a while."

By noon, Elan had reclaimed Tristan from his post but not from his mourning. He was seated across from Elan and Corey in her sunny dinette. She remarked that she had just seen several police cars heading east, a good sign, indicating that they were through searching the Lawson house. No one stopped at her place, either; another good sign! She chatted about Fletcher, how his mean attorney should have the police running for cover by now, and that the phone should be ringing any minute with news that he's on his way. Elan chewed quietly, exchanging glances with her. She shoved potato salad in her mouth. Tristan had his hands in his lap. She slammed her fork on the plate.

"Eat something, Tristan. You look white!"

He stared at his hands.

"Eat something!" She exhaled loudly. "I know you're upset, but the horse was old. It was his time. *It wasn't your fault,* if that's what you're thinking."

Tristan nodded, unable to say a word. To appease her, he picked up his fork and chased an olive. She saw his eyes glisten as he shifted away from her. She told Elan to get up and make some coffee, and then she leaned forward, her forefinger rapping on the table.

"You listen to me, Tristan. I can't tell you how many I've seen come and go over the years: horses, dogs, family, friends. But that's just the way it is. That's nature! Now, if you're going to have horses, you're going to have to deal with the fact that they have a destiny, just like us. *His* was to bring you here and go peacefully, and that's exactly what he did. *Stop blaming yourself!* He had a good life, better than mine, better than most, and, to boot, he lived a long one. Now eat something!"

Elan was just behind the pantry door. Catching Tristan's eye, he mimicked the act of chewing. Tristan stuffed ham in his mouth. Figuring the knot in his throat would make it hard to swallow, Corey tapped on his glass of water. He dutifully drank it and then thanked her for everything. She shrugged.

"Good water here," she commented. "Off the backs of woolly mammoths. Really! That's from an ice age aquifer. That's the oldest. . . ."

The phone rang. She snatched it. Fletcher was free. He was with his lawyer at the police station but would be there soon. Breathing resumed and suddenly, pie a la mode was a great idea.

＊ ＊ ＊

Tom Vicante wasn't happy about the sound of gravel sloshing around his wheel wells. The car was brand new, and he had to turn on yet another washer board road. He scowled.

"This better not be pitting the paint or you owe me a car, Lawson."

"I'm sure I bought this one, Tom."

Vicante laughed, dribbling soda on his Ralph Lauren shirt. "Not this one, the last one. A Porsche, remember?"

"I'd just as soon forget."

They hit a pothole. Tom's golf clubs plunked off the back seat and started clanging around the back, not that he cared. Golf, he complained, was a bore, probably why he wasn't any good at it. Fletcher glanced in the side view mirror. Noticing, Tom did the same. No one was following.

"You gonna be all right, Fletch? You sure you wanna go home?"

"Yes. Thanks, Tom. I must say, you were in rare form."

"Yeah, well, you know the drill. Scare em and run."

"I must admit, that was quite a - what do you call it - whopper?"

"*Alleged* whopper. What the hell. I couldn't let you tell it. Anyway, if you know where he is, don't tell me. So what now? I can't hold 'em forever."

"You won't have to. Tom, I want to give you power of attorney."

"For?"

"I was hoping you could close the house."

"You skipping the country?"

"Well, I. . . ."

"Don't tell me that either. Sure. You'll have to stop by the office and sign a few forms. Where do you want the money? A Swiss account?" Tom chuckled.

"Can I get one?"

The attorney frowned, easing into Fletcher's driveway. "I wouldn't do Swiss. I'll give you a website. You can take it from there." He threw the car in park. "Fletch. . . . ."

"Yes?" His client had one foot on the driveway.

"Look, I know you think he's worth it, but. . . ."

"I know what I'm doing, Tom. But, thanks. Thanks for everything. I can't tell you how grateful I am. I'll drop by." Fletcher shut the car the door.

Shaking his head, Tom steered his brand new, pitted Lexus back down the driveway.

Fletcher swept through his house into the garage. When the deputy had pressed him for car keys, he pretended to be so flustered that he couldn't find them. Ordell was immediately suspicious and had examined the car through the windows. The seats were empty and there was nothing in the glove compartment. And then he got sidetracked, seeing Fletcher's valise on the floor. Fletcher bent down and sifted through his strewn baggage. There was nothing important, so he left it. He leashed Oliver, directing him to sit over the hidden luggage compartment, slammed the rear door and started the car. He backed out a little too fast, not seeing the blockading bumper until it was almost too late. He jammed on the brake, feeling moisture beading his brow, fighting the urge to run over the son of a bitch strutting toward him.

"I see you found your car keys, Lawson. Mind if I have a look?"

"Yes, I do."

"Get out of the car."

"No."

"Lawson, so help me. . . . ."

"I'm in *my car* with *my* dog, doing errands. Does that constitute *probable cause*? You've had all morning to ransack my house! Now I've had enough! Get off my property! Or would you like to face a few charges of your own?"

The young deputy glared at him. Fletcher didn't know what nerve he had hit, but it was a good one. He pressed hard. *"Move your car! Now!"*

Ordell stood fuming with his foot involuntarily tapping. He wanted that job in the Springs. The interview had gone well. He really wasn't supposed to be there and he was alone. Lawson could claim anything. God, he really hated that lying son of a bitch, but. . . . He slowly backed away and moved his vehicle.

Fletcher rocketed down the driveway. The deputy tailed him to Corey Martin's, making a note of the stop. Why there, not all that far from his ranch? Then Ordell remembered. He spit out the window. She was the real estate agent. The lawyer said his place was about to close. Mackey had bought it. Lawson said that the keys on the coffee table were for her, for the inspection. So, that was probably what he was doing: dropping them off.

Cracking open Corey's curtains, Fletcher thanked her for the offer of a sandwich, but said he couldn't eat. He peeked out the window. He didn't see Ordell's sooty sedan but that didn't mean anything. He could be right outside. Pete had called on the cell phone. Ray would haul his tractor over after work. It was insanity, absolute insanity, Pete declared. In fact, given the circumstances, it was suicidal. Elan called it the stupidest thing he'd ever heard. Corey told him that he was being an idiot. If he wouldn't think of himself, think of Tristan; his whole life was at stake. Fletcher said he knew. But then, Tristan wouldn't leave otherwise. So be it, Fletcher thought, closing the curtains.

Ray's tractor was an enormous dinosaur, moaning and groaning as it backed off the flatbed. The timbers popped with every inch of its weight. It was a miracle that he made it, Elan declared. Ray agreed. It took him almost an hour to get there. That box they wanted was in the back of the pick-up: nothing fancy, but it was short notice. His truck still smoking, Ray wedged himself under the hood. There was no time for that, Corey snapped. Would the tractor make it all the way to Fletcher's lugging fifteen hundred pounds? Ray pulled his head into view. Of course it would, he exclaimed, but it would take a while! It's not like it was paved out there. Well, then, she declared, he better get started!

Waiting for Ray's old Deere to advance, Elan mounted Corey's older mare. The tractor belched all the way up the driveway, leaving a thick plume of smoke and a trail of grease stains. Ray had three containers of lubricant taped to the open floor, as well as a stash of bottled water and a bungeed jug of diesel. As the colossus crested the hill, Elan's horse became white-eyed and bolted sideways. The mechanic turned the contraption straight at the western slope. It looked terrifyingly steep. Elan, Corey and Fletcher stared at each other and then at Ray. The diesel fumes must have made him light-headed.

"Wait!" Corey shrieked over the rumble. "You sure about this Ray?"

He leaned forward and peered over the bucket, then planted himself firmly into the seat. "Sure! Look out, baby! *Here we go!*"

In a blast of black fury, the monster plunged over the hill. The onlookers gasped and rushed through the smoke to the perimeter. The tractor was flying down the embankment, clanging, bouncing and leaping over the terrain. Elan spurred his horse and charged after it. Corey cried after Ray, but all she heard over the excruciating din was a high-pitched, "*Yahoooooooooooo!*"

"I hope he knows what he's doing."

Fletcher and Corey spun around. Pete had arrived. His smile was reassuring.

✳ ✳ ✳

As the afternoon waned, Tristan was called upstairs from Corey's cellar, where he had been stowed at Fletcher's insistence. Elan was at the canyon, on a cell phone reporting the latest to Corey. Ray was still at it, digging a ditch that - if it went much deeper - would hit China. It was pretty low on the rise but as far up as they dared go; the tractor almost tipped twice. By the way, Elan added, since they were on their way over, they might bring something to drink. Corey said she'd do better than that, stuffing tuna sandwiches into a plastic bag. Elan then asked for Fletcher. She handed him the phone.

"Fletcher?"

"Yes." He stepped over Oliver and into the hallway.

"I didn't see anyone at your house today, but that doesn't mean anything, you know?"

"Yes, I know."

"This is stupid, Fletcher."

"Yes, I know."

There was a momentary hush. "Did Corey pick up my horse?"

"The gray one, yes . . . and fed the rest."

"Good." Elan took a deep breath. "Tell him to leave at dusk. I'll meet him half way, somewhere in the trees, north. It's a full moon, tonight. You know that?"

"Yes."

"This is a *stupid,* Fletcher! *Really stupid!*"

"Yes."

"I mean it. *He's seriously nuts!*"

Look, I understand. You've done more than enough. I'm very grateful."

Elan exhaled irritably into the phone. "Don't take your car! Tell Pete to keep an eye out. Stick with Corey. She's a hell of a shot."

"I'm sorry?"

"I *said* stick with Corey. She's a hell of a shot!"

Fletcher glanced around the corner. She was still at the counter. "You've got to be kidding," he whispered. "I don't want her involved! And she shouldn't have a gun either! She can't even read a menu!"

"That might be true, Fletcher, but if it moves, she can hit it. And she's already *involved,* thanks to you. Look, the battery's low. Gotta go."

"See you shortly." Fletcher clicked off, sensing someone behind him. He turned.

"Elan?' Tristan queried.

"Yes. He said he'd meet you. Tristan?"

"Yes?"

"Remind me why we're doing this?"

"Because we have no choice. We have to free him."

"Right," Fletcher replied, biting his lip. "I knew it was something like that."

96

The sun hung low in the western sky, searing the brittle pine and parched grass. In its glare, a lone horse and rider were aglow in red, escaping the setting inferno by loping under a canopy of smoldering trees and crumbling rock.

Fletcher demanded that Corey stay behind, fuming while she skirted around him. She was humming as she loaded provisions and set a fully loaded hunting relic on the rear seat. He claimed that it wasn't her affair, that it wasn't a picnic and that she had no right to intrude. Then he was contrite, begging her to please listen. She hiked herself onto the driver's seat and started the truck, asking him with raised eyebrows whether he was coming or not. He glowered, crossing his arms. She threw the truck in reverse. He dashed for the passenger side.

Pete had said that he had an errand to do and that he'd meet them after sunset. As her truck rolled along, Corey sang off-key, while Fletcher - vigilant of the road and the endless prairie – fixed on anything that looked strange. But, then it all looked strange. He realized that his heart was pounding. He wiped the dust from his eyes. There'd be no more terms, confrontations or negotiations, something that as of late, he was regretting. By now, Porter would have unleashed everything he had on Egan, leaving the mariner dangerously isolated. Tristan was wanted on a murder charge, and no doubt, Fletcher's art theft would be the next Interpol transmission. They should be running. Instead they were burying a horse. Elan was right; it was absolute lunacy. It was. . . .

"Fletcher, did you hear me? *Which way?*"

"Oh. Take a right, Corey. In a mile or so you'll probably see Ray."

The tractor was quiet when they arrived. Ray was perched on it, chewing on a stick. Waving hello, Corey and Fletcher decamped from the cab and pulled rations from the back seat. Ray leapt from his rig and sauntered over. Two minutes later, the preacher pulled up. Rolling down his window, he asked if there was any sign of the other two yet. Fletcher said no. Pete said he would wait in the car. A huge moon was rising, so brilliant that it blanketed the summer landscape in spectral snow.

Tristan's horse was picking his way through the woods, following an old deer path. In the ethereal light, the ragged outcroppings were mystically featured, whispering a tongue so ancient that it was lost on the modern stranger. The wind chanted. Branches swayed. Through a canopy of needles, the moon stole glimpses of the interloper, curiously watching as he passed through the night.

In a clearing on a pine covered hill, another was waiting. He was soaked in a lunar glow and astride a grullo horse. He had a broad-brimmed hat, a rifle and a keen eye, and – unlike his contemporary – understood the ancient language around him. He recognized an incongruous rustle and the censure of a startled bird. He detected the crushing of pinecones and the snap of a twig under foot. He descended into the pine swamped valley. The moon held her breath and shrank behind a passing cloud, only to reemerge, as he did, washed in silver splendor with a horseman as his prize.

With well-lit landmarks, Elan and Tristan rode confidently westward and reached the old logging road that would lead them to

Don Christoval's canyon. It wasn't long before they saw the shape of vehicles and heard the timbre of voices in the murky arroyo ahead.

✳ ✳ ✳

With his flashlight wedged between two rocks, Fletcher had toiled assiduously in the dark. Now done, he stood on a boulder, a pensive silhouette against the flashlight's harsh beam. It was as if Tristan was seeing him there for the first time, when he was a sad recluse addressing his only friend, a sixteenth century hidalgo who had managed, somehow, to safeguard a twenty-first century soul. Guided by a son's rare instincts, it was time to return a favor. Fletcher gazed upon the venerable bones that lay in Ray's box.

"Do you need help?" Tristan scaled the incline.

"Just to carry him down."

As Fletcher reached for the lid, Tristan ordered him to wait and sprang to the coffin. He slipped the medallion from under his shirt and around his neck. From its chain axis, it spun like a golden sun, coruscating color across Don Christoval's remains. As Tristan lowered it, Fletcher grabbed his arm.

"I think it was meant for you, lad. I truly do."

Tristan deliberated, his soft eyes tempering the skull's hollow stare. Then he nodded, sliding the gold chain back over his head. He kissed The Falcon's cranium and addressed him in his native tongue. His parting words were in Latin: *mora janua vitae.*

The ancient captain was then transported to his final resting place. It was near the base of the slope, in a deep trough occupied with the remains another: an incomparable eighteen hand warrior, waiting for his caballero.

Ray tapped on Pete's window. The minister gathered up his material and emerged from the car, ignoring the group's gasps. He was overflowing in white satin and gold embroidery, resembling a Medici pontiff.

"What's with the get-up, Pete?" Ray stammered, trying to contain his laughter.

"I'm sure he was a Catholic, Ray, in a time of great formality. The least I could do is dress the part."

The rancher inspected the back seat. "What about the hat?"

Everyone chuckled save Tristan.

Pete surveyed the assembly with narrowing eyes. "I want to remind all of you that we are here to honor a man with our solemn tribute. We are here to observe his final wishes and preside over him in the name of God. He was a soldier in a time of great trial, a devoted father and a man of good character. This is a serious event and I expect conduct *appropriate to the occasion*. Is everyone clear?"

Sobered, the group jostled to the gravesite. Corey lit several candles, having strategically placing them on boulders surrounding the deep pit. The great horse was just beneath the hidalgo, his red coat a muted copper in the astral light. His large head was curled into his chest, his eyes vacant. Upon seeing him, Elan swallowed hard and turned away.

Clipped to his Bible, Pete's tiny halogen lamp highlighted his face so that it appeared flat and gleaming like a medieval icon. His voice echoed through the open air cathedral, while the moon cast it in a ghostly light. He read in Latin and performed the sacraments as well as he could remember, asking the others to join him as per the ritual. Crowding around him, they complied. Then Pete knelt, scattering a bouquet of lilies over the remains of Don Christoval Alcon de Navarre y Marquis and a horse named Little John, wishing them God speed and calling for silent prayer.

For all those present, it was a defining moment, but for Fletcher, it was more. It was his soul's reclamation. Perhaps it wasn't Don Christoval's timeless energy that rushed through him that night; perhaps it was Meredith's - cleansing him of guilt and resurrecting him - for Elan was touched by it, too, left whole and able to love again. Tristan had already been imbued with the ancestral power that had guided him there and to the life he had so desperately wanted. But, in that bittersweet moment, he was strangely aware of his mother, assured of her love. And so it was.

They were all witness to it – an extraordinary force - although there were no tangible signs: no wind gusts, animal cries or unseen touches. Yet it was real: familiar, recognized from deep within, epic and vast, much greater than the scope of their lives. It was cosmic, like the ephemeral brush of a universe with another. It defied extrinsic explanation, yet it was the visceral truth. It was souls sweeping through them, pausing before eternity. It was a flash, a glimpse, a *light*.

Pete squeezed into his car as Tristan and Elan mounted up. Ray was on his Deere. Corey directed her headlights at the crater as the tractor roared back into duty, filling the hole with surprising speed. Fletcher was on the bluff, looking longingly toward his home. He had stupidly abandoned his suitcase and now had no change of clothes. He was filthy. The house was still. It wouldn't take but a minute. He glanced below. Pete was still there, probably waiting for Ray who was now surfacing the area with rock and pine needles. Corey was calling for Fletcher over the din. He sighed and trudged back down the hill.

"Where were you?" she hollered. "We're ready to go."

Ray's machine sputtered into silence. "What about the tractor?" Fletcher asked, passing under its shadow.

"We'll get it tomorrow."

As Corey started the truck, Fletcher strolled to Pete's window and thanked him and the heavy equipment operator just settling into the passenger's side. He reminded them to be vigilant. He slapped the trunk as they sped away. Then, he opened the truck door and informed Corey that he'd be right back.

"Where are you going?"

"To get a change of clothes."

"*Your house? You can't,* Fletcher! No!"

"I'll just be a minute."

"No! *No!* It's not safe! You know it!" She shut off the engine.

"Corey, please! I'll be right back."

She pulled the rifle from behind her seat and shimmied out of the truck. "Idiot," she spewed, slamming the door.

"Corey!"

"I'm going!"

"*No!* I said *no!*"

She flicked her hand at him. He exhaled angrily. "You can come as far as the yard. Then I'm going alone."

As she didn't protest, they proceeded up the slope and across a small field that led to the sanctuary. Scanning his surroundings, Fletcher felt a twinge of sorrow. The barn was lifeless. The house was dark.

They reached the garden's east perimeter. "Corey, stay here. *Right here!*" I'll fetch a few things and be right back."

"I'll be *over there,*" she countered, pointing to the west wall, "where I can see better! You've got four minutes, then I'm coming in."

"Corey, you're pissing me off!"

"Four minutes!"

"*Christ!*" he hissed, trotting across the yard. The kitchen door was unlocked.

Four minutes came and went without Fletcher reappearing. Corey waited another three before venturing into the yard. She peered through the gloom. She hadn't seen a light go on. The house was silent. She crept to the porch, calling softly for him. There was no response. Heart pounding, she tiptoed to the kitchen door. It was yawning into a dark interior. She stepped inside, whispering for him, hiking the rifle to her shoulder. He didn't answer. She groped along the wall for a light switch. The fluorescents flared painfully. There was no sign of him. Her heart beat wildly. She hurried down the hallway, flipping every switch, calling for him. The house was ablaze. There was no reply. She scanned the bedrooms and baths. There was no indication that he had ever even been there. She ran to the front door, flung it open and shouted his name. All she saw were tail lights dipping under the crown of the driveway. She raced across the gravel, bringing the rifle to her shoulder. The car was almost out of range. Feeling dizzy, she forced herself to be steady, aim low and fire. A tail light vanished with the first blast. Again, she squeezed the trigger. The vehicle was gone. She crumpled in the driveway, screaming for Fletcher, screaming for God, for help. Then, she realized she had one more chance. She ran into the house, seized the phone and dialed 9-1-1. She shrieked about a car heading east. Someone had broken into a house. No, no license but it was missing a tail light. Hurry! They could still catch him!

Officer Ordell got the call.

The suspect's car had just passed him. It was a late model Buick with a shattered tail light, clocking sixty along the Rodham Road. Ordell radioed in and sounded his siren. The sedan pulled over immediately.

The deputy knew he should wait for assistance, but it might be another ten minutes. He was near the edge of the county. He was brimming with excitement. Might it be the Spaniard? Extending his arm out of the window, he kept his flashlight high, using a loudspeaker to order the two visibles out of the car. They complied with hands raised, offering identification. Ordell stepped from his vehicle with his gun level and instructed them to lie on the ground. One buckled obligingly while the other immediately dashed into a grove of cottonwoods. Ordell hollered after him, whirling around to the prostrate suspect when he heard a blast. As he fell, he felt his wife touching his arm, saying that he had forgotten his dinner. He smelled her freshly shampooed hair. He saw the wide eyes of his infant daughter, formula escaping her smile, and then he saw a shadow. It was his executioner.

The state and local police searched obsessively for the Buick but to no avail. The plates were stolen. They had no registration. What they did have, however, were fingerprints, lifted from a .45 discarded at the scene. They belonged to one Ryan Lawson Egan, better known as Fletcher Lawson, wanted in connection with an art theft in Great Britain.

Relentlessly grilled, Corey kept repeating the same story. She never saw the driver, just the car. All she knew was that Fletcher went into his house for clean clothes and never came out. He wasn't a murderer. He wouldn't kill a bug! Her interrogators became more denigrating by the hour. Not only did they not believe her Lawson story, they certainly didn't buy the mad-scientist crap she kept reciting. Faller intervened. She may have been played for a fool, he said, but was innocent all the same. She was released.

Corey had made one other phone call that night: to her answering machine, telling Elan to pick up. Of course he didn't; he wasn't there yet, but apparently he got the message. When she arrived home that morning, there was a note on the counter. He had to leave town for a while with an old pal. Don't worry, he wrote. Exhausted, she collapsed on a chair, stroking Fletcher's dog as tears soaked his tousled hair.

Elan escaped with Tristan so irate that the only way to get him into his tack trunk was to promise that they would head directly for Zephon, Inc. The idea was to get into the building any way possible and see how disruptive they could be before getting either killed, arrested or an answer to Fletcher's whereabouts. It wasn't much of a plan. Elan didn't hold out much hope, but Tristan had saved his life, so what the hell.

Despite the hour, the warehouse had plenty of cars in the lot. Elan parked a couple of blocks away and released his charge. Tristan emerged better humored. He had an idea. When Elan heard it, he laughed out loud; it was *that* ridiculous. But that was exactly what Tristan liked about it.

So they walked to the depot at three in the morning, Tristan carrying his .45 handgun, his pockets bulging with ammunition, and Elan with an old pistol, sure he'd never get a shot off. But, then, that was the plan, and there was no talking Tristan out of it. Elan's stomach ached. At the edge of the lot, Elan tried to stop him, but Tristan yanked his arm away and trotted across the asphalt in full view. He took aim and exploded a light over the docking area. Sparks rained down like meteors. Elan was forced into action. Tristan fired two rounds into a window. The alarm sounded. He jogged to the door in full view of a brand new camera, and - shouting Spanish obscenities - obliterated the lens. In the meantime, Elan had raced across the north lawn and down the east side of the building where he was crouched at the corner. Tristan was waiting just ten feet away, but he might as well have been a mile.

Incredibly, the alarm was silenced and the door opened without gunfire. Two men greeted the troublemaker. They were right there, a clean shot from Elan, breathing vapors into the cool air. The bald one - built like a wrestler - shoved Tristan to the ground. The other one – wearing an enormous ring – disarmed him, hoisted him up and shoved him through the door. Tristan had been right. First and foremost, Eckhart was a business man, and having Tristan alive was too good a deal to pass up. No one bothered to have a look around, but, then, Tristan had predicted that, too. They'd think he was brash enough to come on his own. Elan licked his lips. So far so good. Now for the hard part.

Tristan's hands were zip tied behind him. He was steered through the front office into the huge space known as the work room. Porter's electronic map was ablaze with color and rapidly modulating with data input. The place was buzzing with the sound of voltage, voices and typing. The extended table was dotted with reading lights and piled with papers. There were eight people manning the computers: four men and four women in lab coats, none of whom Tristan recognized. He was shielded from view by the bald man as he was hustled to the rear quarters. Tristan's ringed escort then squeezed him through the entry and shoved him to the floor. He was told not to move. The heavy guard left.

Tristan gazed up at the gleaming stainless steel panels spanning the wall behind Porter's kewpie doll face. The scientist remained glued to a computer, acknowledging his new arrival with a mere nose flare. As he attacked the key board, Tristan twisted around to see if there was anything under the covers on the cot. His heart leapt. Whatever it was, it was breathing.

Porter slammed the Enter key, sighed, and peered around the screen.

"Tristan! I could hardly believe my good fortune! Naturally, I sent a few people to look around outside. Let's start with: *where are they?*"

Tristan remained silent.

"My guess is it's just the Indian." Porter stood up, taking off his glasses. "Well that shouldn't be too hard." He dropped his glasses on the desk and rubbed the bridge of his nose. "How long have you known him, Tristan . . . your Indian? A month or two? Something like that?"

"Why?"

"Just curious. How long have you known Mathew? How long have you been paling around? Four or five years now, right?"

Tristan shifted his weight off his shoulder and onto his hip. "How is he?"

Porter smirked. "Good of you to ask. As of yesterday, better. I went to see him, thinking of you, thinking how ironic it was that after cleaning up all your messes, keeping you alive, not to mention *sane* – no easy task - that he should be rewarded with a stroke, all because you shot him in the chest and left him there bleeding like an animal. Tell me, Tristan, did you step over him on your way out? Did your Indian? I mean, he's what you traded Matt for, isn't he?"

Tristan closed his eyes. The ringed man was standing directly over him. He was wearing boots. It was going to hurt and it did. It was a vicious kick; a rib cracked.

"That'll do!" Porter barked. "So, what was your plan, to find your padre and go home? Was that it? Well you certainly have found him. He's right over there. Apparently, he wasn't at all cooperative, so he's not doing very well. In fact, he hasn't budged since last night."

Tristan could hardly breathe. The pain was excruciating.

Porter crouched over him. "After all the crap I've put with, and all the trouble you've caused, this day is your last, you ungrateful *shit!* But before you go, you're going to smile for the camera - a family portrait - just you and Dad for grandpa. Then, you're going to e-mail him with that clever code of yours, and tell him to release my daughter or God help me, I'll make your father's last hours so miserable, he'll beg me to kill you!" Porter's hands trembled; his face flushed. He stood up and rubbed his forehead. "God, I hate this! But it's the only way to deal with scum like you! You reduce us all, Tristan! Now, get up! *Get him up!*"

Tristan was hoisted to his feet. Porter's cell phone was vibrating off the desk, caught by the guard supporting Tristan by the armpit. He handed it to Porter, who thanked him by name: Trevor.

"Yes? Well, keep an eye out, Claude. I'm sure there's only one. Have Rolf come in. You stay out there. The delivery should be here any minute. I don't want any problems."

Porter clicked off, sighed and informed Trevor that it was time for the photograph and a few vials of blood.

Tristan was told to sit on the cot. Fletcher was propped up, buttressed between him and the wall. His face was gray and caked with dried blood. His mouth fell open. His teeth were brown. His right ear sent a trickle of red down his neck. He sagged to Tristan's shoulder. Porter shook his head. There was a rapping at the door. It was Rolf. Trevor directed him through an Aussie accent. Rolf withdrew and then reappeared with an armful of white towels.

"Is he still alive?" Porter grimaced.

Rolf nodded, vigorously wiping Fletcher's mouth.

"Well, he doesn't look it. Put his hands in front of him, and try to keep his head up. Christ! You can thank yourself for this, Tristan! Poor idiot, listening to you! That'll do." Porter threw a newspaper on Fletcher's lap, pointing at it. "Make sure we can see the date. Trevor, here's the camera. You know how to work it?"

"Yeh."

"Tristan, smile for your grandfather or we'll plaster one on your face." Porter glanced at Fletcher and turned away. "Poor bastard. Take the damn picture!"

The camera whirred and clicked. Trevor parked himself at the desk, quickly loaded the digital into the computer, and rose as Porter took his place. Porter then instructed him to get a woman named Sarah from the main room. He needed the blood samples now, and then he'd have Tristan e-mail the good captain.

An overweight woman arrived with a small satchel, asking how much blood was needed. Pulling out a desk drawer, Porter said he wanted at least six vials from each and slapped them on the desk. She pulled on plastic gloves and extracted needles from her case. Then, standing over Tristan, she looked questioningly at Porter. He barked at her to go ahead. She announced that she needed Tristan's hands untied, or at least in front of him to get enough. Porter motioned to Rolf to untie him, but to shoot him if he so much as flinched. She then proceeded. When it was Fletcher's turn, she dallied, muttering something about his not being able to spare much. Porter glared at her. She averted her eyes and tapped a vein. Porter's cell phone rang. He received the news with a grunt.

"The delivery's here. How long will you be, Sarah?"

"I'm almost done. Where do you want these?"

"In the walk-in." Porter sorted through a ring of keys. "Label them please! Lawson Egan on that bunch; Tristan Egan on the other." Porter fumbled with the locks on the refrigerator and pulled the steel panel open. "Put them on the second shelf in the corner. Careful! *Don't touch anything!*"

Porter's phone rang again. This time he rang off red-faced. "Trevor, get out there!"

"What happened?" Trevor rushed toward the door.

"Some damned fracas around the truck. Probably the Indian! As if we have time for this! Tristan, I can't *wait to be rid of you!* Sarah, *hurry up!*"

She scribbled on the last vial and gathered up as many as she could safely carry. She scurried into the walk-in and dashed out. Fletcher slumped forward. Tristan used his shoulder to block his fall. Rolf tapped his gun against Tristan's forehead and grabbed Fletcher by the hair. Pushing him back against the wall, Rolf suddenly hollered, crumbling with a kick to the groin.

Fletcher leapt over him, sending a torrent of papers airborne as he vaulted over Porter's desk. Tristan foiled Rolf's shot and grappled for the gun. Sarah collided with Fletcher as she darted for the exit while Porter yelled into the intercom for help, simultaneously pressing a digit on his cell phone. Fletcher slapped the mobile from his hand and dove into the freezer. Tristan had both hands on the guard's pistol while the man beat him pitilessly with his free fist. Porter threw himself against the walk-in door, but it wouldn't latch. He kicked the cell phone from the breach, and repeatedly slammed his weight against the door, but it was too late. Fletcher was braced on the other side, his arm wedged painfully in the gap with an icy test tube dangling from his fingers. Rolf wrenched the gun free and held it to Tristan's temple, waiting for Porter's ruling but it didn't come. With a stricken look, the scientist shook his head and backed away from the stainless steel aperture. Trevor and Claude burst into the room. Fletcher's exposed fingers continued to wiggle the test tube as he slowly splayed the door. Porter spun to his security force with a frantic signal to stop.

Fletcher held the tube out in front of him, staring at Rolf. "Put the gun down. Slide it to me and get away from him."

Rolf glanced at Porter, who bobbed his head. Tristan rolled on his side, groaning. The guard placed the gun on the floor and pushed it toward Fletcher. Tristan weakly intercepted it.

"Porter," Fletcher rasped with a ruby smile, shaking the tube. "Tell them to do the same and stand very still."

Porter stared apprehensively at his security team. Pistols were slowly placed on the floor.

"Good. Tristan? Can you come here, Lad?"

Tristan rose haltingly to his feet, limped around the desk and stood hunched at his father's shoulder.

"Well, I'm astounded!" Porter exclaimed. "Fletcher - if you don't mind my asking – just how long *have* you been awake?"

"Long enough. You like ironies, Porter? How about this one? You wanted blood to prevent the precise situation you're in right now: someone threatening you with your own stupid concoction, someone immune, while *you're not!*"

Porter smiled. "So, what makes you think you've got the right stuff, Fletcher? From here, I can't tell. There're all kinds of formulas in there."

"Well, there's only one way to find out." Fletcher rolled the glass over, raised his arm, and diminished his hold to two fingers.

"*Don't!* Fletcher, don't."

"Up to you."

The bio-engineer threw up his hands. "There's too much at stake. You've seen it! I know it's hard to comprehend. Life as we know it. . . ."

"So you've said, but tell me true, Porter. Isn't it really a power grab?"

"No." Porter licked his lips. "All right, Fletcher. You win. Take your boy and go home. Live your life. If you have a long one, you can thank me for it. I'm sorry they hurt you, I *truly* am, and you know it. Why did you resist? I wouldn't have let them do that if I had been there, but these men . . . well, war is war. That's what this is and everything - and I mean *everything* - is at stake. In the end, you'll thank me for it."

"Tempting, Porter. But there's no home to go to, remember? Besides, I don't think I want you in charge."

"*In charge?* I have no interest in politics. My interest is in preservation and - for a change - serving the greater good."

"Right, although I think you're just as keen on toppling the powers that be."

"And you're opposed to that? You're opposed eliminating the very people who would keep you groveling, Fletcher? The very people who are poisoning an entire planet *for profit* and robbing men like you of a future?"

I'm opposed to all of you."

"Where's Elan?" Tristan muttered.

Porter shrugged, glancing at Trevor. "Well?"

"He's all right," Claude interjected. "He's out there, in the front office."

"All right, Fletcher," Porter crooned. "there you have it. You can take him, too. I'll fix your problem, though it might take some time. The hounds are loose now - as you know - and not so easy to call home. All I want, for the sake of civility, is my daughter. She's not responsible. You can do that much."

Fletcher stepped forward. "Tell them to move away from the door." He thrust the tube at Porter. "I mean it."

Porter stepped backward. "Gentlemen. . . ."

Fletcher took another step. "How many will this little vial kill, Porter? What's the *optimum efficiency?* How many? Fifty? A hundred?"

"More. And for your information, at that concentration, I doubt *you'd* survive it."

"Tell them to get out of the way!" Fletcher shouted. "All of you! Stand over there by the bed. Not you, Porter. You stick with me. You boys, slide your keys over here to Tristan."

Tristan aimed his pistol at Rolf's head. The latter kept a wary eye on him and moved slowly, bending down to dispatch his keys. He exchange glances with Trevor and Claude who followed suit. Tristan snatched the sets from the floor, and, backing toward the door, kicked the surrendered pistols toward the exit.

"Come on, Porter, out!" Fletcher ordered. "Tell them to stay here, keep quiet and not to call anyone! The first sign of trouble, I'll drop this thing. Stay close, Porter. And don't bump my arm."

Fletcher shadowed the scientist while Tristan gathered up the weaponry, slipped from the office and locked it. Fletcher surveyed the cavernous hall. The map was alive, its modulating screen licking color over the staff like a flicking tongue. Most of them were on their feet, gaping at their captive leader. Fletcher inspected them; it was the wrong count. There was someone else there: him - the one in a loud cabana shirt - rising from the work station.

"Shame on you, boys!" Pete's voice boomed across the rafters. "Not telling us a thing! But it's all right. Thanks to the intercom, we heard the whole thing!"

Fletcher stared at him. Tristan trained on him like a rattlesnake.

"Elan's O.K," Pete quickly added. "Ray's with him, in front there. Fletcher, how about you?"

"I'll manage, thanks to a hard head. How did you know. . . ?"

The minister strode toward him. "Where else would you be!"

"Stop there!" Tristan ordered.

The big man halted and shifted his attention to the scientist. "Well, Porter. Evidently, there's a new plan."

"So there is. Needless to say, it's not mine." Porter tipped his head Fletcher. "He's got a better one, one that would doom us all to extinction. If you look closely, Peters, you'll see he's about to do *just that*."

Pete scanned Fletcher.

"What's going on?" A lab coat suddenly blurted. *"Where's security?"*

Thumbing his revolver, Tristan yelled, "Sit down. All of you *sit!* Keep your hands flat on the table!"

The personnel rushed to their seats. Pete stood squarely in front of Fletcher. "If that's what you've got, Fletch, maybe you should set it down."

Fletcher glared at him.

"Or at least sit down," Pete suggested, assessing his friend. "You need as doctor. Let's get you some water. Then in a hushed voice, he continued, "Fletcher, I can see that you don't understand but try to bear with me. You're in the company of our greatest minds. Surely we don't want to lose them."

"What?" Fletcher shouted at him. "Stand back, Pete! I mean it! *Stand back!*"

Tristan pointed the gun at him. The big man didn't budge.

"*What the hell's wrong with you?*" Fletcher snapped. "*Whose side are you on?*"

"Easy Fletch," Pete whistled softly. "There's only one side." Then he turned to Porter Eckhart and thundered, "When was the last time you sat through a sermon?"

"*What?*" Porter squinted at him.

"A sermon!" Pete grinned.

"Sunday. Yours. It was awful. Have you lost your mind, Peters? I don't buy any of that."

"I have a proposition. A chess match. I win: you and your colleagues give me an hour of your undivided attention. You win: my brethren and I leave safely but without your formula. What say you Eckhart? A chess match. You were good. Are you still?"

Porter tilted his head quizzically. "Peters?"

"Seems to me there's a set in front there," Pete quipped.

Tristan shot Fletcher a wild look, but Fletcher was staring at Pete, smoldering. Suddenly, he turned to Tristan and whispered, "I have no idea what he's doing. But, *we're not a part of this.*"

"How about *this*, Peters?" Porter's delivery was sing-song, as if indulging a child or a lunatic. "*I* win; I get *my daughter* and the vial. *You* win, same deal, you get *them,* safely out the door."

Pete nodded his head. "I like it." He looked to Fletcher for approval but didn't get it. He shrugged and extracted a cell phone from his pocket. "You ready, Eckhart?"

"I. . . .Whatever you say," the scientist sputtered.

The minister thumbed numbers on his cell phone. Soon after, Ray appeared with the set. Elan trailed behind him, dragging a chair for Fletcher. Pete sidled up to his companions. Fletcher seized him by the shoulder. "*What are you up to?* Look, I don't want to leave you here, but. . . ."

"What are you going to do with the vial, Fletch?" Pete whispered gruffly. "Toss it in the garbage? Please, just take it easy. Sit down. Have a little faith! And careful with that stuff!" The Reverend winked and unhitched himself. He ushered Porter to the work station. The bewildered staff made room as the opponents faced off.

Pete was expressionless. In fact, he looked like he was falling asleep, barely acknowledged Porter's opening move. He lazily advanced a pawn. Porter unleashed his knights, alternating their play with his bishops. Fletcher winced as Pete sacrificed piece after piece. He exposed his major players, skirting them around the board in a haphazard fashion. Porter chased, claiming a knight, a castle and now cornering Pete's queen.

Tristan poked Fletcher in the arm. "Isn't he *losing?*"

"So it would seem," Fletcher muttered.

The reverend advanced his rook, threatening Porter's dark knight in a cross-fire. Porter thought little of it and seized the minister's white lady. Fletcher groaned softly. Pete's king would be next. But, then, something happened. It was as if Fletcher was able to distance himself, and see the game – for the first time - in its entirety. He gulped, elbowing Tristan and nodding. Pete advanced his knight. Check. The geneticist leaned over the board, adjusting his glasses. He fingered his queen but - anticipating the next move, and then the next - groaned loudly. Pete would have his hour.

The victor took center stage and waited while Fletcher and his troupe arranged themselves before the world screen. Its blue light washed their bruised and furrowed faces, making them seem ageless and pure. Pete made sure that every eye was on him, returning each impassive stare with intense focus, taking extra time to engage Porter. The scientific elite watched Pete circumspectly, not sure they weren't witness to a madman. But as per Porter's decree, they indulged him as they would their own adored leader.

"Are we a universe of dimensions? Something on the order of membranes?" Pete thundered, his arms sweeping the space. "The recent M-theory reacquainted us with the fantastic yet cogent possibility that there *is* more than one universe. Maybe infinite! Imagine that! But, then it's just an equation, an exploration . . . an attempt to mathematically prove Big Bang's feasibility . . . to explain the birth of our universe and back, back beyond this simple place we know. Still, it's remarkable, isn't it? That our greatest minds – *your minds* - are posing such formidable questions: questions difficult to *ask*, much less answer! Yet, you do! *We* do! We ask! We ask because we have to know! We're driven to know!" Pete began pacing back and forth. "*How did it all happen? Where* did it begin? *When* did it take place? *What* is the origin of life? *How* did we come to be? And . . . *how* can we achieve immortality – maybe with a little genetic alteration - so we can ask even *more* tortuous questions!*"

There was a flurry of laughter as Pete halted, stooped and plucked a tiny pebble from his sandal.

"We don't have the answers but we're sure working on it! *You're* working on it: the hows, the whats, the whens, the wheres, even the *what-ifs!* We pose questions just that way: *how, what, when, where* because the solutions – however difficult or seemingly impossible - are in fact, tangible, *material, physical: can be* and *will be* found right here on our *very own secular plane!* It's true! You're proof-positive! You're digging deeper and deeper into our formation and the structure of life. You can clone, fuse, and create new life-forms. You can estimate the distance of a star and calculate its energy. *What, when, how, where.* . . . We're learning, because of *you,* and it's monumental. It's awesome!" Pete's gaze settled momentarily on Porter, and then he continued.

"But, what of the question we don't dare ask? What of the question so incomprehensible, so agonizing that we avoid it, even as it speaks to our very core? The question of *why. Why? Why* did we come out of nothing? Why evolve from algae? Why become multi-celled life forms? *Why?* Why would an infinite void suddenly swirl with gasses to form galaxies, black-holes, stars, planets, carbon, nitrogen, oxygen, microbes, *life? Why?*

We've got a pretty good idea of *when*, even *what* may have happened. We're working on *how*; we're pretty comfortable with *how*; but we don't like *why*, because *why* takes us out of our corporeal dimension, our world, our universe, our nest, so to speak, and forces us into *real flight*, beyond mere logic and the security of our conscious existence, beyond our physical limitations into a transcendental reach. And we're not ready yet, or so we tell ourselves. So what do we do in the interim? We endure in our finite realm; we explore and exploit it. We try to master its structure, its content, its gifts. And maybe," Pete scanned them, "*if* we can preserve it long enough, we can someday work on *why*. But we mustn't delay. *Why* is *the* question, the essential question, the crucial question because it can explain *everything*. So however frightening it is, it's imperative that we not be anchored by the physical questions, that we see beyond our horizon and understand that we – each of us - are a part of something greater than our limited awareness, a part of the *why*. And that, ladies and gentlemen, *is what faith is*. It's our intuitive recognition that there's more to us than this mere moment - this temporal place - and it is what keeps us reaching!"

Porter's staff seemed mesmerized, their shiny, rapt faces mirroring the huge electronic display. Pete loomed before them - a pastel Olympian against the hemispheres – and took a deep breath.

"Einstein forever transformed us, forced us into a staggering evolutionary leap with a single concept. He didn't alter our genes or our environment; he simply changed our perception of what had always been. Staggering! An idea, an equation and we're forever changed! And that's just the beginning! What a fantastic time to experience this plane!"

Pete stopped pacing. His large finger outlined the African continent as he reflected quietly.

"I don't doubt that we're here because some little quadruped climbed down from a tree and walked upright on a savannah. That a mother – somewhere during a Roman siege or the plague of the

Middle Ages - subsisted long enough to see her offspring into adulthood, and so on through the centuries. Biology. That's the process. That's *how* we are here, in this form. But is our survival all that important? Is any? When you really think about it, we suffer a great deal to endure a lifetime. It's a lot of work. Why do we do it? Wouldn't we happily drop right here had we not been instilled with a fierce drive to go on? That instinct, residing in *all life,* infused in every cell is there to keep us all from *giving up,* because frankly, it would be a lot easier if we did! But we don't because we were *endowed* with that drive. We persevere! We learn, we adapt, and we evolve. *Why?* We don't know yet. The reason lies somewhere out there and in here," Pete tapped his heart, "and in the realm of God and physics. And, ladies and gentlemen, we're going to have to make a few more gigantic evolutionary leaps - in the tracks of Galileo, Newton and Einstein – to find it. In the meantime, we have to assume – *logically* assume - that if all of life is compelled to succeed and does - against the odds and against the *void* – that it must have a *reason,* and that *reason* - albeit intangible - gives it value beyond what we can measure or comprehend at this moment."

The Reverend paused and then resumed. "During our development, we've been guided by those connected to *the reason*: prophets, seers, saints, philosophers, scientists and so on. Collectively, they gave us a map, marking our path to enlightenment, marking it with compassion, *curiosity* and *ideas,* instinctively guiding us to transcend our tiny sphere - that dot that Einstein demonstrated - of what we know. Unfortunately, we're at a critical juncture, not quite ready to take flight, but not sure we can endure the mess we've made in this nest we're so rapidly outgrowing. So, the obviously solution is primal: to compete and destroy, especially the group taking up too much room. But that flies in the face of the code that we were given, the one that assures us of finding the way. So what other solution is there? *Faith,* ladies and gentlemen: *faith* that if we *work together*, we'll make it. And *we will, all* of us! We will!"

Porter rose as if to say something, then simply shook his head and sat down.

Pete ignored him. "Look, we're just now adjusting to the idea that particles waft in and out of other dimensions. *Other dimensions.* And regarding faith, we're certainly not shy of evidence! It's just that the proof to our purpose, our calling, our connection to something greater will not be borne out of archeology. Our answers don't lie in the past; *they lie in the future!* We're growing! What was quantum physics a hundred years ago? We have fantastic theories that may launch us into a fantastic future, but even as they're yet still theories, I'll tell you what's indisputable: *miracles.* And I'll tell you why. We came from algae, and we build jets. We can span the globe in hours. We killed each other in wholesale slaughter and yet we exist in unprecedented numbers. Fifty years ago, we knew little of Mars other than it existed; today, we have soil samples. We've uncovered the essence of matter and mapped the entire human genome! More to the point, there are potentially infinite universes to go with infinite possibilities, already speaking to the odds of eternity! And, ladies and gentlemen, there's a collection of minds sitting in this room right now, so brilliant that they're able to forecast an entire planetary collapse! Think about it! You're gifted! But, you're only here because you were valued by what came before and perhaps *even after* you. Your essence was derived from something that connects us all, something you've already acknowledged by selflessly trying to make this world a better place. There's no doubt that you're here because life matters, and thus, you matter; and despite all our personal definitions of who's important or what, life *can* be saved – all of it – and by you: the very same species that clung to tree limbs! And if that's not a miracle, *I don't know what is!*"

Pete paused. Only Porter moved. He folded his arms, his glasses refracting the bright primaries of his world. He cleared his throat.

"So, Peters: your solution is faith. Faith and somehow, we'll fix it. Well, it better be soon. In the meantime, we should continue to support all the greedy thieves and so-called world leaders that brought us to this point. We'll make sure that they have another hour to check their stock prices, to pump more fossil fuels into the air, to count their greenbacks while dumping chemical waste. We'll make sure they have every gadget for their kids. Hell! We'll even give them our kids, to sacrifice in wars in the name of excess … in the name of *Exxon!* I've met these people, Peters. I've walked among them, and they're a scourge."

Pete tilted his head. "True, Porter. But, out of that scourge came you with your billions. Out of that very scourge could come our salvation."

Porter scowled. "I'm certainly not one of those. . . ."

"I know," Pete concurred softly, tapping his forefingers together. "Yes, plenty of self-serving people run the show. But, eventually they're deposed, replaced by some that are worse, but mostly better. We're evolving. We really are. Besides, Porter, the bad ones are only here because we get lazy, and you're not the first to notice we can ill afford them. But it doesn't take eradication, it takes education. It takes a new perspective." Pete winked.

Porter gazed at his map. "Power's not irrelevant, Peters, if that's what you think. Even if we forestall this mess we can't continue on the current path, which effectively means an end to human freedom. We'll need laws and regulations for every action just to keep the greedy bastards from starting it all over again."

The Reverend shook his head. "I'm not worried, Porter. For every selfish person, there are ten who comport themselves within the parameters of common human decency … and don't need a directive to do it. It's called a conscience, gifted to them a long time ago. And I've met those people, Porter. I've walked among them. And in the final analysis, you can trust them to get it right."

Porter reflected upon his staff. They returned his gaze with the kind of telepathic commiseration acquired through years of working together. Pete weighed their reaction quietly, and then turned abruptly and strode toward Fletcher.

"The vial please," Pete commanded, his palm outstretched.

Fletcher deliberated and then shook his head.

"Please," Pete implored.

Fletcher studied the glass in his hand, and then tacitly sought the reaction of his allies. Ray shrugged and nodded. Elan did the same. Tristan waved him on to proceed. Fletcher handed it to the clergyman. Pete's flip-flops made a smacking sound as he paddled to the bio-engineer.

"Well, I guess I've had my hour. So here's to yours, Porter. Your finest is yet to come." He carefully placed the formula in Eckhart's hand. "You know where to find me if you need me."

Pete mustered his troops; time to go. Sweat flashed across Porter's face as he gingerly wedged the vial between two notebooks and shouted after the departing group.

"What about my *daughter*? Where are you going, Peters?"

"Home." Pete paused for a moment and considered Tristan. "And I'm sure your daughter will be released. In fact, I can promise it."

Porter surveyed his distressed coworkers as they backed away from the vial. "Lawson!" he suddenly shouted, "Remember, I can't stop what's happened, not for a while. It will take time. The warrants are in the system now."

Fletcher nodded wearily.

Porter seemed momentarily confused by the multifarious blinking of his electronic empire. His eyes cast around the floor. Pete put a firm hand on Fletcher's s back, propelling him toward the room's exit. The scientist suddenly glanced up. "Peters, what if we can't...?"

"You *can*," the minister bellowed without looking back. "You've got everything you need!"

And then he left, sweeping out of Porter's delicate blue orbit.

Between Pete's reverential presence, Elan's rusty Silverado and Ray's real, live driver's license, a multi-vehicle caravan managed to make it to Corey's without incident. Released from the trunk, Fletcher apologized for his appearance. Corey was horrified. Tristan crawled out from Pete's rear seat sporting every shade of black and blue. Elan helped him to the house. Corey dawdled by the car with an eye on Fletcher, but he said he needed a minute and would be in shortly. She said he had five minutes - tops - and then allowed Ray to drag her to the kitchen. Fletcher eased in beside the driver, who had remained seated in anticipation of the tête-à-tête.

"That's a hell of chance you took."

Pete rolled his eyes. "Well, I. . . ."

"A hell of chance, Pete! Everyone, including your own family at stake! What were you thinking?"

Pete lifted his eyebrows. "What were *you* thinking? *You* gave me the vial!"

Fletcher threw his hands up in the air. "I don't know! God, I don't know! I must have been insane! You must have had me hypnotized! I guess I actually believed all of that *crr*. . . . Anyway, correct me if I'm wrong, but if he wakes up tomorrow and decides on his original course, millions will be murdered, including *you,* and no doubt, *us.* If he doesn't, then the world as we know it will be destroyed while he waits for divine intervention. How do *you* see it?"

"Well. . . ." Pete licked his lips. "I suppose that if he wakes up and decides on his original course, nothing's going to happen. Once he realizes nothing's going to happen, he'll redouble his efforts to make his earthly home habitable, because he's too cynical to wait for divine intervention. He *is* the intervention. He's got everything he needs right here: an extraordinary brain, a huge bank account, an incentive by the name of Sandy, and a remarkable staff."

Fletcher gaped at him. "What do you mean, *nothing's going to happen?*"

"It's nothing. It's harmless, well . . . almost." Pete grinned, shifting in his seat. He extracted his wallet from his back pocket.

"Faith, Fletch. I told you. In the end, we'll get it right." He handed Fletcher a card.

It was a very official looking card with a very official looking phone number under which was printed a very long French name beginning with C for *Claude*. . . .

Fletcher sat in Corey's living room with his bare feet on an ottoman. He was sipping tea, wondering why it didn't feel like morning. Despite all the aspirin, his head ached terribly. Elan had showered and was snoozing on the couch. Tristan was on the floor with a leg folded against the coffee table. His eyes were deep, bruised sockets, his nose swollen and his jaw midnight blue. He arms were locked over his ribs. He was sound asleep.

"Fletcher, you should be in a hospital. At least see a doctor," Corey murmured, plopping into the recliner opposite him. "Tristan, too. I know someone."

"It's all right. My teeth have stopped wobbling. That's a good sign." He tried to smile. "You know I can't, Corey."

She shook her head and sighed. "So what happened, Fletch, at the house?"

"You know, I don't remember. I can't remember a thing."

"It's not important." Corey touched his arm. "You're exhausted. Do you think you can sleep?"

"I can't. I've got to sort things out."

The television was droning the news. It was still on, six hours later, when he woke under her shawl.

* * *

Fletcher was pacing back and forth in the kitchen, holding Corey's cell phone away from his ear. Tom Vicante was yelling, a habit he had when he wasn't in control of the situation.

"Listen, Fletcher, don't call my cell *ever!* They can track it! What a mess! You need to turn yourself in."

"God, no! Can we discuss the matter at hand?"

"The *matter?* Which matter would that be? *Theft? Harboring a fugitive?*"

"Actually, the closing."

"Oh! Of course! Leave it to you, Fletch! *The closing!* They'll freeze your assets anyway. You're a fugitive, wanted for. . . ."

"I know, murder."

"I didn't say that! They know you didn't kill that cop. The prints don't mean anything. The ballistics don't match. Whoever did *that:* what a couple of dummies! But there's still harboring a terrorist and stealing some painting, which you have yet to explain. You need to come in now so we can straighten this out! I'll negotiate something. They've called my office a dozen times."

"Tom, listen to me! I need to talk to Mackey, to revise the contract."

"Are you crazy, Fletcher? *Now?* Why?"

"It's personal."

"What do you mean, *personal?*"

"Please, all I want you to do is close the house. Close it for me! Can you do that?"

"You know you're certifiable?"

"Please, Tom. As soon as you get the new terms."

"Which are?"

"I'll let you know or Gordon will. I mean, if he still wants the house. If he's heard I'm a criminal. . . ."

"Even if has, he won't care. When it comes to business, nobody cares what you do, unless you're a child molester. Besides, you haven't been arrested yet. How can they? They can't find you! But it won't be long, and this is not a game!"

"You'll close, then."

"If you sign a power of attorney."

"Oh, come on, Tom! I *can't come in!* Be reasonable. Just do it!"

"*No!* Find a fax machine! I could be disbarred!"

"Tom!"

"I mean it. Now listen, I've got something for you. This is my last freebee. Got a pen? Just in case we actually see your money, here's a phone number: country code. . . ."

✳ ✳ ✳

Corey was insistent that Ray and Elan stay for supper. She wanted a packed house for her stuffed pork chops and three bean salad, but no one was particularly hungry. Fletcher was back in the car with Pete, lost in the pastor's tale of recent events. Pete had met Claude yesterday morning. As it happened, the broken-nosed ruffian cornered him in the chapel, scaring him – he confessed – witless. Claude reassured him by gently recapping their saga, presenting himself in the somewhat ambiguous role of *sympathetic advisor*. All he hoped for was a little cooperation. Pete was more than receptive, so Claude told him about Egan and tipped him off about Fletcher's kidnap. Then, bit by bit, other blanks were filled in. Claude had in fact discovered Fletcher's high-tech transmitters but left them intact, giving Fletcher the leverage he needed for release. And it was Claude that enabled the group to break in to Zephon, Inc. Fortunately, he was manning security that night, allowing them all the time they needed to dig their ridiculous hole. After they cut the power, he stalled the system's alarm long enough to see to their escape. He came close to being fired after that one, he chuckled, but Porter chalked it up to painkillers - Claude tapped on his bandaged nose - and let it go. The vandals' identities, however, were unavoidably compromised. Elan was tracked down, resulting in the unfortunate aftermath.

Pete just wanted to know *why*: why all the subterfuge? It was complicated, Claude had said. The *agency* realized that it was critical Porter keep working. There was no doubt the planet was in jeopardy, and Eckhart was its best bet. But Porter was not only too powerful, but too fanatical to threaten. Thus, all the *agency* could do was contaminate his virus and hope that he could be redirected. As it turned out, Fletcher was a big help buying them time, thanks to his supernatural survival. Then, with Egan snatching Porter's only daughter and Pete's timely introduction - reviving what was left of Porter's flat-lining conscience - the scientist wound up exactly where they wanted him. Thus, the *agency* was grateful and phoned Pete just an hour ago with a message. Fletcher could depend on a pass regarding a certain stolen painting and any other charges like harboring a fugitive. Tristan, on the other hand, was a different story. He was wanted for two murders abroad. He was dangerous; it would be better if he surrendered directly. Since he had demonstrated surprising probity in abandoning Porter's dark quest, the *agency* would give him twenty-four hours in good faith to submit. All he had to do was call. *'Did they know where he was?'* Fletcher demanded. Pete didn't know. *And what about Egan?* Concerning him, Claude was evasive, leading Pete to believe that he was still missing - an embarrassment not readily admitted - making Sandy's debut all the more urgent. With her return, the old smuggler could probably count on the same apathetic pursuit he had enjoyed for years. After all, he was over seventy, maybe not guilty –a possibility no one wanted to hear - and there were far more pressing matters in the Middle East. Fletcher pledged Sandy's liberation, but asked Pete not to divulge their conversation to Tristan or anyone else. The killer they sought was gone, Fletcher asserted. *His* Tristan – this one – was not going to spend the rest of his life caged like an animal. Pete exhaled quietly and nodded.

Whoever Claude was, he should have had it in for Elan – who, after all – was the one who restyled his nose. Instead, Claude had probably saved his life. As Elan told it, he couldn't make it through Zephon's shattered office window. Desperate, his only other recourse was to become a distraction in the hopes of buying time for Tristan. Claude spotted him almost immediately and used a stun gun to paralyze him, then dragged him to the side of the building and tucked him in its shadow. Minutes later, when the delivery truck arrived, it was Claude that shot a few holes into the cargo bay area, drawing out security. In all the commotion, Claude shouted that he had captured the troublemaker and reached Elan just seconds before Trevor rounded the corner. Claude bent down, whispered to Elan that he'd be O.K., then knocked him out, after which Elan was apparently hauled into the building

On his way out, Ray declared that the pork chops were the best stuffed pork chops he had ever had. Corey snaked her arms around Ray's waist and kissed him on the nose, producing an unexpected tightness in Fletcher's chest. The party filed out on the porch. Before they left, Ray wanted to make a quick stop at the barn to say hello to his old dog, having insisted Corey keep him. When he returned, he informed his hostess that he'd call later, much to Fletcher's baffling irritation. Then, the entire company departed.

Ruth couldn't be delayed another hour and was driving like a fury on I-70. They had had a miserable time in Maine. It rained nearly every day, and the mosquitoes ate them alive. She was due in the following night. Pete was elated.

That afternoon, Corey had left Mackey an urgent message: Fletcher had a proposal. Returning the call, the CEO insisted on a face to face meeting tomorrow at his office. Gritting his teeth, Fletcher agreed.

Elan was glad to be home. He unloaded his mailbox, petted his cat and helped himself to a beer, offering the same to his underground guests. He strode out to feed his horses. Fletcher had never been in Elan's house and had no intention of staying, especially given the prominent photo on the side table. Tristan stood in the hallway, finishing his Dos Equis with an eye on his father.

"Your wife."

Fletcher averted his eyes and eased on to a stool. "Egan all set?"

"Yes. Sandy will call."

With the slap of a screen door, Elan reappeared. "Listen, the rental's here. They want me to run back to sign the papers. They forgot 'em. I'll be about an hour. Sit tight."

"Elan, I have some cash."

"Later. I'll put it on my credit card. It'll look better that way."

Tristan peeked through the blinds and groaned.

"Told you, Tristan." Elan smirked as he changed shoes. "Nothing fancy."

"Does it at least have a cd player?"

"Are you kidding?" Elan chuckled. "I doubt it has a radio! See ya!"

Fletcher smiled and pulled the cell phone from his pocket. He had exactly three more requests of Ray.

97

G ordon Mackey had set the appointment for 11:00 a.m., which gave Fletcher ample time to make a stop at the bank, withdraw his remaining funds and close the account. Expecting the police to burst in at any minute, it was the most nerve-racking thirty minutes of his life. The teller was excruciatingly slow and - to make matters worse - he had less money than expected. Trying not to rush her, he filled a small satchel with bills and then left at a brisk walk with a headache and a raw stomach. He drove to a department store, bought himself and Tristan two weeks' worth of nondescript clothing and got his hair cut. When he arrived at Gordon's citadel, he was careful to park in an adjacent lot. His stomach was in knots. He wiped his hands on his pants, devoured three more antacids and departed the anonymity of his rented van.

Fletcher was ushered into Gordon's executive suite on the hour. The CEO was standing at his desk, finishing a call when he motioned his appointment toward a chair. The office was surprisingly dull. Every shred of upholstery was neutral; the desk, a Victorian repro; the prints commonplace. The singular point of interest - jarringly out of character - wsas an enormous, ornately carved coo-coo clock, marking every second like a Black Forest ticker tape.

Gordon hung up. He seemed leprechaunish, skipping around the desk in khakis and a wool sweater to shake Fletcher's hand. It was absurdly cold. The air conditioner must have been set on fifty.

"Fletcher, good to see you. My Lord, did you have an accident?"

"A rather silly fall. I'm fine."

"Good. . . . Good. I just ordered sandwiches." Gordon gestured at the clock. "A gift from my daughter. What do you think?"

"Quite beautiful, Gordon."

"*Isn't it?* Normally, I try to keep personality out of the office; work is work. But, she gave it to me on condition that I think of her every minute. I must admit, I do."

Fletcher nodded mechanically. "She sounds charming."

"She is. Hard to believe, married and a mother of two. So can I get you something to drink? Coffee?"

"No, thank you."

"Please. Sit down. You sure you're all right? Must have been quite a fall."

"It's nothing."

"All right. Well, then, what's on your mind?" Gordon eased into a club chair near his guest.

"Uh, Gordon, assuming you're still planning on closing. . . ."

"In a few days if I'm not mistaken. I can check to be exact."

"No, no." Fletcher met his piercing gaze and took a deep breath. "Actually, I was hoping you'd be interested in a price reduction."

"A *reduction?* That's a first. Why? What's wrong?"

"Nothing's wrong. It's just that there's a complication: three to be exact."

"Go on."

Gordon listened dispassionately as Fletcher disclosed the existence of the conquistadors, the manuscript outlining their last wishes and his subsequent proposal. At exactly eleven-forty, lunch arrived. The CEO was mute as he ate his turkey club. Fletcher forced down toast, praying that the man would say something. Gordon cleared his throat. Fletcher dropped his crust.

"Fletcher, I do have a question. I hope I can count on your honesty."

"Of course."

"Have you been mining that area for gold?"

Fletcher blinked at him. "No."

"Have you seen any?"

"Frankly, Gordon, I haven't been looking. Probably everything that was found was sent with the son of the Spanish captain."

"And the bodies? Do they have anything of value, historic or otherwise?"

"I don't know. Possibly armor, but obviously, they should be reinterred with their belongings. I mean it's a question of dignity."

"Of course. But, if there's anything of *value*. . . ."

"Gordon, I don't think you understand. I'm offering you a substantial discount on the property – more than whatever their trappings could be worth – to see them back to their native country intact. You have the resources. I'm not sure I can explain, but these people are important to me."

"I understand, Fletcher. Really I do. But, I'm sure you can see my position. I think a price reduction is warranted anyway, based on the fact that there's little gold left if any. Obviously, you've had a pretty good look around, and, frankly, that was my interest in your property. Now, you tell me that there's a manuscript, but you have no intention of relinquishing it, although it could be sold – maybe through Sotheby's - at a considerable sum. You have three bodies, though you won't tell me exactly where, which I suppose is prudent for the time being. But whatever artifacts they might have with them, you don't want to include in the sale! Surely, you can see my point. Now I'll be happy to see them back to Spain, to these Franciscans you've mentioned, but I think I have the right – if I'm to buy your place – to make the most of my investment. Fletcher, wait! Sit down! Where are you going?"

Fletcher strode past the receptionist, his head pounding and his stomach churning. He slammed his fist into the elevator button. How could he have been so stupid! He should never have. . . .

"Wait!" Mackey shouted behind him.

Fletcher wheeled around. "Look, Gordon, I'm sorry. We're obviously not on the same page. I'm sorry I brought the whole business up. If you don't want it, I understand. I'll let Tom know. The deal's off."

"Fletcher, please understand. As a business. . . ."

"I don't care about business, Gordon. At this point, the money's inconsequential. I understand your position."

"Fletcher, if you'd just calm down. I'll buy your property, but I do want three hundred off. I think that's fair."

"So, essentially, you're buying grazing land."

"And water rights. The market's soft, and I don't need another house."

Fletcher tried to rub the throbbing from his temples. "And the Spaniards?"

"If you leave them with me, I have a right to their *trappings* which I'll probably donate to the state museum. Naturally, while they're here, they'll be studied if they're of interest. But, I'll see the bones back to your Franciscans. That I promise."

"And if I don't . . . leave them with you?"

Mackey shrugged. "I'll buy your land. And your antiques."

"You'll contact Tom Vicante?" The elevator chimed its arrival.

"Sure. So, what about your Spaniards? It might be worth fifty grand if you leave them."

"They won't be there, but thanks, Gordon." Fletcher stepped in the elevator.

"Fletcher, before you go, I've heard something of your situation. . . ."

"If you don't mind, Gordon. . . ." Fletcher pushed *lobby*, leaving the CEO to ponder him as the doors sealed.

Fletcher rushed across the parking lot and out of the building's austere shadow. The van was blessedly hot. He climbed in, letting his hands warm up on the dash, furious with himself. How could he have been so stupid? Mackey was a predator, had been all his life. When presented with a heartfelt mission, he didn't respect it, he pounced on it! The meeting had been an obscenely expensive waste of time, not to mention dangerous, and it was entirely due to a complete lapse in judgment: *his own!* It must have been all that business about Pete and his faith. What a load of. . . .

A tap on the window sent Fletcher's pulse rocketing. "Mr. Lawson?"

Fletcher stared at the out-of-breath young woman in a gray suit. He rolled down the window.

"Mr. Lawson, this is for you . . . Mr. Mackey." She offered him an envelope.

"Thank you." Fletcher took it. She left, eyeballing him a couple of times as she trotted back to the building. The note was hand-scrawled.

I'll see to it that the remains with all their effects are safely returned to Spain without publicity or delay. Please provide the appropriate contact. Have Vicante draw up something you're comfortable with.

I'd like to have a copy of the manuscript. Naturally, I'd like to know more as I'm sure would local historians, but it's your decision. Good luck. Gordon

Fletcher gripped the steering wheel, his eyes wet, wondering how it was that Pete knew so much. Then he wondered if the Colorado billionaire had made Porter's list. He grimaced, then shook his head and chuckled as he pulled away from Gordon Mackey's mighty fortress.

Taking the back roads to Elan's added another half hour to the trip, but, Fletcher noted, it was worth every minute. There were no problems. By this time, Corey should be supervising the cleanup at his house, watering the sanctuary, and transferring his boxes to a storage unit. She had already called Lieutenant Faller, telling him that the department would be paying for the Merry Maids. He didn't argue. Ray had promised three more caskets, and would leave them by the canyon sometime near nightfall. Tristan was still at Elan's, hold up in a shed with the manuscript, editing his notes.

After Pete celebrated the return of his family, he began working on a sermon. This time, it would be without any thought to financial security. On Sunday, he would rock the house.

Elan was just turning out a new colt when Fletcher arrived, parking the van in the center aisle of the barn. Tristan's grin evidenced his amusement at his father's butchered hair. Fletcher noticed that he was still holding a rib, but that his face wasn't so swollen. Fletcher waved a few bags of fast food in front of him. Tristan crawled out of the hay bales to snag one.

Nibbling on French fries, Fletcher called Tom on his home phone.

"Tom? I bought a fax machine."

"Hallelujah. Mackey's attorney called an hour ago; he just forwarded a release on the first contract."

"Good. Then, as you know the price of the house has changed."

"Yep. Three hundred less. You're a great negotiator," Tom sniggered, "not to mention, full of surprises. So, outline this whole bit about the stiffs and their stuff."

"You mean the conquistadors."

"Whatever! Tell me exactly how you want it. I'm standing here in my swim trunks with pen in hand."

98

Fletcher was lying down in the back of the van with the doors open, enjoying - of all things - a glass of port and a cigarette. Corey had dropped off his decanter so he was savoring every drop. It was nearly seven o'clock. She had also remembered Oliver's kibbles. The dog was stretched out next to him, hardly recognizable, having been sheared into a Shepherd. Creamy peach clouds were swelling across the sky. A tangerine spill was seeping across the horizon. It would be his last sunset here. Elan appeared with a beer and balanced it on the bumper.

"Pretty night."

Fletcher propped himself up on an elbow. "Yes it is. I suppose we should be heading off."

"You sure you're up to it?"

"Yes."

"Look, Fletcher, if you don't mind my asking: why? You don't trust him or what?"

"Mackey? Oh I don't know. I trust him, I guess. It's just that - if I leave it to him - he'll have to use some kind of team to get the remains. And, it would just be too tempting not to filch a few things, don't you think? To me, the place is - well,

I know it sounds strange - but . . . well . . . sacred. And Ray's coffins are nondescript and can be sealed. No one sees them until they reach the Franciscans. They'll see to it that they're buried properly."

"Ryan!" Tristan was striding from the house. "We should go."

"Yes, just give me a minute. Saddle up. Isn't that the proper jargon? Saddle up?" Tristan rolled his eyes and headed toward the corral.

Elan," Fletcher resumed, "I haven't had a chance to thank you, and I know I can't repay you, but, I'd like to give you something for all your trouble."

"Don't."

"Elan. . . ."

"I mean it. Don't. It would be insulting." The horseman crossed his arms, surveying the sky. "You know, you were talking about the cave, how you felt. For what it's worth, I'm glad I got to know you better."

"Likewise."

The Native American stood quietly, his ear to a nearby Meadowlark. "Fletcher, there's been something I've been wanting to say . . . about Meredith."

Fletcher held his hand up. "Please. Don't. It would be insulting. And the truth is, you were the better man, Elan. I always knew it."

99

Despite all the years of caring for Little John, Fletcher had never been on a horse, nor was he looking forward to it, but it was the only practical way. He had adamantly refused to let Elan join them. If he and Tristan were caught, the horses would be declared stolen, and Elan shielded from complicity. The hope was to secure the remains quickly, return to Elan's directly and depart. The coffins would be left near the road. Ray would recover them sometime before sunrise. Give or take a few days, they would be shipped.

At eight o'clock, they set out. Fletcher's unease was soon replaced by a strange sense of peace. It was as if they had escaped into another time. They reached the canyon without incident. Fletcher wriggled from the saddle while his guide swung off like an old pro. The horses tied, Tristan unloaded supplies from the saddle bags while his partner went in search of Ray's boxes. He found them near a washed-out gulley. As requested, they were narrow, therefore manageable, and sturdy. Thankfully, the night was just bright enough to work without flashlights, but that had its own set of problems. The trickiest part would be the trip to the barn where Elan's rope ladder lay. Fletcher called softly that he would be right back.

Although a wall of clouds had obscured Denver's glow, the barn's high pitched roof was drenched in moonlight, leaving the surrounding grass in a moat-like shadow. From the rim of the gorge, Fletcher surveyed his former homestead. There was no movement, not even a breeze to wave the overgrown grass. He rushed through the clearing, braced himself against the side of a stall, and edged around to the tack room ingress. He squeezed through it and saw the ladder piled up like a knotty hill near the window. He seized it, heaved it across the floor and fled. He had forgotten how heavy it was. Snagging on every weed, it was perilously slow-going. He was grateful to see Tristan clambering over the hill. Together, they reached the security of the pine laden slope.

"You should've waited for me," Tristan scolded.

"I know," Fletcher panted. "Did you uncover the hole?"

"Only enough to fit through. And I tested a stake. I think they'll hold."

"Good." Fletcher navigated around a boulder. "We'll fasten this thing right below the rim, that way it'll be long enough to pulley the boxes up. That should save us some time. Could you see down? Is there any water?"

"I think there's just a little, you know? Like before."

"Good. All right. Let's give it a try. Hand me a spike."

"I'll do it." Tristan dropped the ladder with a groan. He reclaimed the sledge and metal stakes he had left there and drove four long spikes into the scarp. Testing their fastness, he nodded approval. He and his father fastened the ladder, then quarreled about the best way to detangle it before being forced into a mutual, methodical effort. It was finally straightened and heaved into the grotto.

They were able to haul all three caskets to the cave in one trip. Ray made them from pine so they were surprisingly light. They looked like crates.

"Do you think they'll fit?" Tristan asked.

"They're skeletons," Fletcher responded breathlessly. "We'll make them fit. The monks can rearrange them later."

"I mean down the hole! Should I widen it?"

"Oh. No. Plenty of room if they go longwise." Fletcher drew a yellow rope from their gear pile. "I'll string them together and feed them down to you. Wait about half way. This rope is too short, but it should make it that far. Once down, tie your end to the ladder. Then, let it drop. They should make it the rest of the way. All right?"

"Right."

While Fletcher tied the caskets, Tristan stuffed their gear under a leafy mound. He then slipped into the grotto. Fletcher fed the containers down to him. After ten minutes, Tristan signaled their successful landing with a wave of his flashlight, and then trained it on the ladder. Fletcher smiled; it shouldn't take too long. He jammed a few necessary tools in his pockets, planted his feet on the first rung and froze. Above him, two beams were sweeping toward the canyon rim, a low discussion in progress.

"Come on!" Tristan yelled.

"*Cut the light!*" Fletcher shouted hoarsely.

"*What?*"

"The light! *Cut the light!*" Fletcher found his voice, hurtling down the ladder. "Tristan! *The flashlight!*"

He banged his elbow on the first tier as he scrambled past it and jumped, plunging onto the dark cavern floor. Water seeped through his jeans. Kneeling, he peered up at their only exit, his heart pounding. There was no sign of anyone.

"Did they see you?" Tristan whispered anxiously.

"I don't know."

"How many?"

"Two, at least."

"Waiting . . . at the house?"

"Not likely," Fletcher rasped. "They would have been right on us. I must have tripped an alarm, maybe a motion detector or something. It's been at least an hour since we were up there. They had to have come a ways."

A shaft of light swept across the cavity. The ladder flared white and then vanished into darkness. Murmurs were audible. The two shrank back toward the wall.

"Ryan," Tristan muttered under his breath.

"Keep still."

They stood motionlessly, up to their ankles in cold slime. All they could hear was their own breathing and an occasionally drop of water.

"I think they might've missed us," Fletcher whispered. I think....."

A brilliant ray burst through the breach, defining the ladder and illuminating the boxes in a halo of dazzling white. "Shit!" Fletcher hissed. They reeled out of the glare.

"*Here!*" A deep voice sounded. The middle of the chamber lit up like daylight. "*Down here!*"

In the clamor that followed, Fletcher identified three distinct voices: one Australian, one American, and one undoubtedly French. What they were saying was indiscernible until they started hollering. Fletcher crouched. The ladder was ominously still, hanging like a spider web. There was no way out, but it was a stalemate for the time being. They wouldn't be coming down, no one anxious to dangle like a hapless fly in Tristan's sight. Their only alternative was to wait it out, unless somebody happened to have a grenade. Fletcher had a sinking feeling. Sure enough, that's exactly what they were being threatened with.

"Tristan!" The Australian hollered. "Give your old man a break! He'll be fine! Promise! Come on out of there! Come on, Mate. Do us all a favor. We'd hate to have to warm things up down there!"

"*Don't answer!*" Fletcher barked under his breath. "They don't know anything right now."

"Ryan, *what did he say?* They would let you. . . ?"

"Of course not!" Fletcher snapped. "It's a lie. Fuckers! Tristan, eventually they're going to drop something down here. Our only chance is up there."

He flashed his light at the eastern tunnel and quickly doused it. Tristan started wading the opposite way. Fletcher lunged for him.

"What the hell are you doing?"

"Shhh!" Tristan commanded, pushing him away. Keeping to the shadow of the overhang, Tristan snagged the faint yellow rope with his boot and floated the three boxes toward him. He slit the cord holding them together. Towing one behind him, he slogged toward the craggy shaft. "Ryan," he croaked, "come on!"

"What are you doing? Are you mad?"

Tristan pivoted. *"What else are we going to do?"*

"Think of something! Find another way out!"

"There isn't any! The letters would have said."

Tristan clicked on his flashlight and quickly rounded the corner. Fletcher stared after him, then, hoisting a box over his shoulder, tracked after him.

"This is a pointless exercise," he grumbled.

"Maybe. Maybe not," Tristan retorted. "Maybe they'll make it out of here, even if we don't."

The Australian's admonitions were getting fainter. "These boys don't sound *official,*" Fletcher muttered, trying to keep pace. "Do you know who they are, Tristan? Do you have a guess? Damn!" He stumbled to a knee; the container slamming into his already sore ribs. The tunnel was glazed with slime.

Tristan stopped and turned toward him, his cargo hanging from his shoulders like a backpack. "Why don't you use your flashlight?"

"The batteries. *Remember?*"

"Right." Tristan hunched over, shifting the weight of his cargo. "Look, Ryan, I don't really see a way out of this."

"I don't either, but we're here now. Let's push on."

The corridor climbed and grew steeper. They could no longer hear their tormenters. They reached the cross and high water mark nearly out of breath. Fletcher fought the claustrophobia by resting with his knees up, laughing at Tristan's sorry jokes.

"So, Tristan. . . ." He stood, rearranging the box on his shoulder. "Do you know who's after us?"

Tristan rose, brushing by his partner as he trudged ahead. "Not really. Probably government agents but acting on their own, you know? Hired."

"Mercenaries with credentials. Why do they want *you* so badly?"

Tristan scrambled up the last incline. "I don't know. Maybe revenge. I hurt some people. I told you. Maybe I know too much. Maybe it's reward money. That's usually why they go it alone." His bright beam skittered across a large yawn in the rock. "We're here."

Now dry and dusty, the duct funneled into the tomb where Don Christoval's friends rested. Turning on his flashlight, Fletcher followed Tristan as he scaled the short wall and dropped into the chamber.

"Well, lad," Fletcher chirped, casting off his freight, "if this job doesn't get done, it's not for lack of trying!"

"You know," Tristan mumbled, scanning the room, "maybe there is another way out. Maybe some place in here."

Fletcher craned his head back toward the passageway. Tristan read his mind. "I'm sure we'll know. They won't come down without clearing the deck. Probably a grenade. Don't worry. We'll hear it."

Fletcher tried to imagine where they were in respect to the canyon. Although the tunnel entrance was east, it had actually twisted south and west most of the way. They were probably fairly high on the slope, and yet the dome they were under was at least ten feet high. They had ascended well beyond the canyon, which would leave them . . . southeast of the barn, under the house?

Tristan was examining the middle remains, calling softly to his father. According to the inscription, it was Alexandre's best friend,

Arias de Rio. Fletcher approached the figure. Stepping into the halo of Tristan's halogen, he was anchored by a strange sense of fellowship. The youth before him was tall for the time, easily five foot seven, and had been partially clad in armor although it had fallen away. There was no sign of a helmet or shoulder plates. The remnants of his clothes suggested the typical rough linen shirt, but he also must have been draped in animal skins; tufts of fur were still there. The hard leather of his shoes was remarkably preserved as were his teeth, white and complete. Tristan reached down, feeling the soft hair nestled under the neck, wiping away the dust of five centuries. It was reddish blonde. It was a surprise attack, Tristan murmured, running his palm over the sternum and across the fractured ribs. Dawn, he continued, thumbing a fragment of the spear that killed the boy, now resting loose in the rib cage. He possessed no armor, Tristan explained, but Alexandre – being the same build – would share his. Rio had dreamt of a complete suit of his own, with a coat of arms. But that morning, he wore none when he rushed to his friend's defense, and was killed almost instantly. He was buried with what armor Alexandre had gifted him. Tristan leaned over and kissed the dark cranium. Then, the modern day Spaniard reclaimed the small silver cross that had fallen from the sixteenth century hand and replaced it in the bony palm. It was a gift from Rio's mother.

To the right lay Mateo de Aguirre. He was a pious man who, despite his name, detested war. He was small, perhaps only five foot three and wore no armor, just animal hides. A large cross – green with age - hung to the side of his neck. He was cherished not only for his mining expertise, but for his knowledge of scripture. Although he could not read or write, he knew the verse as well as any priest. Prior to his marriage, he had considered a monastic life, but had no regrets. He loved his family and was determined to lift them from poverty with New World gold. Don Christoval described him as the closest friend of his life. Mateo suffered greatly. During an ambush by the Acomas, his leg was punctured by an arrow. The injury never healed. Tristan pointed to the femur just above the right knee. There was a ghastly cavity.

Tristan crossed the vault to the last of the men, whispering the name as if royalty. Jcan Lopez, he declared, was the consummate warrior and the strongest of them all. Fletcher was astonished; Jcan's armor was in near perfect condition, as was the elaborate sword by his side. He still wore a gold ring and a gold cross. The favored but bastard son of a Spanish aristocrat, Jcan was described as clever but quick to temper. Understandable, Tristan said. He was treated like king, only to be denied a kingdom. Jcan channeled his frustration into becoming a master of the blade and an expert horseman. Even in a weakened state, he fought fiercely. He was the last Don Christoval laid to rest.

Tristan swept his hand over the ancient helmet.

I suppose we'll start with him," Fletcher bugled, startled by the sound of his own voice. "He'll be the most difficult, on the account of the armor."

Ducking into the darkness, Fletcher reemerged with a pine chest and dumped it in front of the remains. "We really should hurry. There's only so much battery. We'll have to be somewhat unceremonious about this. He has to fit in here." He pried the lid off, then scanned the ceiling with his flashlight. "What we *should* be doing is finding a way out."

As expected, Jcan and his effects had to be crammed into the casket. Tristan did his best to arrange them properly. The armor was overlaid, the helmet placed on the skull; the lid nailed shut. Arias de Rio was next. He was too long; they had to overlap bones. Tristan fussed with them until Fletcher reminded him that it was temporary. He checked his watch. It had been well over an hour and they still had Mateo to go. Unfortunately, the last casket was in the main cavern. Fletcher eyed the corridor. He was coated with dust and sticky with sweat. It was sickeningly stuffy. "Tristan. . . ."

"I'll go."

"No thanks, I'll go. It's worth getting shot for a breath of fresh air."

They both went, hearing nothing but their own footsteps as they retraced their way to the main hollow. Where the passageway narrowed, they extinguished all light, feeling along the ceiling and walls. It was quiet and maddeningly black, but they persisted, stumbling over the rough rock as stealthily as possible.

Fletcher felt the familiar overhang give way. He crouched and whispered to Tristan to wait. He heard nothing but drops meeting a watery mantle. The darkness impenetrable, he had to rely on memory. He stole across the liquid floor, groping for the box until he found its edge. He tapped on it lightly, signaling success. Then, he felt for the cord, feeling it adrift in the slime. Carefully drawing it toward him, the crate lurched into his grasp just as he was immersed in a searing white glare. There was a sizzle by his ear, then another, and then a hard crack; and suddenly, he was in scorching pain.

Tristan slammed Fletcher aside, firing four rounds before shattering the light and plunging them into obscurity. He hollered *this way*. Fletcher bolted toward his voice, blindly running up the tunnel, feeling fluid racing down his shirt. Reversing, Tristan squeezed past him, his gunfire ricocheting into the blackness before he barreled back up the slope. Fletcher ran without thinking. Tristan was on his heels, propelling him to *go*, move, *move!* Then, Fletcher hit something with his shin and catapulted onto the jagged ground. Tristan tumbled over him. With labored breath, they froze, listening. Echoing up the duct, the Australian's threats were muffled and getting no louder. With a shaking hand, Fletcher switched on his flashlight. Tristan pulled himself up to a squat, using the light to reload, but was paralyzed mid-task, stricken by the sight of his father.

"*Oh God!* Ryan! Let me see! Look at your arm!" Tristan focused the light. Fletcher had ceased to feel pain, inspecting his arm as if it weren't his own.

"Can you move it?" Tristan demanded.

"Somewhat."

Tristan ripped the bottom off his shirt and applied it as a tourniquet above the bicep. "You've been shot! Can you stand?"

"Yes."

"Come on then. Hurry. Just a little more."

The two stumbled a short way into the conquistadors' chamber. Fletcher felt light headed. Tristan helped him sit, then dropped next to him and tightened the bind. Blood dripped slowly onto Fletcher's jeans. Tristan jumped up and began to frantically scour the walls.

"Ryan, I'm going to have to go back."

"*Don't, Tristan.* It'd be suicide. Please. I'll be all right."

"You're bleeding bad."

"Not so much now."

"I have to go back!"

"Tristan, don't. *Please!* Don't make my life a waste. Give it a little time. Faith, remember? Now listen to me. They may blow the main entrance. But they don't know where we are or how far this shaft goes. You listening?"

Tristan was rampaging around the vault, testing every crevice. Fletcher let his head drop back, searching the darkness for the faith he couldn't seem to muster. Weakness crept into his legs and he felt a spasm of cold. He squeezed his eyes shut against Tristan's dancing beam.

"I'll find a way," Tristan vowed. "We'll get out!"

Fletcher nodded. As Tristan's ranting faded and the light dimmed, he opened his eyes, face to face with a familiar visage. His features were sharp. His golden hair defied the gloom, falling like flames across his marred chest. Fletcher reached for The Falcon, but his hand was cast away. Then, others appeared in the haze. A small wiry man approached. He had sable curls, large sad eyes and a heavy beard. From his neck dangled a bronze cross that Fletcher recognized: Mateo. Another loomed nearer. He was taller, with a Roman nose, white skin and pale eyes. He seemed melancholy and exhausted until he smiled, then he looked like a young Apollo: Rio. The last to emerge was in armor, his helmet off. His hair was a massive auburn mane, his rugged face square, his nose crooked. He was badly scarred from smallpox; his red beard was scant. He fingered a gold ring and peered into Fletcher's eyes: Jean Lopez.

Don Christoval leaned closer to Fletcher and cocked his head. He fingered his scabbard, and then drew his sword and waved it above him. The blade was polished, shimmering like water running down a window.

"Escuche," the captain murmured, pointing toward the ceiling. "Escuche." He tapped his ear with his forefinger. "Llueve."

Mateo crouched beside him. "Pobre hombre." He lifted his arms. "Llueve." The other two came closer, their arms outstretched. "Llueve," they chanted. "Llueve."

Fletcher's eyes filled with tears, stretching a hand toward Christoval. The specter brushed his palm with a kiss. "Mi hijo amado . . . adios."

He vanished as a sudden quake rocked the vault. Adrenaline sent Fletcher to his feet, shouting for Tristan, hearing a faint cry over the din of falling rock. It was pitch black. Another explosion crackled down the corridor. Fletcher fumbled for his flashlight and switched it on but saw nothing but a veil of dust. He yelled frantically for his son, just as he materialized out of the vapor, stumbling to his knees as a tremor fissured the floor. Fletcher grabbed his arm.

"Ryan!" Tristan hollered. "They're blowing us up!"

"Stay with me! Right here! *Right here!*"

"We'll be trapped!"

"No, we won't! It'll be all right! Stay right here!" Fletcher doused his flashlight.

They hunkered against the wall in the dark and covered their mouths with their shirts. To their surprise, there were no more blasts, just the distant rush of sand and debris. As it grew quiet, they tried to control their convulsively coughing, listening for a voice, a footstep, anything. . . . But there was nothing.

"Are you all right?" Tristan rasped. "How do you feel?"

"I'm all right." Fletcher sniffled, wiping the stinging refuse from his eyes. "Tristan, *llueve*. What does it mean?"

"Llueve?" Tristan spat. "It means rain, raining. Why?"

Fletcher pondered it, and then erupted with laughter. He shouted *llueve* over and over into the dust filled cavity. Tristan tried to hush him until, desperate, he shook him. *"What's the matter with you? Stop it!"*

Steadying his beam, Fletcher focused it on his son's appalled face. "Tristan," he choked, wiping the tears from his eyes. "It's raining. Did you hear me? *It's raining! Raining!"*

Tristan stared at him and then closed his eyes, a slow smile eroding the grit off his face.

They filed down the passageway, and found – as expected – their saving grace: Acheron lapping at the high water mark. Still, it might be twenty-four hours before the cistern drained. They had no potable water and their batteries were waning, soon to leave them in the infuriating dark. Fletcher wouldn't consider swimming, recalling the last nightmarish attempt. Tristan, on the other hand, was more than willing. He was worried about his father, examining his arm under a dimming orb. No longer bleeding, it was horribly swollen. Fletcher said the throbbing was a good sign: if he could feel it, he was alive; and for the moment, the pain wasn't unbearable. They finally agreed to give the water an hour to recede. In the meantime, they'd have to stuff Mateo's skeleton in with Rio. Tristan was skeptical that he would fit, but without a third casket, there was no choice. This time, it was Fletcher who insisted that *none stay behind*, even if he had to shove a tibia or two in his pocket.

They marked Mateo's remains with limestone chalk and squeezed him in around Rio. Miraculously, he fit. Tristan used the remainder of hides as packing material, and the casket was sealed shut. As they dragged the container to the high water mark, Tristan's flashlight failed, Fletcher's shortly after. Thankfully, Tristan had a lighter which he used to fire up a cigarette. Fletcher smoked one, too, finding it a measure of relief. The throbbing had turned into a nauseating ache.

"Ryan, we can't stay, not with your arm like that."

"Did you check the water?"

"It's down a lot more than I thought."

"Good." Fletcher shifted. "We'll wait one more hour, then we'll give it a try. In the meantime, why don't you tell me more about these fellows. I could use the distraction."

Tristan took a deep breath. "Let me think. I'm not sure where to begin."

Fletcher stubbed his cigarette out. "How did they discover this place?"

"By accident," Tristan answered, settling back in the dark.

Five hundred years ago, the canyon floor was not a dry strip of sand, but a rushing rivulet. It was Jcan - scouting ahead - who discovered it. The gorge was a deserter's paradise: rich in grass, naturally enclosed and easily defended. Jcan gathered his comrades and returned by dusk. Although they slept hungry, the following morning, Jcan had them dining on fish. But it was Mateo - filtering sand through his fingers - who made the prophetic observation that would inaugurate their new home. He hobbled up the slope where the cave's entry, at that time, was visible. Rio and Alexandre fashioned a yucca rope to gain access. It took only three days before gold was being sifted from the cavern's watery floor. Not knowing the full potential, everyone was near ecstasy. Remembering Cortez and his calculated rebellion, Don Christoval envisioned a royal reprieve with his own bullion presented at the king's feet. His family name would be restored; his comrades: New World hidalgos. But the captain was soon to discover that – for all he lay claim in the name of Philip – there was another contender, one with an equally compelling cause.

It was on a Sunday after Mateo said mass that the Spaniards first set eyes on him. He stood atop the ravine with four scouts. Don Christoval shouted a greeting, but the stranger vanished, only to return the following day with a larger retinue. This time, he sent an arrow into their smoldering camp fire, another into a saddle. Undeterred, an armored Don Christoval marched up the incline. Again, the strangers withdrew. It was troubling. The Iberians slept at the mouth of the fissure, alternating as watchmen, with their horses nearby and secured. Three days passed before they saw him again. This time, he descended down the slope with four others. Although Alexandre objected, Don Christoval - anxious to establish good relations - approached alone, taking his sword and shield at his son's behest.

Don Christoval described the man as magnificently adorned in necklaces of red, white and yellow crystals. He had large feathers interwoven in his long, straight hair, and not a blemish on his brown skin. His pants and vest were a tawny hide, decorated with curious forms. Despite the cool weather, his companions had bare torsos and geometric patterns painted across their faces and chests. The leader greeted Don Christoval with a simple gesture, then crouched immediately and began scratching the grit with a stick. When finished, he put his hand to his heart, tapped his drawing and uttered what Christoval presumed was his name. The Spaniard repeated it, taking several minutes to interpret the picture, and from then on, referred to the man as el Lobo de L'Arroyo: the Wolf of the Stream. The Spanish captain pointed to his shield, at the falcon presiding over the coat of arms. El Alcon, he said, his hands crossing his chest as he bowed: El Alcon de Navarre.

The man seemed pleased with Don Christoval's title as well as his own: el Lobo. He was also fascinated by the shield. In a gesture of good faith, Don Christoval presented it to him. The Wolf received it with great solemnity, then acknowledged the rest of the Spanish retinue before withdrawing. The following morning, high on the east rim, was a stick figure of a flying bird. When Jean investigated, he exclaimed that there were baskets of plums and berries. There were also five hide blankets and a wrapping of much coveted salt. The berries were bitter, but greatly appreciated, fruit having been a rarity for nearly a year; and the blankets proved their salvation when the cold arrived. But despite the surface geniality, the Wolf kept a close eye on the Spaniards, each day sending a band to watch them, preying on their European nerves.

As time wore on, the Iberians grew closer and their cache larger, but the gold was increasingly hard to find. Further exploration revealed no mother lode. Mateo explained that there may not be one, that what they had could have come from far upstream. He proposed that they head toward the mountains. But, with the peaks already white with snow and Mateo not well, Don Christoval opted to take their good fortune and depart for Mexico City. Because of God's great goodness, they had enough to buy a fair hearing and probably a pardon. Once absolved, they could return, properly equipped, with the support of the Viceroy, a proper company of friars, the blessing of the King and Mateo in good health. Everyone agreed; everyone, that is, but their absentee warlord: el Lobo de L'Arroyo.

With frost upon them, the Spaniards prepared for their journey. The horses were well rested and strong. Jcan surmised that if they kept to low ground, they would travel quickly, avoiding the worst of the winter. They packed their mounts with what provisions they had, the gold secured in a blanket. God willing, they could reach the city in two months. But when the morning came – regardless of God's will – no one was leaving. Hemmed in by twenty warriors, Don Christoval parlayed with the Wolf, beseeching him to let them pass. El Lobo was perfectly amenable, as long as they returned the gold to the cave and the ancestral spirits residing there. Without the gold, all was lost, so the Spaniards skirmished for eleven days without gaining ground, losing two horses in the process. Don Christoval ordered restraint, hoping that diplomacy, rather than carnage, would triumph. However, staples were running low. There was no game; there would be no more berries; and El Lobo was resolute. Thus, Christoval devised a ruse. Someone needed to escape unnoticed with the gold, that the rest - unladen - might pass later. Alexandre was unanimously chosen. With great ceremony, the Spaniards mourned the youth's contrived passing and consigned him to the cave as the natives watched. They let two days pass. Then, in the freezing hours of dawn, Jcan crept to the canyon rim. It had flurried. Alexandre's tracks would be discovered, but he could easily outride the enemy. Don Christoval ordered his immediately departure, issuing him a letter for the Viceroy. Alexandre was also given provisions and a warm endorsement by the others. They told him that they would fight for their lives knowing that he was on route to their redemption. Sick with fever, Mateo begged him to remember his family and to save a little gold for his children. Alexandre promised, and then rode to the edge of the gorge. His horse pawed the snow as he tearfully looked back at his father. Don Christoval flicked his hand in dismissal. But as Alexandre spurred his horse, a Wolf was waiting.

The assault was stunning, erupting from the silver rocks all around them. Rio was killed almost immediately, rushing to save Alexandre from an intended arrow. Jean and Don Christoval fought side by side until so exhausted that they were forced to retreat to the cave where Mateo lay unconscious. He would pass the following day. There was no food, having sent their last scraps with Alexandre. So, Jean and Christoval huddled together that long and terrible night. Their sole consolation was that the last they had seen of the fledgling Falcon, he was in a full gallop south.

The following morning was iron gray as they crawled out to claim Rio's body. They were not impeded. The red rime was a testament to the ferocity of the prior day's fighting. The enemy had vanished. Two hours later, under el Lobo's s gifted hides, Mateo expired. His attendants prepared the frontier tomb where he and young Rio would rest.

Don Christoval mentioned the cistern flood only once, but must have experienced it several times, as he knew exactly where to inter his companions. He also knew where to store his manuscript, that it would survive the water's effects. Evidently, Alexandre had been told where to find the letters, should the company not follow him. But as there was no record of the youth ever reaching Mexico, it could only be assumed that Alexandre met his own dark fate somewhere in the vast west.

Don Christoval wrote the last two pages after Jean fell. Lopez and his cross bow slaughtered several, as did his sword before he was overrun. Badly wounded, Don Christoval was taken prisoner. He was strung to a tree resembling the cross on his shield. There, el Lobo carved the flying falcon into his flesh, spitting on the coat of arms that served as his model. Then his party withdrew. However, the Wolf would not desert his prey for long. Hours later, as Don Christoval languished, the chief returned and cut him down. For reasons Christoval would never know, he was transported to the mouth of the cavern and supplied with food and water. The natives carted off his armor, but left Jean's intact. By the grace of God, the Falcon's most valuable possession, his medallion, remained around his neck. It was an heirloom, given to his grandfather by none other than the royal emperor, Philip I of Spain.

Don Christoval ate a little, drank and slept for what was probably days. When he woke, the only surviving horse was standing over him, nibbling on dried grass. Don Christoval caught the animal but was too weak to hold him. It dashed off into the trees. Garnering what was left of his strength, the captain dragged Jean into the tomb. There, he finished his letters. Tristan believed he spent his final hours at a post outside the cave, hopeful that he might see the horse through the frozen pines. He carved his name in an ice-capped rock. It was probably el Lobo de L'Arroyo that buried him.

The narrator rose to check the water level. "Ryan, it's draining quickly. We can go."

"Sure?"

"Yes. It's probably waist high in the main room, you know? It'll be all right. Maybe the ladder's still there. Come on."

Cording the caskets together, Tristan and Fletcher carried them, hammock-style, down the shaft. They were heavy now, and Fletcher – with minimal use of his arm - struggled for balance. By the time they reached the water, it was only hip deep. Whatever had happened had actually aided the drainage. But, it was slow going as they slipped over loose rocks and debris. It was dark, save for the timid glow of a veiled moon exposing their ladder. Unfortunately, it was nothing but a detached heap: a pearly island in a murky lake. The coffins floated silently across the mire like ghost ships as Tristan scanned the water with his lighter.

"Do you see any signs of them?" Fletcher rasped.

"No. But, I think I just felt one."

It surfaced. Tristan held the flame to the grisly face of Trevor, the Australian of their internment. Tristan pushed him away and snorted. "I guess he can't swim either."

Fletcher folded to relieve his sick stomach. The ache in his arm had spread to his chest.

"You all right?" Tristan asked anxiously.

"I'll make it."

"Heh, Ryan," Tristan cried softly. "You know what?"

Fletcher spit phlegm. "What?"

"You're a rich man."

Fletcher looked up and spied Tristan's shape. He was wading southward toward a spectacular new fracture. As he climbed, the water receded to his ankles, his splashy footsteps echoing through the chasm. He held the lighter's flame to the jagged breach. Fletcher sensed his huge smile. "What do you think, Ryan?"

And there it was, sparkling like a wildfire on a high plains desert night: the mother lode.

100

Fletcher was stricken by the excruciating pain. Tristan quickly sloshed back to him and held him as he retched. They could climb out now, the Spaniard whispered . . . through the new breach, over the gold. *Could he make it?* Fletcher nodded. As they ascended, Tristan tagged him closely. Then, at his father's insistence, Tristan clambered back down into the chasm and cut the ladder to a third of its original length. He tied the caskets to the tangled rungs. With a Herculean effort, he climbed back to the star-studded sky, dragging the boxes out with him. He heaved the whole pile to Ray's designated retrieval site. Out of breath, he still had to find the horses. He spotted them grazing in the thicket. Fletcher was worse but said he could still mount up, although - as it turned out - he didn't have to. Ray's truck had sidled to the edge of the road. He was just untangling the boxes when Tristan and his blood-soaked father burst through the willows. Ray rushed Fletcher into the cab. Tristan rode toward Elan's with the other horse in tow, met by his worried mentor on route.

✳ ✳ ✳

It was five o'clock in the morning. Pete's cell phone sounded like a hornet under his pillow. He seized it, glanced at Ruth, and then, tip-toed into the hall. Moments later, having raided the medicine cabinet, he was hastening down the corridor when he heard, "*Dad?*"

He spiraled around. "Ellen! What are you doing up?"

She was in sweatpants and a tee-shirt, rubbing sleep from her eyes. "I don't know. It's late back east. The question is: what are *you* doing up?"

"Keep your voice down. I have to go see someone."

"Who? *Wow!* What happened? Why do you have all that stuff?"

"I'll explain later. Go back to bed."

"No. I'm going with."

"No, Ellen, and that's an order."

She was suddenly on red alert. "It's Tristan, isn't it? That's why you're being so sneaky. *I'm going or I'll follow you!*"

"You can't. Please."

"I'm starting my car right now. You can either let me change or I'll follow you dressed like this."

"*Keep your voice down!*"

"No! I'm gonna wake the whole house."

"Ellen!"

I'll get Mom!"

"No! No! All right. *Hurry up, then!* I must be insane."

"I can't believe you, Dad! After our talk last night...."

"*Shhhhhh!* Just go change. Hurry!"

"What about you? Are you going *like that?* In your pajamas?"

Pete looked down. "Oh! No. I'll meet you in the car. Be quiet!"

Pete pulled a pair of pants from the dryer, dashed off a note and scurried out of the house. He dumped his first aid on Ellen's lap. "Sweetheart, I have something to tell you," he began, as he quickly pulled the car out of the driveway.

Fletcher was shocked to see Ellen. He tried to smile, muttering something about his embarrassing state. He was in fresh clothes. Ray forced him to drink water. The up side,

Ray informed them glumly, was that the bullet looked like it had missed the bone and exited. Pete rolled up his sleeves and dragged the casualty to the kitchen sink. He needed serious attention, Pete growled; the most an old missionary could do was to load him up with aspirin, antibiotics and booze. He could pray, Fletcher added wryly.

"Works better if you do it yourself," Pete retorted, scrubbing around the wound, then running it under water for what seemed like hours. Fletcher nearly passed out, gnashing his teeth as he sputtered about their pursuers. Ellen gripped his wrist to keep his arm still.

"In a very short period of time," Fletcher winced, swallowing phlegm, "those boys will go missing, and then Tristan and I will have the honor of topping the ten most wanted. We never harmed those fellows, you know, never wanted trouble, but they'll blame us. . . ."

"Now you know how Egan felt," Tristan exclaimed, barging through the screen door. Elan swept in behind him, adding that there was unusual activity on the road. As they began arguing exit strategies, Tristan was suddenly struck dumb. Ellen was staring at him from behind her father.

"This is going to need serious attention, Fletch," Pete announced. "I mean it. You don't want gangrene. And you've lost a lot of blood. You're white."

"I know. I'll see someone. I will . . . just not right now. Thank you." Fletcher straightened. "Tristan, we should be going. If you'd be so kind as to gather anything that remotely looks evidence. Put it in a bag, and we'll take it with us. Garbage, anything. Pete, Ellen, you, too, Ray: you need to be on your way. In case you didn't know, what you're doing is a crime."

Tristan fingered a "come here" at Ellen, and then withdrew into the living room with a plastic bag. She slipped in behind him, shutting the door.

Pete sighed. "That son of yours is going to be my undoing."

"Mine, too." Fletcher smiled weakly.

"Not to change the subject," Elan chirped, "but you won't be driving out of here, Fletch. That's the third time that car has been up and down this road. Somebody's looking all over hell for you."

"I could get them out," Ray piped. "The problem is, where to?"

"Well, wherever it is better be a long way." Elan stared out the west window. "And remember what happens if you're caught."

Ellen tipped her head through the kitchen door. "Ray! Isn't Tabor off today?"

"Um, yeah."

"So, it's just Nick this morning?"

"Yeah, why?"

"I've got an idea. You're supposed to be at work in like a half hour?"

"Yeeaah . . ."

"Can you take them with you?"

Pete stiffened. "Oh no, Ellen! No! Absolutely not!"

"What's she talking about?" Fletcher demanded.

"No, Ellen!" Pete bellowed. "They're fugitives!"

"Well, I can't do it without *you*, Dad. I mean, I have to have a reason."

"Oh, I get!" Ray smirked. "You're going to fly them out?"

"Why not?" she snapped.

"It's out of the question, Ellen," Fletcher interjected. "There's no point in discussing it."

She ignored him and zeroed in on Pete. "After everything I told you!"

Pete crossed his arms, only to open them again and then shove his hands in his pockets, gradually slumping in defeat. "All right, wait a minute. Hold on, Fletch. We didn't come all this way to see you. . . . There's got to be a way. Let's think about it for a minute."

"There's no time to think about it," Elan barked. "Take a look! See those cars? They'll be stopping here *any minute*; then we're *all* going to jail! They're looking for them! Right here! Now, if she's got a plan, let's do it!"

"Easy, Elan," Ray murmured. "It'll be all right."

"I'm not doing time, Ray!"

"Get your stuff, Fletch," Ray ordered. "Elan, I need a few bales of hay. Come on, everybody! Hurry up!"

"What if they follow you?" Pete demanded.

"What if they do? I'm going to work, remember?" Ray winked. "I didn't know they were in the back of truck!"

"Dad, are you going to help or not?"

"Ellen, honey, it's you're whole future."

"*Fine!* Ray, I'm riding with you."

"No, no," Pete stammered. "Come with me."

"Tristan?" Elan shouted. "Where the hell are you?"

"Here!" Tristan appeared at the doorway with a garbage bag.

Elan steered him toward the door. "Come on. Forget that. I'll get it. I've got something for you."

"We're leaving?"

"Obviously!" Pete brushed past him. "I'll tell you, Tristan. You're one pain in the. . . ."

101

"Dad, you've got him wrong."

"No, I don't!" Pete retorted, checking his rear view mirror. Ray was following at a healthy distance. They had already been pulled over by two men identifying themselves as F.B.I. The reality of the situation was sinking in. He licked the perspiration over his lip. Ruth should divorce him.

"Ellen, you have no idea what he is. *He's using you!*"

"It was my idea! I told you!"

"It doesn't matter! If he cared at all, he would've said no. He wouldn't have. . . ."

"Dad, last night, I told you I loved him, and you were fine with it! *Now I know why!* Because you thought I'd never see him again. You treated me like a kid! Well I love him, like it or not!"

"Ellen, give it time. You're young. You have college, a future, a whole world of people to meet. For heaven sakes, he's a felon! He's not even American!"

"So why did *you* help him?"

Pete stared ahead. The car was shuddering. He was going too fast. He glanced in the mirror. Ray's truck was a veritable cyclone of dirt, Fletcher's dog riding shotgun on the passenger side. Pete slowed down. "I didn't *help him*, per say, Ellen. It's complicated. I thought I was serving a greater good. In the process, I thought I might be helping Fletcher."

"Well, in the *process*, you helped Tristan, too. You helped him a lot. He's different now. I know you see it. Wasn't it worth it?"

"*Worth it?*" Pete blasted. "*No!* Not at the expense of my family!"

"Look, Dad! *It's too late for that!*"

"No it's not, Ellen. I swear to you I'll see them both safely on their way. I promise you, all right? Now, once we get to the airport, you take my car. Tell your mother. . . ."

"Dad, I'm flying them out, with or without your help."

"No you're not, Ellen."

"*Yes, I am!* I already called Nick. He's renting me a four seater. So, it's all done. I'll get them to Nebraska. I'll rent them a car and come home. It would make it a lot easier if you'd come, but if you don't want to, I understand."

"Ellen, please don't do this to me. Please. Think of your mother."

"I am! I'm also thinking of *my child*, Dad! *Get it? I'm pregnant! I'm not giving it up*, and I'm not going to live the rest of my life wondering how his father's doing, *rotting away in prison!*"

Pete clung to the steering wheel, his heart missing beats. Tears welled up in his eyes as he tried to recall where he was, how to drive, how to breathe. The airport was right there, but Ellen had to tell him to turn, gushing how sorry she was for everything, and that she hadn't meant to tell him that way. She begged him to be all right. He couldn't look at her. She directed him toward the front lot. He didn't remember parking the car. He had a crushing pain in his chest.

"I'm sorry, Dad. I'm so sorry! Please, tell me you'll be all right." She choked back her tears and fanned her face. She pulled a Kleenex from the glove compartment. "I'll be back late this afternoon. Dad? Say something! Are you all right? Dad? Look, I'll call if I'm running late."

Pete's head bobbed. Still glued to the steering wheel, he was staring at the glass doors. "Don't we have to fill out something?"

Ellen wiped her eyes. "Yes. Nick will have it."

"Well then." He cracked his door.

"Dad, are you O.K?"

"No." He smiled feebly, examining his expansive torso. "What's the weight limit, anyway? Do you think we can get off the ground?" Then he turned to her, tears running down his face. "Here's flying with you, kid . . . both of you, I guess." And then his long arm reached for her. She dabbed his face with a Kleenex and then hugged him fiercely, thanking him for being the greatest old man anybody could ever have, *ever.*

Ray pulled into the hanger, leapt out, and mumbled something to the truck bed. Feathered with timothy, Tristan and Fletcher squirmed out from under the bales. The designated plane was right outside, so, after a good look around, Ray was able to load the stowaways while Nick was otherwise occupied. Everything was going great until Sparta emerged from the office escorting the Peters, chatting amicably, heading straight for the covert operation. Ray caught Ellen's eye, rabidly shaking his head. She abruptly halted, hooked her arm around her father's, then gushed to Nick that it was a special occasion, something of a *private* one . . . *thank you for everything! Bye-bye!* Nick insisted on giving the plane a once over, but by that time, Ray had jogged over to them, cheerily announcing that he had just inspected the chosen Cessna thoroughly, and *everything* was in perfect order! *Everything! Perfect!* Nick stopped, blinking at the maniacal grins surrounding him. Then he slowly nodded and wished Pete and Ellen a great flight. He turned back toward the building to a collective sigh of relief.

The little plane was jam-packed, and since neither Pete – too large for his seat – nor Fletcher - awkwardly hunched over - were fond of flying, it was shaping up to be a long journey. Regardless, Ellen was ecstatic. All her cherished men were in her hands. At its weight limit, the aircraft taxied a long way before becoming airborne. Fletcher bolted up, shouting a little too loudly that the take-off was superb. Pete turned around, laughing deliriously that they appeared to be in flight. With Oliver under his elbow, Tristan sat quietly. The sky was as pure and blue as he had ever seen it. He leaned forward and hooked an arm around Ellen's shoulders, unable to express his inexpressible gratitude. They were free.

It was a perfect day to fly. Despite his pitiless quarters, Pete found himself enjoying the crystal clear expanse, while Fletcher, feeling infinitely better on pain killers, was mesmerized by the geometric farm fields below. Using a jacket as a pillow, Tristan leaned against the window and shut his eyes. The little plane hummed through the morning and across state lines. Starting her descent in the eastern half of Nebraska, Ellen grinned, feeling supremely complimented. Each passenger had conveyed his utmost confidence in her by snoring.

They landed on a little airstrip outside of Lincoln. Pete used a pay phone to hail a taxi. Fletcher walked the dog and watched from a distance as Tristan - curled up with Ellen - drank a soda under a magnificent old English oak.

Tristan received her news without expression, staring through a canopy of glittering leaves. When he finally turned to her, he caressed her cheek, and told her not to waste her life on him. He told her things he had never told anyone, about terrible nightmares, unpardonable sins and unrequited prayers. He said that even if he hadn't been a felon, he would have been nothing more than a fisherman, without the means to give her the life that she deserved. Tears in her eyes, she swept the hair from his face. He gazed at her, then drew her to him and admitted all that he had never dared say to such a Renaissance jewel: that he loved her and that he would return for her and his child, a promise he would make on his life.

Pete arrived back with an old SUV from Rent-A-Wreck, the only thing he could find with tinted windows and no tracking system. It was perfect, Fletcher exclaimed, murmuring that in case it wasn't returned . . . and stuffed a wad of cash into Pete's front shirt pocket. For a long while, the two said nothing, staring at the asphalt. It was better that way, Pete thought later, remembering Fletcher's stiff embrace. Goodbyes were never said.

As Ellen boarded the plane, Tristan shook Pete's hand and asked him to wait for just a moment. He reached under his shirt and pulled the fabulous medallion from around his neck.

"Oh no! No. I can't, Tristan. Really, I can't."

"Please. Keep it for Ellen and my son. Please."

Pete considered him, and then bowed, allowing him to slip the incomparable cross over his head.

"In hoc signo vinces, Pete."

"Until we meet again, Tristan. By the way, what makes you think it's a boy?"

"Family tradition, Padre."

The suddenly tearful minister wrapped his arm around him. "God bless you, Tristan. God speed."

The Cessna's propellers spun into a blur as the engines roared and Pete squeezed into the cabin. Two generations of Egans watched as Ellen – more beautiful than Raphael's Madonna – paused to blow them a kiss. Then the vision taxied, and – lifting from the tar like a white dove – transcended the earth and disappeared into the sun drenched heavens.

102

Tristan did most of the driving, using the long days to teach his father Spanish. They also talked of poets and painters; Tristan quoting Cervantes and Jimenez; Fletcher reciting his favorite poem: Wild Geese. Tristan so adored it that he immediately consigned it to memory. When they arrived in Maine there was a half-moon speckling the salty docks of Casco Bay. They slept in the car. The following morning, Fletcher made five calls from a hard-to-find pay phone: one to Corey, one to Elan, one to Pete and two to Tom Vicante, who rang him back a total of four times. Their business was settled with a fax, a couple of letters and a package shipped from a local UPS store. After lunch, the two Egans loitered conspicuously on Commercial Street, tossing fried clams into the slimy water as the gulls fought over their New England leftovers. Within an hour, a thin, unshaven, reddish-haired man approached. He asked Tristan what he knew about Portuguese stew. Tristan replied in Portuguese that only one man could make it, and offered a name. The stranger issued directions to Rockport and told them where to find an old lobster boat named the Enchantress. Moments later, the Egans were traveling north.

Early that evening, on a bleak, ravaged waterfront, the Enchantress was located, although her captain was not. As it grew later, the mist rolled in, blunting the gleam of the salt-pitted lanterns into a firefly's luminance. Dew dripped from peeling shacks and creaking boats, melding distinct shapes into vague shadows. A fog horn blew. With eyes on the old vessel, Tristan and Fletcher waited, parked near the pier until nine p.m., when the same wiry messenger of the afternoon brushed by their vehicle and rapped on the door. As they lit, he demanded the car keys and tossed them to a younger version of himself emerging from the fog. The teenager barely waited for Tristan to unload before whisking the rental car into the night. The older man threw a duffle bag on the Enchantress and flicked on her lights.

"Nobody said anything about a dog," he growled and disappeared into the wheel house. He returned with three cans. "My name's Stoner: Stan or Dan for short. If it pees or anything, you clean it up." He tossed them each a beer.

Fletcher thanked him and held out his hand, but Stan or Dan didn't take it. Pulling up fenders, the captain ordered Tristan to throw over his gear and get in, and motioned to Fletcher to do the same. Tristan tossed everything aboard but the manuscript, asking Fletcher to hold it while he hoisted Oliver astern. Then, he hopped back on the dock to retrieve the journal. The engine started. Fletcher dispatched the letters.

"Ryan, come on. Come on!" Tristan held out his hand. "*Come on!* What's the matter?"

Fletcher contemplated the oily planks. "I can't, lad."

"*What?* What do you mean? You have to!"

It was low tide. Fletcher was gazing at the contiguous pylons supporting the adjacent centipede-like wharf. "I'll find another...."

"Ryan, stop it!" Tristan leapt from the boat. "What's the matter with you? *What is it?*"

"Tristan, I can't, that's all. I'm just not ready."

"Ready? What are you talking about? We have to go! Are you scared?"s

"No, no. Nothing like that."

Fletcher folded his arms against his son's pleading eyes. He sighed. "I'm not ready to see him, you understand? I can't. I won't know what to say."

"Then say nothing! Ryan, I know it's hard, but I won't go without you. If you won't come, I'll get our things."

"No, Tristan. Go."

"*No.*"

Fletcher licked his lips, tasting the briny air. He wasn't ready, but then he never would be. He'd do it for Tristan, he resolved; he owed him that. He scanned the blurry stars, took a deep breath, and stepped off the wet laths and onto the boat. It would be his last footprint in North America, his perdition and now his past, consigned, like his vaporous exhale, to the murky shore.

The Enchantress rolled out into the ocean where the cold cleared the air and the night sky became a wash of fiery light. It was Ryan's first encounter with an aurora borealis. The wind picked up as did the boat's pitching, but it didn't faze Stan or Dan a bit. He was back lit in the wheelhouse, listening to talk radio, occasionally cackling at some call-in. Tristan was smoking with his head tilted to the sky, his legs braced over the nervous dog. He offered his father a cigarette. Fletcher refused, keeping his face to the wind, not risking a prolonged whiff of the malodorous fish slime sloshing back and forth under his boots. Stan hollered something about taking the wheel. He had to pee. Tristan handed his father the leash and ducked into the cabin. The captain teetered across the deck with a beer in his hand and relieved himself aft. Zipping up his pants, he paused to examine his passenger.

"You hurt bad?"

"No."

To Ryan Fletcher's dismay, Stan took a seat. "You know how I met Marino?"

"No."

"He fished me out of the Bay of Biscay."

"Oh. Well, that was good of him."

"Damn right, it was. Nobody else would've!" Dan swilled his beer and burped. "So, maybe cargo like you makes us even. Then again, maybe nothing will." He shrugged. "I mean, what's your life worth?"

He abruptly departed and resumed his post with a fresh six-pack. Tristan returned with a pair of binoculars.

"God, I think he's drunk." Ryan rose, but a sudden lurch slapped him down. "Do you have any idea where we are?"

"Just north of Matinicus Island. He lives there. Don't worry. He's all right."

"Are those ship lights?"

"Yes, but not what we're looking for. I'll let you know."

Nearly two hours passed. The sea grew calmer, the white swells reduced to rippling furrows. The Enchantress droned on, cutting through the water like a razor through crinkled silk. Stars blanketed the late summer sky. Occasionally, Stan could be heard on the radio. Tristan would intermittently slip into the amber lit wheel house and chat with him. Then he would return, clutching binoculars, sitting opposite his father, who was now hunched over, succumbing to both pain and sea sickness. Stan sent something back for the nausea. Once again, he was on the radio, clicking through a spectrum of channels, trolling for an answer in the night. This time, he got one. The radio crackled with a hail from The Reveler. Tristan jumped up. Scanning the ebony sea, he yelped. Despite her name, he would know her running lights anywhere. A Tiger was stalking the horizon.

It was another forty minutes before the noiseless shape materialized into a trawler that could be heard chugging toward her intended. Slapping on the flood lights, Stan got busy on the radio, sporadically spitting orders to his one-man Spanish crew. The charging vessel looked like an ominous glacier as she cut her engines and drifted toward them. Tristan was scurrying back and forth, unfurling thick coils of rope. Not knowing what to do, Ryan jumped up, grabbed one, and tried to obey the commander's imprecise instructions. The captain came about twice before he was comfortable with his position. Then, with the fenders down, he sidled up to the larger craft. It was a dangerous maneuver, especially on the open sea, but the seamen knew it well. Ropes flew back and forth and were winched so tightly that the two vessels became one. As the commotion subsided, Dan bellowed across to the Tigre that they were secure. There was silence while a short ladder dropped. Three figures loomed above them, one hollering, *"Tristao! Tristao!"*

Tristan eyes widened as he cried "Luis!" and hurtled up the ladder to the open arms of Marino's Portuguese ex-partner, reinstated.

Ryan loitered in the shadow of Stan's wheelhouse as his son's exuberant reception resounded across the empty Atlantic. Then Tristan returned to the Enchantress, using a winch to pulley up their belongings before shouldering the trembling dog. He glanced at his father, tacitly urging him to follow. Ryan thanked Stan, who held the ladder for him while regarding him thoughtfully.

"You don't know him, do you?"

"No."

"Well, don't worry. You're in good hands. That I'll guarantee. Good luck."

Ryan was grabbed by Luis and Tristan and hoisted over the rail of the Tigre. Luis' broad smile and warm hand shake was instantly followed by a hot cup of coffee, freshly made by Pablo, the only hired help. From far below, Stan whined about hurrying up. Fighting a nervous stomach, Ryan reached down for the reassuring feel of his dog. Then he heard her. He spun to see her gliding toward Tristan. She dropped a tapestry bag before wrapping a long Calvin Klein leg around him, delivering a kiss to his lips.

Murmuring something to her, Tristan detangled himself.

"Did you miss me?" She cocked her head.

"Go on, Sandra!" A menacing brogue boomed. "You're nothin' but trouble!"

She kissed Tristan again. "Bye, Baby. Everything's all right, isn't it? You seem a little strange."

He nodded.

She pivoted around, addressing the figure in the shadows. "Tell me the truth, Egan: would you really have killed me?"

"You better hurry up before you find out."

She giggled, picked up her bags, and - slinking to the astonished dog handler - cooed "Helloooo, Ryan Egan."

Luis winked at him, then relieved her of her luggage and hurled it down to the Enchantress.

"I don't understand." Ryan stammered. *"What are you doing here?"*

"Your *Da* wanted to be on the safe side, so we're running a little late. Don't worry. I've been in touch."

"But. . . .You mean. . . . You're not. . . ?"

"Oh! You thought he was a *real kidnapper?*" She rolled her eyes affectedly. "Bye boys! Bye, Tristan! Miss you!"

Below them, Stan held the ladder as she descended. Then, with the whirring of winches and a frenzy of activity, the Enchantress was set free.

Ryan stood with a coffee mug cooling in his hand, waiting for Tristan to approach. "I don't understand, Tristan. I just don't."

"She didn't like his plan, either, Ryan, but, you know, he's her father. I guess she played along to protect him. Anyway, maybe Pete was right. We might need him, you know?"

"Why didn't you tell me?"

"It was tricky enough."

"So, you and she were, uh. . . ."

"Friends," Tristan interposed. "She always wanted me out of it. So I got out, but it was really for other reasons. She thought we'd all be safer if she was. . . ."

"Held as collateral; a phony kidnap. Her idea."

"Pretty much." Tristan lit a cigarette. "She's really smart. Smarter than him."

"And those men in the cave?"

"I told you. Probably agents, maybe on to Porter, but they had their own ideas, you know, about making money."

"You mean blackmailing him? Stealing the virus? Is that what you mean? Why did they want you, Tristan?"

"I can't say for sure. Probably for Porter's list."

"You have *the list?*"

Tristan shook his head. "Not any more. Listen, you all right for a few minutes?"

"Yes."

"Have a look around. I'll be right back."

Ryan was void of curiosity. His only impulse was to make himself small, hunkering down with Oliver while the smell of diesel and the thunderous engines claimed his thoughts. From high above, a rusty lantern cast a sickening green pallor, spilling its phosphorescence across the stern until it dripped overboard into blackness. He missed Corey. She had refused to say goodbye, maintaining that nothing was forever. He could still taste her kiss. He longed for the rhythm of his chores, the prairie sun, the comfort of his books and the scent of the old horse. He closed his eyes and wilted against the bulkhead, his dog resting his head on his knee. He was drifting away, thinning lilies in the pond when Oliver growled and knocked into his arm, an excruciating reminder of his whereabouts. He opened his eyes to a pair of shoes wading into his periphery, kicking away the asylum of his past.

"Let me have a look at you."

The dog yapped twice but his handler was heedless, remaining seated as he gazed into the darkness.

"Ryan!" the man barked. "If you don't mind. . . ."

"I do mind!" Ryan snapped and swallowed hard, struggling to his feet. Cloaked in olive, the figure before him stood firmly against the ocean's sway and his palpable anger. The intruder took an audacious step closer, the eyes an astonishingly vivid, unyielding blue in the lime glare. He was lean, his features chiseled in sharp symmetry. His white hair framed his neck in thick waves. He looked like Tristan, or rather, Tristan looked like him. But then, Tristan was nowhere to be found, leaving Ryan Fletcher Lawson Egan to stand alone, setting eyes - for the first time - upon the Irish heathen that spawned him nearly a half century ago.

"What do you want?" Ryan choked on a frightening inner stir.

"Come with me." Egan responded calmly.

"Why?"

"I want to see about your arm."

"It's all right."

"No. I think not. It's fifty degrees and you're sweatin'. It's fever."

"I have pills."

"They're not doing much good, then. And it doesn't make much sense, to spend the rest of your days with one arm."

"I'm fine!"

"Suit yourself. Either way, you're not dyin' on my boat. So, you'll either give me your time now or your arm in a day or two."

Ryan snorted, waving a dismissal. But Egan was locked in place, an obdurate nuisance.

"Look," the Irish captain sighed, "Even if the weather's with us, if it's festerin', it'll be too late. Don't be a damned fool."

"So, what are *you* going to do?"

"I'll start by having a drink with ya. Then we'll have a look. I heard you like port. It just so happens, I have some . . . Spanish."

Ryan deliberated, the pain arcing through him like a thousand volts. He blew his resignation into the Atlantic's cool vapor. "I don't need *a look*. But I could use a drink."

The captain grinned, his chipped teeth gleaming like rough pearls. "Tristan! *Where are ya?* Come get your damn dog."

The galley was immaculate, its stainless sink brassy under an array of yellow lights. Across the table, Luis joined Ryan with a glass of port while Egan donned his spectacles and arranged his remedial munitions on the counter. As the passenger was placated with liquor, Egan carefully cut the soggy bandages from the arm.

Ryan knocked back his third. "So, what do you think, Egan? Am I going to die on your boat?"

"I told you, I won't have it."

"So, how is it?"

"Could be worse. For now, I'm going to clean you up and give ya two shots: one's for the pain. The other's for infection. I don't dare suture it now." Egan glanced up, shaking his head at a refill. "No mas, Luis. Not for him. Have you eaten anything?"

"I'm not hungry."

Egan chuckled. "You will be. Luis, por favor."

The first mate rose, extracted a large pot from an ice chest and lit the stove.

The pain killer effective, Ryan withstood the bullet hole's savage scouring while the galley filled with the smell of seafood and saffron. The heavenly pot almost boiled over but Luis caught it in time, and set a bowl of the divine concoction in front of the wounded voyager. It looked like bisque, and - Egan was right – was irresistible. The aroma drew Tristan, who visited long enough to exclaim *Portuguese stew*, served up two dishes and returned to night watch with Pablo and Oliver.

Egan directed his guest toward his sleeping quarters. It was the only actual room. Ryan refused it, easing down on a nearby bunk with a narrow chest of drawers and a curtain.

"The head's over there," Egan informed him.

"Right. Thanks."

"And if you don't have any shirts, those should do."

A stack of white sweatshirts were strapped into a shelf opposite the cot. Ryan nodded.

"You all right, now?"

"Yes."

"Good." Egan crossed his arms. "When you wake up, you'll be feelin' it. I had to go pretty deep. So, if I'm sleepin', you wake me. I'll give you another shot."

"I'll be all right."

Egan studied him skeptically. He drew the curtain and left.

Ryan tucked the pillow under his head, comfortable for the first time in days. His heart was beating normally while the engines hummed hypnotically, propelling the Tigre toward the dawn. He eyed a clean shirt but was too tired. Everything smelled of bleach. The sheets were smooth and sterile, the blankets freshly laundered, the floors, he noticed, spotless. Egan, like himself, was compulsively clean. His lids grew heavy. Genetics. . . .

He didn't know how long he had slept, but the pain that woke him was so excruciating that he barely made it to the head before vomiting. The Tigre was more active now, punching through waves that sent a tremor through her and slapped him into the water closet's wall. He crawled out of the suffocating confines toward the galley. It was dark. His clothes were soaking. Perhaps they were sinking. He thought he heard someone shouting, but was so ill that he all he could do was curl up on the cold floor and pray for nothingness.

He was being driven by a frigid wind. He was airborne, skimming the angry Atlantic like an albatross. He heard whispers while a terrible gale kept him aloft, cradling his head, chanting mystical incantations. He was swathed in warm seaweed and bound with rope. He saw Jean Lopez in full armor, slicing through the monsters born of his shame: distorted visions of his mother, Palter, old lovers and past friends. They charged toward him, their curses lodging like embers in his soul. Appearing as a monk, Mateo held his cross against the fiends, but the internal flames had already been planted and stoked, and the stricken sinner screamed. Little John swept above him, an emerald Pegasus with fins for feet. Don Christoval was astride him, defying the storm, dousing the inferno with a pass from a liquid blade, wailing to the dreamer that he was only dreaming . . . dreaming . . . dreaming . . . and that he must wake . . . wake . . . wake now. . . .

Ryan's eyes fluttered open. He was on deck cocooned in blankets and a tarp. He saw fat gray clouds pressing slowly like geese toward a cobalt horizon. The wind feeding his lungs was cool and moisture laden, as if after a storm. Tristan was peering down at him, his pale face drawn, his cold hand applied to his father's forehead.

"Ryan? Can you hear me? Do you know me?"

"Yes. Yes, I do, Tristan."

The young man slumped with relief, wearily nodding at the figure crouched by Ryan's shoulder. He asked if he could sit up. Ryan said yes, struggling from under the layers, surprised that he was so weak. Tristan had to free him. The figure ordered him to keep a blanket on and not to stand, not yet. Then, the seaman rolled to his feet and turned away. He braced himself against a rail, intent on an invisible shore.

Tristan stood. "Abuelo, the fever's gone. I'm sure."

Egan's head bobbed. He stammered something about water and waved him off.

Ryan rubbed his eyes and took a deep breath before addressing the mariner's back.

"You all right, Egan?"

The captain nodded.

"Nice morning."

"Morning?" The seaman spat. "It's dusk."

"Oh? Oh. So, how long. . . ?"

"Two bloody days!" The Irishman clenched the rail.

"Oh! I see. Well, I'm sorry." Ryan rubbed the back of his neck. "You sure you're all right?"

"*Are you?*"

Egan wouldn't face him. He used a sleeve to wipe his eyes, and then jammed his hands in his pockets. "I thought," he whispered, "I thought it was my punishment, ya see . . . for leavin' ya the way I did. All those years . . . never knowing ya . . . that I could ever hope. . . . Never dreamin' I'd deserve it. And then . . . before I could to tell ya how sorry I am. . . ." Egan gasped for breath, "that I thought . . . you'd . . . that I could never make it right, even to tell ya. . . ." He shook his head, unable to go on.

Ryan struggled to his feet. Tristan arrived and handed him a glass of water. He peered at his grandfather. "Abuelo, estas bien?"

Egan didn't answer, riveted on the placid waves. Tristan stared after him. "Grandpa?"

"Tristan," Ryan murmured, "give us a minute, would you?"

Tristan stood still, appraising them both before moving out of ear shot. Ryan shuffled across the deck to the rail, using it for support as he monitored the same water as Egan in silence.

"I thought the infection. . . . I thought you were finished," the seaman blurted out flatly.

"Not on *your* boat, Egan."

The captain bit the side of his cheek. "Christ, I'm sorry." As the sun dropped below a cloud, it torched the horizon, flooding the ocean in antique gold. Egan squinted. "Listen," he muttered softly, "I want to tell ya something. You have a right."

"*No.* You don't have to. You don't owe me anything. You have nothing to. . . ."

Egan raised his hand. "Just hear me out. I want you to know."

"You mean, just in case. . . ."

"*Don't, dammit! This is important!*" Egan thumped the rail. From the east, a timid star previewed the night. The mariner licked his lips, scanning the leagues around him. "I just want ya to know that those things in the newspapers, it didn't happen that way. I didn't plant that bomb. I know what you were told, but I swear to ya. I swear to God, I didn't. Someone was rattin' on 'em, see? They figured maybe it was me, me with my proud English wife. It was different after I married her. I was different. But they didn't understand. How could they? God, I was so wrong. Wrong about everything! Wrong to take her there. But I thought she . . . that I could . . . Anyway, you came along and all I wanted was peace. That's all. They set me up. I swear to God. And I want you to know that I came back for ya, but she wouldn't hear me out. I came again when you were sixteen, when she couldn't hold ya anymore, but you were already gone, and I couldn't find ya. I couldn't find ya anywhere."

Ryan shivered and folded his arms across his chest.

"You better get below, into warm clothes. Can you make it all right?"

"Yes."

"I made a mistake." Egan added, trailing him to the stairs. "I didn't know how sick you'd be or I would've held to the coast, but I wanted to get out of Canadian waters. I didn't want trouble. They don't like foreign trawlers. So we headed out, ran into rough weather. You never been on a boat, have ya?"

"No."

"Well, you'll sleep in the cabin from here on. There's plenty of air. We'll keep up on the shots until we're in port. Then you'll see a doctor."

"So, where are we?"

"Where do ya think? The middle of the Atlantic. We should make Lisbon in no time. Do you have decent clothes? There're sweatshirts down there. Luis will show you. He's makin' dinner, something special."

"I could use a shower."

"Help yourself. I'll see to a new bandage when you get out. Tristan! Where are ya? The dog peed over here!"

"Egan?" Ryan posed quietly, lingering on the first stair.

"What?"

"I . . . I thought I heard singing. I was just curious. Was it. . . ?"

"Everything I knew."

Pablo was Luis' eldest son. The good-natured lad took the helm while the others ate in the galley. Luis fished for compliments on his latest specialty: a seafood omelet. Although he spoke little English, he was elated when Ryan declared it a masterpiece. Tristan had three helpings. The captain barely ate at all, content with his ale, tucked in the booth smiling while Tristan prattled on to him in Portuguese. Egan suddenly interrupted, growling that out of deference to his father, he should speak English. Tristan winked at Ryan and slid from the table to fetch his grandfather another brew. Ryan felt a twinge of jealousy. Tristan obviously adored the old salt.

After dinner, Ryan was installed in the captain's room. He was administered another dose of antibiotics and painkillers without protest. The arm was better. The tissue was no longer a spongy yellow and the bicep was shrinking to normal size. Even Pablo could stand to look at it, munching on biscotti as he watched. Taping the new bandage, his boss grumbled something to him in Portuguese. He promptly disappeared. Minutes later, Tristan arrived in his stead with Oliver and a smirk of astonishment. It was *incredible* that the skipper would even allow a dog on board, much less in his room! Well, Egan sputtered, as long as it didn't bark or piss, it should stay with its master.

Ryan was surprised to find his new quarter's home to a library. The walls were lined with old walnut shelves where the books – everything from Homer to an old set of Encyclopaedia Britannica - were neatly strapped in with a leather cord. He scanned the collection. Much of it was classics or nonfiction, history and philosophy, a lot of political commentary with a few leftovers from Tristan's childhood. Wall space was at a premium so the only artwork there was signed by the boy. One was of a horse, done when he was twelve; the other was of his grandfather, done later. There was a shoebox of photographs. Mostly, they were of Tristan as an adolescent and teen, Egan and Luis when they were younger, several of a dark-haired woman, a few miscellaneous, and – strangely – a browning Polaroid of his mother holding him as an infant. He examined it closely. No wonder he married her. She was radiant. There was a small Davenport desk, a lamp and an outstanding sterling decanter set. He smelled the contents: port. Above the desk were two small sliding windows, already cracked. Oliver growled. Egan was at the doorway.

"Everything all right, then?"

Ryan hastily replaced the photograph. "Fine, thank you. Quite a collection. You're an ardent reader."

"There's a lot a time on a boat."

"I see Tristan's handiwork, an excellent artist."

"So are you from what I hear. So was your grandfather."

"Oh? I didn't know. I don't know much about. . . ."

"I know. If you'll allow me," Egan motioned toward the decanter, "I'd like to tell ya a little about yourself."

Ryan propped himself up on the bunk as the captain took a seat and poured two glasses.

Egan asked twice if his listener was weary, and twice the answer was no. It was well past eleven when he retired, leaving Ryan Lawson Egan with an aunt, an uncle, four cousins, and a family tree dating back to the seventeenth century. Lying in the dark in the middle of the ocean, Ryan Lawson Egan found himself on solid ground and unexpectedly tearful. Prior to his leaving, the Captain had requested a favor. His asked that his only son call him Nolan, a name reserved exclusively for his family.

Over the course of the next few days, the seas were cooperative and the crew in good spirits. A good amount of Ryan's time was spent with the skipper. Nolan had a biting wit and kept everyone off guard and laughing. He didn't talk much about himself or his sins, admitting only that he owned them. But, then, Ryan Egan II understood all too well that those denied justice tend to make their own.

Oliver adjusted to his limited territory and was free to roam. Pablo grinned a lot but said little, while Luis conjured up all the English that ever stuck – which wasn't much – and tried to converse with the company. Despite Tristan's shrieks and constant corrections, Luis was undaunted. When interrupted, he would simply frown, inhale, and resume chattering nonsense.

A night before landfall, Egan asked to see Ryan alone in his cabin. He shut the window and closed the door, making the space hot and confining. It couldn't be helped, he said, drawing up a chair. He told Ryan to sit down. They had to face facts. Nolan's preamble was that Tristan would be forever, mercilessly hunted. The odds were, bluntly put, that they wouldn't make it for long.

Ryan stared at him. "What makes you think that? Porter got his daughter."

It wasn't that simple, Nolan replied. Although the scheme with the girl worked temporarily, in the long run, it would only serve to enrage Eckhart, especially when he discovers his daughter was complicit. He'll never blame her; he'll blame Tristan. To make matters worse, Tristan stole a disc of his list. He'll be looking for Tristan as soon as he realizes it. He'll certainly never intercede on the charges even if he could. And, Nolan surmised, regardless of Trans-Origin's infiltration and the contamination of the virus, Eckhart was fully capable of producing it again. Unlike Pete, Nolan doubted Porter would be denied his new world order.

Ryan rubbed the back of his neck. He examined Tristan's artwork, his timid signature scrawled on the bottom. He glanced at Nolan, and then back at the portrait. It was a good likeness. He hated the cramped space and wanted to punch the door open but he didn't. He knew there was more. He felt prickly and deceived and yet calm. He had a feeling that R. Nolan Egan was a very smart man. The old mariner's eyes locked on his. He had a way out, he whispered. It just might work, but no one could know. It would be tough-going for a while: no communication, no internet, no phones, no trace. But, then, they just might make it. They just might.

Nolan assessed Ryan's reaction and smiled. He poured the first drinks of the evening. "Open the door, would ya? It's stuffy in here."

103

They weren't in Lisbon for long. Ryan saw a doctor and was declared on the mend. Within two days, the Reveler left port with plenty of provisions, but without Luis or Pablo. This time, the captain did not take a circuitous route. He was headed straight to North America, to do a little fishing off the Grand Banks.

An expert in clandestine operations made it all the easier for Egan to draw attention when he wanted to, and it wasn't long before he had the attention of authorities. He was flagrantly using illegal netting, taking cod and American plaice - both protected species - right under the noses of Canadian authorities. He and his shipmates were positively identified. Cutters were fast approaching when the Reveler exploded. There were dozens of boats in the water that day so there were plenty of eye witnesses. Everyone said that she had shredded to splinters. It was a horrific scene leaving refuse for miles and fishermen scrambling in shock. Hence, no one seemed to notice a little craft named the Enchantress coursing south. And, although an investigation yielded no specific cause - knowing Ryan Nolan Egan - it was probably a mishap with contraband explosives. Needless to say, no survivors were found. Thus, after fifty years, the Irish terrorist got his due, or so said the evening news.

104

Within six weeks and without fanfare, two caskets cleared customs in Bilbao and were met by a troop of Franciscan monks. The remains were carefully sorted and interred: one in San Sebastian, one in Burgos and one in an ancient plot located somewhere in the Pyrenees. With the exception of the names, the stone inscriptions were the same: *A Noble Servant of God and Country Rests Here.*

Ten months later, Pete was sound asleep when Ruth's shrieks rocked him to his feet. Her children wrapped around her, she was in the hallway, sobbing inconsolably. Pete read the letter. She wrote that she loved them so much that she didn't dare face them, afraid she wouldn't be able to leave. She enclosed a picture of herself and her baby taken yesterday, in exchange, she said, for the family photo in the living room. She swore to them that she'd be all right and be in touch as soon as it was safe. Pete put an arm around Ruth. He knew this day would come.

The partnership that owned the Lawson land and mineral rights wrangled with the authorities for nearly a year before the dust finally settled. When it did, it was 24 karat. Fletcher never signed the revised contract with Mackey, nor did Corey ever sell his furniture. Instead, she took up residence in Fletcher's house so that she could supervise operations full time. Elan transferred his training prospects into Fletcher's lush fields, and Ray visited Corey so often that he eventually just moved in. He asked Corey to marry him. It took him three more times before she finally accepted. Despite the news accounts, Corey still wires money every month to an account offshore. She also forwarded Gordon a copy of the Navarre manuscript, one she received from Maine prior to the accident. Despite the deal's collapse, Gordon is delighted. He has plenty of money. What he needs now is a translator.

Dana Tabor has filed for divorce and is poised to receive a hefty settlement. She works part-time for Corey Martin.

Tom Vicante represents Lawson Mining, Inc. and continues to hate golf.

Nick Sparta always loved his life in Colorado, but ever since Bill gave notice, he's been euphoric. He's now the official airport manager. It's rumored that he and Dana are an item.

Mathew Kraft has found God and walks with a cane.

Sandy Eckhart can still do no wrong in her father's eyes.

Only two bodies were ever recovered from the cave, one an ex-C.I.A operative and suspected hit man, and the other an Australian tied to a drug cartel. The Australian drowned. It was assumed that Tristan murdered the American as he was shot at point blank range. If there was a third man, he was never found. But, it wouldn't surprise anyone if a Swiss-borne mole is enjoying all kinds of accolades at an undisclosed location.

Shortly after Fletcher's disappearance, Pete Peters was fired. He used a portion of his mining revenue to establish a non-profit organization dedicated to elevating the world poor with sound, profitable, earth-friendly vocations. Ruth is his top administrator. His organization enjoys substantial contributions by none other than Trans-Origins, Inc. The Peters family has since moved to New England, Pete spending much of his time teaching as an adjunct in two institutions, forging new inroads into human understanding by weaving history, theology and science – particularly physics – into a binding force. Nurturing imaginations and delving into the unexplored, he is a beloved professor with a profound impact on students and faculty alike. However, he was only hired with the indomitable pressure of Porter Eckhart, who liked him in the vicinity. The billionaire bio-engineer has reestablished his headquarters in Massachusetts, although he spends a great deal of time abroad. When he's stateside, though, a chess match with Peters is mandatory. He has yet to win.

In a semi-remote tropical area, an Irishman presides over his dynasty with all the love that a man could tender. He is married to a graying haired woman named Matilda, who speaks Portuguese and attends mass every day. His son has made a paradise out of the muddy acreage they occupy. The hacienda is replete with exotic flowers and supplies fruits and vegetables to the neighborhood. The gardener also tends grounds for wealthy people in the suburbs. They adore him and ask him to stay for drinks, but he never does. His father often accompanies him. A third generation drives a taxi and dreams of horses. He takes art courses at a university at night. It's hard for him to be away, but his father encourages him to continue, as does his young wife, secure in his love. When the time is right, her father-in-law will withdraw the funds that a devoted friend has deposited. His son will ride again and his precious daughter-in-law will fly. But, it doesn't take that long. A nonprofit organization dedicated to elevating the world poor with sound, profitable, earth-friendly vocations, needs a rural pilot and a trailblazing horseman.

105

On a rainy night in a steamy city somewhere in South America, a taxi waits. When a tall man slips into the cab, it's not the man the cabby expects. Seeing the driver's reaction, the man explains that he's had a heart attack and had to lose weight if he was to finish his life's work. Then, he asks about the eagle feather dangling from the mirror. The driver winks and replies, *"in hoc signo vinces."* The customer chuckles and asks where they are going. The driver smiles. It's a memorable smile. "To the naranjos," he replies.

The passenger reaches forward to throw a long arm around the chest of his guide. "To the naranjos, then!" he exclaims, consigning a priceless gold medallion to his chauffer's lap.

Two men are playing chess in a semi-remote tropical area. It's a raging battle between a clergyman and an Irishman. A toddler named Sonsoles Ruth Egan y Peters upsets the board twice before becoming mesmerized by the prolific, intoxicating, irrepressible blooms snowing from the orange trees. As the child fingers a star-like flower, somewhere in the immeasurable cosmos, across the folds of time, there is a life to be fulfilled. It is there a conquistador has found his horse. It is there a conquistador rides.

Made in the USA
San Bernardino, CA
23 December 2013